THE
GOOD LIFE

THE
GOOD LIFE

SUSAN KIETZMAN

KENSINGTON BOOKS
www.kensingtonbooks.com

KENSINGTON BOOKS are published by

Kensington Publishing Corp.
119 West 40th Street
New York, NY 10018

ISBN-13: 978-0-7582-8132-6
ISBN-10: 0-7582-8132-3

First Kensington Trade Paperback Printing: March 2013
10 9 8 7 6 5 4 3 2

Printed in the United States of America

*To Teddy, William, and Henry
for their encouragement*

CHAPTER 1

~

She was in the tub when her mother called.

After receiving the message, Ann sat back against the warmed, white porcelain and closed her eyes, wondering what her mother could possibly need at 8 p.m. on a Tuesday night that couldn't wait until tomorrow. She had just talked to her, what, two, three weeks ago? Ann rose from the bubbles, stepped out of the tub, and descended the two steps to the heated floor, where she slowly towel dried her body and hair, all the while looking at herself in the mirrors that covered the walls. She rubbed moisturizer into her arms, legs, face, and neck and blotted almond gel around her small hazel eyes. She approached her pedestal sink to tug the few errant hairs from her shaped, light-brown eyebrows and floss and brush her teeth. Afterward, she slid into her silk pajamas and matching robe and calfskin mule slippers. She grabbed the bedroom phone from its plastic holder and walked down the stairs, through the foyer, and into the study, where Mike had buzzed her on the intercom about her mother's call. "Will you get me a glass of champagne?" she said to him as she pushed the buttons on the phone. "I'll join you in the living room in five minutes."

"Let me know when you're off, and I'll pour the drinks then," said Mike, who, in similar situations with his wife, had been kept waiting more often than not.

"Okay," she said, leaving the study and walking into the neighboring den, where she sat down in a large Italian leather armchair.

"Hello?" asked Eileen tentatively.

"Mother, it's me," said Ann. "What's up?"

Eileen took a deep breath. "I have some news," she said. "Meadowbrook cannot take us until the spring."

"Meadowbrook?"

"The assisted-living community your father and I were hoping to move into."

"Yes, yes, yes," said Ann. "I just forgot the name for a moment."

"Anyway," said Eileen. "We were hoping to get in there before Christmas."

"What, exactly, did they tell you?"

"They said the unit they had set aside for us was no longer available. I think they made a mistake."

"Oh Lord," said Ann, running her fingers through her chin-length blond bob so it would curl under rather than flip out.

"I don't think I can wait until the spring," said Eileen, her voice wavering. "I need some help." Ann leaned back in the chair, tucked her legs up underneath her, and closed her eyes. Her mother had become increasingly emotional in the last six months or so. Before this, she had always been strong, distant even, with an almost mechanical ability to keep her emotions in check. And while the transformation had been gradual, the needy person on the other end of the phone was not the mother who had organized the annual Grange picnic for forty years and won its women's chin-up contest until she was fifty. "Your father seems to be getting worse every day," she said. "The adult day care at the Lutheran church is threatening not to take him anymore."

"How can an adult day-care facility refuse a patient?" asked Ann.

"They can when he becomes too much for them to handle," said Eileen, clearing her throat. "He tried to escape twice today."

"Escape?"

"He gets these notions, Ann, notions that people are conspiring against him. Today it was the day-care kitchen staff. These are the sweetest bunch of volunteers you could imagine. They cheerfully cook a delicious lunch five days a week. And normally your father sings their praises. Not today. Instead, they were representatives from the farmers' union, ready to string your dad up for his evisceration, his word, of their fair work policies. He told me they came after him with a lynching rope, so he ran for the door."

"The staff can stop him, can't they?"

"Well, yes," said Eileen, "if they see him. But basically, they tell me it's their job to take care of him, not to imprison him."

"They don't go hand in hand?" asked Ann, retucking her hair behind her diamond-studded ear lobes.

"Apparently not," said Eileen.

"Where is he now?"

"Watching television. He seems relaxed and calm at the moment, but it's getting to the point that I just don't think I can manage him alone anymore."

"Take the phone to him, Mother," said Ann. "I want to talk to him."

"You don't believe me."

"Of course I believe you," said Ann. "I'd just like to talk with my father."

"Hold on," said Eileen.

Ann picked up the remote from the table next to her and clicked on the flat-screen TV. After hitting the MUTE button, she sank further into the soft back cushion and flipped through the channels. She stopped at a gardening channel featuring an outdoor living area with a kidney-shaped pool much like theirs. Ann looked at her watch, and then heard her parents' voices through the phone. "Who would want to talk to me at this time of night?" her dad said. "Is it something about the meeting tomorrow?"

"It's Ann," said Eileen. "She wants to talk to you."

"Ann who? There's no Ann at the office, unless she's the new girl."

"She's not the new girl, Sam. She's your daughter."

Nothing, and then, "Whose daughter?"

Ann next heard what must have been her mother's hand covering the mouthpiece. Seconds later, she heard her father, his voice reedy and tired. "Hello?"

"Dad, it's Ann."

"Yes, I understand. But it's a little late in the evening to be phoning someone at home. Can't this wait until the morning?"

"It's Annie, your daughter."

"Thank you for calling, young lady. I'll take up your concerns with the president tomorrow."

Ann turned off the TV and sat up in the chair. Eileen got back on the phone. "What in the world was that?" asked Ann.

"He's disoriented, honey," said Eileen, walking back into her kitchen, where some hot chocolate was warming on the stove top for Sam. "He had fallen asleep."

"Is he always like this, Mother? And if he is, when the hell did this happen? He wasn't like this last Christmas."

"The last few months," said Eileen, retrieving the bag of mini-marshmallows from the cupboard next to the oven. "In the last few months, he has gone downhill very quickly."

"Why didn't you say something?"

"I did mention it a couple of times, Ann. When you live with someone every day, it doesn't seem dramatic until it suddenly is."

"Do you have any outside help?"

Eileen hesitated. "I don't want that," she said. "I don't want an underpaid, devil-may-care county health-care worker coming into my house."

"So get private agency help," said Ann.

"Oh Ann," sighed Eileen.

"What do you want then?"

Eileen took a moment, and then said the words she had rehearsed before making the call. "I want to come live with you."

Ann felt like she had been in a car accident, the air bag slamming into her chest. She inhaled deeply, frantic for air. "What?" she finally said.

"Your father and I would like to come live with you," repeated Eileen. "It would be temporary, of course. As soon as Meadowbrook has something available, we'd be happy to leave. We need that kind of facility at this point anyway." Ann tried to corral her thoughts as they flew around the room. "I know this is an awful lot to think about," said Eileen.

Her head buzzing, Ann said, "Yes."

"Sleep on it," said Eileen. "My father always told me to sleep on important decisions."

"Granddad was a wise man," said Ann, her imminent conversation with Mike taking shape in her mind.

"We need you, Ann," said Eileen. "You're our only child and your father is sick."

Ann swallowed the saliva that had pooled in her mouth. "I'll call you tomorrow," she said.

Ann walked back into the study where Mike was still at his computer. She stood behind him, put her hands on his muscled shoulders, and looked down at his manicured hands on the keyboard. "So," he said, eyes on the screen, "what's up with your mother?"

"Let's go into the living room," said Ann. "We'll talk there."

Mike hit the SAVE button and slowly stood. As he did, Ann backed up, feeling the presence and pressure of his six-foot-four frame filling her space. He loosened his tie, undid the top button of his custom-made dress shirt, and stretched his long arms out in front of him, arching his broad back like a taut bow. He then wrapped one arm lazily around Ann and led her through the doorway and into the entrance hall. "One drink," he said, yawning. "I'm exhausted."

When they reached the living room, Ann sat down on the white linen couch in the east sitting area, and Mike walked to the marble wet bar to make their drinks. Ann put her legs up on the adjoining seat cushions and lay back, one of two antique needlepoint pillows supporting her damp head. She stared at the eighteen-foot ceiling, searching for words like constellations in the sky. The pop of the champagne cork startled her. She looked over at Mike, who was pouring one of the splits from California. "I thought you were going to order the new champagne I wanted," she said.

"And I did," said Mike, carrying the drinks to the couch. "It takes more than four days to get here from France, Ann. Plus, you have a dozen of these splits—chilled to your specifications—still in the fridge."

"I'm tired of the splits," said Ann, sitting up and moving her legs so Mike could sit.

"The splits are perfect. You don't need any more than two drinks in an evening."

"Tonight I do," said Ann.

"There is always an excuse, Ann."

"And tonight, it's a good one."

"Well," said Mike, setting the glasses down on the table in front of them on the Audubon bird coasters that never made it back into the side table drawer. He sat on the opposite side of the couch. Ann took her crystal champagne flute from its Great Horned Owl perch and lifted it to her lips. She was as thirsty for the bubbles and the fizz on her tongue as she was for the warmth in her stomach and the downshift in her brain. Perhaps the French champagne, available only in glorious full bottles, would arrive along with her parents. They would be watching the evening news at the same time she was pouring her first glass of the evening. They would be getting into their pajamas just as she was getting into her second glass. And with the third glass, they would be turning out their bedside table lamp, just as the light of recognition and reason in Ann's head was beginning to fade. The timing couldn't be more appropriate. "Dollar for your thoughts?" asked Mike, crossing the ankle of his right leg over his left knee and settling in.

Ann looked at her husband of twenty-two years. She had met Mike in college. He was known then, at least to the women who tracked his whereabouts on campus, as 3G, the gorgeous and gifted goalie of the university ice hockey team. Ann had been well aware of him from the first hockey game she attended, but she did not make herself available for a staged introduction until the beginning of her sophomore year. By then, she had achieved her goal of weighing ten pounds below what the doctor advised, and her blond bob, freckled nose, and slim legs—her most alluring features— were beginning to attract attention from the players on campus. She carefully planned her happenstance meeting with Mike, and by the beginning of his third hockey season, they were an item. While

Ann pursued Mike because he was great looking and powerful, she soon grew attached to him because they wanted the same things out of life: security and freedom. Plus, they were both only children; they understood each other's histories and motivations. When Mike was a senior, he asked Ann to marry him. This was not necessarily because she was the one true love of his life. Could he know at twenty-two? No, it was more because his parents both died in a head-on collision with a log truck on the road that led to their country retreat, and Mike knew Ann would understand both his needs and his responsibilities. The week after his impromptu proposal and Ann's eager acceptance, his parents' fortune, made a generation before in the timber industry, became theirs.

"My mother," began Ann, shifting her body to face him, "wants to come live with us."

"What?" said Mike, stopping his heavy crystal glass of single-malt scotch halfway between his lap and his lips.

"I think you heard what I said."

Mike lifted the glass the rest of the way and took a long drink. "Start from the beginning," he said, leaning forward with his forearms on his thighs, scotch straddled between his legs, and dark blue eyes drilling into Ann's. She pushed back six inches on the couch cushion, sipped her champagne, and relayed the story her mother had just told her—that Meadowbrook, the assisted-living facility, had no room, and that alone Eileen could no longer care for Sam, her husband of forty-eight years. "This is not a problem," he said dismissively. "We can easily get someone in there to help. If money is an issue, we can certainly help them with that." Ann explained her mother's desire to live with them, reiterating how old-fashioned she was, and how much she believed in family. "Family is different now," said Mike, finishing his drink. "We live in a global world; the multigenerational living arrangements of the past have gone the way of the family farm. Your parents ought to know that, their farm being anything but profitable for its final ten years."

"They were never in it for the money," said Ann.

"They were to some extent, Ann. It was their livelihood," said Mike. "My point is how different life is today. Our lives, our expectations are so far removed from where theirs ever were. It would be

a monumental adjustment to have them here, even temporarily."
Ann said nothing. "I don't need this right now, Ann," Mike continued. "I've got a million balls in the air at work. I need my home life
to remain relatively stable." Ann nodded in agreement; Mike was
right. Her parents were both seventy-two years old and lived, mentally and physically, in another era. Her mother's desire to move
into their life was unrealistic. Ann could easily refuse her request
and send her a large check to cover their increased expenses.

"Nobody needs this right now," said Ann. "This would affect
me the most. I have no interest in playing nursemaid."

"So say no," said Mike, getting up from the couch to make himself another scotch. "It's as simple as that."

"It's not as simple as that," said Ann, downing the rest of her
champagne, then setting the empty glass back down on the watch-
ful owl in front of her. "They're my parents."

"Whom you've had very little to do with for the last twenty
years. We see them at Christmastime and that's it," said Mike, his
massive back to her. "And every year, you moan and groan, along
with the kids, about spending three days on the farm."

Ann thought back to the previous Christmas, trying to remember their visit. "What was my dad like last Christmas?" she asked.

"He was okay," said Mike, returning to the couch with his drink
and the bottle of champagne, which he emptied into Ann's glass.
"He interacted with the kids a bit. He was certainly a part of the
celebration."

"He was quiet."

"Yes," said Mike, "he was quiet. But your dad's always chosen
his words carefully."

Ann swallowed half her glass and then said, "They would live
here for six months."

Mike set his glass down on the Scarlet Ibis and looked search-
ingly at his wife. "Are you even entertaining this?"

"Hear me out," said Ann, scrambling. "We could give them the
guesthouse."

"We *use* the guesthouse," said Mike. "That's why we have one."

"Mike, we don't have a lot of overnight visitors, especially during the winter," said Ann. "Our entertaining is ninety percent drinks and dinner, with overnights thrown in occasionally. That guesthouse is underused. You know that." Mike picked up his glass and took a sip. Three feet from Ann, he was miles away. "There are two bedrooms back there," she said, talking faster. "One could be for my parents and the other could be for the live-in help, quality help, which I would get in place before their arrival. And they would be all set. They would live their lives and we would live ours. Of course, I would spend a bit of time with them every day, and we would ask them here for dinner once a week—maybe on Sunday afternoon—and that would be that."

Mike scratched his head, then finger-combed his tight black curls back into place. His eyes roamed the room, as if the secret to ending this discussion lay underneath a chair cushion or behind a burlap drapery panel. His gaze returned to his wife's face, bright and focused on his. He could see, anyone could, that she wanted this, as much as she wanted another vacation in Tuscany or a Tiffany necklace at Christmas. "You're kidding yourself if you think a live-in aide is the only cost of your parents living in your backyard for six months," he said, not ready to surrender. "First of all, they have to leave their home. Someone—most likely you—has to help them pack up whatever they might want or need at this Meadowbrook, and then you'll need to sell the house. Then, we'll need to get your parents here. Then we'll have to assess their needs and hire the right people. The list is endless. You can't just fix this, Ann. This is not like organizing a Christmas party."

"I know that," said Ann, softer and slower. "But I also know we can get through this."

"Then you've decided," said Mike, stiffening.

"No, honey," said Ann, extending her legs so her bare feet touched Mike's thigh. "I'm still trying to decide. But you tell me what you'd do if you were the only child and your seventy-two-year-old mother, who has been single-handedly taking care of your seventy-two-year-old father, called you and asked for help."

Mike's concept of parents and what they represented had become clouded and dark since their accident and death. Their untimely passing had made him a very wealthy twenty-two-year-old man, and he wasn't sure he would give up everything to have them back. "I don't know," he said, looking at the melting ice cubes in his glass.

"I know," she said, gently digging her toes into his leg. "You would help them. And though you can no longer help your parents, you can help mine." Mike rubbed his forehead with his thumb and index finger. "You know this falls on my shoulders, Mike," said Ann. "I will do everything. You will have to do nothing."

"This is bigger than you think."

Sensing a slip in his defenses, Ann began making a mental list. Mike stood and crossed the room. He dumped the remaining half of his drink in the bar sink, and then faced her again. "This conversation is not over."

"I know," said Ann, hiding an inner smile.

"I've got some more work to do before turning in," he said. "Let's sleep on this and talk more about it tomorrow."

"Come here," said Ann, standing. And when Mike again crossed the room to stand beside her, she wrapped her arms around his waist and laid her head momentarily on his chest. "You're a good man."

"Not necessarily," he said. "I'm a businessman. What, if anything, is in this for me?"

"My happiness," said Ann, the champagne working its way through her system like electricity through a circuit.

"Umm," said Mike, kissing her on the mouth.

As soon as he left the room, she scurried over to the bar and silently opened another bottle. She downed half a glass, then ran to the kitchen for a legal pad and mechanical pencil. Back on the couch with her champagne in arm's reach, she started her list. She scribbled notes and drank for an hour, then she turned out the lamp beside her and lay down for a moment. She awoke early in the morning, with the cashmere blanket from the armchair draped over her.

Two hours and three Advils later, Ann showered, dressed, drank a supplement shake, and drove her fifteen-year-old daughter, Lauren, to the public high school. They rarely talked on the ten-minute drive, so it was easy not to tell her the news. Ann would tell her and Nate, sixteen, as soon as everything was in place. She would also have to tell their housekeeper, Emma, whose duties would be affected, at least temporarily. After the drop-off, Ann called her mother on her cell phone, fumbling the numbers twice in her haste. She kept meaning to add her phone number to her contact list; this new arrangement would finally prompt her to actually do it.

"I hope we won't be too much trouble," said Eileen, picking up on the third ring as she always did.

"No trouble at all," said Ann. "I'm going to set you up in the guesthouse, with your own caregiver."

"Oh, we don't need all that," said Eileen, sucking in her stomach. "We'll be fine. And we can come to you if we need help."

"This will be better for both of us, Mother," said Ann. "The only thing you'll have to come to us for is dinner on a Sunday afternoon." On her way to the coffee drive-through, Ann told her mother to pack winter clothes for herself and Sam. "We'll arrange to have more sent as we need them," she said. "And you won't need anything else. The guesthouse is completely furnished."

"This is all happening so quickly," said Eileen.

"I thought this was what you wanted," said Ann.

"It *is* what I want, what I need," said Eileen. "There are just so many details to work out."

"Like what?" said Ann, switching lanes.

"Like the house," said Eileen. "What do we do with our house while we are living with you?"

Ann told her mother they had a couple of options. They could rent the house. It was only ten minutes from the local agricultural college and would certainly attract a professor or staff member with a family. Or, they could simply sell it. Since they would be moving from Ann's guesthouse to Meadowbrook, they wouldn't need it anymore. Eileen could think about it, and then Ann would call a Realtor, either way. All Eileen had to do was tag the pieces of furniture she would take with them to Meadowbrook. The rest would stay with the house as part of the package. "Meaning we'll be moving from Meadowbrook to Oakdale Cemetery," said Eileen, grimly.

"Oh God, Mother," said Ann. "There's no need to get morbid here. Hold on a moment. Yes, I'll have a large low-fat caramel latte. And make it hot."

"Are you still there?"

"Mother, I'm ordering a coffee."

"In the middle of our conversation?"

"Welcome to the twenty-first century."

"I miss the twentieth," said Eileen. "Life was simpler. I can barely find what I need in the grocery store, there are so many products crowding the shelves. The other day, I was looking for a block of cheddar cheese, you know, to grate onto my tuna casserole? Well, the blocks are gone, replaced by bags of already shredded cheese, coated with something to prevent the pieces from sticking to one another—corn starch, I think it is. Who in the world needs that?"

"Many people prefer that, Mother. It saves time."

"What are people so busy doing they can't grate cheese?"

Ann breathed heavily into the phone as she took the cardboard cup from the girl with a nose ring at the window. She immediately set the latte down in her cup holder, handed the girl a dollar, and then cradled the phone between her shoulder and neck so she could sanitize her hands with Purell. "Thank you," she called as she zoomed out of the drive-through lane.

"Well, thank *you,* Ann," said Eileen.

"For what?"

"For taking us in," said Eileen. "Are you talking to me again, or are you still distracted?"

"Yes, I'm talking to you," said Ann, pulling the car out into traffic. She blew the horn at a teenage driver who tried to pass her on the right.

"Ann?"

"I've got to run, Mother," said Ann. "People drive like maniacs in this town. I'll call again in a few days to see how you're doing. Try not to worry. Everything is going to be okay."

* * *

As soon as Ann got off the phone with her mother, she called her decorator and asked her to come immediately. Dede Devore expeditiously rescheduled all of her appointments that morning and arrived at Ann's front door, fabric books in hand and lipstick retouched, forty-five minutes later. "My parents are coming," said Ann by way of greeting, leading Dede quickly through the foyer and into the kitchen.

"So, you want to redo one of your spare bedrooms?" asked Dede, trying to hide her disappointment.

"I want to redo the guesthouse," said Ann, handing her an espresso.

"For a weekend visit?" she asked, taking a sip.

"For a prolonged stay," said Ann. "Let's take those books out back."

Ann and Mike had built the guesthouse along with the main house three years earlier. The combined 8,500-square-foot structures stood majestically at the end of Foxwood Lane, number sixteen, accessed by a divided crushed shell driveway. The house was a white 7,000-square-foot stucco box, with a semicircular, columned portico attached to the front. Looking at the house from the street, the living room was on the left, the dining room was on the right. The kitchen, Mike's study, and a den ran along the back of the house, as well as a bathroom large enough to hold a sauna, which, in the end, Ann decided belonged in the basement next to the workout room. It looked remarkably like the White House in Washington, D.C., so much so that everyone in town referred to it as White House West. The guesthouse was less grand in appearance, but spacious enough to accommodate two couples or a family of four for a weekend.

Before moving to Foxwood Lane, the Baronses lived on the other side of town, adding onto an aging house in an old neighborhood three times in ten years. The house eventually outgrew the neighborhood, as did the Baronses when Mike became CEO of Dilloway. The construction of the new house took nine months, but everything was ready when they moved in, from the landscaped flagstone patio and pool area to the painted walls, window coverings, and furniture Ann had meticulously chosen with Dede. The guesthouse matched the main house in its traditional decor—Ann loved floral chintzes, subtle stripes, and rich colors—but it would never do for simple, elderly people like her parents. Ann was convinced they needed a country look if they were going to feel at home. "The walls should be a cream color, I think," said Ann, opening the guesthouse door and walking down the hallway into the living room. "Something soft and soothing, an antique white maybe."

"How about some stenciling on the kitchen walls along the ceiling?" asked Dede, laying her books down on the coffee table in front of the couch and adjusting the waistline of her shirt, making sure the fabric camouflaged the small mound of flesh at her middle. "Some hearts or ducks, something pastoral."

"That sounds great," said Ann. "My mother would *love* that. Let's go with hearts."

The living room furniture, they decided, was too formal and would have to be put in storage. Dede would replace it with inexpensive wood composite furniture that Ann could simply donate to the Salvation Army after her parents' departure. The furniture in the bedrooms could stay, but the duvets would be replaced with quilted, washable bedspreads, and the window treatments would be scaled back to simple, pinch-pleat panels that could be drawn closed in the evenings. Dede jotted down notes as they walked back into the living room, where she asked Ann about a budget. "Don't worry about that," said Ann. "I don't want you to go overboard, of course. Keep in mind these are farm people. Spend more time and energy on the larger bedroom, where my parents will stay, than the other one. And make sure the fabrics you select are washable. God only knows what kind of spills and accidents will happen back here."

"Would you like to look at some fabrics?" asked Dede, her green eyes wide and attentive.

"I'm going to leave that to you," Ann said. "Give me three choices for everything and we're in business."

"Great," said Dede, smiling at Ann through pink frosted lips as she mentally calculated her profit on the job. "When do you want to get started?"

"The sooner the better," said Ann, leading Dede back out the door. "They will be here in as soon as two weeks. Is that enough time?"

With an unlimited budget, Dede knew she could find painters to work that very night. "Yes," she said. "I'll get things rolling as soon as I get back to my office."

Yellow legal pad in hand, Eileen stood in their bedroom closet, looking at Sam's sparse half: three button-down flannel shirts, four white button-down broadcloth shirts, two pairs of stained khakis and one reasonably clean pair, two pairs of navy blue sweatpants, a flannel bathrobe, a dark gray business suit, and a rack of outdated neckties. Everything hung on wood hangers spaced inches apart along a six-foot chrome bar, like clothing in an expensive women's boutique. The painted pine shelves at the end of the bar housed Sam's favorite navy blue, V-neck sweater that had worn through Eileen's darning job at the elbows, a light gray cardigan sweater, two faded sweatshirts, a pair of Cloud 9 walking shoes Sam used to wear when Eileen took him to the mall for some exercise, and his favorite brown wing tips. However, his feet had become so swollen from medication and disuse that he spent most of his time in a pair of ancient sheepskin slippers that Ann had sent from L.L.Bean the Christmas after she married Mike. When he went to the Lutheran day care, Eileen shoehorned his red, scaly feet into a pair of soled moccasins she had picked up at the mall several months ago. They were undignified, as Sam had called them when he insisted on wearing the wing tips that first day, but they were comfortable and would keep Sam's feet dry on the way from the car to the church parish hall. Eileen decided she would pack the flannel shirts, two of the white shirts, the sweatpants, and the blue sweater. She would also take the moccasins and slippers, as well as socks, boxer shorts, and pajamas from his dresser—and his gray fleece bathrobe hanging on the hook in their bathroom. He would need some new items though, which she jotted down on the pad: two pairs of khaki pants, a gray sweatshirt, and one pair of comfortable shoes—size eleven, not ten! When Eileen turned, realizing she ought to check the condition of his boxers, she just about ran into Sam, who had silently traversed their bedroom carpeting and was standing less than a foot behind her. "Oh!" she said, putting her free hand to her chest. "You scared me."

Sam frowned, his full head of white hair looking like it had lost the war. "Why in the world would you say a thing like that? I have every right to be here."

"Of course you do, dear. I guess I was just lost in thought," said Eileen, combing his hair with her fingers. She would have better luck after his shower.

"Not a bad place to get lost," he said, turning away from his wife. He moved slowly back into the bedroom. When he reached their double bed, he sat down. "What's on the docket for today?"

"Errands."

"I hate errands."

"That's why you're going to the center," said Eileen. "They need you today."

"They sure do," said Sam, pushing himself up off the bed. "Frankly, I don't know how they run that outfit when I'm not there."

"Let's get you in the shower," said Eileen, looking at Sam's damp pajama pants. "And then we can get dressed and be on our way."

Eileen walked Sam into the day-care center and left him with Janice, an always optimistic fifty-five-year-old nurse and Eileen's favorite volunteer. Eileen watched them walk to the armchairs, where Janice helped Sam sit before getting him a donated copy of yesterday's *New York Times*. As usual, Sam turned immediately to the business news. Eileen watched a moment longer, then walked back down the hallway to the director's office and knocked on the door. Penelope Jennings looked up from her computer screen, her black round glasses resting on her pink round cheeks. She smiled genuinely, and waved Eileen in. "How's our Sam today?" she asked, standing. "Can I get you some coffee?"

"No thanks," said Eileen. "And Sam's okay. He seemed happy to come today."

"That's good. That's what we like to hear," said Penelope. "I'm sorry about all the trouble last week."

"Don't be," said Eileen, holding up her hand. "You offer a wonderful service here for clients who match your criteria. Sam is moving into another category."

"Do you have plans?"

"Yes," said Eileen. "We are leaving in a week or so to live with our daughter in Michigan."

"No kidding," said Penelope, folding her arms across her chest. "I'd forgotten about your daughter."

"She's far away," said Eileen.

"Yes," said Penelope.

"So, I'm here to thank you, for everything you've done for Sam. Next Tuesday will be his last day."

Penelope walked out from behind her desk and hugged Eileen. "We will miss him," she said into the space behind Eileen's left shoulder. "Underneath his disease, he is a good man with a good heart." Eileen's eyes began to tear up. She looked at the muted industrial-quality drapes covering half the window behind Penelope's desk. "And you are a good caregiver," said Penelope, releasing Eileen and moving two steps back. "One of the best I've seen. You'd be surprised at the number of people who drop their husbands, wives, grandmothers, and grandfathers at the door without a word. They don't have to say anything; the burden and resentment are written all over their faces. They've forgotten the good days."

"I understand that," said Eileen. "Sometimes they're easy to forget."

"Hold on to them," said Penelope, putting her hand on Eileen's shoulder.

"We try," said Eileen, struggling to sound cheerful. She then shook the director's hand.

"If your plans change and you stay in town, call me. I'll help you find the right place for him."

A sad smile on her face, Eileen thanked the director again, and then walked out the door, closing it quietly behind her.

* * *

The guesthouse redecorating was finished eight days after Ann first spoke with Dede, and cost Mike Barons $20,000. During that week, Ann had been successful in hiring a caregiver, a retired nurse who lived up north but had a sister in town who had responded to Ann's ad in the local newspaper. Only two things remained on Ann's list: renting her parents' house and physically getting them from Pennsylvania to Michigan. Charlene Dennis, the real estate agent in Clearwater, was optimistic about renting the house. Not only was the college close by, but so was a large agricultural processing plant in need of experienced shift supervisors. Between the two, an outsider would surely get hired and need to relocate. And, Charlene said, offering a furnished home was a bonus. A single man or family pressed for time could sign the contract in the morning and move in that afternoon. Ann grabbed a hot pink sticky note from the kitchen counter and stuck it to her list. On it, she wrote: *Call Charlene!* Her biggest worry was getting her parents from point A to point B. She had no doubt her mother was a fine driver—she did everything well—but a trip across two states was radically different from a trip to the corner market for milk.

CHAPTER 2

That Saturday was the annual Cancer Society Charity Ball. Ann got out of bed earlier than normal and slipped on black yoga pants and a tank top. She exercised in their home gym for ninety minutes, watching two recorded episodes of *The Real Housewives of Orange County*. After a hot shower and a low-fat protein shake, Ann told Mike, who was in his study, that she had a number of things to do and that he should be ready to go by seven o'clock. Keeping his eyes on the red numbers on his computer screen, he nodded his head. Fifteen minutes later, Robert, head massage therapist at The Serenity Spa, was easing the tension out of Ann's back with his exquisite soft hands. His Brazilian rainforest soundtrack played quietly in the background. "You are tight today, Mrs. Barons," he whispered.

"I know, Robert," said Ann into the donut-shaped pillow. "Don't get me started."

"Hard week?"

"My parents are coming to live with us."

"Oh my," said Robert, rubbing oil into Ann's bare shoulder.

After her massage, Ann nibbled at the spa lunch: a chilled shrimp, peeled cucumber, and arugula salad drizzled with raspberry vinaigrette. When Ann left the salon, she drove immediately to the Coffee Station for a double espresso to go. She stopped at the new women's boutique for French hosiery and a quick poke around before heading home. When she walked through the kitchen door at just after three o'clock, she washed her hands and then went to find Mike. As she suspected, he was still in his study. "Okay," she said, walking behind him and wrapping her arms around his neck. "Time for a break."

"I did have some lunch," Mike said, focused on the screen.

"Good," said Ann. "Now, go for a run and take a hot shower. You'll feel better."

Mike rubbed his eyes. "You're right," he said. "I've been staring at these numbers all day and still can't figure out a viable way to change them."

"More bad news?" asked Ann, examining her French manicure.

"No," said Mike, "the same bad news. I just want to make sure I'm looking at better numbers next quarter."

"Isn't that what you pay Terry for?" asked Ann, referring to Dilloway's chief financial officer.

"Ultimately," said Mike, standing and stretching his arms out in front of him, "that's what they pay me for."

Ann smiled at her man. "And you're worth every million. Now, get out of here and get some exercise."

Mike grabbed Ann by her hips and pulled her in to him like a fish on a reel. "I know another way I could get some exercise."

"Later," said Ann, putting her hands on Mike's chest.

"When?"

"Tonight," said Ann, "after the ball."

Mike kissed Ann on the mouth, then let her go. "Okay," he said. "But that means you have to watch what you drink. What time are we leaving?"

"Seven sharp," said Ann, though the cocktail hour started at six thirty. "So get going."

"I'll be back in an hour."

Ann walked up the stairs to their living area. She walked into her closet, undressed, and then, naked, approached the gown she had purchased for the evening. She slipped her hand underneath the protective plastic covering and gently touched the seafoam-colored silk before running her fingers along the mink trim at the collar and sleeve cuffs. She moved to the bathroom, weighed herself, and ran the tub, pouring two generous capfuls of bubble bath under the faucet. She climbed in and lay back, closing her eyes and concentrating on the heat of the rising water. She ran her right hand over her stomach, wondering if her mother would insist on cooking Sunday dinners. If so, she would prepare meals out of Ann's childhood—fatty chuck roasts with calorie-laden gravy and egg noodles and tuna casseroles topped by a generous half-pound of sharp cheddar cheese.

Ann had not lived with her parents in rural Pennsylvania since she was twenty-two years old, eighteen really, when she first left home for college. As a young teenager, Ann was a chubby, awkward girl with few friends and a mother whose idea of a proper weeknight dinner was meat loaf, baked potatoes, buttered green beans, buttered rolls, and a homemade dessert. The rib-sticking meals at the end of the day made sense for Ann's father, who worked alongside his day laborers six days a week to squeeze a living from their dairy farm, but not for a girl who wanted to blend in with her thinner, urban-minded contemporaries. But when Ann complained about the amount of food on the table to her mother, nothing changed. Eileen had grown up in another generation, when food was sometimes hard to come by, when an abundant table was a blessing.

So, the kitchen was the center of Eileen's life. She spent most of the day there. And when Ann was home, she was tacitly expected to join her mother. It didn't occur to Eileen, patient and chatty as she worked, that Ann might want to be doing something else—going to the movies, shopping, or gathering with girls at one another's houses. No, Eileen and her daughter, side by side, scrubbed their seven-room farmhouse on Saturday mornings and the rest of the time hovered over the stove, making homemade jellies, pies, hearty beef stews, and starchy side dishes, sampling whatever they made.

Ann continued to put on weight. By her sophomore year in high school, she was thirty pounds more than what the county doctor called ideal. When he put her on a diet, when her mother finally began to understand, it was too late. She had already been ostracized by her trimmer female classmates, and the boys had simply stopped looking at her. Because she was invisible at school, Ann turned to her mother, not only for baking tips and comfort but also for social interaction. Ann even went with her parents to the potluck dinners at the Grange, where, when other mothers lamented about their teenagers' recalcitrant behavior, Eileen happily boasted about the close relationship she had with her daughter.

Ann managed to shed several pounds before heading off to college on the East Coast. After being away from home cooking for nine months, she lost even more weight, gaining a sense of independence in its place. Until now, she had never been away from home for more than a weekend. By the time her parents picked her up in May, she was weighing what the doctor called "very close to normal." Taken aback by her daughter's diminished body, Eileen served Ann farmhand portions and encouraged her to snack between meals. But achingly aware of how difficult it was to lose weight, Ann pushed her plate aside, rebelling against her mother's efforts to fatten her up, newly suspicious and disdainful of her mother's controlling behavior. Ann and Eileen fought that summer. Sam often supported Ann, telling Eileen that she had to let go. But it was a women's battle that he at times didn't understand. By early August, both Ann and Eileen couldn't wait for school to start again in September.

In the tub, Ann parted the bubbles to look at her stomach. With the exception of three small fuzzy lightning stretch marks, it looked like something out of a teen magazine: smooth, flat, and toned. It had looked, more or less, this way since Ann was twenty, and it was not going to change. If Eileen wanted to cook, Ann couldn't stop her. But she couldn't make Ann eat. No one could. Again closing her eyes, Ann relaxed for another ten minutes before running the razor over her hairless legs and the bare pits of her arms.

As soon as she had dried and moisturized, Ann wrapped her body in her robe and her head in a towel, and then sat in one of two bedroom reading chairs and flipped through *Architectural Digest.* She checked her watch. Amanda, her hair stylist, was scheduled to arrive in fifteen minutes. On occasions like tonight, Ann wished she wore her hair longer; there wasn't much Amanda could do with a bob. Yet, she got more volume out of Ann's hair than anyone else in town. Plus, Ann trusted her. Amanda was young, but she was able to walk into the Baronses' house, up the stairs, and into Ann's private sanctum without making a big deal about it.

An hour later, Ann's hair was perfect. Even strand fell into place and was ever so subtly held with spray. It was soft and flexible, nothing like the helmet-headed styles of previous generations. Ann gave her head a quick shake as she looked in the bathroom mirror. Boom, back into place; it was flawless. Ann walked back into the bedroom and returned to her chair and magazine. When she finished reading an article about a sunroom she thought might be perfect for the back of the house, she pushed the house intercom button to call Mike. He was back from his run, no doubt with the towel he'd used to wipe his face hanging around his neck. "It's almost six, honey," she said. "You need to shower."

As Mike tied his bow tie in the mirror, Ann, facing him, ran her hands down the silk lapels of his Armani tuxedo. He quickly kissed her mouth, and then coaxed his thick black curls into place with his fingers. Even though he was beginning to gray at his temples, he was as arresting now as he was in college, more so, really, as the most powerful man in town. Plus, something about a man in formal wear made Ann's breasts ache.

"You look great," Mike said, looking at Ann's exposed back in the mirror.

"Do I?" asked Ann, turning around so he could see her from every angle.

"Do I want to know how much I spent on that dress?" he asked, kissing the tip of her nose.

"You've spent more," said Ann, standing on her toes to wrap her arms around his shoulders.

"You know you're worth it," he said.

"Yes," she said, "I am."

Mike laughed and gently spanked her bottom. "Let's go," he said, "your public awaits your arrival."

When they walked into the Grand Ballroom of the Hilton, the men straightened their spines and their ties, and the women, hands at their throats and lips slightly parted, inhaled simultaneously. An instant later, the crowd moved toward them. Like children drawn to a school-yard fight, they pushed forward enough to almost touch Mike and Ann, but left adequate space for them to move. As the Baronses made their way to the bar, Ann winked, smiled, and waved, and Mike, one hand on Ann's back, used his other to pump the outstretched hands of the few comfortable enough to approach him. A warm spotlight shining on them or a band playing a grand march would not have seemed inappropriate for their arrival.

The $1,000-a-plate sturgeon was tender and delicious; Ann ate almost half of it before pushing her plate away. She took a sip of her third champagne, arching her eyebrows at Mike across the table. Mike dutifully rose from his seat, approached her, and asked her to dance. He led her around the floor in a seamless waltz, holding her close enough to feel her backbone with his fingers. She could feel everyone's eyes upon them.

"Are you okay?" he asked.

"I'm bored," said Ann, surveying the crowd as they danced. "All this business chatter gets tedious."

"Welcome to my world, honey."

"And I'm happy to keep it in your world."

Mike kissed her forehead. The women in the room who noticed whispered their approval and envy to one another. "Do you want to go home?"

"No, no, no, it's early," said Ann. "I'm just ready to get up from the table and mingle a bit."

"So you can go find your higher society friends?" Ann laughed at Mike's joke.

They walked back to the Dilloway table, and Ann sat back down next to John Patterson, Mike's head of human resources. He was a nice enough man, but his wife, Lisa, rankled Ann. Ann admired Lisa's youthful chestnut-brown ringlets and her tiny runner's body, but nothing interesting ever came out of her mouth, which was frozen in an omniscient grin. When Ann first met her, she thought she'd had a bad face-lift, but each and every time Ann had seen Lisa since, the smile was there. No matter what the occasion, from funeral to stockholders' meeting to gala, she grinned like an amused toddler. John sat between them, but that didn't stop Lisa from leaning forward every several minutes to share her perpetual amusement with Ann.

When the key lime pie arrived at the table, Ann ordered another glass of champagne and then excused herself to go to the women's room. She washed her hands to remove any trace of sturgeon scent and then fluffed her hair with her plum-colored fingertips. She reapplied her matching lipstick and checked her profile in the mirror. She was making her way toward the door when Joan Stanton, a Dilloway by marriage, breezed in. Joan was a former beauty pageant queen, having spent eight years on the state and national circuits and coming incredibly close to being crowned Miss America in the early nineties. She had a gorgeously thin but at the same time voluptuous body and thick, wavy blond hair that fell just past her shoulders. She was in an Oscar de la Renta gown that accented her sizable breasts, and Ann's momentary jealousy heated her cheeks. It was gone in an instant, however, when Ann focused her attention on Joan's prominent nose—her one flaw. A nose job, Ann thought every time she saw it, a plastic surgeon's dream. "Ann," said Joan, approaching her with a practiced smile on her face. "How are you?"

"Wonderful," said Ann, leaning forward to accept a shoulder touch and a midair kiss. "And you?"

"Couldn't be better," said Joan. "We've just returned from the islands. The weather was spectacular."

It was always this way, whenever they chatted. It was always about money. Vacations, cars, clothes—money—and who had more. *"Fabulous,"* said Ann. "I hope we have the same for our cruise next spring."

Joan smiled at her reflection in the mirror. "Why wait until spring, darling? The best cruising weather is winter, when it's so terribly terrible here."

"Too true," said Ann.

"Will I see you at the fund-raising meeting?" asked Joan, meeting Ann's eyes in the mirror.

"You know I wouldn't miss it, dear." Ann blew out the door and walked with a determined gait down the hallway and into the grand foyer of the hotel. She stopped in front of an immense arrangement of white lilies that sat on a central table in the most magnificent cut-crystal vase she had ever seen and took a deep breath. Intoxicated by the fragrance, she lingered a moment.

"They are beautiful, aren't they?"

Ann whirled around and saw her friend, Jesse White, standing next to her. She smiled genuinely. "Where did you come from?"

"A catfight in the lower level powder room," said Jesse. "Two women just discovered they have the same dress." Ann covered her smile with her hand. "It was ugly in there," said Jesse. "I'm lucky to be alive." Ann laughed. "And your dress," said Jesse, reaching out to brush the back of her fingers against the fur trim at Ann's shoulder, "is one of the prettiest I've ever seen. Good choice."

"Thank you," said Ann. "And you look darling, too, my dear. Are you having fun?"

"I am," said Jesse. "Everyone at my table is drunk and uninhibitedly telling childhood stories. When Amy Claussen was seven, she caught her father and mother, pants and pantyhose around ankles, having sex in the laundry room one morning before breakfast."

Ann laughed again. "I want to be at your table. Mine's boring."

"That's because you're with the boss," said Jesse.

"And I should be getting back," said Ann. "Do you have time for lunch this week in your do-gooder schedule? I need your opinion on a few things."

"Yes," said Jesse. "How about lunch on Thursday? My pick this time, though, which means real food."

Ann smiled at her friend. "My parents arrive on Friday, so that sounds like perfect timing," she said, turning to walk back to the ballroom. When she reached her table, she sat down and picked up her champagne glass. Lisa leaned forward and grinned at her.

When Eileen called the following Monday morning, she reported to Ann that she had packed their belongings into two suitcases and three duffel bags that a neighborhood boy agreed to load into their station wagon. She had cleaned the house and washed the curtains and bedspreads. And she and Sam had packed up the canned and dry goods in the cupboard to be taken to the soup kitchen at the Congregational church in town. They could start their journey on Wednesday afternoon, after the real estate agent did her final walk-through to make sure everything was in order. Apparently, Charlene had several potential tenants lined up. Eileen and Sam would take their time, stopping along the way to enjoy scenic vistas and spending two nights in off-highway hotels. Charlene had even printed out a few suggestions from the Internet, Eileen told her daughter. That would make Friday their arrival date—just two-and-a-half weeks, Ann quickly calculated, from her mother's original phone call. In seventeen days, Ann had done everything necessary to move her seventy-two-year-old parents into her backyard. She praised her mother and told her to drive carefully. And then she made herself a latte and walked out to the guesthouse for the final inspection.

The one task remaining was telling Nate and Lauren. They had noticed the painters' truck in the driveway, but that was nothing new; Ann routinely redecorated rooms in the main house. She had no idea what her children would say, but she was certain it would not be positive. Ann looked at her watch, shut her notebook, and grabbed her purse from the back of the kitchen chair. In ten minutes, she would be at the gym, where she would dazzle her friend, Sally Butterfield, with the final details of the project. She'd invite her back to the house afterward for a latte and a tour. Once Sally saw the guesthouse, she would know just how ready Ann was to welcome her parents into her life.

Sally couldn't believe it was done, even though Ann had been in contact with her almost daily about the progress. They had chatted about fabrics and wallpaper, but Ann, wanting complete credit, hadn't shown Sally any of the samples.

"They won't be any trouble," said Ann, walking with Sally down the path from the kitchen to the guesthouse. "The caregiver is moving in tomorrow. I think we're all set." Ann pushed open the door and stepped into the entranceway. "Keep in mind," she said, gliding into the living area, "that this is a home for two old farmhouse dwellers. It's simple, it's country, and yet it's everything they need."

"Oh, look at the cows in the kitchen," said Sally, covering her cheeks with her French-manicured hands. "Cute, Ann. Wherever did you find paper like that?"

"In one of the hundreds of books I pored through," said Ann. "*Country Elements,* I think."

"And the furniture," cooed Sally, "perfect."

"I wanted something simple," said Ann, "something they would find comfortable instead of intimidating. The cherry in here is beautiful, of course, but it's polished and sophisticated. I wanted furniture they could set their coffee mug down on."

"And you've certainly done that."

"Of course, it's out of here the day my parents move out," said Ann. "Can you imagine housing guests with this decor?" Sally chuckled.

Ann showed her the bedrooms and bathrooms, which Sally agreed were more than adequate. And she also agreed with Ann that the quilted bedspreads and simple window treatments were as good a match with the bedroom furniture as what had been there before. "It works," said Ann, walking back through the front door with Sally in tow. "They'll be very comfortable. Now, how about a caramel latte?"

Sally nodded her head enthusiastically and then, heeling like a well-trained dog, she followed Ann back into the big house.

After Sally left, Ann called Mike and left a message, reminding him to meet her and the children at Tony's for dinner at seven o'clock. She then called Nate and Lauren and left the same message on their cell phones. That would give them more than an hour after football and volleyball practice to shower and drive to the restaurant. Ann told Nate to give his sister a ride, if he wanted his exorbitant car insurance paid that month. Nate would be furious with her interference, but Ann didn't give this a second thought. She had no time to go to the high school to fetch Lauren.

At four o'clock, when Tony's opened for the evening, Ann

called to make a reservation. She recognized Tony's voice. "It's Ann," she said.

"Well, hello, Mrs. Barons," said Tony playfully. "Where have you been? Are you eating at The Chart House?"

Ann blushed. "Just once," she said. "We went once, and the food was *terrible.*"

Tony laughed. "What can I do for you?"

"I need a table for tonight," said Ann.

"I think I can arrange that."

"We need something off to the side," said Ann. "We've got some news for the children and there may be some noise."

"Oh," said Tony, "are you leaving them?"

It was Ann's turn to laugh. "My parents are moving in with us," said Ann, "temporarily."

"In that case," said Tony, "I'd better put you in the back room."

"I'll see you tonight," said Ann. "Seven o'clock."

"We'll be ready," said Tony before he hung up.

Ann ran the bathwater and slowly took off her clothes. Naked, she walked into her closet. Hands on her slim hips, she glanced at her wardrobe. She chewed on her bottom lip; she had no idea what to wear. She walked back out of her closet and into the bathroom. She stepped onto her scale, already knowing she weighed 105 pounds. At five feet, five inches, she was considered very thin. Her doctor routinely advised her to gain ten pounds and warned her about osteoporosis, but Ann dismissed her advice. She would rather suffer a long list of ailments than put on ten pounds of blubber. She gazed at her reflection in the wall mirrors. While perimenopause was beginning to thicken the waists of some of her friends, Ann's stomach was flat. Her breasts were circular, firm. Her muscular legs were void of fat, even her inner thighs. Her arms looked like they were cut from flesh-colored limestone. She spun around and looked at her backside. Her rear end was tiny and tight with no sign of flabby, disgusting cellulite, a miracle at her age.

Ann walked up the two steps to reach her tub, and then stepped down into it. She lay back and let the bubbles envelop her. She closed her eyes and tried to predict the kids' reaction to her news. Would they protest? Would they shrug and return to their dinners? Nate wouldn't care; Ann couldn't figure out what he cared about, if anything at all, except his independence. He had always been an independent child. As soon as he learned to walk, at eleven months, he wanted to be on his own. Ann used to chase him around the living room of their old house, both of them laughing as he increased his distance from her. He shunned his crib at two, preferring a "big boy bed" and a dark room for sleeping. There had been one episode of nightmares just past Nate's fourth birthday that drove him into his mother's arms. He cried out in the middle of the night, insisting on sleeping next to her and then moving his body into hers, attaching himself, so that they were more like one person than two. And while Ann had tried to whisper away his fears, she was selfishly grateful for the few months he needed her.

Lauren was more verbal, more needy, than her brother. In high school, she had become more circumspect, preferring to confide in her friends, Ann guessed, than share secrets with her. But before that, as late as seventh grade, Lauren chatted eagerly about everything from boys and who liked who to teacher personalities and homework. And Ann had just as eagerly listened, often spending several minutes with Lauren sitting on her bed before Lauren became silent with fatigue. Lauren still opened up to Ann, rarely. But mostly, Lauren—and Nate—chose to talk, eat, and spend most of their time with their peers. They're normal teenagers, Mike and her friends told her. But Ann felt discarded and discredited nonetheless.

Ann decided to dress casually, in moss green suede pants and a black and white striped angora sweater. She took some new black shoes out of a box in the back of her closet and slipped them on her bare feet. As if the shoes had been hand-sewn to conform to every contour, the soft Italian leather gently clung to her skin, from her narrow heel to her lacquered big toe. Back in the bathroom, she applied her makeup and then rubbed cream into her hands before reaching for the ring she removed to bathe. Women could barely keep their eyes off the six-carat diamond and sapphire trade-up engagement ring Mike had bought her when she turned forty; their gaze ping-ponging from her face to the ring, face and the ring. She looked at the ring and then herself in the mirror one last time before turning out the light.

Tony's was crowded, but, as promised, a table was ready when Ann walked through the door. It was just before seven when she sat down. Five minutes later, Mike joined her. "I had a four-hour meeting today," he said, sitting down and loosening his tie. "I've never needed a drink more."

"I beat you to it," said Ann, holding up her glass of champagne.

"Are the kids coming?"

"Yes," said Ann. "At least, I hope they're coming. I left messages with both of them."

Mike ordered a scotch, which arrived just as Nate, glaring at Ann, and Lauren, ponytailed black hair still wet from her postpractice shower and dressed in jeans and a button-down pink oxford cloth shirt, approached the table. Mike took a long drink. Lauren gave her parents a tight smile, then sat down. Nate stood behind his chair. "That's blackmail," he said to his mother. "Ordering me to drive my sister around in exchange for insurance payment is blackmail."

"Sit down, Nate," said Mike, putting his white cloth napkin in his lap. Mike was increasingly ordering Nate to sit. Nate had grown six inches in the past year, and while he was nowhere close to Mike's height, he was closing in.

"I'm serious," said Nate, yanking his chair out from under the table and flopping down onto the seat. He jerked his head to coax his blond bangs out of his eyes, a frequent maneuver with results lasting only seconds. Ann had stopped riding him about cutting his hair, heeding Mike's advice to pick her battles. Big or small, she seemed to lose all of them. "She's a big girl. She can find her own rides."

"And you're a big boy," said Mike. "So you should understand that you, too, can find your own rides. Your car can certainly sit in the garage until you're mature enough to pay for it." Nate knew a threat when he heard one. His father would never follow through, but it nonetheless hung there, fouling the air, until Nate took a sip of water from the glass their server just filled.

"I'm Mario," he said. "Would you like to hear the specials?"

"No," said Ann. "I'll have poached salmon and a house salad with raspberry vinaigrette on the side."

"And I'll have a Caesar salad and tortellini Alfredo," said Mike.

Ann frowned and said, "Call nine-one-one when you put in that order."

Mario smiled agreeably. "And for the young lady?"

"I'll have what my dad's having," Lauren said. "I'm starving." She put her napkin in her lap and straightened the flatware at her place setting.

"There goes your waistline," said Ann, taking a sip of her drink.

"Ann," said Mike, "she's just come from a two-hour volleyball practice."

Lauren, who wore a size six contentedly, made eye contact with her dad, a mirror image.

"And I'll have a cheeseburger and fries," said Nate.

"I'm sorry, young sir," said Mario. "We don't have cheese-burgers."

"You're kidding," said Nate. "It's the twenty-first century and you don't have cheeseburgers?"

"Can you check in the back?" asked Mike. "See if they can make him one. If not, bring him a plate of spaghetti and meat-balls."

"If they can make meatballs," said Nate, folding his arms across his chest, "they can make a burger."

"Good point," said Mike.

"Yes sir," Mario said, and then left the table.

"So," said Ann, "how was everyone's day?"

"Perfect," said Nate sarcastically. "All the teachers praised my work, and I got three touchdowns in football practice. How about you, Ann? Yummy massage at the spa?"

Ann took a sip of her drink. She tried to remember when Nate had first started calling her by her first name. It was in the last year or so, before he had his license, because they were in the car together and it had begun as a joke. And it seemed appropriate then, funny even. He used her name differently now, when he called her anything at all.

"That's enough, Nate," said Mike. "How was your day, Lauren?"

"Fine, Daddy," she said. "I got a B+ on a math test."

"Good girl," said Mike, looking at the menu even though he'd already ordered.

"Good girl?" said Nate, flipping his hair that had fallen back into his eyes. "You blow a gasket every time I get a B."

"Shall I stock up on gaskets?" asked Mike, looking across the table at his son. "When do report cards come home?"

"Next week," said Lauren, at the same time Nate said, "I don't know." Nate shot his sister a look.

"Just before Thanksgiving," said Lauren softly, finishing her sentence.

"I'm looking forward to Thanksgiving," said Ann, jumping into the conversation. "We're going to have some very special guests." Nate and Lauren looked at their mother.

"Your grandparents are arriving at the end of the week. They'll be here for Thanksgiving and for some time afterward."

"What are you talking about?" asked Nate, his hazel eyes boring into his mother's matching set.

Ann savored the last few bubbles of her champagne and then set her glass down on the table. She pushed the words through her lips. "Gramps and Gran are coming to live with us for a while," she said. "They need temporary housing until the spring, when they can move into an assisted-living facility."

"What?" said Lauren. "When did you decide this?"

"Thanks for asking our opinion," said Nate, refolding his arms across his chest.

"And what is your opinion?" asked Mike.

"Gran and Gramps living with us twenty-four/seven, parading around the house in forty-year-old but 'perfectly good' bathrobes and mismatched slippers? What do you think?"

The remark about slippers was in reference to their visit with Ann's parents last Christmas. Her father had come into the room on Christmas morning with a sheepskin slipper on one foot while the other was unsuccessfully crammed into Eileen's penny loafer. They had all laughed, thinking Sam had done it on purpose. And because he was adept at concealing and compensating for his disease, no one had questioned it.

"They're going to live in the guesthouse," said Ann. "You'll only see them at Sunday dinner."

"Since when have we had Sunday dinner?" asked Nate.

"I don't even know them," said Lauren, reaching for her water glass. "And now they're living with us?"

"You will get to know them," said Ann.

"I don't think so," said Nate.

Ann unfolded her napkin and laid it in her lap. Mike checked his BlackBerry. Mario arrived at a silent table with their dinners, including a cheeseburger and fries for Nate.

"Your grandparents need us right now," Mike said to his kids after their plates were set down in front of them and Mario had retreated to the kitchen. "I know you have your friends and your activities. We all do. And, for the most part, we can carry on. We will have to make an effort every now and again, however, to spend some time with our guests. Remember that most of the burden will fall on your mother, not on you." Ann forced a smile. "Everything is going be the same, basically," said Mike. "They'll live in the guesthouse. We'll live in our house. It couldn't be a better arrangement."

CHAPTER 3

$\approx$

Ann got a large, extra-hot, fat-free caramel latte at the Coffee Now drive-through on her way to the mall. She had her nails touched up and bought a dozen Godiva chocolates and six Gerbera daisies before racing to the salon for her weekly bangs trim. When she arrived home, she jogged down the path to the guesthouse. She put the chocolates, which she had temporarily stored in her car cooler, in the refrigerator, and set the flowers in the cute white milk-jug vase she found at T.J.Maxx, and then placed them on the living room table. She took a quick look around to make sure everything was in order. The caregiver, Selma Jackson, drove in just as Ann was walking out the front door. Ann jogged to the driveway to greet her. "Good morning, Selma," said Ann cheerily as soon as Selma opened the car door.

"Good morning, Mrs. Barons," said Selma, meeting Ann's gaze.

"Today is the big day."

"Yes, it is, Mrs. Barons."

Ann looked into the backseat of Selma's 1994 Ford Taurus and saw several cloth bags filled with food. "I see you did the grocery shopping."

"Yes," said Selma, easing herself out of the car. Standing, she put her hands on her lower back and leaned back briefly before righting herself. "It doesn't matter if I'm in a car five minutes or five hours," she said, explaining, "my back is not was it used to be. Too many hours on my feet in too many hospital rooms." She was shorter than Ann expected, and slighter, making Ann wonder if she could handle a man her father's size. But she was younger looking than her sixty years, with barely a wrinkle on her brown face and clear dark brown eyes that didn't require glasses. She reached for Ann's hand. "It's nice to meet you," she said. "I'm fine with the telephone, but I don't feel like I really know a person until I have a chance to look them over."

Ann took her hand and shook it. "Yes," she said. "I completely agree. Are you all moved in? I'm sorry I wasn't here earlier; I had to run some errands."

"Yes. And as soon as I get these groceries in the house, I'll change into something more presentable. I thought I'd make chicken noodle soup. After traveling today, your parents will want something easy to digest," she said.

"That sounds delicious," said Ann, hands pressed against one another in front of her chest.

Selma looked at the man's watch on her wrist. "I expect they'll be arriving soon."

"Yes," said Ann, looking at her Rolex. "You should *officially* be on duty in about an hour. My mother called from the hotel this morning. They're right on schedule."

The pleasantries behind them, Selma turned her attention to the groceries sitting on the backseat of the car. She opened the door of the car and grabbed the handles of four cloth grocery bags, two in each hand. "Well, I'd better get started then," she said, pushing the car door closed with her right foot. Ann watched with pride as Selma trudged along the path with the bags and disappeared into the house.

Ninety minutes later, Eileen pulled their Ford station wagon into the driveway. Ann, who was on the phone in the kitchen, hung up and ran out the back door as soon as she saw the car. Eileen waved through the windshield as she shifted into PARK. Ann opened her door. "Is everything okay?" she asked. "I've been worried about you."

"Hello," said Eileen, lifting herself out of the driver's seat. "We're fine. Your father wanted to stop at the dairy thirty miles back for ice cream."

"Oh," said Ann.

"We've had quite a morning," said Eileen, giving her daughter a hug. "Ice cream was just the ticket. Your father has always loved ice cream, vanilla ice cream. We had it every afternoon in the summer when you were growing up. Do you remember that?"

"How could I forget," said Ann, wrapping her arms around her mother's sloping shoulders. "It's taken me a thousand trips to the gym to work it all off."

Hands on Ann's bony arms, Eileen took a step back and looked at her daughter. "You're too thin, dear," she said. "Next time, I'll bring some back for you."

"I never eat it," said Ann, shaking her head.

"Well," said Eileen. As she launched into a colorful description of the acres of farmland they drove by, Sam, still imprisoned in the car, fiddled with the door handle. Unable to lift it, he knocked on the window. Remembering him, Eileen walked around the front of the car to open the door for him. "It's not easy to work these handles, honey," she said.

"You have no idea," said Sam as Eileen bent down to undo his seat belt. She then grabbed his wrists and planted her black tie–shoed feet shoulder-width apart on the driveway. "Swing your legs around now." Sam quickly lifted his feet from the car floor, as if he had just stepped in something distasteful, and moved them in the direction of the door. Eileen dropped one wrist and used that hand to guide her husband's legs over the metal trim and his feet onto Ann's driveway. "Now duck your head." And with Sam scooting himself forward, and Eileen pulling from outside the car, it took just thirty seconds or so to birth Sam from the car's cavity. Like a newborn calf, he was unsteady on his feet. He took hold of the car door to regain his balance, blinking his eyes in the bright sunshine. Ann studied him a moment before walking around the front of the car to greet him. She hugged him quickly, careful to avoid the dollop of melted ice cream on his flannel shirt, and then stepped back to look at his face. It was as cold, white, and lifeless as a vacant ski slope. The muscles in his cheeks had gone limp, had simply abandoned their job of holding up his mouth. His deep blue eyes, formerly keen and focused—he had not needed reading glasses until he was fifty-eight—were watery and empty. "Who's this young girl?" he asked, turning his face to his wife for clues.

Eileen smiled and put her hand on Ann's shoulder. "It's Annie," she said, "your daughter."

"Really?" said Sam, looking back at Ann. "It's been a long time, hasn't it?"

"Well, since Christmas," said Ann. "We were at the farm last Christmas. How was your trip?"

"Very good," said Sam, "except for the fog this morning." Ann looked at her mother.

Eileen waved her hand dismissively. "It's always somewhat foggy, dear."

"Let's go inside," said Ann. "We can get settled and then have a nice chat."

Ann was halfway to the guesthouse before she realized that her parents were not right behind her. She stopped, turned, and watched her father shuffle from the driveway onto the brick path, kicking the crushed shells onto the grass with his worn moccasins that never lost contact with the ground. When they finally reached the front door, Ann waited a dramatic moment before leading them inside.

"Oh Ann, this is lovely," said Eileen, following her daughter into the living room. "Isn't this great?" she turned to ask Sam.

"Swell," said Sam, taking in the room with slow, deliberate head turns. "It's going to cost me a bundle, so I'm glad you like it."

"I sure do," said Eileen, kissing her husband's cheek. "Why don't you make yourself comfortable on the couch while Ann gives me a tour."

"I wouldn't mind having the grand tour myself," said Sam.

"And you shall have it," said Eileen. "I just need to use the powder room."

"Oh well," said Sam, sitting down hard on the couch.

Ann waved her mother into the bedroom, half-closed the door behind them, and spoke in an urgent whisper. "Mom," she said, "Dad didn't recognize me."

"Don't worry about that, dear," said Eileen, rubbing her daughter's arm. "He's like that sometimes, especially after a long day. He mixes me up with his mother, of all people."

"Why didn't you tell me about this?" asked Ann. "It happened on the phone a couple of weeks ago, and it's happening again."

Eileen took a deep breath, sucking in her stomach, and then slowly exhaled. "I don't know," she said. "I guess I didn't think too much about it at first. As I've told you, when you live with someone, change is gradual. It wasn't until summertime that he really started going downhill."

"He seems pretty close to the bottom of the hill," said Ann. "I wish I had known."

"And what could you have done, Ann? This is not a solvable problem. This is permanent."

Ann lowered her eyes. "I don't understand how this could have happened."

"It's just rotten luck," said Eileen. "Nothing more than that."

"And you've been handling this, handling him on your own, for the last six months."

"Not anymore," said Eileen, brushing away the stray gray strands of hair from her forehead with her fingers. "I can't do it anymore. And that's why I called Meadowbrook. When I talked to them in July, they said they'd be able to take us before Christmas. I figured I could take care of your dad until then. I've been doing it for forty-eight years."

Ann put her hands on her hips. "Have you had *any* help?"

"Here and there," said Eileen, looking out the glass sliding door at the woods behind the house. "Our friends have been wonderful. For the most part, we've just been doing less. He's best at home."

"How did you get out, to get groceries, or get your hair cut?" asked Ann.

"He went to day care when I needed some time off," said Eileen. "But he's been more agitated in the last month or so. Remember, I told you he tried to escape."

"Yes, I remember," said Ann, a searchlight in her brain, sweeping for the facts.

Eileen smiled slightly at her daughter. "We'll be okay," she said. "It's so good to be here."

"It's good to have you here, Mom," said Ann, accepting a hug.

"Now, let me use the bathroom and then we can get down to the business of unpacking. I never feel at home until my suitcase is empty."

"The bathroom's right there," said Ann, pointing to a doorway in the corner of the room. "I'll meet you in the kitchen." Ann walked back into the living room, where her father was tracing the plaid pattern on the couch with his right index finger. Ann lingered a moment, then moved quickly and quietly behind him to the kitchen. She moved as close to the stove as possible, so that her father couldn't see her if he turned his head. She lifted the lid of the soup pot, closed her eyes, and inhaled.

"Now what smells so good?" said Eileen, a few minutes later, as she walked through the living room and into the kitchen. "I must be hungry."

"Chicken noodle soup," said Ann, again lifting the lid to show her mother the diced carrots, celery, and onion simmering around bite-sized pieces of chicken and egg noodles in a clear yellow broth.

"You were always a good cook," said Eileen, "and you were sweet to make it—and to remember that it's your father's favorite."

"I didn't make it," said Ann, replacing the lid. "Believe it or not, I hardly ever cook now, Mom. But Selma, your caregiver, is supposed to be wonderful in the kitchen."

"Is she here?" asked Eileen, peeking through the space under the cabinets into the living room, as if she'd missed seeing her on the way in.

"She was here a while ago," said Ann. "Maybe she had to run out for something."

Together, they walked back into the living room. Eileen sat next to Sam on the couch and Ann sat in the chair facing them. She looked at her father's face, both familiar and foreign, and couldn't think of a single thing to say. She looked down at her hands in her lap.

"Everything looks so fresh and clean," said Eileen.

"Yes," said Ann, happy for conversation. "I've redone it."

Sam looked at Ann. "When will the others arrive?" he asked.

"Who?" asked Ann.

"Don't tell me they've canceled," said Sam, switching his gaze to Eileen.

"No one's canceled," said Eileen, patting his hand.

Just then, Selma came breathlessly through the door carrying a baguette. "I'm sorry," she said. "I forgot the bread."

"No trouble," said Ann. "Come in and meet my parents."

Eileen stood and extended her hand. "Nice to meet you, Selma."

"And you, too, Mrs. Sanford," said Selma, shaking it.

"Please, please call me Eileen. You're awfully nice to be here with us."

"That's my job," said Selma. "I think we'll get along just fine."

"Well, if that's your soup I smell, I know we will," said Eileen. "This is my husband, Sam."

Sam scooted forward on the couch cushion, readying himself to rise. Selma approached him and set her hand gently on his shoulder. "Please stay seated," she said.

"Have we met?" he asked, searching her eyes for signs of recognition.

"I don't think so," she said. "But it's nice to meet you now."

"When do we eat?" he asked. "I'm as hungry as a black bear in spring."

"Soon," said Selma. "I'll go check on things in the kitchen."

Silence filled the open space. "Well," said Eileen, after a moment. "I'm going to grab a few things from the car and start unpacking."

As soon as her mother turned to go, Ann stood. "Let me help you," she said.

"I'm fine," said Eileen, calling over her shoulder as she walked to the door. "I'm just going to get my duffel bag. I'll get the other bags after lunch."

"What can I do?"

Her hand on the doorknob, Eileen called to her daughter, "Stay with your dad. It will take him some time to adjust to these new surroundings."

Ann sat back down in the chair facing the couch, her father, and the string of saliva hanging from his chin. She looked at the floor. Forcing her eyes to his face, Ann said, "So, Dad. How was your drive?"

"Fine," answered Sam. "How was yours?"

"I didn't have a drive," said Ann.

"How did you get here then?" asked Sam.

"I live here. This is my house."

Sam smiled at her. "You're putting me on."

"No," said Ann.

After a moment, Sam again shifted his bottom to the edge of the couch cushion. "Well, I've had a nice stay," he said, "but I've got to get home now. My wife will be looking for me."

Alarmed, Ann stood and put her arms out in front of her, to give herself time to think, to stop him from moving. She called for Selma, who appeared from the kitchen just as Sam, who was more off the couch than on, slid to the floor and covered his face with his hands. "Leave me alone!" he shouted in a raspy, warbled voice.

"What is it, Dad?" asked Ann, frozen in place.

"They're out there again," said Sam, pointing at the large living room window. "They've followed me here!"

Ann glanced at the window and saw nothing but clear glass, the grass, and the back of her house. "Who, Dad," she asked urgently, "who do you see?"

Selma stepped forward and touched Sam's arm. "I've got some cookies," she said gently. "Come into the kitchen with me."

"What about them?" asked Sam, breathing hard and again pointing at the window.

"They won't bother us," said Selma. "They don't like cookies." Sam looked at Selma, back at the window, and then back at her. Her smile ran around her face in a circle, from the edge of her mouth through the tiny laugh lines at the corners of her eyes and back down to her to soft brown lips. "Let's get something to eat," she said. Sam slowly shifted to his hands and knees and then used the couch, with Selma holding on to his free elbow, to lift himself off the floor. Ann watched as he followed Selma into the kitchen. She helped him sit at the table before reaching into the end cupboard and pulling out a red tin. Ann watched her take two oatmeal cookies from the tin, put them on a paper napkin, and calmly set them down in front of Sam. The incident was over, but Ann's chest still thundered. Moments later, Eileen walked through the front door carrying a duffel bag. Ann followed her mother into their bedroom, tears and terror in her eyes, and told her what she just witnessed.

"Honey, honey," said Eileen, rubbing Ann's back. "It's okay. Well, I mean, it's not okay. He's not okay. But we can handle this."

"I don't understand what's going on," said Ann, holding on to her mother. "I don't know how this happened. Why it happened."

Eileen pulled a tissue from the pocket of her dress and handed it to her daughter, who accepted it, took a step backward, and blew her nose. "What happened out there, what you just saw, is what the doctor calls hallucinations. Your father sees things—people mostly— that aren't there. He imagines things. Remember I told you about the kitchen staff at the Lutheran church? These flashes of fantasy are, unfortunately, happening more frequently," said Eileen, "but thankfully they don't last terribly long. And I'm getting better at distracting him. It sounds like Selma did the same thing."

"Yes," said Ann. "She seemed to know exactly what she was doing. But how can we change this, Mom? What did the doctor say about that?"

"The doctor thinks this is partially the disease, and partially a side effect of his medication."

"Can we change the medication?"

"We have fiddled with it, here and there," said Eileen, lifting her duffel from the carpet to the bed. "But, in the end, the good outweighs the bad."

"What is the good?"

"He can move. The tremors in his hands and feet are under control. The rigidity that struck his entire left side has softened."

"Good God," said Ann, putting her hand to her chest. "I've never seen anything like that."

"Well, yes," said Eileen, unzipping her bag. "I would imagine it's terrifying."

"And is that why he drools?" asked Ann. "The medication?"

"He drools because he's lost the use of some of his facial muscles," said Eileen, taking three sweaters out of her bag. "Plus, he can have a hard time swallowing. I always carry a handkerchief with me."

"Well," said Ann, taking another step backward, "you must be hungry. Would you like some soup?"

"I'm just going to unpack this duffel and I'll be ready," said Eileen, putting several cotton turtlenecks into an empty bureau drawer. "I'll be there in a minute."

"Oh, I can't stay," Ann lied. "I've got a few things to take care of at the house."

"Will we see you for dinner?"

"Of course," said Ann, backing out of the bedroom. "I'll come and get you."

"Come back anytime," said Eileen. "We're here all afternoon."

"Okay," said Ann, over her shoulder. She flew out the front door and jogged up the path to her house. In her own kitchen, Ann locked the door behind her, then raced to the sink to wash her hands. She dried them on a fresh towel from her linen drawer and made a mental note to change her kitchen hand towels every day. She scooped two spoons of coffee into her cappuccino machine and grabbed some skim milk from the refrigerator. Her father was in another world. She steamed the milk for her coffee, wondering how her seventy-two-year-old mother had been taking care of someone in that condition. Thank God for Selma. She seemed more than capable. Ann took her drink to the island and pulled the stool out from underneath. She sat there, staring out the back window at the guesthouse, glad for the seventy yards between her parents and herself.

After a few sips from her mug, Ann called Mike. When she got his voice mail, she hung up and called his secretary. If anyone could find Mike, it was Peggy. At fifty-five, Peggy had more energy than anyone in the office, Mike included. And she was unusually loyal to Mike for a woman not interested in seducing him. Mike depended on her for booking his travel, his meetings, and his manicures, putting the right people through on his phone, finding the perfect gift for Ann, ensuring his long days didn't get any longer, and, on some days, making sure he ate lunch. Plus, she knew how to keep her mouth shut. And for this he paid her three times the salary of the other Dilloway executive assistants. "Yes, Mrs. Barons," said Peggy. "And how are you today?"

"Fine, Peggy. Do you know where he is?"

"In a meeting," she said. "It's scheduled to run another hour. My guess is it will go over." Ann sighed. "I can text him, Mrs. Barons." Mike, Ann knew, would not consider her father's condition an emergency, so she asked Peggy to tell Mike to call her as soon as he could.

Next, Ann called Sally, who answered the phone on the third ring. "Sally, it's me."

"Hello, darling," said Sally. "Where have you been? We missed you at the gym this morning."

"I exercised here," said Ann. "My parents arrived today."

"Yes, yes, of course they did," said Sally. "And how is everyone?"

"Terrible," said Ann. "My father is completely out of it. I don't know how in the world he got this way. Last Christmas, he seemed fine."

"What do you mean by 'out of it'?" asked Sally.

"He's gone, Sally, mentally and physically," said Ann, massaging her forehead. "He has no idea what's going on. He drools constantly. Sally, he didn't know me when he saw me."

"Oh God," said Sally. "You poor thing. What are you going to do?"

"I don't know," said Ann. "I had no idea what I was getting into. My mother didn't tell me any of this."

"Do you need a cappuccino?" asked Sally.

"I just had one," said Ann.

"Do you want me to come over?"

Ann thought about Sally's offer. On the one hand, she would

love Sally to keep her company. They could talk about Ann's problem and Sally would provide enough sympathy to quell—temporarily at least—Ann's anxiety. On the other hand, Sally wasn't completely trustworthy. If Ann wanted her innermost feelings spread all over town, she could do it herself. Still, Sally was always so affirming. Ann was just about to invite her when she heard her mother tapping on the back door. "I'll have to call you back," she said, hanging up the phone. Ann walked to the door and opened it. "Is everything okay?"

"Yes," said Eileen, crossed arms holding her thick wool cardigan sweater in place. "We're fine. Your father fell asleep on the couch, so I thought I'd sneak over here and have a chat with you. You looked like you were in shock, honey."

"Well, yes," said Ann, closing the door behind her mother and pulling a chair out from underneath the kitchen table so she could sit.

"He's not as bad as he appears," said Eileen, removing her sweater and then tucking the hem of her floral traveling dress underneath her before she sat.

"That's good," said Ann, "because he appears to be pretty bad."

"Well, you're right," said Eileen, cradling her hands in her lap. "He doesn't think like you and I think. He forgets what he's doing in the middle of a task. He loses everything, mostly because he puts things down in illogical places and then can't find them later. He spends some days walking around the house in circles, looking for this or that. But he's docile and, except for his hallucinations, relatively content."

"Tell me more about his hallucinations," said Ann.

"Well," said Eileen, "as I said, most of the time they're people, somewhat troll-like in nature from what he has told me. He thinks they're spying on him. It's paranoia gone haywire, really. The doctor recently altered his medication, though, so things should change for the better."

"I hope so," said Ann, glancing out the window behind her mother.

"I'd love some tea," said Eileen. "Selma and I looked in the cupboards, but we didn't see any."

"I'll have her pick some up at the store."

"That sounds good," said Eileen. "Do you have any tea here?"

"Of course I do," said Ann.

"I'd love a cup."

"Now?"

"Lovely," said Eileen. "If you have the time. I know you have things to take care of this afternoon."

Ann retucked her hair behind her ears. "I've got time for a cup of tea," she said. She lifted herself out of the chair and walked slowly to the stove for the teakettle. She filled it with water, ignited the gas burner, and then set the kettle back down to boil. "So," she asked, returning to the table, "where does he see these people?"

"Outside, mostly," said Eileen. "They sit in trees or in parked cars. Sometimes they wave or take notes."

"Good God," said Ann, closing her eyes.

Eileen reached across the space between them and touched Ann's hand. "It's okay," she said. "Sometimes his hallucinations are good. Sometimes he sees children."

"You should have *told* me," said Ann earnestly.

Eileen's smile was tired. "He'll be okay," she said. "With all of us looking after him, he'll be okay."

Ann looked into her mother's blue eyes. She wanted to see behind them, to know what enabled her to care for such a sick man. What would Ann do if Mike got sick? What would he do if she got sick? The water boiled. Ann removed the kettle from the burner and extinguished the flame. Then she walked into the dining room to retrieve the china teapot she kept in one of the corner cupboards. She returned to the kitchen and rinsed out the dust with hot soapy water. No leaks. She poured in the water from the kettle, dropped in two tea bags, and then watched the liquid turn brown. Eileen studied her from the table. "Do you still drink tea?" she asked her daughter.

"No," said Ann. "I drink coffee."

"You used to drink it. Remember?" said Eileen. "You and I had it every afternoon, in the wintertime, when we were preparing dinner."

"Tea and cookies," said Ann, bringing the pot to the table. "I'd forgotten." Ann went back to the china cupboard in the dining room for two cups and saucers. She rinsed them in the sink and then brought them to the table. She sat and again looked out the window at the guesthouse.

"You changed the color of the walls in here," said Eileen, breaking the silence.

Ann looked back at her mother. "That's right," said Ann, pouring out the tea. "You haven't seen the house since it was just done, have you? We've made a lot of changes."

"Let's enjoy our tea," said Eileen, "and then I'd love a tour."

Ann gave her mother a tour that included almost everything: the home gym, spa, and game room on the lower level; the living room and dining room, Mike's study, and the family room on the main level; and the master bedroom suite, guest bedrooms, and two of the other four bathrooms on the second story. She avoided Lauren's and Nate's rooms and their bathrooms because she knew what condition they were in. As a child, Ann had been expected to keep her room tidy. "Well," said Eileen, as they walked back into the kitchen from the hallway. "You certainly do have a beautiful home."

"Thank you," said Ann. "We're proud of it."

"Yes," said Eileen. "I can see that."

"I hope you'll be comfortable in the guesthouse," said Ann.

"How could we not be comfortable?"

"It's a bit small," said Ann, "for a prolonged stay. It's meant to be a weekend retreat."

"It's perfect," said Eileen. "Your father and I don't require much."

Ann's cell phone, sitting on the kitchen counter, rang Mike's tune. "I've got to get this," she said, already reaching for it.

"Thanks for the tea and the tour," said Eileen, grabbing her sweater from the chair before slipping out the back door. "We'll talk more later."

Mike had just five minutes for Ann. He was in a financial status meeting, his third that day. Knowing she shouldn't burden him, but unable to stop herself, Ann poured out her woes, fears, and concerns in sixty seconds. Mike listened to his wife while he thought about what the latest numbers would do to their annual target. When she was done, he assured her everything would be okay. He had to get back to the meeting, but he would come home after that, certainly in time for dinner. He suggested she call Nate and Lauren to ensure their presence at the table. It would be their first night as an extended family.

Nate answered his cell phone, even though he knew it was his mother. He was sitting at Burger King with his best friend, Josh Petersen, having a late lunch in lieu of physics class. He balked when she told him to be home early for dinner; he had already made plans to go to the library with his girlfriend, Jenny Garr, to watch her study. Ann told him to be home by six o'clock, if he knew what was good for him. Nate told his mother she had no idea what was and what wasn't good for him, but he would consider her request. After he hung up, he called Jenny. She told him under no circumstances should he go to the library. She could study better without him, and grandparents, she said, were important. After he hung up the phone, Nate took a sip of his chocolate shake and announced that women were sentimental idiots.

Lauren called her mother back when she got out of chemistry. She promised to be home by six. She did, however, have a lot of homework that night and would not be able to stay at the dinner table long. Lauren hesitated just a moment before beefing up the fib, telling her mother that she had three tests the next day. Ann told her dinner would last thirty minutes, tops. From her brief visit that morning, Ann couldn't imagine her father lasting more time than that.

Emma Lindholm, Ann's stout housekeeper, walked into the kitchen just as Ann was finishing her conversation with Lauren. Emma reported that the quail, wild rice, and spinach salad would be ready whenever Ann needed them. White wine would be served with dinner and pecan pie afterward. Feeling on top of things again, Ann gave Emma a rare pat on her substantial shoulder, then left the room. She would call Sally back from her speakerphone in the basement while she rode her Lifecycle.

* * *

Just before six, Mike walked through the garage door into the kitchen, carrying his briefcase, with Lauren, backpack on one shoulder, who had been driven home by a friend. Ann gave them both quick kisses and told them to wash their hands for dinner, which would be ready in five minutes. They both walked out—Lauren to dump her stuff upstairs and Mike to turn on his home computer—just before Eileen, trailed by Sam, walked in the back door. "Doesn't something smell delicious," said Eileen, peeling off her camel-hair overcoat to reveal a pressed white blouse and a string of pearls paired with a pair of plaid wool slacks. She helped Sam out of his coat and then steered him to a window seat cushion, onto which he slowly lowered himself.

"Yes," said Ann, giddy with the evening's early successes. "Our Emma has outdone herself, once again." Emma, who was putting the finishing touches on the salad, turned from her task and smiled.

"Hello, Emma," said Eileen, walking toward her and extending her hand. "It's been a long time."

"Yes," said Emma, wiping her hands on her apron before taking Eileen's hand and shaking it once. The women, about the same age, took one another in with swift glances—checking for color in the face and eyes, stooped posture, or swollen ankles—quickly calculating physical strength and mental acuity. "It's good to have you here. I've always liked cooking for a crowd."

"Oh, did you make our dinner?" asked Eileen, kidding her.

"I'm happy for the opportunity," said Emma, returning her attention and hands to the salad. Her knuckles, Eileen noticed, were plagued with osteoarthritis. Emma had stopped trying to hide this deformity, as her fingers were involved, and therefore visible, in every task she performed, from finely mincing scallions to guiding a dust cloth around the curves and corners of Ann's furniture.

"And I'm happy, too," said Ann. "All I can do well in the kitchen is boil water."

"That's not true," said Eileen. "You used to be quite a good cook."

"That," said Ann, taking a sip from her half-empty glass of wine, "was a long time ago."

"I'd like to say something," said Sam abruptly from across the room. Eileen and Ann turned to look at him. For a moment, Ann had forgotten he was there. "This is a lovely place we're staying in."

"Yes," said Eileen, going to him and patting his back. "We're lucky to be here."

"Hi, Gran," said Lauren, twirling a strand of her black hair around her index finger in the kitchen doorway.

"Lauren!" said Eileen, leaving Sam and crossing the kitchen to hug her granddaughter. "How nice to see you, dear. Did you have a good day?"

"I did," said Lauren. "How was your trip here?"

"Fine," said Eileen. "You're sweet to ask. Come say hello to your grandfather." Lauren walked with Eileen to the window, where Sam was still sitting, looking up at them. "Sam, you remember Lauren, your granddaughter." Sam looked at Lauren blankly.

"It's your granddaughter, Lauren," Eileen said again.

"Well, so it is," said Sam, struggling to get up as he extended his hand. "Hello, Lauren."

"Don't get up, dear," said Eileen. "It's okay."

Lauren took his dry hand and gave it a gentle shake. As soon as he let go, she stepped backward and then quickly turned to face her mother. "Where's Nate?" she asked.

"Late," said Ann, looking at her watch. "We're eating in five minutes."

"Well," said Mike, walking into the kitchen. "I hear we have company."

"Hello, Mike," said Eileen, smiling at her son-in-law. "You look younger every time I see you."

"It's your daughter," said Mike, giving Eileen a hug and a kiss on the cheek. "She keeps me young."

"I'll bet she keeps you hopping," said Eileen.

"That, too," said Mike, turning to look at his father-in-law. "Hello, Sam."

"Hello, young fellow," said Sam, brightly. "Thanks for having us to the party."

"You can come to our parties anytime," said Mike, taking Sam's hand and shaking it. "How was your trip out?"

"Excellent," said Sam. "The food was delicious."

"That's good to hear," said Mike. "Let's move into the dining room because I know we've got more delicious food coming."

"Nate's not here yet," said Ann.

"Then Nate will join us when he arrives," said Mike, escorting his mother-in-law into the dining room. When she was seated, Mike walked back into the kitchen to get Sam. Helping him out of the chair was like lifting a 180-pound bag of sand instead of a man with moving parts.

"Where are we going?" asked Sam when his feet were planted on the Mexican tile floor.

"Into our dining room for dinner," said Mike, steering him toward the doorway. Sam scuffed along slowly like a windup toy, shifting his bulk from one side to the other and lifting his feet only enough to move them forward. Out of habit, Mike looked at his watch, which he immediately regretted.

"Will we be late for our appointment?" asked Sam.

"We're doing fine," said Mike, ushering him through the doorway and toward the side chair next to Lauren.

"He does better in a chair with arms," said Eileen.

"Mike sits at the head of the table," said Ann.

"That's all right," said Mike. "Sam is our guest. I'm happy to give him my seat." As soon as Sam was planted in Mike's chair, Mike sat down next to him and across the table from Eileen. Mike suggested a blessing and they all bowed their heads, except Sam, who said he'd love some dressing. Mike said a quick grace, then put his napkin in his lap. On cue, Emma entered the room, her orthotic shoes silent on the carpet. Carrying a bottle of chardonnay, she poured half a glass for everyone. Ann's she filled; Lauren's she excluded.

"When can I have some wine?" Lauren asked.

"When you stop whining about it," said Mike.

"Very funny, Dad."

Emma brought in her spinach salad with hot bacon dressing on individual plates, as Ann requested. Ann preferred being served to scooping the contents of a family-style bowl onto her dinner plate. As soon as they all had salads in front of them, Ann lifted her fork. "Let the feast begin," she said gaily.

"Oh," said Eileen, pushing her chair back from the table. "I almost forgot your bib, Sam." She reached into the pocket of his gray cardigan sweater and took out and unfolded a white cloth and plastic bib big enough to fit a baby elephant. She placed it on his chest, and then wrapped the ends around his neck and snapped them together. As soon as it was in place, a glob of Emma's dressing dripped out of the corner of Sam's mouth and landed on his unprotected lap. Lauren involuntarily shuddered. "Obviously, it's not a foolproof system," said Eileen, apologetically.

"That's okay," said Mike, moving his eyes from Sam to Eileen. She chatted about the drive as the rest of them ate their salads. Lauren, who had lost her appetite when her grandfather had spittled out his salad dressing, drank water slowly from her glass as she stole glances at him. He was barely able to manage his fork, once stabbing his lip with the tines and making it bleed. Eileen reached over and wiped away the tiny dots of blood with one hand while she ate her salad with the other.

"This is delicious," she said. "I can tell Sam is enjoying it, as well." No one looked at Sam, perhaps all fearing that, by now, his bib would be covered with masticated Bermuda onion and avocado. Lauren, who couldn't get the image of giant cartoon character Baby Huey out of her head, unsuccessfully stifled a giggle. Ann reached under the table and squeezed her knee. Mike simply shot her a stern look. As soon as they were done with the salad, Emma cleared the plates. Ann excused herself from the table when she saw Nate steal past the doorway. She caught up with him at the bottom of the stairs.

"And where do you think you're going?"

"To my room," he said. "I'm not hungry."

"I don't care whether you're hungry or not," whispered Ann urgently. "You will wash your hands and come into the dining room. There, you will be as civil as a diplomat to your grandparents and then you will join us for dinner."

"I'd love to," said Nate, sarcastically, "but I've got a ton of homework."

Ann put her hands on her hips and grinned falsely at him. "That is the most ludicrous thing that's ever come out of your mouth," she said. "You've got one minute to get in that dining room, if you know what's good for you." The moment those final few words left her mouth, both she and Nate knew they were false. She had said them too often; they had no meaning. And Ann knew that Nate actually did know what was good for him. He didn't seek trouble. Sure, his room was always a mess, and his homework was done poorly, and his disrespectful attitude was tedious. But he was not driving his car when drunk. He was not doing drugs—at least Ann had found nothing in her periodic jacket and pants pocket searches. Ann and Mike had never been frantic in the night, seconds away from calling the police because he was not home and might be in danger. Other mothers worried about that. Instead, Ann worried about the distance between them. When he had pulled away, farther away than he had already been, Ann had done nothing to bring him back. It was as if they were attached by a large rubber band, stretched to the point of breaking.

"But you always tell me that I don't know what's good for me," said Nate, jerking his head to shift his bangs.

"In this case I think you do," said Ann, turning her back to him. She returned to the dining room just as Emma was putting a dinner plate in front of her seat.

"Nate will be joining us shortly," Ann said to Emma. "You can just put the salad on his dinner plate." Emma nodded her head, then returned to the kitchen.

"Nate's home?" asked Eileen. "I didn't see him."

"He's just washing up," said Ann, sitting. "Apparently, his after-school plans took longer than he realized." They all returned to their dinners. Sam coughed, launching several rice grains into the air like miniature artillery fire. They landed, six of them, on Ann's white tablecloth. No one said anything. Nate walked into the room looking bored already. He hesitated a moment, and then sat down next to his grandmother in the only empty chair.

"Hello, Nate," said Eileen, reaching over to hug him. "You've grown since last Christmas."

"Hi, Gran," said Nate, arms at his sides.

"I need a hug, young man."

Instantly reddening, Nate lifted his arms and draped them loosely around his grandmother's rounded back. He lifted his eyes to meet his father's. Mike winked. As soon as she let him go, Nate pulled away. He glanced at his grandfather, whose bib was newly spotted with rice grains and gravy, then shifted his gaze downward. "Hi, Gramps," said Nate to his salad. Sam said nothing.

"He didn't hear you," said Eileen, gently squeezing Nate's arm. "Try again, Nate."

"Hi, Gramps," said Nate, a little louder. Sam continued to push grains of rice onto his fork with his finger.

"Sam," said Eileen, reaching over and touching her husband's arm. "Your grandson is saying hello." Sam looked at his wife with a puzzled expression. "Your grandson is saying hello."

"It's okay," said Nate, still embarrassed.

"He gets tired at the end of the day," said Eileen. "Tomorrow, he'll be better."

I'll bet, thought Nate, looking at his watch. He lifted his fork and shoveled in some rice.

"How was school?" Eileen asked him.

"Fine," said Nate, thinking the last time someone had asked him that question in earnest was second grade.

"What are you studying?"

"Lots of things," said Nate, finally giving his grandmother a look loaded with the weariness he felt. "As a matter of fact, I've got a huge physics test tomorrow, so I should hit the books." He pushed his chair back and stood.

"We've got pecan pie for dessert," said Ann with forced cheerfulness.

"That's okay," said Mike, feeling Nate's discomfort. "You get to your studying. You can have some dessert later if you want to take a break."

"Me too," said Lauren, standing. "I've got a history test. My teacher this year is brutal."

"No pie?" asked Ann, already knowing the answer.

"Let them go," said Mike gently. Dismissed, Lauren and Nate bolted from the room. They moved quickly up the stairs to the landing, where they stopped and looked at each other.

"Oh my God," said Lauren.

"Did you see his bib?" asked Nate. "It's a national disaster area. For every piece of rice he actually got into his mouth, there are two on his bib."

"How about just the fact that he has a bib?" said Lauren, following her brother down the hallway to their bedrooms. "I mean, what is he, a baby?"

"And Gran is acting like nothing's wrong," said Nate. "Do me a favor and shoot me if I ever get like that." Nate disappeared into his room and shut the door behind him. Lauren lingered a moment. Seconds later, she heard music. She turned from his door and walked the rest of the way down the hallway to her room.

Downstairs, the four adults ate their dessert in the kitchen, at Mike's suggestion. He told them he found the kitchen atmosphere much more conducive to quiet conversation. While this was true, he moved everyone mostly because he had seen too many bits of food bounce and slide off Sam's bib onto his $50,000 Oriental rug. When they finished, Eileen lifted her napkin from her lap and gently wiped a blotch of whipped cream off her husband's chin. "That was delicious," she said. "What a lovely meal."

"Thank you," said Ann, looking at her watch.

"Well," said Eileen, getting out of her seat. "Sam and I had better hit the dusty trail home. Let me just take these dishes over to the sink."

"Leave them, Mom," said Ann. "Emma will get them on her way out."

"That seems silly," said Eileen, collecting the plates and forks. "I'm heading that way anyway."

"That's what I pay Emma to do," said Ann.

"Just because you pay her doesn't mean you shouldn't help her out."

"Then by all means, do whatever you want."

They all waited silently until Eileen returned to the table. "There," she said. "That just took a minute." Mike stood and helped Sam up. Eileen removed his bib. She folded it, stained and damp, and put it in the pocket of his sweater. She brushed the piecrust crumbs from his pants. "Ready to go?" she asked her husband.

"Yes, I am," said Sam softly before turning to Mike. "Thank you for a wonderful evening." Mike looked into Sam's eyes, wondering if he had missed something. He took his father-in-law's hand and shook it.

"You're welcome, Sam."

Ann opened the back door, and then she and Mike watched her parents amble down the brick path to the guesthouse. "My God," she said, "I had no idea what a nightmare I was getting myself into."

"It's not a nightmare," said Mike unconvincingly.

"No more dinners in the dining room," she said. "From now on, we eat in the kitchen."

"We're not eating together every night."

"Absolutely not," said Ann. "Sundays only. Maybe a few other nights, sprinkled in here and there. We'll see. The rest of the time, they'll eat in the guesthouse." Ann wrote a note to herself on the yellow legal pad she kept by the phone. "I'll reconfirm the meal plan with Selma in the morning. Even though we've gone over this, I want to make sure she expects to do the majority of the cooking for my parents. She told me she loves to cook, so it's not an issue."

Mike kissed Ann on the forehead. "I'm going to do a bit of work before bed," he said. "I'll be up in a couple of hours."

"And I'm going to make an Irish coffee and take a bath," said Ann. "It's been a terribly long day."

"Skip the Irish," said Mike. "And if you're making decaf, I'd love a cup."

CHAPTER 4

Ann walked from the garage into the kitchen to the unwelcome sight of her mother in an apron stirring something in a pot on the stove. Ann set her pastel shopping bags down on the floor and took a deep breath. The day had not gone as she planned. Her favorite treadmill at the club had broken down in the middle of her workout. She had lunch with Sally and had to listen to her brag about her kids and their academic achievements. While Sally talked about tough honors courses and the burden of extra homework, Ann made a mental note to ask Lauren for her report card and to ask Emma to search Nate's room for his. And after lunch, Ann endured an endless budget discussion at the most tedious hospital board meeting she had ever attended. As a reward afterward, she hit the mall, which lifted her mood some. But now her mother, uninvited, was in her kitchen, using her expensive copper pots and humming a hymn Ann vaguely remembered from Sunday school. "What are you doing?" were the first words that came out of her mouth.

"Oh, hello," said Eileen, turning around to face her daughter. "I was lost in thought and didn't hear you come in. I'm trying out a soup for Thanksgiving. I hope you don't mind."

"Is your stove working all right?" asked Ann, tossing her keys noisily into the wicker basket on the counter.

"It works like a charm," said Eileen. "Selma is making our dinner and I didn't want to get in her way. Thanksgiving is only a week away, Ann. We have to start preparing. Come taste this."

"We have nothing to prepare," said Ann, peeling off her coat and hanging it on a peg. "I have it catered."

Eileen's eyes became full moons. "You're kidding me, Ann. You cater Thanksgiving?"

"I'm not kidding, Mother. Thanksgiving is an underappreciated meal that's devoured in seven minutes."

"Thanksgiving is an American tradition, honey."

"It's way too much work."

"Not if we roll up our sleeves and work together," said Eileen. "We could spend next Wednesday in the kitchen, just you and me. It would be fun."

"That," said Ann, lifting her shopping bags and walking across the kitchen floor, "is *not* my idea of fun."

"What is your idea of fun?" Ann stopped and turned to face her mother. "It seems like every day you leave here early in the morning and return late in the afternoon with a bunch of shopping bags," said Eileen, turning off the burner.

"How would you know when I come and when I go?"

"I have eyes, Ann," said Eileen. "Our little house has that beautiful picture window."

"So," asked Ann, reddening, "you've been spying on me?"

"I'm not spying on you, honey," said Eileen, laying the wooden spoon down in the sink. "I'm interested in you. I want to know what your life is like."

"Look around you," said Ann, gesturing with her free hand. "This is what my life is like. It's a fabulous life, and I love it."

"That's good," said Eileen, moving the pot to the granite countertop. "I just want you to be happy."

"I'm ecstatic," said Ann. "I have everything I want. Who wouldn't be happy?"

"Sometimes you seem a little edgy, dear."

"I live my life on the edge," said Ann grandly.

"Well, good for you," said Eileen, looking into her daughter's eyes. "I just hope you don't fall off." Ann was immobilized for just an instant by her mother's remark. And then she slowly smiled, and—never breaking eye contact—backed the rest of the way out of the kitchen. She jogged down the hallway and up the staircase to her room. She shut the door behind her, sat down on the bed, and called Mike. He didn't pick up.

"Damn it!" she said, sitting on the edge of her king-sized bed and breathing as if she'd just stepped off a treadmill. She sat for a moment, and then walked into her bathroom to wash her hands. When she returned to her bedroom, she emptied the contents of her bags onto the bed and stared at what she had bought. She took a permanent marker and a pair of scissors from her bedside table drawer and clipped the tags from the buttery cashmere sweaters and wool tops. Holding the marker, she turned to the shoes and labeled the box: Br Drive Moc w/ G Bkl. She took both the box and the clothes to her closet and put everything in its proper place. She hesitated at the wall of shoe boxes, and then sat on her chrome stool to count her fall/winter collection. She had seventeen pairs of everyday shoes in brown, including the new moccasins, twenty-three pairs in black, and sixteen pairs of what she called "funky everyday." She had fifteen pairs of suit shoes, suitable for upscale charity meetings and business receptions, and thirty-five pairs of party shoes, her favorite. She got up from her seat, walked to the party section, and removed a box from its slot. Inside was a pair of Italian black satin sling-back pumps, with the daintiest heel she could stand upon without toppling over. She ran her fingers across the miniature toe box and along the skinny heel strap. She remembered Mike telling her how sexy she looked at Susie Dalton's Christmas party the year before. She would have to find a reason to wear them again. She walked out of her closet and back to her bed, where she sat and removed her shoes. She grabbed the phone from the table next to the bed and called Jesse. "My mother is driving me crazy."

"Hmm," said Jesse.

"And I don't want to hear, 'I told you so.' "

"What do you want to hear?" asked Jesse.

"I want sympathy."

"You poor thing," said Jesse. "How's that?"

Ann lay back on the bed. "She's down in my kitchen making a concoction for Thanksgiving."

"And?" asked Jesse.

"She's got her own kitchen, for God's sake. She doesn't need to be nosing around mine."

"As if you ever use your kitchen," Jesse pointed out.

"I *do* use my kitchen," stated Ann. "Just because I don't cook very often doesn't mean I don't use my kitchen. I'm in it all the time."

"You can be there when she's there, you know," said Jesse. "That's probably what she's looking for. She wants to spend some time with you."

"And I want to spend some time with her," said Ann, draping her free arm across her forehead. "But I want to do it on my own terms. If I spend the entire day with her, I'll snap. Honestly, Jesse, I'll just let her have it."

"Why?"

"Because she's my mother and all mothers drive their daughters crazy," said Ann. "And because she'll want to crawl into my head and into my life in a last-stab effort at getting to know me better. I don't want her to know me any better. I want her to live in the guesthouse out back and come to me when she needs help."

"I don't think that's how it's going to work," said Jesse.

Ann closed her eyes. "I've made a huge mistake."

"No, you haven't," said Jesse. "You're just going to have to be more flexible, Ann. We all do, at certain times."

"I hate being flexible," said Ann.

"Work on it," said Jesse. "In the meantime, go be with your mother."

When Ann walked into the kitchen fifteen minutes later, her mother was gone. On the counter was a plastic container filled with a thick orange liquid, still steaming. The blue lid sat next to it, plastered with a wide piece of masking tape and the words *Mama's*

Butternut Squash Soup written in her mother's handwriting. The shining copper pot was hanging in its usual spot over the island, and the other dishes and utensils her mother used had been washed and dried and were sitting on a dish towel on the counter. A note in her mother's handwriting lay on the counter next to the dishes. Ann picked it up and read: *I'm sorry I used your kitchen without asking you. I hope you like the soup. It's your grandmother's recipe.* Ann put the note down. "I hate this," she said.

She put the soup in the fridge, then picked up the phone and called Mike's office. She left a message with his secretary to have him meet her at the club at seven o'clock for dinner in the bar. She then called Nate's and Lauren's cell phones and left messages about where she and Mike would be for dinner and when they would be home. She told them to order whatever they wanted from The China Palace and to do their homework. She then put the menu and $40 in the middle of the kitchen table. She looked at her watch. She had enough time to do sixty minutes on the StairMaster, shower, change, and drive to the club. Mike would be late, but that didn't matter. She could taste her first glass of wine already.

"Yes!" said Nate as soon as he listened to his mother's message.

"What?" asked Jenny.

"My parents," said Nate, selecting his sister's cell phone number from his contact list. "They're not going to be home tonight."

"Want to have dinner at my house?" asked Jenny, flipping her long blond ponytail over her shoulder.

"No way," said Nate. "We're going out."

Jenny opened her mouth to speak, but Nate held up his hand. "Lauren," he said into his phone. "I'm going out, too. You go into my room, I'll kill you."

"I can't go out tonight, Nate," said Jenny as Nate put his phone back in his pocket. "It's a school night."

"A school night?" said Nate, feigning horror. "Why didn't you tell me? I can't go out, either. I've got to get home, take a shower, do all my homework—double-check my math answers—and get into bed early so I can get a good night's sleep." Jenny laughed. "Call your mom," said Nate. "She'll let you go out."

Jenny looked at her watch. "She's not home."

"Even better," said Nate. "Leave a message. Tell her we're going out for pizza, and I'll have you home early. Tell her it's our six-month anniversary, or something."

"It's not our six-month anniversary until next week."

"I know that," said Nate.

"Crap," said Lauren, after she listened to her messages.

"Who was that?" asked Pammy, an on-again, off-again friend from the volleyball team who was currently on.

"My mother and my brother," said Lauren. "Everybody's going out to dinner tonight."

"That sounds like fun."

"Yeah, for everybody but me," said Lauren. "I hate it when my mom does that."

"Goes out to dinner?" asked Pammy, looking at her hand, onto which she was writing a phone number with permanent marker.

"Blows me off," said Lauren, shoving her school books into her backpack. "They do it all the time." It was when Lauren was twelve, she decided, that her mother had chosen to be elsewhere rather than at home, preferring the gym, shopping malls, and nice restaurants to dinner at the kitchen table. Before that and before Emma, when Lauren was in elementary school and they lived in the old house, they had eaten at home most nights. And her mother had produced pretty good meals, routine stuff like spaghetti and meatballs, chicken dishes, and the like. Back then, when Lauren walked into the house after school, the kitchen smelled like something to eat rather than disinfectant. It was when they moved into the new house, the building of which had seemed to require her mother's daily supervision and input, that she was suddenly never home anymore. Her father had never been home much for as long as Lauren's memory could reach back. He had often arrived just in time for a late dinner, but he had a defendable excuse.

"I think you're lucky," said Pammy, drawing a heart next to the phone number. "I wish my parents would go out once in a while. They're always around, dinner after dinner after dinner."

"Want to come to my house?" asked Lauren. "We can eat take-out, just the two of us. It will be really cool."

"I can't tonight," said Pammy. "It's my little sister's birthday. My mom is making her favorite dinner and then we'll have cake and stuff."

"Now *that* sounds like fun," said Lauren, redoing her ponytail.

"Oh, it will be," said Pammy, capping the marker and putting it into her jeans pocket. "Sometimes my mom gets my brother and me a present, too, just so we don't feel left out."

"You've got the coolest mom."

"Yeah," said Pammy. "Hey, I've got to run. Do you need a ride home or anything? My mom should be out back by now."

"No thanks," said Lauren, not wanting to go home yet. Her mother would be dolling herself up for an evening out, which Lauren had no interest in witnessing. She shrugged her backpack onto her shoulders, walked down two flights of stairs and out the back door of the school, where other mothers were waiting in warm cars for their kids. They would take them home, make them a nutritious dinner, and probably pour them a huge bubble bath or something equally nice. Lauren turned away from the line of cars and walked along the sidewalk. She was almost to the street when she heard someone call her name. It was Katie, another friend from the team, looking at her from the passenger side seat of their family minivan. "Do you need a ride?" she yelled.

"No," shouted Lauren back. "I'm going to the library." Katie waved and then raised her tinted window. Lauren crossed the street and walked the four blocks to the public library. She chose a table in the Catherine Whitfield room, down a narrow hallway from the main desk. It was a small, relegated quiet space—named after the daughter of the town's founding father—with comfortable upholstered chairs, brass reading lamps, and walls covered with glass-doored, wooden cases filled with old-looking books Lauren had not wondered about enough to examine closely. She lowered her pack to the carpeted floor, took off her new North Face down jacket, and settled in at one of the four empty tables.

Ninety minutes later, she had done seventeen algebra problems and finished the rough draft of her English essay, tentatively titled "The Myriad Merits of Mediterranean Literature." She called a cab, which arrived fifteen minutes later and took her home. She got out of the car and jogged up the front steps, where she used her house key to open the front door. She reset the alarm and then walked quickly through the dark hallway to the kitchen. The light over the table was on, illuminating The China Palace menu and the money. Lauren pocketed the bills, put the menu back in her mother's file, and opened the fridge. Just as she was taking out the squash soup, she heard a knock at the back door. It was her grandmother. Lauren put on a smile. She pushed the alarm release code and opened the door. "Hi, Gran," she said.

"Hi, honey," said Eileen, hugging herself from the cold as she stepped into the warm kitchen. Both about the same height—the high school volleyball programs listed Lauren as five feet, six inches—they were quickly eye to eye. "How was your day?"

"Pretty good," said Lauren, taking a step back.

Gran looked around the room. "Are you here alone?"

"Yes," said Lauren. "My parents went out. So did Nate."

"Have you eaten?" asked Eileen.

"No," said Lauren. "I was just going to have this soup."

"I made that soup," said Eileen, smiling. "It's your great-grand-mother's recipe. You sit, and I'll heat some up for you."

"That's okay," said Lauren. "I'm fine."

"No trouble at all," said Eileen, taking off her Irish-knit cardigan. "You sit at the table, and I'll have this over to you in a jiffy."

Unaccustomed to being alone with her grandmother and her easy, unprompted cheerfulness, Lauren was silent. When the Baronses visited the farm every Christmas, holiday activities filled the awkward spaces. There was the carol sing at the Grange, the moonlight sleigh ride at the Gundersons' farm down the road, the creation of a gingerbread house, last-minute gift wrapping and cookie baking, and hot chocolate around the woodstove in their immaculate but lived-in-looking country kitchen. Now, with nothing but a plastic container of soup as a conversation starter, Lauren couldn't think of anything to say. She looked over at the stove and watched her grandmother, in Emma's starched white apron, stirring a portion of the soup in a pot and humming. "Tell me about volleyball," said Eileen, turning to face her.

"It's fun," said Lauren.

"Do you have a game I could come and watch?"

"As a matter of fact, I have one tomorrow," said Lauren. "It's my last one before the state tournament begins."

"What time does it start?" asked Eileen. "I can see if Selma can take care of Sam so I can tag along with your mother."

"My mom doesn't come to my games," said Lauren. "She says they make her nervous." This is what Ann had told her daughter when Lauren made the varsity team her freshman year after a series of very competitive tryouts, the results of which were posted daily on the wall outside the girls' locker room. Each morning, Lauren, with her stomach feeling like it had turned itself upside down on the car ride to school, ran to check the list. Other players were always there, some smiling, hooting even, while others openly wept and received hugs from the more talented and fortunate. Day after day, Barons was at the top of the alphabetical list. And on the final day, when it was still there, Lauren called her mother with the news. "I'm thrilled for you," her mom had said, promising to go to every game she could fit into her schedule. And she had gone to a few, when Lauren was first starting out, first learning the playbook, making mistakes. When Ann started missing more home games than she attended—and she had never gone to an away game in a car caravan with the other mothers—Lauren stopped telling her when one was coming up. Ann was happy to know when the team won, but she didn't seem much interested in the details.

"Oh," said Eileen, tasting the soup. "Well, maybe if she goes with me, she'll be able to handle the pressure." Lauren shrugged her shoulders. "I'll talk to her tomorrow," said Eileen as she brought a bowl of soup to the table. "We'll see what we can do." After Eileen set the bowl down in front of Lauren, she walked back to the counter for a spoon. She poured Lauren a glass of milk, then pulled a napkin from the elaborate wire holder next to the refrigerator. She grabbed a pad of paper and a pencil from Ann's desk on her way back to the table and sat next to Lauren. "There," she said, handing the spoon to her granddaughter. "I'll say a short blessing and you can begin." Lauren closed her eyes in an effort to tone down her grandmother's level of caring. "Bless the Lord and the bounty He bestows upon us," said Eileen. "Make us forever grateful. Amen."

"Amen," said Lauren dutifully before lifting a spoonful of soup to her mouth.

"Now," said Eileen, picking up the pencil, "what time and where is your game?"

"Three thirty," said Lauren. "At the high school."

Eileen wrote the game time on the pad, then set the pencil down and looked at her granddaughter. "How's the soup?" she asked.

"It's really good," said Lauren.

"My mother was a good cook," said Eileen. "She was one of those people who didn't need a cookbook. She just made recipes up in her head."

"We go out a lot," said Lauren between spoonfuls.

"Do you like to go out?"

"Well, sure," said Lauren, shrugging. "You can special order anything you want. And it frees up my mom's time for other things, I guess."

"Your mother was a wonderful cook when she was your age," said Eileen, sitting back in the chair.

"She used to cook," she said. "She's too busy now."

Eileen waved her hand. "She's not too busy. She's just let it go."

"Maybe you could teach her again," said Lauren, taking another spoonful of soup from her bowl.

"Maybe I could at that," said Eileen. They sat for a few moments in silence while Lauren ate the rest of her soup. It was the best soup she'd tasted in a very long time, including what was served to her in restaurants and at the club. "Can I get you some more?" asked Eileen.

"No, thanks," said Lauren, pushing back her chair. "I should get to my homework."

"You run along then," said Eileen, standing. "Put your spoon and bowl in the dishwasher and I'll take care of the soup."

Lauren, who was unpracticed at chores of any kind, did as she was told. She then grabbed her backpack from the floor and slung it over her shoulder. "Thanks, Gran," she said.

"My pleasure," said Eileen. "Do you want me to stay here until your parents get home?"

"I'll be okay," said Lauren. "The alarm's on. When you walk out, just make sure you close the door within thirty seconds."

"I'll be right next door if you need anything," said Eileen, washing out the pot.

"I've got plans," Ann told her mother, who was standing in Ann's kitchen with her heavy sweater on.

"What kind of plans?" asked Eileen. "Are you able to break them?"

"The point is, I don't want to break them," said Ann, in the middle of making a cinnamon, double-shot latte.

"This is her last game," said Eileen. "And you haven't been to one all year."

"That's not true," said Ann, spilling the cinnamon. "I got to the first one, I think. Look, Mother, they just make me nervous. I can't stand sitting there and watching Lauren mess up."

"How about her good shots?" asked Eileen. "Wouldn't you be proud to sit and watch her then?"

Ann faced her mother, crossing her arms over her chest. "I think those are few and far between."

"How would you know if you don't go to the games?" said Eileen, crossing her arms over her chest.

Ann looked at her mother, who was still staring at her. No one spoke. "All right," said Ann, finally. "I'll go to the game. How I'm going to get everything done by—what time does it start?"

"It's at three thirty," said Eileen, smiling, "at the high school. I think we should leave here by three."

"We'll leave at three fifteen and not a minute sooner," said Ann, looking at her watch. "Already, I'll be pressed for time."

"Then I won't keep you any longer," said Eileen. "You have a good day, honey. And thanks for going with me."

Ann waved her mother off as she pretended to read the front page of the *Wall Street Journal* that was sitting on the island. As soon as Eileen was out the door, Ann called Gretchen, her manicurist, and rescheduled. She gulped down the rest of her coffee, then dashed out the garage door to her car. After her usual Wednesday workout, Ann met Sally for lunch at Bagels 'N' More. They both ordered sesame bagels with low-fat, veggie cream cheese and sprouts—Ann's favorite—ice waters, and sugar-free caramel cappuccinos. They sat in a small booth next to the front window so Ann could see who was coming and going. Just as she was about to take her first bite, Marge Simon charged through the door. "Ann!" she said, approaching the table. "I've been thinking about you. We've got the annual fashion show coming up in January, and I'm hoping you'll model for us again."

"What's the theme this year?" asked Ann brightly.

"It's the same theme every year, Ann," said Marge, penciled eyebrows scrunched in incomprehension. "We give the proceeds to local charities."

Ann gave Marge a patronizing smile. "Of the *fashion* show," said Ann, glancing at Sally before returning her gaze to Marge. "What's the theme of the fashion show?"

"Oh, of course," said Marge, her large bosom shaking as she laughed. "Yes, well, this year just happens to be furs, Ann. We've got some beautiful coats coming in that I know you'll enjoy showing."

"Put me down," said Ann, taking her BlackBerry out of her purse. "What's the date?"

"The twenty-sixth," Marge announced. "But I'll talk to you before then. All the ladies will meet in early January and decide who's going to wear what."

"Perfect," said Ann.

"I'll be in touch," said Marge, already on her way toward the short line of customers. Ann turned to Sally and winked.

"So," said Sally, slighted by Marge's consistent refusal to acknowledge her and anxious to change the subject, "what are you up to today?"

"Oh my God," said Ann, "I didn't tell you?"

"What?" asked Sally, leaning in to share the secret.

Ann lifted her bagel out of its purple basket. "I'm taking my mother to Lauren's volleyball game."

"I'll bet I know whose idea that was," said Sally, grinning.

"She won't take no for an answer," said Ann. "She's the most stubborn woman I know." Sally nodded. "So," Ann continued, pulling a sale flyer out of her purse, "as a pregame pick-me-up, I thought I'd run over to the mall and stock up on cashmere sweaters. Do you want to come?"

Sally thought about the discussion she had with her husband the night before about her spending habits. Jack wanted her to be happy, but he didn't see why she needed a different outfit for every day of the month. He told her to settle down and to let Ann do some shopping on her own. *We cannot keep up with them,* he had told Sally, referring to Mike and Ann Barons. *It's a game we will lose and lose badly.* "I'd love to, Ann," she said, "but I've got a million errands to run."

"You're no fun," said Ann, feigning a pout.

"Next time," said Sally.

Ninety minutes, three sweaters, two skirts, and a silk blouse later, Ann ran through the kitchen door. Eileen was sitting at the table, reading the newspaper. "Make yourself at home," Ann snapped.

"I have," said Eileen, looking up from the paper. "Are you ready to go?"

"Three minutes," said Ann. "I'll be down in three minutes."

Ten minutes after that, they were backing Ann's Mercedes SL600 Roadster out of the driveway. Ann was freshly resentful about being talked into going to a high school volleyball game, so they rode most of the way in silence. As soon as she drove behind the school and caught her first glimpse of the parking lot, jam-packed with American-made cars, she abruptly hit the brakes. "Where are we supposed to park, for God's sake?" she asked, looking left and right.

"Out there," said Eileen, shielding her eyes from the sun with one hand and pointing with the other to several empty rows at the far end of the lot.

Ann sighed. "This is ridiculous." She drove the length of the lot and parked the car five spaces from the end of the pavement. She and her mother briskly zigzagged through the cars toward the back of the enormous brick structure that Dilloway Company money had built just three years earlier. Dilloway High School stood as a testament to corporate largesse, with its state-of-the art smart classrooms, media center, and gymnasiums, one of which was magnificent enough to occasionally draw the Pistons north for a razzle-dazzle fund-raiser. Ann opened the heavy metal and glass door for her mother and led her into the hallway crowded with backpacked teenagers and conversation. Eileen asked about the volleyball game and was directed to the little gym. Down another corridor and around the corner, the little gym was just as impressive as the larger version, with its gleaming wood floor, bleachers with padded seating, and revolutionary lighting and sound systems. Three minutes before the start of the volleyball game, it was bustling with uniformed volleyball players warming up, people finding seats in the stands, students selling popcorn and candy, and the buzz of two hundred people occupying the same room. Just inside the door, a woman seated in a metal folding chair at a plastic banquet table shouted the price of admission at them. "We have to buy tickets?" asked Ann. "You're kidding, right?"

"All the sporting events cost four dollars," said the woman. "The money goes right back into the school athletic program."

"Here," said Eileen, pulling her thin wallet out of the ancient leather handbag around her wrist, "let me treat you."

"Don't be silly, Mother," said Ann, reaching into the front pocket of her jeans for a twenty-dollar bill. "I can afford four dollars. I'm just surprised, that's all. And I'll treat you."

"Thank you," said Eileen, putting her wallet away, then looking at the woman handing Ann two tickets. "We're here to watch my granddaughter."

"She's a good player," said the woman, who apparently knew who Ann was, "and she's a friend of my daughter. I'm Joanne Rogers."

Eileen shook Joanne's hand. "I'm Eileen Sanford, visiting from Pennsylvania, and this is my daughter, Ann Barons."

"Nice to meet you," said Ann, looking beyond Joanne at the bleachers. Where in the world were they going to sit?

"You'll find some space at the top," said Joanne. "If you're far-sighted like me, that's the best seat in the house."

"How do we get up there?" asked Ann.

"You climb up the side and say 'Excuse me' a lot."

"Thank you," said Eileen, smiling at Joanne. "You've been very helpful."

Ann and Eileen slowly made their way through standing, sitting, and shifting bodies juggling backpacks, babies, purses, popcorn, newspapers, needlepoint, cell phones, and crosswords. Halfway up, they found an unoccupied section of bench and plopped down. Eileen was out of breath. "My goodness," she said. "The last time I climbed bleachers, *you* were in high school. Remember? The sta-dium at the back of the school had bleachers that went almost to heaven."

"Of course I remember," said Ann, pulling her left arm from her jacket sleeve.

"People still talk about the 4-H fair the summer you graduated. It was spectacular. Do you remember the size of the Grundys' cows?"

"That was a long time ago," said Ann, checking her cell phone messages to see if Mike had called.

"Look!" said Eileen, pointing at the gym floor. "There's Lau-ren."

Just then, Lauren, on the sidelines and scanning the crowd, spotted her grandmother. Eileen stood and waved, and Lauren waved back. Seconds later, she bounded onto the court, taking the place of a teammate in the back row. Ann pocketed her phone and turned her attention to her daughter. She watched her return a hard serve by bumping the ball to the front row. One of her team-mates tapped it over the net to win the point. Lauren was shorter than many of her teammates, but this didn't appear to be a disad-vantage. Lauren next received the ball in the front row and sent it straight up into the air for her teammate to slam onto the opposing court. She appeared calm and confident, Ann noticed. Her next four shots were dead-on, perfect.

At the end of the first game, which Lauren's team won 15–9, Ann looked around the gym. She saw several people she knew, including her son. He was leaning against the entranceway, unwilling, Ann guessed, to pay the $2 student fee to get in. Two boys were with him; they were all talking. Meeting his eyes for a second, Ann raised her hand in a half-wave that Nate didn't acknowledge. Didn't he see her? Ann returned her attention to the court just as Lauren, who was standing in the front row, jumped and sent a ball screaming to the far end of the opposing team's court. Lauren's teammate gave her a double high five.

After the match, Ann and Eileen waited outside the gym in the hallway, even more crowded and aromatic than before the game. Ann stood with her back up against the wall, trying to avoid contact with teenage sweat, dirt, and cigarette breath. As soon as Lauren emerged from the locker room, Ann ushered them quickly outside. Just beyond the doors, Eileen stopped Lauren and hugged her. "You are a fantastic volleyball player," she said. "I'm so proud of you. What an exciting game!"

Lauren beamed. "Thanks, Gran. And thanks for coming. What did you think, Mom?" Ann's heartbeat echoed in her ears as she opened her mouth to speak. Nothing came out. The game and Lauren's well-placed and powerful shots were running through her mind like video. Her daughter was not the failure she feared. The other players on the team looked to her for direction, grateful for her presence on the court with them—Ann could see this, read this on their faces from afar. She thought about all the games she had missed.

"She's speechless," said Eileen, wrapping her arm around her granddaughter's shoulder.

Ann leaned down and kissed Lauren's cheek. "You were amazing."

"Thanks," said Lauren, looking into her mother's eyes for a connection. Ann broke away first.

"The car is out back," she said. "Let's hurry, so we'll beat the rush."

* * *

That night, as Ann lay in bed reading *Midwest Living,* her thoughts kept drifting back to the volleyball match. As soon as Mike walked into their bedroom, she started talking about it. "Didn't we run through every point at dinner?" he asked. "Your mother would have made an awesome sports writer. She knew every detail." He got into bed beside his wife. "I didn't know you cared about volleyball."

Ann turned out her bedside light. "I had no idea she was so good." She lay thinking in the darkened room. The moon, just out of sight as Ann glanced over at the windows, softly lit the panes of glass. On another night, she might have called it peaceful, but on this night it was unsettling, an intrusion. "Mike?" she said.

"Ummm?"

"Why haven't I gone to Lauren's volleyball games?"

Mike slowly rolled over to face his wife. "You're busy, Ann."

"Too busy to go to her games, or to Nate's football games? What kind of busy is that?"

"Regular busy?"

"Do you remember when she was little?" Ann said. "She used to follow me around like a duckling follows its mother. And at first, I found it endearing and then, at some point, I found it annoying. God, I was craving space back then. And now I have all this space."

"You're lucky," Mike said. "I have no space."

"You've created that condition."

"As have you, Ann," said Mike.

CHAPTER 5

For a good reason that Ann could not recall later, Eileen had been able to talk her out of a catered Thanksgiving dinner and into a homemade meal. Eileen proposed buying all the groceries—it was the least she could do, she said—if Ann and Lauren would join her in the kitchen. Ann told her mother she would absolutely not cook all day Wednesday as well as Thursday, so Eileen agreed to preparing, serving, and eating the meal in one day. They would have to start early, however, right after a crack-of-dawn breakfast. If they worked steadily, they could have dinner on the table by 5:00 in the afternoon. Mike, who had not seen his wife spend more than five minutes cooking in the kitchen she custom-designed, requested cornbread stuffing. And Nate, who said the thought of his mother's cooking scared him, declared he would rather eat at McDonald's on Thanksgiving than die of food poisoning.

And so the process began. Just as Ann was finishing her Fiber One, she heard a knock at the back door. There, with a cloth grocery bag in each gloved hand, stood her mother, a thin red woolen cap on her head and a determined look on her face. Ann looked at her watch and slowly got up from the table. She opened the door, and Eileen charged past her and set the bags down on the floor. "I hope I'm not too early," she said.

"Would it matter if I said you *were* too early?" asked Ann, taking a sip of black coffee from her mug.

Eileen unloaded potatoes, squash, celery, onions, and the piecrusts she had made the night before onto Ann's island countertop. "There are more bags on the counter in my kitchen. Would you be willing to walk over there and grab them? We'll get Mike to bring the turkey. I got an eighteen-pounder. I thought we could have soup and sandwiches over the weekend. How does that sound?"

"Interesting," said Ann, who had not thought beyond the chores of the day except to know that she did not want to spend the entire weekend with her parents, playing Scrabble, taking short walks that her mother would call exercise, and eating leftovers. She dumped her tepid coffee into the sink and put on her coat.

"Tell your father to come up to the house," called Eileen as Ann walked out the door.

Ann wrapped her coat tightly around her as she walked down the frost-covered brick path to the guesthouse. She knocked on the door once, opened it, and walked in. She found her father in the kitchen, rooting though the silverware drawer. "I can't find my car keys," he said, a half-dozen forks in one hand. "I need to go out."

"You don't need to go out, Dad," said Ann, approaching him tentatively. "We've got everything you need right here."

Sam turned his head in Ann's direction. "You have your coat on," he said, "so apparently you're going somewhere."

Ann lightly put her hand on his shoulder. "I've just come down to grab the groceries Mom bought for Thanksgiving. It's time to start making the meal."

"Let me help you," said Sam. "Where are we taking them?"

"Up to my house."

Sam reached for the bags on the floor and, with effort, lifted them. "Okay," he said. "Where to?" He was dressed in an old flannel nightshirt, his bulbous, scaly feet stuffed halfway into his sheepskin slippers.

"I've got an idea," said Ann. "I'll run these up to the house while you get some clothes on. And then I'll come back to get you."

"Is this a formal affair?" asked Sam.

"No," said Ann. "Just a bit more formal than you are now."

"Right-O," said Sam. "I'll be ready in a jiffy."

Sam scurried off to the bedroom, and Ann grabbed the bags. She walked quickly up the path and into her warm kitchen, where her mother was already dicing celery on the center island.

"You found everything?" she asked, still chopping.

"I just grabbed the bags on the kitchen floor," said Ann. "Dad was looking for car keys."

"Yes," said Eileen, looking up from her task. "He can spend hours doing that. I've had to hide all kinds of things from him. It seems cruel to me sometimes, but I know it's for the best."

"When did he stop driving?" asked Ann, unloading corn bread, cranberry sauce, mushrooms, green beans, and dinner rolls from a bag.

"Last winter," said Eileen, tipping the cutting board of chopped celery into a large ceramic bowl. "I told the doctor I didn't feel safe with him driving, and the doctor agreed. Your father hasn't taken it too well. Remember when I told you he thought the kitchen staff at the day-care center was plotting against him? Well, that was just the latest in a string of incidents that began with the doctor. He doesn't trust Walt at the hardware store because he wouldn't sell him a chain saw, and he doesn't like Jim Townsend, the attractive new bank manager, because he wouldn't let him take twenty thousand dollars out of our savings account to buy more cows. We've had just two cows for the last ten years, but your father thinks he's still in the business."

"I don't know how you handle this, Mother," said Ann, removing the plastic wrapping from the pan of corn bread. "I don't know what to do with him."

"I didn't know what to do, either, at first," said Eileen, reaching for an onion. "I learn day by day, every day."

Both women looked at the back door when they heard a knock. It was Sam, his white hair sticking out in all directions, dressed in a woman's pink bathrobe. "Oh God," said Ann.

Eileen put her knife down and, wiping her hands on her apron, walked to the door and opened it. "I'm looking for a place to stay," said Sam.

"You can stay with us," said Eileen, pulling him in out of the cold and sitting him down at the kitchen table. "But we've got work to do."

"We've all got work to do," said Sam to the far kitchen wall.

Eileen walked back to the island and the half-chopped onion. Ann approached her and whispered in her ear, "What are we going to do now?"

"Make Thanksgiving dinner, dear," said Eileen, patting her daughter's shoulder. "He won't be any trouble."

Sam stood. "I've got to go," he said.

Ann, who couldn't imagine where he thought he had to be dressed in his wife's terry-cloth bathrobe, stared at him.

"How about some coffee, Sam?" asked Eileen calmly.

"I'd love a cup, thanks," he said.

"Settle into that chair right there and I'll get some for you," said Eileen, pouring a cup from Ann's pot. She brought it to the table and set it down. She patted his arm. Ann looked at her mother and then at her father and then back at her mother. "Help me chop these onions, Ann," said Eileen, returning to the island. "We need to finish the stuffing so we can get our bird in the oven."

"I'll get the bird," said Sam, spilling his coffee in his haste to stand, turn, and head for the back door.

"Mother!" said Ann.

"Go get Mike, dear," said Eileen, rinsing her hands in the sink. "This is precisely where I've run into trouble."

Ann ran out of the kitchen, up the stairs, and into the master bedroom, where Mike, dressed in his favorite work jeans and a flannel shirt, was brushing his teeth. "My father is outside wandering around in my mother's bathrobe," said Ann breathlessly. "Come quickly."

Mike followed Ann back down the stairs and into the kitchen, where Eileen was buttoning up her coat. "I think we're okay," she said. "He's just gone into our house out back."

"What happened?" asked Mike.

"When he gets it into his head that he has someplace to go, I can't always stop him," said Eileen. "I've had a couple of really good scares. Sometimes, I just can't reason with him."

"What does he want to do?" asked Mike.

"He thinks he needs to be somewhere," said Eileen. "He talks about meetings with grocery store executives as if they are still a part of his life. Or sometimes he just wants to run errands like he used to. He wants to stop in at Bill's store for a gallon of milk or mail bills at the post office."

"What do you want me to do?" asked Mike, taking his coat from a peg on the wall and putting it on.

"Bring him back here," said Eileen, taking off her coat. "Without Selma there, this is probably the safest place for him. Oh, and would you grab the turkey from the fridge while you're there?"

"Can do," said Mike on his way out the door.

"Let's finish up the onions, honey," said Eileen, pushing the sleeves of her white cotton turtleneck over her elbows. "They'll be back in a jiffy."

Five minutes later, they were back. Sam, dressed in his own bathrobe, opened the door for Mike, who was carrying the turkey as if it were an infant. "Sam decided not to get dressed," said Mike, setting the turkey down on the counter.

"That's okay," said Eileen. "It's such a process. Sometimes, if we have nowhere to go and aren't expecting to see anyone, we just don't bother."

"That sounds good to me," said Mike, taking off his coat.

"Is anyone listening to me?" asked Sam.

"We're all listening," said Eileen. "Let me warm up your coffee and you can sit down and tell us all about it." When Eileen set the mug of coffee down in front of Sam, he stood up.

"No more for me," he said. "I've got to get going."

"Oh God," said Ann, hand to her forehead.

"Let's see if there's something good on the History Channel," said Eileen, taking Sam's arm in hers. "Ann, where can your father watch television?"

"In the den," said Ann. "Follow me."

They walked out of the kitchen and into the hallway, past Mike's study and the bathroom to the den. Eileen sat Sam down in the large leather chair, covered him with a leopard chenille throw, and turned on the television. She flipped through the channels until she saw World War II battleships. "There," she said to her husband, smoothing his recalcitrant hair into place with her hand. "You watch a bit of this and you can tell me about it later."

"Will you watch with me?"

"You start," said Eileen. "I'll be back in a little while."

"Will he be all right in there?" asked Ann in the hallway, thinking about her expensive furniture, coffee table books, and table adornments as much as her father's troubling condition.

"I think so," said Eileen. "Let's lock all the doors to the house anyway, just in case. He's agitated today."

"Why?"

"I'm not sure," said Eileen. "Some days he's fine and others he's a real handful."

Ten minutes later, as Ann was dumping her onions into the large ceramic bowl with the other stuffing ingredients, Sam walked into the kitchen. "I'd like to help," he said.

Ann looked at her mother. "I've got an idea," said Eileen. "Do you think Mike would take him back to our house for a while and keep him company? I've got a new jigsaw puzzle for him."

"You can ask him," said Ann. "He's working in his study."

As soon as Eileen left the room, Sam spoke to Ann. "What's your name, young lady?"

"I'm your daughter," said Ann, her temples pounding.

"You're kidding," said Sam, the beginning of a smile on his chapped lips.

"No, I'm not," said Ann, returning her attention to the bowl with the stuffing.

"You *are* putting me on, because my daughter lives far away," said Sam. "She's so important now that she never calls or visits." Ann lifted her face to her father. "There you are, Annie," he said, approaching her. "It's so good to see you." Ann accepted his hug, and then she slowly put her arms around him and laid her head against his chest. His bathrobe smelled like home. "We thought we'd lost you." When she was little, there was nothing her father's broad, solid chest couldn't cure, from a scraped knee to a troublesome dream in the night to a disappointing afternoon. She spent most of her time with her mother, in easy conversation with ready affirmation, but it was her father's approval she sought. He had not been effusive with praise, neither to his farmhands nor to his family. This was not because he was tough and mean; rather, he had strict standards and high expectations. A "job well done" from him made her feel euphoric, like, she would learn later, being drunk. This man in her kitchen now? Her mother was doing a good job of pretending, but Ann's real father, she could see every time she searched his eyes, was either deeply hidden, like a hibernating bear in a den beneath layers of snow and ice, or had simply chosen to vacate his body.

"Here they are," said Eileen as she and Mike walked into the kitchen. "Is everything all right?"

"Fine," said Ann, who had pulled away but was still examining her father's face.

Mike stepped forward and put his arm around Sam's shoulder. "Let's head down to your house," he said. "I hear we have some puzzling to do."

"Now there's a capital idea," said Sam, allowing Mike to turn his shoulders and steer him toward the back door.

Ann kissed her husband on the cheek. "Thank you," she said softly.

Mike nodded and then looked at his watch. "In one hour, wake Nate and tell him to come see me."

The time passed quickly. Ann and her mother stuffed the turkey and put it in the oven. Eileen peeled five pounds of potatoes, and set them on the stove to boil. Ann peeled, chopped, and boiled the butternut squash, following the instructions on the *Mama's Butternut Squash Soup* recipe card Eileen had handwritten for the occasion. While it cooled, she chopped an onion and minced some fresh sage. Eileen washed the lettuce for the pear and cream cheese salad. All the while, she resurrected stories about their life together decades before. "Remember that Saturday when your dad took you fishing?"

"Fishing?"

"You were twelve or thirteen at the time," said Eileen, over the metallic scraping sound of Ann whisking the onions into the soup.

"Oh yes," said Ann, adding salt and pepper. "We went to that river in the next county, with the silly name."

"Fish River," said Eileen, gently breaking apart the lettuce leaves. "I can't remember what the real name is, but everybody called it Fish River."

"Yes," said Ann, sprinkling in the sage. "And the banks of the river were packed with fathers—and sons. There wasn't another daughter in the crowd."

"And everyone looked at you," said Eileen, blotting the moisture off each leaf with a tea towel. "I remember you telling me you could have just died of embarrassment, right on the spot. So, instead, you just glowered at your dad."

Ann chuckled. "I sure did. I was furious."

"But then things changed, didn't they?"

"In a hurry," said Ann, turning to face her mother. "I cast out my first time and pulled in a fish a minute later."

"And a minute after that, from what I understand," said Eileen.

"And a minute after that," said Ann. "All of the fish in the river swam to one spot and just waited in line."

Eileen laughed. "You came home with the most fish I had ever seen," she said, "and then I had to clean them."

Ann smiled. "That is so gross."

"Those fish were the best I've ever tasted, to this day," said Eileen.

"They were pretty good, weren't they?" Ann remembered that day now, brilliant with sunshine. Her father had announced the night before that he had a hankering to catch a few fish, and that he was willing to shirk his Saturday morning chores if Ann was willing to abandon hers. They would leave the farm at dawn. Ann's sleep that night had been restless, like a child on the eve of Christmas or a birthday. And when they set out the next day in her father's truck, fishing rods and tackle box in the back and a picnic basket packed by Eileen between them on the seat, Ann felt like she had lived for that very moment. He talked to her that day, in quick, effective bursts of words, asking about school, friends, and her plans for the future. And when she caught all those fish, while the other fathers and their hapless sons stood by with dormant poles, he just kept nodding his head. Good girl.

Eileen smiled at her daughter as she brushed the hair off her face with the back of her hand. "Let's take a break," she said. "Do you want more coffee?"

"Definitely," said Ann. "But not that coffee. It's been sitting there for two hours."

"Just the way I like it," said Eileen, pouring more into her mug.

"I need a latte," said Ann. "But first, I'd better wake Nate."

When Nate didn't answer Ann's knock, she walked in. His room looked like it always did, cluttered with dirty clothes, damp bath towels, video game paraphernalia, and individual pizza boxes. Ann turned her face from a half-eaten slice of pepperoni sitting on his laptop keyboard. She would have to remember to tell Emma to disinfect everything in here, floor to ceiling and wall to wall. Tiny red lights danced on Nat's elaborate music system, but Ann heard nothing. She flicked on the light next to his bed and found her son, naked to the waist, sleeping with headphones over his ears. She gently lifted one of the headphones and Nate stirred. "What?" he said, opening one eye.

"It's time to get up," said Ann.

Nate looked at the clock next to his bed. "In another time zone maybe."

"I'm not kidding," said Ann. "Your father needs you."

Nate rolled over. "Nobody needs me before noon on a holiday."

"Get up, take a quick shower, and put some clothes on," said Ann. "Dad's in the guesthouse with Gramps."

"Don't tell me it's time for a three-generation chat," said Nate, still facing the wall.

"All I know is it's time for you to get up. I wouldn't want to have to send your father up here."

"He hasn't been in here in two years," said Nate, farting.

Ann ignored this, waited a moment, and then said, "With good reason."

"Ten more minutes," said Nate. "I need at least ten minutes."

"Ten minutes," said Ann, looking at her watch. "If you're not downstairs at quarter after, I'm sending your father up to get you."

Twenty minutes later, Nate, looking like he had just gotten out of bed, appeared in the kitchen doorway. "Hello, dear," said Eileen. "Did you sleep well?"

"Hi, Gran," said Nate, scratching his head.

"Sit down at the table, Nate," said Eileen, "and I'll get you some breakfast."

Nate held up his hands. "I can't eat before noon. It turns my stomach."

"No breakfast?"

"Never," he said, "unless it's lunch." Eileen looked at Ann, who shrugged her shoulders. "Where's Dad?"

"He's down in the guesthouse," said Ann. "Put a coat on. It's cold today." Nate saluted his mother and then walked out the back door coatless.

"You've got to give him a good breakfast, Ann, if he's going to start his day on the right foot," said Eileen.

"Let's not start, Mother," said Ann.

Nate walked through the front door of the guesthouse and found his father and grandfather in the living room. Mike was watching CNN from the chair, and Sam was dozing on the couch. The table in front of them was covered with puzzle pieces, a half dozen of which were attached in a line. "Great timing," said Mike, getting up from his chair and looking at his watch. "I'd like to chop some wood for a fire this afternoon."

"If you're going to chop wood," said Nate, "what do you need me for?"

"I need you to stay here with your grandfather."

Nate looked at the old man sleeping on the couch. "You mean, like babysit?"

"That is exactly what I mean," said Mike, putting on his coat.

"No, no, no," said Nate, backing up two steps. "You've got the wrong guy for the job."

"Oh, I don't think so," said Mike.

"Dad, be reasonable," said Nate, feeling oddly nervous. "He can work with you at the woodpile."

"Do you honestly think your grandfather is in any kind of shape to be near an ax?"

"I'll get Lauren up," Nate said. "She's had a lot more baby-sitting experience than I've had. Give me five minutes. I'll run back to the house and get her."

"Nate," said Mike, putting his arm around his son's shoulder, "you're overreacting here. He's just an old man. And besides, he's your grandfather."

Panicking, Nate thought he'd try a line he'd heard from his guidance counselor at school. "I'm not comfortable with this situation," he said, as calmly as he could.

Mike smiled at his son's effort. "A little bit of discomfort in our lives is not a bad thing."

When Mike started for the door, Nate followed him, asking, "Why does he need to be babysat anyway?"

"Because he wanders," said Mike. "Your mother and grandmother are trying to put a nice Thanksgiving meal together, and they don't need the distraction."

"Mom's really cooking?" asked Nate.

"Didn't you just walk through the kitchen?"

"Dad, I just got up. I'm not awake yet."

Mike patted Nate on the shoulder and opened the door. Nate looked back at the couch. His grandfather was still asleep. "It's going to be okay," said Mike. "He's been asleep most of the time I've been here."

"Tell Mom to make me a double espresso," said Nate. "I'm going to need some juice for this job."

"Will do," said Mike.

Nate watched his father walk up the path to the house. Then he walked back into the living room and sat down in the chair his father just vacated. He picked up the remote and turned to the music video station. Five minutes later, he heard a knock at the door. It was his grandmother, holding a travel mug and a bagel. "Here's your expresso," she said.

"It's *espresso,* Gran," said Nate, taking it from her hand. "With an *S*."

Eileen shrugged. "It's all just coffee to me. And here's a bagel. You've got to eat something, dear. I don't want you to waste away to nothing."

"I'm fine," said Nate.

"Is your grandfather still asleep?"

"Yes. Dad said he's been sleeping for a while."

"Good," said Eileen. "He's been tired lately."

"Thanks for the coffee, Gran," said Nate, wondering what he was missing on *I Love the 80s.*

"You're welcome," said Eileen. "Just call or dash up the path if you need anything."

"Will do," said Nate, turning away from her.

Just as he sat back down in the chair, his grandfather opened his eyes. Averting his gaze, Nate willed his grandfather to go back to sleep. Sam blinked several times, and then struggled to right himself. "Can someone help me?" he said.

"What do you need help with?"

Sam stared at his grandson, searching for recognition. When he couldn't place him, he decided it didn't matter. He simply needed someone's help. "Getting up," said Sam. "I can't seem to get up."

Nate got out of his chair and approached his grandfather. He took Sam's outstretched hand and pulled. Nothing. Nate squared his body to his grandfather's. He braced his feet against, but not on top of, Sam's and pulled again, both arms this time. He was able to get him halfway up before Sam flopped back down on the couch, like the heavier kid on a seesaw. The density of his grandfather's body surprised him. He was twice as heavy as he looked. "You have to help me here, Gramps," said Nate.

"I am helping," said Sam, scooting his bottom closer to the edge of the cushion.

Nate grabbed his grandfather by both wrists and pulled again. "That's good enough," said Sam. "Put that fancy pillow behind me, would you?" Nate followed his grandfather's gaze, and grabbed the large checked pillow from the other chair. He put it behind Sam's back. "There," said Sam, now sitting up straight on the front half of the cushion, "that's better. It's a good thing you happened along, young man, or I would have been in a jam."

"No problem," said Nate, returning to his chair.

For a minute, they both watched the TV. Then Sam asked, "Who are those girls?"

"They're dancers, Gramps," said Nate.

"They're naked, for Christ's sake," said Sam. "What kind of show are we watching here?" Embarrassed, Nate changed the channel. He stopped when he saw Katharine Hepburn and Spencer Tracy in black and white.

"Are you hungry?" asked Sam.

"No," said Nate, his eyes on the screen.

"Well, I am," said Sam, trying to push himself up off the couch. "Help me up here and we'll see if we can find some treats."

Nate again positioned himself in front of his grandfather. He grabbed his wrists and fell backward, as if he were going to lie down on the floor. As Nate dropped, Sam rose. When his grandfather was standing, Nate put a foot back and righted himself. *This,* he thought, *must have something to do with physics.* Mrs. Marsten was always going on about weight distribution. Maybe he would tell her this story. Maybe she'd give him extra credit. Nate followed Sam into the kitchen, where the old man began to root through the cupboards. When he found a red tin, he took it down from the shelf and pried the top off, revealing several chocolate chip cookies. "Here's the jackpot," he said. "Your mother thinks she's so clever, but I can find them every time. Do you want one?"

"Sure," said Nate, taking a cookie from the tin.

Sam took two and shoved them into his mouth, which he couldn't quite close around the sweets. Crumbs immediately fell through his open lips, down his pajama top, and onto the floor. "Gramps," said Nate. "Slow down. There's no rush."

"I don't know when your mother will be back," said Sam, looking past Nate into the hallway.

"Trust me, it will be a while," said Nate. "Here, let's sit down at the table." Nate steered his grandfather toward a kitchen chair, then got him a glass of milk from the fridge.

"Thank you," said Sam, when Nate put the glass down in front of him. "Tell me again, what branch of the service are you in?"

Nate closed his eyes for a moment, scanning his mind for patience, and then opened them.

"I'm not in the service, Gramps. I'm in high school."

"High school?" said Sam. "It's time you moved along, son."

"It sure is," said Nate, eating his cookie, wondering how his grandmother put up with this nonsense day in and day out. He had been with him for twenty minutes and was ready for relief.

Sam finished chewing his cookies and drank his milk. As soon as he was done, he put his hands on the table and pushed himself up and out of his chair. "Thanks for your hospitality," he said. "I've got to get going."

"Going?" asked Nate, standing. "Where are you going?"

"I've got a meeting downtown," said Sam, shuffling out of the kitchen. "I shouldn't be more than an hour."

Nate followed him into the hallway. "I forgot to tell you. Someone called while you were resting. The meeting is canceled."

"Canceled?" asked Sam, shifting his watery gaze from the floor in front of him to Nate's face. "Who called?"

"I can't remember," said Nate.

"It was probably Ted Masterson," said Sam. "We're always rescheduling around his needs."

"I think it was Ted," said Nate.

"Well, God damn it, what are we supposed to do now?" said Sam. "What the hell do we do now?"

Nate studied his grandfather, a lost boy in a grown man's body. "We could go back into the living room and watch TV. I think that Spencer Tracy movie is still on."

"I love Spencer Tracy," said Sam. Nate ushered Sam to the chair, figuring it would be easier for his grandfather to get in and out of, and sat him down. Nate took Sam's place on the couch. "You won't leave me, will you?"

"No," said Nate, getting comfortable. "I'm not going anywhere."

An hour later, back at the main house, Lauren was putting the brown sugar crumbly crust on the second of two apple pies. "Those are beautiful," said Eileen, looking over her shoulder. "I can't believe you've never made a pie before. You're a natural."

Lauren smiled. "My mom doesn't like messing up her kitchen."

"That's not true," said Ann, who was stirring the squash soup on the stove.

"It is true," said Lauren, emboldened by her grandmother's presence. "No one cooks in here."

"Emma cooks in here all the time," said Ann defensively.

"How about with supervision?" asked Eileen, who had walked back to the griddle where she was browning lunch sandwiches.

"Mom would have no more interest in supervising me in the kitchen than she would in eating anything I made," said Lauren. "She's much too busy for that."

"That's enough, Lauren," said Ann, moving the pot of soup to the granite countertop to cool.

"You can ask me, then," said Eileen, flipping four ham and cheese sandwiches on whole wheat, revealing perfectly toasted undersides. "Anytime you want to cook something, find me and I'll do it with you. I love to cook."

"Thanks, Gran," said Lauren.

"Is anyone hungry?" asked Eileen, looking at her watch.

"I couldn't eat a thing," said Ann, hand to her stomach. "We've been looking at food all morning."

"I am," said Lauren.

"Good," said Eileen. "Put a coat on and find your father. He said something about chopping wood. And then stop by the guesthouse for Nate and your grandfather. I'm just about done with these sandwiches. I'll set the table. Ann, will you find the condiments? I think we'll need ketchup, pickles, and maybe a little mustard. Do you have any potato chips?"

"Chips?" asked Ann, washing her hands. "I haven't eaten chips since I was eighteen."

"How about the rest of the family?" asked Eileen, moving the warm sandwiches onto a porcelain serving plate with the others.

Lauren walked to the large cupboard next to the fridge and pulled out a big bag of corn chips. "Will these do?" she asked.

"Where did those come from?" asked Ann.

"Perfect," said Eileen to Lauren. "Now run along and get those boys."

Lauren did as she was told; Ann stared, blankly, after her.

"Well," asked Eileen, putting the platter of sandwiches back into the warm oven, "are you going to get the condiments or not?"

Ann looked at her mother crossly. "I don't think pickles *are* a condiment."

"How about just getting them anyway," said Eileen, putting the chips into a large plastic bowl.

"Coming right up," said Ann, with false cheerfulness. "But don't count me in for lunch. If I don't get some exercise, I'm going to explode."

"I would imagine," said Eileen, her back to her daughter.

Mike, red-cheeked and smelling like the fresh cold air, walked into the kitchen just as Lauren returned from the guesthouse. "They're on their way," she said. "Nate said to tell you that Gramps is vertical and moving."

"Excellent," said Eileen.

"Something smells good," said Mike, shedding his barn coat and then rubbing his hands together. "Eating after working outdoors is such a treat."

"That's what Sam and his boys used to tell me," said Eileen. "You should have seen the lunches they put away after a hard morning's work."

"Where's my lovely wife?"

"Exercising," said Eileen, taking plates down from the cupboard.

"Well, good for her," said Mike, taking the plates from his mother-in-law and setting them down on the table.

Nate opened the back door and walked in, followed by Sam. "What kind of restaurant is this?" asked Sam, looking around. "I hope it's casual."

"Very casual," said Nate, helping his grandfather take off his coat. "You'll be happy to know, Gran, that I'm actually hungry."

"I'm glad," she said, retrieving the platter from the oven and setting it down on a pot holder at the center of the table. "Everyone please sit."

Sam took a sandwich from the platter and moved it directly to his mouth. After he had taken too big a bite, he said, "Where's that woman?"

"Exercising," said Eileen, grabbing a stack of napkins from the holder next to the fridge before sitting down.

"No surprise there," said Nate. "She'll have to get a couple of hours in if she's even going to *look* at Thanksgiving dinner."

"Is that much exercise good for you?" asked Eileen, passing the chips to Nate.

"No," said Lauren, "but it's essential if you want to remain a size two."

"What's a size two?" asked Eileen, just before she took a bite of a sandwich.

"Think thin and then cut that in half," said Nate. "It's a prerequisite for rich, attractive women." Mike smiled.

"You know, it used to be just the opposite," said Eileen, squirting mustard onto her plate. "If you were prosperous, you showed it by your girth. Wealthy women were rotund."

"No kidding?" asked Lauren, taking another half sandwich.

"No kidding," said Eileen.

"I would love to have lived back then," said Lauren. "I get so tired of watching my weight."

"That's because it only goes up," said Nate, chewing.

"Very funny, jerk," said Lauren, narrowing her eyes at her brother.

"I can't remember the last time I had a sandwich like this," said Mike, putting more chips on his plate.

"What do you normally eat for lunch on the weekends?" asked Eileen.

"Whatever we feel like," said Nate. "We grab a menu and order in. Just about everyone in town delivers."

"I don't know if anyone delivers grilled ham and cheese," said Mike, who usually stopped at a deli when he was running errands.

"Anytime you want a homemade sandwich, just ask me," said Eileen.

After he had eaten another half sandwich and handful of chips, Mike stood, thanked Eileen, and then put his coat back on and walked out the door. Next, Nate stood and announced he needed a shower. Lauren took the lunch dishes to the sink, and then headed into the dining room to set the table as promised. And Eileen was left alone with her husband and the glob of ketchup on his pajama top.

* * *

Dressed in casual but clean clothes, everyone gathered in the living room at four o'clock for a cocktail. The wood Mike had chopped was blazing in the fireplace, and a silver platter of Ritz crackers topped with liver pâté and corn relish sat on the coffee table—an hors d'oeuvre Ann remembered having at her grandmother's house on Thanksgiving. When everyone had a drink, Sam stood and lifted his glass. "I'd like to say something," he said. Everyone looked at him, fooled for a moment by his thick white hair wet-combed into place and his flannel shirt ironed and tucked into pressed khakis. "The vote was unanimous. I was elected the new chairman of the board," he said, a humble smile momentarily lifting his lifeless cheeks.

"Hear, hear," said Eileen, raising her glass in Sam's direction.

"And to the rest of you," Sam said to the others. "Watch out, change is coming."

An hour and two drinks later, Mike ushered the family from the living room to the dining room. They all lingered a moment behind their chairs, giving Eileen a chance to snap Sam's freshly laundered bib into place. As soon as everyone sat down, Mike popped up, insisting on serving the soup. Protesting, Ann followed him into the kitchen. "I don't know why you're doing this," she said, closing the swinging door behind her. "If it's an attempt to humiliate me, it's uncalled for, Mike."

"I'm doing it because I want to do it, Ann."

"You've never wanted to serve anyone before. Why start now?"

"Maybe I don't want my seventy-two-year-old mother-in-law to have to do it," said Mike, removing the lid from the pot of soup on the stove.

"Oh, here we go," said Ann, holding on to the edge of the counter. "Now we're getting at it."

"Getting at what?" asked Mike, looking at his wife.

"The fact that she does everything and I do nothing," said Ann, tipping the last of her fourth champagne into her mouth.

"Did I say that?"

"You didn't have to," said Ann.

Mike took the empty glass from Ann's hand. "Enough," he said.

"Are you cutting me off? In my own house on Thanksgiving?"

"Let's not make this about you," said Mike, setting the glass down on the island. "We've had a wonderful day. Four people we love dearly are in our dining room waiting for a meal. Let's focus on that."

"I'm not hungry," said Ann.

"You will be," said Mike. "This looks and smells delicious. Here, you can help me. The bowls are next to the pot; do you want to ladle the soup or bring the filled bowls to the table?"

Ann narrowed her eyes at her husband. Still sullen, she said, "I'll ladle."

Soup in front of everyone, Mike and Ann sat down. Mike suggested they all hold hands for the blessing. Nate made a face at his father before slowly reaching out to his mother and grandmother. Lauren held her father's hand firmly and her grandfather's hand gently. "Thank You, Lord," began Mike, "for this wonderful, home-made meal. Thank You for the hands that prepared it and for the mouths that will enjoy it. Help us to remember how very fortunate we are, and that the less fortunate need our help." Ann looked up at her husband. "And help us to be truly thankful," added Mike, looking at Ann, "for our special guests this Thanksgiving. Help us to welcome them into our hearts as well as our home. Amen."

"Amen," said Eileen aloud. "Thank you, Mike. That was lovely."

"And thank you, Eileen," said Mike, "for preparing our Thanksgiving dinner."

"I couldn't have done it without Ann and Lauren," Eileen said.

"And thank you as well, Lauren and Ann."

Ann tasted her soup; it was warm and buttery, with satisfying texture. The nutmeg and cinnamon subtly presented themselves mid-tongue and lingered, and a quick bite of pepper hit the back of her throat as she swallowed. The soup at the country club wasn't this good.

"Unbelievable," said Mike after his first spoonful.

"Ann made it," said Gran, smiling at her daughter.

"This is really good, Mom," said Lauren. "You should cook for us more often."

Ann smiled at her daughter. "That's why we have Emma."

"Without Emma," said Nate between bites, "we'd starve."

"Your mother's a wonderful cook," said Eileen to Nate. "She's just out of practice."

"Yeah, she'd get cut from JV at this point," said Nate. Lauren laughed.

"That's enough, Nate," said Mike.

Ann stood, laid her napkin on the table, and walked into the kitchen, closing the door behind her. Mike told everyone to continue eating and then followed Ann. He found her leaning against the counter, arms crossed over her chest. "What's going on?" he asked.

"I've had enough," said Ann. "I've had enough of the graces filled with innuendoes. I've had enough of the cracks about my cooking, and I've had enough of the adulation for my mother, who's put on no less than forty Thanksgiving dinners in her life. It's not a huge deal, for God's sake."

"Let it go, Ann," said Mike. "We're in the middle of Thanksgiving dinner and you're in here moping because you're not getting the kind of attention you want."

"That's not true," said Ann.

"It is true," said Mike, putting his hands on his wife's tiny shoulders. "You have to put your needs aside today and focus on your parents, your mother in particular. She needs all the praise we can give her. Do you think your dad's been thanking her for taking care of him? I don't know about you, but I'm starting to get an idea of how difficult her life has been—and continues to be. I know it's hard on you, but think about how hard this has been on her." Ann looked at the floor. "Take a good look at your father, Ann," said Mike. "Does he look anything like the man you grew up with? Does he look anything like the man your mother married?"

"No," said Ann quietly.

"Okay, then," said Mike, "can we just move on for now? I know you have issues and we can discuss them later."

"It's always later, Mike," said Ann. "You spend more time with your computer than you do with any of us. Maybe if you gave us more attention, we wouldn't have issues."

Mike ran his hand through his hair. "I don't think we want to have this discussion now. Let's go back with the others and eat our dinner."

"Fine," said Ann, walking past Mike toward the dining room.

"Is everything all right?" asked Eileen when Ann stepped into the room.

"Yes," said Ann. "I just have a bit of a headache."

"Well, no wonder," said Eileen. "You haven't eaten all day."

"And I'm about to change that now, aren't I?" asked Ann, sitting down and putting her napkin back in her lap.

"Who's ready for turkey?" asked Mike, opening the swinging door from the kitchen just wide enough for his head. Like a schoolboy with the answer to a classroom question, Sam raised his hand. "Great," said Mike. "I'll carve that good-looking bird. Lauren, will you get everyone some salad while they wait?"

"I'll do that," said Eileen, pushing back her chair.

"No, I'll do it, Gran," said Lauren, standing. "You sit."

As Mike carved, Lauren spooned the pear, cream cheese, and iceberg lettuce salad onto her mother's Spode wedding china. She brought the salad plates two at a time into the dining room. When she was done with that, she donned the oven mitts sitting next to the stovetop, took the matching casserole dishes out of the oven, and set them along the top of the granite counter. "Keep the lids on," said Mike, turning to his daughter, "so your culinary efforts will stay warm until we're ready to eat."

"Okay, Dad," said Lauren.

"Let's go enjoy our salads." Mike put the foil back over the turkey and sliced meat and then he and Lauren went into the dining room, where Sam was drawing circles on his plate with lettuce leaves tined onto his fork, and Ann was pouring herself a glass of wine at the sideboard, and Eileen was asking Nate about his physics class. Minutes later, they all filed through the kitchen, filling their plates—Eileen helping Sam—with turkey, mashed potatoes, stuffing, gravy, and green beans. Everyone including Ann and Nate, a picky eater since early childhood, took a hearty portion. Back in their seats, they ate eagerly. Lauren talked about her upcoming volleyball tournament. Nate talked about his football game on Saturday. Eileen discussed the simple ingredients for turkey soup with Ann. And Sam occasionally glanced up from his plate and nodded his head, seeming to absorb bits and pieces of the conversation around him. An animated table full of relatives, temporarily void of misunderstandings, sarcasm, and awkward silences, their Thanksgiving dinner reminded Mike of a scene in a holiday movie he had seen several years before.

It was a bitterly cold Saturday morning. Two inches of snow covered the ground and swirled around the house, carried by an angry wind that howled at the windows and bent the tops of the evergreens behind the guesthouse. Ann got out of bed and walked to the windows. "There's no way I'm going to that football game," she announced, arms across her chest.

Mike rolled over to look at his wife, and then beyond her to the blowing snow. "It's perfect full-length mink coat weather," he said, rubbing the sleep out of his eyes. "And I'll bet a hundred dollars you have boots to match."

Ann stared at the snow. "I'll still freeze."

Mike threw back the covers and sat on the edge of the bed. He stretched his arms out wide and then stood and walked to the bathroom, where he urinated loudly. "It's a two-hour commitment," he called. "You've suffered through worse."

Ann shivered, then got back into bed and pulled the duvet up to her chin. She felt the beginnings of a cold in her nose and throat. She swallowed; her throat was definitely scratchy. She put the back of her hand to her forehead, which felt slightly warm. Going out in this weather would be a mistake. Mike walked out of the bathroom and glanced at Ann before he walked to his closet. "We don't have a lot of time," he said. "The game starts in ninety minutes." Ann said nothing. She would wait until he was dressed and on his way to the kitchen before she verbalized her plans. Nothing and no one could make her go out in that weather to that game. Five minutes later, Mike walked back into the bedroom from the closet. "Let's go, sleepyhead."

She turned to face him. "I'm not going. I don't feel well."

Mike frowned. "I think Nate will be disappointed."

"I don't," said Ann. "Seriously, I have a sore throat and a headache and I think I should just stay home and rest. I've had a crazy week."

"And too much wine?"

"I'm just tired, Mike."

"We're all tired, Ann. And my week, I would imagine, has been just as crazy as yours."

"Yes, but you're not ill, are you?"

"No," said Mike, on his way out of their bedroom. "I'm not."

Downstairs, Eileen, Sam, and Lauren were sitting at the kitchen table eating something that looked and smelled like Mike's grandmother's cinnamon buns. He hadn't had one since his early childhood, but he instantly remembered the warm, sweet taste. "What wonderfulness have you prepared today, Eileen?" he asked, pouring himself a mug of coffee from the pot on the counter.

"Gran made cinnamon swirls," said Lauren, frosting on her upper lip. "They are the best thing I've ever tasted."

"Well, that's high praise," said Mike, sitting down. "Pass one to me, please." Lauren handed the platter of buns to her father. He put two of them on his plate.

"Where's Ann?" asked Eileen.

"She's not feeling well," said Mike. "She thinks she has a cold coming."

"Don't we all," said Sam, his mouth full.

"She's going to Nate's game, though, isn't she?" asked Eileen.

"I don't think so," said Mike. "She's in bed. Eileen, this cinnamon roll is amazing. You've done it again." Eileen said nothing. "Where's Nate?" asked Mike, chewing. "He's up, isn't he?"

"Up and gone," said Eileen. "His team is having breakfast at Bob Evans before the game."

"Unbelievable," said Mike, looking at his watch. "Football is the only thing that can get that kid up before noon on a Saturday."

Eileen pushed her chair back from the table and stood. She put a cinnamon bun on a plate. "Maybe this will cheer Ann up," she said. "Do you think she'd mind if I paid her a visit?"

"Go ahead," said Mike.

Eileen walked out of the kitchen, through the hallway, and up the stairs. She walked the few steps to Ann's closed door and knocked. Hearing no response, Eileen knocked again and then walked in. "Why in the world would you knock on your own bedroom door?" called Ann, still in bed.

"Because it's not my bedroom," said Eileen, approaching the bed.

Ann rolled over and faced her mother. "What are you doing here?"

"I heard you were sick and not going to Nate's game and thought I'd check up on you," said Eileen. "I brought you a cinnamon bun."

"I'm not hungry," said Ann.

Eileen set the plate down on Ann's bedside table. "Perhaps it will make you feel better," she said.

"I doubt a butter-laden cinnamon roll has any medicinal qualities whatsoever," said Ann.

"Well, think about it," said Eileen, turning to leave. "You have an hour before we have to leave."

"I don't have to think about it," said Ann, rolling back over. "I'm not going."

"I think Nate will be disappointed," said Eileen.

"That's the second time I've heard that this morning."

"That's because it's true," said Eileen.

"You don't know Nate very well," said Ann. "He couldn't care less if I'm at the game or not."

"You know as well as I do that that's not true," said Eileen. "It certainly wasn't true with Lauren. She was thrilled to have you at her volleyball game." Ann said nothing. "We'll be downstairs if you change your mind."

"Why can't I just stay here? I don't feel well. Doesn't anyone believe me?" said Ann.

"Of course, we believe you, dear. And if you absolutely can't go, everyone will understand. However, if there's any way you can find the energy, even for an hour, I think Nate would notice."

Eileen walked out of Ann's room, closing the door behind her. She quietly descended the stairs, walked into the kitchen, and sat back down at the table, where Mike, Lauren, and Sam were still eating. She forced a smile. "Any luck?" asked Mike.

"I don't think so," said Eileen. "Poor Nate."

"He'll understand," said Mike, taking another bun from the platter. Eileen took a sip of her tepid coffee.

Mike, Sam, Eileen, and Lauren, huddling under the Dilloway wool stadium blankets Mike kept in the trunk of his car, watched the marching band maneuver around the field. Their black boots lifted the snow, like a gust of wind shifts sand, as they formed themselves into a tiger, Dilloway High School's mascot. Dressed in black pants and orange jackets and berets, the musicians played the theme song from a *Rocky* movie. Sam clapped to the music and then sang along with the national anthem in a clear, resonant tenor. As soon as the players ran onto the field, the crowd cheered and applauded. Mike, who hadn't been to a game since the previous Thanksgiving, felt his chest swell with anticipation. Just after the kickoff, Lauren excused herself to sit with friends. Mike, Sam, and Eileen immediately filled in her space, leaning closer to one another for warmth. From a large canvas bag she carried from the car, Eileen extracted an old-fashioned, red plaid pattern thermos. "Hot chocolate, anyone?" she asked.

"Oh boy," said Sam. "I'll take a large."

Hands wrapped around their plastic cups of cocoa, they turned their attention to the game. Five minutes in, Nate jogged out onto the field. Two minutes after that, he made one of the cleanest, most effective tackles Mike had ever seen. And in the second half, he helped score the touchdown that cemented the game.

Ann opened her eyes and immediately looked at the clock on her bedside table. She had fallen asleep for what had seemed like minutes but had been more than an hour. She sat up, pushed her hair out of her face, and took a deep breath, which she was able to do through her nose. She swallowed; her throat, while still sore, felt a bit better. She got out of bed, stripping off her pajamas on her way to the closet. If she got dressed quickly, without showering, and made a quick latte to go, she might be able to make the fourth quarter. Silk long underwear on the top and bottom, wool socks, jeans, a cashmere turtleneck, a wool sweater—she was dressed in two minutes. She jogged into the bathroom to brush her teeth and wash her face. Her hair, looking like it had no master, she would hide under the fur-trimmed hat that matched her coat. She scurried down the steps and into the kitchen, where she made herself a vanilla latte, tapping her foot as the milk warmed. When it was warm but not as hot as she liked it, she poured the milk into a travel mug with the espresso and snapped on the lid. She glanced at the microwave clock, and then dashed down the hall to the front closet that held her furs. She chose the full-length mink, as Mike had suggested, and threw it around her shoulders. She grabbed her hat, scarf, gloves, and her warmest boots, and rushed back to the kitchen to put everything on.

Coffee and car keys in hand, she stepped out into the garage and could, immediately, see her breath. She could feel the cold working its way, like a determined lover, through her layered clothing. She wrapped her arms around herself as she ran to her car. Inside, she started the engine and pushed the remote button affixed to her visor to open the garage door. Nothing. She pushed the button again, but the door refused to rise. This had happened before, once, when the mechanism had frozen. Ann looked over at the opener connected to Mike's bay. He had had to release the spring and raise the door manually to get his car out. Ann looked at her watch and then rested her head, briefly, on the steering wheel before turning off her engine, getting out of her car, and walking back into the house.

CHAPTER 6

"I'd like to go to church," said Eileen, dressed in khaki pants and a cream-colored cashmere cardigan sweater over a navy blue cotton turtleneck, sipping coffee at Ann's kitchen table.

"Go for it," said Ann, in exercise clothes, reading the newspaper and drinking a large mug of latte.

"I mean with you," said Eileen. "Do you ever go to church?"

Ann lowered the newspaper and looked at her mother. "I don't have time for church."

"It's only an hour on Sunday mornings, Ann," said Eileen. "What do you mean you don't have time?"

Ann sighed loudly but kept the newspaper in place between her and her mother. "We're busy people," she said. "We have a lot going on in our lives. Since you've been here, we've been home, but it's not usually that way. Sometimes, Mike and I go out for brunch on Sundays. Or, we go away for the weekend."

Eileen finished her coffee and put the cup down on the saucer. "I can understand that," she said. "And you can go away anytime, Ann. Your father and I didn't mean to change your life."

Ann lowered the paper again, just enough to see her mother's eyes over the top edge. "That wasn't my point," she said. "We run all week long. When we're in town, we like to sleep in or just relax on Sunday mornings. Didn't the Lord himself call it a day of rest?"

"That's not what He meant and you know it," said Eileen, out of her seat and pouring herself more coffee from the pot on the counter. "Growing up, you went to church with us. You even seemed to enjoy it."

"I didn't *enjoy* church," said Ann. "Children go to church because their parents make them."

"Well, nobody makes me go and nobody makes my friends go," said Eileen. "The people I know enjoy church very much."

"And the people you know are all in their seventies and eighties," said Ann. "What else is going on in their lives?"

"Actually, they aren't all in their seventies and eighties," said Eileen, returning to the table, to a face-to-face conversation with her daughter, who had set the paper aside. "There are a number of young people at our church. They go, even though they are busy like you, because they want to go. They are thankful for what they've got."

"Oh," said Ann, "and I'm not thankful, right?"

"I don't know," said Eileen. "Are you?"

Ann lifted her mug and sipped her latte. "In addition to not having time for church, I don't have time for discussions like this," she said. "Life is different now, Mother, plain and simple. Children have activities. Men work twelve-hour days. Women have lives outside of the home. When I was growing up, people weren't busy like we are today. There were many days, I remember, you never left the house, for God's sake. You cleaned, you cooked, and you sewed. I mean, no wonder you wanted to get out on a Sunday morning. It's the exact opposite now. We're out all week and on Sundays, when we're home, we want to stay home."

"So, church is irrelevant now?" asked Eileen. "Is that what you're saying?"

"In some ways, yes," said Ann, getting up to reheat her coffee in the microwave. "People have since found other places to gather and socialize."

"How about worshipping God?" asked Eileen. "Can you do that at the mall now?"

"I get enough sarcasm from my children," said Ann. "I don't appreciate it from you."

Eileen brushed the hair from her face with her fingers. "Go with me," she said gently. "Go with me just once. If you hate it, you don't have to go back."

When the microwave beeped, Ann removed her heated mug. "And I won't have to listen to you harp about it?"

"No," said Eileen.

Ann waited a moment.

"Okay," she said, hardly believing she'd consented. "But I'm telling you right now, once will be more than enough."

That Sunday morning, Eileen, wearing a gray wool skirt, pressed white cotton blouse, navy blue cardigan sweater, and pearls under the camel-hair coat she'd had for thirty years, knocked at the back door. Mike, dressed in jeans and a Brooks Brothers shirt, got up from the table where he was eating a bagel to let her in. "Don't you look nice," he said.

"Thank you," said Eileen. "Is Ann ready?"

Mike looked at his watch. "She's in the shower. She didn't think the service was until ten o'clock."

"It is at ten," said Eileen. "I like to get there a little early."

"Well, it's nine now," said Mike. "How about sitting down for a few minutes? I'll get you a cup of coffee and something to eat."

"Coffee would be great," said Eileen, shedding her coat. "I'll wait to eat, though, until after the service."

"Ann was thinking about going out to brunch afterward."

"That sounds delightful," said Eileen. "Will you let Selma know I'll be gone a bit longer?"

"Will do," said Mike, putting a mug of black coffee down in front of his mother-in-law.

"And how about you?" asked Eileen, using the fingers of both hands to coax some life into her still damp hair. "Can you come with us?"

"For brunch or for church?" asked Mike, amusement in his eyes.

"Both," said Eileen.

"You two head off on your own this morning," he said, sitting. "I'll catch up with you when you get back."

"We'd love to have you come," said Eileen.

"And I appreciate that," said Mike, taking a bite of his bagel.

"You were raised a Catholic, weren't you?"

"I was," said Mike, chewing.

"But you don't go to church at all now?"

Mike wiped the cream cheese from his mouth with a paper napkin. "I had a lot of religion early on," he said, "and that was okay because everyone else did, too. As soon as I went to college, I needed a break. When Ann and I moved here, and I was getting my MBA at Michigan, there simply wasn't enough time for church. We all worked so hard. In the rare instances when we weren't studying, we wanted to relax. Throughout my childhood and teenage years, I found church to be many things, Eileen, but relaxing wasn't one of them."

Eileen smiled. "Perhaps you'd feel differently now."

"Perhaps," said Mike, looking at his watch as he took his last sip of coffee.

Upstairs, Ann couldn't figure out what to wear. She wanted to look good but not sexy. She wanted to be comfortable but not casual. She wanted to impress those around her but not appear overly ostentatious. Classy was the look she needed. Her mother, Ann knew, would be mortified if she wore pants. Women from that generation didn't understand dress pants and never would. Ann ran her hand along the multicolored row of skirts hanging on the lower bar of her winter closet section. When she spied the bottom half of her camel-colored suede suit, she pulled it out. *Perfect,* she thought as she removed the plastic dry cleaner bag. She found the suit jacket on the top bar and removed its protective covering as well. Crossing the closet, she surveyed her section of black blouses and sweaters and chose the cashmere turtleneck she had bought the week before. Satisfied, Ann dressed, put on as little makeup as she could bear, brushed and sprayed her hair, and grabbed her black pearl necklace and earrings from her safe. She hurried down the stairs and into the kitchen, where the first word out of her mother's mouth was a loudly whispered "Finally." Ann said nothing in return. Wishing she had worn pants, Ann walked to the counter to pour herself a cup of coffee. "I don't think we have time for that, Ann," said Eileen, getting out of her chair.

"We do if I bring it with me," said Ann. "I don't go anywhere without a cup of coffee first."

"I would guess not," said Eileen, walking toward the door to the garage.

"For God's sake, Mother," said Ann. "I know what time it is. It takes exactly four minutes to get to church."

"How would you know?" asked Eileen.

"Okay," said Mike, "off you go."

Ann snapped the lid on her travel mug and took her car keys from the basket on the counter. "Let's go," she said.

St. Paul's Episcopal Church was more crowded than Ann would have guessed. They arrived ten minutes ahead of the scheduled service, but it took them half that long to find a parking place and walk into the church. Eileen frowned as she stood on her tiptoes, looking for a place to sit. The only seating available was in the front, the first two pews on both sides. "Up front," she said in a loud whisper, discreetly pointing an index finger.

"I'm not going up there," Ann whispered back.

"And I'm not standing back here," said Eileen. "They're going to process right past us if we don't get moving."

Behind them a robed teenage boy with sleepy eyes and flyaway hair held the worn wooden handle connected to a polished bronze cross. Behind him were two younger boys, dressed in the same white robes, solemnly carrying lit candles. And behind them was an adult choir, several members looking more annoyed, Ann thought, than anointed. She moved forward. "I *hate* sitting in the front," she said.

"Most people who don't go to church feel exactly that way," replied Eileen.

They scurried down the center aisle. Ann's heels tapped loudly on the slate floor, even though she tried to walk on her toes. People's eyes followed her as she made her way down the aisle, as if she were a bride. "There's Ann Barons," someone said in a hushed voice. When they reached the second pew, Eileen ducked in and Ann followed. As soon as Eileen sat, she removed her overcoat, and then quickly knelt on the mossy green rectangular cushion on the floor in front of her and closed her eyes. Ann, too, closed her eyes, picturing the Bloody Mary she would be sipping by eleven thirty. *Thank You, God, for alcohol.* The first organ blast startled her. She glanced at her mother, who was already standing with her hymnbook open. Ann grabbed a hymnal from the rack and stood next to her mother. As Eileen sang, Ann read the lyrics extolling a virtuous, God-fearing existence. This, she thought, was the reason she quit going to church. Afterward, they sat and listened to the priest ramble through the announcements before a young woman in dress jeans strode to the front and read a lesson from the Bible. Ann tried to listen, but she was distracted by voices behind her.

"That's Ann Barons," said a woman.

"I can't believe she's here."

"Why?"

"Well, for one, I thought they worshipped at the bank."

Ann face warmed. She glanced at her mother, wondering if she'd heard their spiteful remarks. If she had, however, Eileen gave no sign. She appeared content, her eyes fixed on the reader. Ann looked at her watch; the service was already dragging, and they had been there only seven minutes. Sometime later, when Ann was making a mental shopping list of Christmas presents she needed to pick up for Mike, the man next to her cleared his throat in a meaningful way. She looked at him and he glanced downward. He then handed her the silver offering plate, already holding a white pledge envelope and a $5 bill. Flustered, Ann took the plate and set it down in her lap while she dug through her purse. She found her wallet, which contained three fifties, a five-dollar bill, and three ones. Sweating, Ann put $5 in the plate and then handed it to her mother.

"Would you look at that?" whispered one of the women behind her. "All the money in the world, but only five dollars for the Lord."

"Don't be too hard on her, dear," said the other. "She simply spent all of her money yesterday—on herself."

Ann stiffened, but refused to turn around. She took a travel bottle of hand sanitizer from her purse and rubbed a few drops into her palms. The husbands of the gossipers behind her probably worked for Mike's company in low-level management jobs. They would never amount to anything. Ann glanced at her mother, again wondering if she had heard anything. But Eileen was busy pulling a $20 bill out of her wallet. She passed the plate back to Ann and then dropped to her knees again. Ann handed the plate back to the usher and then knelt beside her mother and looked at the words Eileen pointed to in the prayer book. They were familiar, although they didn't seem to be the same words Ann remembered from her childhood. She found interesting the resurrected notion of being held accountable for things she hadn't done as well as things she had. Could anyone get it right? After a fifteen-minute sermon about a poor widow, communion—including the interminable Prayers of the People—and the final hymn, Ann felt like a sprinter seconds before a race. She turned to her mother. "Let's go out the side door. The line is building quickly in the back."

"I want to say hello to the minister," said Eileen, grabbing her coat. "He gave a good sermon, don't you think?"

"If you mean good as in trite and predictable, yes, it was right on target," said Ann, standing.

"The line moves quickly," said Eileen. "It won't take more than five minutes."

Ten minutes later, she was shaking Father David's hand. "Hello," he said warmly. "Welcome to St. Paul's."

"Good morning," said Ann politely.

"Are you new to us?" he asked.

"Yes and no," said Ann.

"Are you new to town?" Father David asked gently.

"Oh no," said Ann. "We've been here for years."

"Well," he said, "I'm so glad you've come to pay us a visit. There are green newcomer cards on the table in the narthex, on the other side of the glass doors. Take a few moments to fill one out and tell us about yourself. We'd be happy to have you join our family."

"Thank you," she said, releasing his hand.

"Lovely sermon," said Eileen, next in line. "It's a familiar message, but a good one, especially this time of year."

"Thank you," said Father David. "Are you new to us today, as well?"

"Yes," said Eileen. "My husband and I live in Pennsylvania, actually. We're temporarily living with our daughter, Ann, who has graciously taken us in. My husband is not well, and we're on the waiting list for an assisted-living facility. We're hoping a spot will open up some time in the early spring."

"Well, I'll keep you and your husband in my prayers," said Father David. "In the meantime, if there's anything St. Paul's can do for you, please don't hesitate to call us."

"That's very kind," said Eileen.

Ann looped her free arm through her mother's and steered her out the doors and into the crowded narthex. "You forgot to mention your high school graduation and wedding day," said Ann as she urged Eileen forward.

"Ministers are interested in their congregations," said Eileen, slowing to put on her black leather gloves.

"I'm sure they are," said Ann, squeezing her mother's arm with hers as she cut a path through the forest of people. "But you aren't a member of the congregation, are you?"

"Oh look," said Eileen, stopping at a table near the front door. "Here are those green cards he was talking about. Shall we fill one out?"

"Put it in your purse and you can write your life history on it at the Omelet House," snapped Ann. "If I don't get out of here this very second, I'm going to explode."

Ann's spicy Bloody Mary, which she ordered as soon as they walked into the restaurant, was exquisite. The Tabasco sauce bit her taste buds while the vodka warmed her blood, instantly relaxing her. Eileen, who told Ann she couldn't remember the last time she'd had a drink at lunchtime, asked for a glass of white wine when they were seated at their table. By the time it arrived, Ann was done with her drink and ordered a second. "It couldn't have been that bad," said Eileen, after their waitress left.

"What?"

"Church," said Eileen. "Was it so bad that you need two drinks?"

"I don't need a reason to have two drinks other than desire," said Ann. "And yes, church was that bad."

"What was so bad about it?"

"The congregation is full of hypocrites, and the minister lectures rather than preaches," said Ann, biting her celery stalk.

"Hypocrites?" asked Eileen.

Ann told her mother about the two women who had sat behind them. Eileen said she hadn't heard a thing and wondered aloud if Ann could have imagined it. "A guilty conscience can do that," she said, looking into her wineglass.

"I don't have a guilty conscience," said Ann. "And I don't need to go to church on Sundays to know I'm a good person."

Eileen looked at her daughter. "What makes you a good person?"

Ann halted the ice chip she was pushing around her mouth with her tongue. "What kind of remark is that?"

"It's a question, Ann," said her mother, straightening the flatware in front of her. "It's meant as nothing but a question."

"Why would you ask a question like that?" asked Ann. "What that question tells me is you don't think I'm a good person and you'd like me to prove differently." Ann's second drink arrived. She drank a third of it as the waitress read the daily specials, all full of fat. Eileen ordered eggs Benedict. Ann ordered a poached egg on dry whole-wheat toast with ripe cantaloupe and strawberries on the side. Eileen unfolded her napkin and put it in her lap. "Do you still need me to prove my goodness?" asked Ann as soon as they were alone again.

"Of course not," said Eileen, reaching for her wineglass. "You just seem different to me."

"Different from the last time we were together, or different from my childhood?"

"Well, I haven't spent much time with you in recent years," said Eileen, pushing a gray curl from her forehead, "so I guess it must be from your childhood."

"It's called growing up, Mother," said Ann, finishing her drink.

"How sad would it be if I were still that innocent little hayseed whose idea of a good time was a strawberry milkshake after fishing with Dad?"

Before Eileen could stop them, tears welled up in her eyes.

Ann's outermost layer melted. "I'm sorry," she said. "I didn't mean that."

"No, it's nothing," said Eileen, dabbing her eyes with her napkin. "It's the wine."

Ann looked out the window. Moments later, their food arrived. Eileen said a quick blessing, and then they ate the first few bites in silence. "I'm sorry, too, if I said something to upset you," said Eileen. "I can't tell you how thankful I am to be here. I know your dad is thankful, too."

Ann waved her hand dismissively. "It's okay," she said. "It's not a big deal."

"It *is* a big deal," said Eileen, leaning in toward her daughter. "You have no idea what taking care of your father has become."

"I have some idea," said Ann.

"It's a tragedy," said Eileen, the words catching in her throat on the way out of her mouth. "It's not fair. He was such a good man."

"Let's not do this," said Ann, tucking her hair behind her ears. "Let's not talk about this now."

"When do you want to talk about it?" asked Eileen.

"I don't," said Ann. "I just don't."

"So you like having your head in the sand," said Eileen, straightening her spine.

"It's not that, Mother," said Ann. "It's just hard."

"Talking about hard things can be good."

"It can also be painful," said Ann. "Please. Let's just eat our food and talk pleasantly. I hear it's supposed to snow tomorrow."

Eileen nodded her head and then lowered her gaze and concentrated on her eggs.

They both were quiet on the car ride home. As soon as Ann pulled the car into the garage, Eileen got out, repeated her thank-you for brunch, and headed directly for the brick pathway that wound around the garage and led to the guesthouse. She was anxious to see Sam, especially since she hadn't been allowed to discuss him. Ann walked into the house, through the kitchen, where she washed her hands, and into Mike's study. He was focused on his computer screen, a yellow legal pad under his right forearm and a mechanical pencil in his hand. "Well, hello," he said as soon as she appeared beside him. "How was your morning?"

"Church was ridiculous," said Ann. "And my mother is driving me crazy."

Mike hit the SAVE button on the computer, then wheeled halfway around to face his wife. "So what else is new?" he asked with a smile on his face.

"I know you find it hilarious," said Ann, "but you have no idea what it's like. You don't spend time with her like I do."

"Honey," said Mike, yawning, "you've got to learn to relax with her. She's an old woman and she's your mother."

"And she pushes my buttons every time she gets a chance."

"Everybody pushes your buttons, Ann," said Mike. "Maybe you've got too many buttons."

Ann folded her arms across her chest. "I need to get away," she said. "We haven't done anything since their arrival. As soon as we're done with Christmas, we're out of here."

"Sounds good to me," said Mike, turning back to his computer. "You work out the details and I'll pack. Just a weekend, though; I'm really busy at work right now."

"So what else is new?" asked Ann, walking out of the room.

CHAPTER 7

$\approx$

At this point, Ann's Christmas party happened almost by itself. She had called her favorite caterer just after Labor Day with menu ideas, which were finalized before Halloween. She had chosen a design for the invitation, which the printer had made 100 copies of and she had proofread the weekend before her parents arrived. She had gone over the guest list, making the additions and subtractions that suited her, before driving the invitations to the calligrapher at Heavenly Hand, who had mailed them the day before Thanksgiving. Ann's party planner, Stephanie, had called that very morning to give Ann the latest count: 168; eight more than the year before. On Monday evening, December 23rd, the Baronses' house would be filled with the most powerful and interesting people in town.

It was almost lunchtime on Saturday, but Ann was not hungry. She had spent an hour on the Precor machine, done three hundred sit-ups and twenty five push-ups, showered, dressed, and was enjoying a double latte and *Architectural Digest* at her kitchen island when Lauren walked into the room. "Hi, honey," said Ann warmly.

Dressed in flannel pajamas bottoms and a Nike T-shirt, Lauren yawned and lifted her hand in greeting. She walked directly to the fridge, grabbed a can of Diet Coke, and sat down at the sunny end of the kitchen table. Lauren popped open the can, angled her face toward the morning sun shining through the glass, and closed her eyes. "How was the party?" asked Ann.

"Okay," said Lauren.

"Who was there?"

"Lots of people."

"Name one."

"Judd Acker."

"Ah," said Ann, looking up from her magazine, "and how is Mr. Acker?"

"Gorgeous, as usual."

"And did you talk to him?"

"For about three seconds," said Lauren, opening her eyes and taking another sip of soda. "Then his annoying insect of a girlfriend showed up and pulled him away for a dance."

"Girlfriends always seem to get in the way," said Ann, turning a page.

"Tell me about it."

"Did you dance with anyone?"

"No," said Lauren, "unless you count Emily, Nicole, and Hannah."

"No boys?" asked Ann.

"No," said Lauren, "unless you count Josh."

Ann smiled because she did count him. Nate's friend Josh was tall, over six feet, trim, and had thick, curly hair the color of Kraft caramels. And he was polite, unlike most of Nate's friends, who treated Ann's house like a cheap summer rental. Those boys ordered food that Ann suspected she paid for and then left a trail of chips, pizza grease, and spilled soda behind them. And if Ann, by chance, walked into the kitchen as they unabashedly sat on her custom-made cushions in their dirty jeans and walked on her floor in their soiled sneakers, they stopped talking. Ann didn't speak to them either, never asking their names, never encouraging Nate to invite them back. Equally uncomfortable with these accidental encounters, the boys often asked Nate if his mother was going to be home before agreeing to go to his house. Since Nate didn't much like being around his mother either, he was mostly elsewhere, which suited both of them. "Did Josh ask you to dance, or vice versa?"

"Of course he asked me, Mom," said Lauren. "How else would I dance with him?"

"I think he likes you," she said.

"I'm his best friend's sister," said Lauren, flipping through the *TV Guide*. "He has no choice."

"Oh yes, he does," said Ann, walking to the table and sitting down next to her daughter. "He talks to you and dances with you because he likes you."

Lauren blushed. "I don't think so," she said, not looking up from her magazine.

Ann took another sip of her latte, then set her cup down. "What do you say to a little shopping today?" Ann didn't offer up a mother-daughter shopping trip often. She preferred shopping alone or with her friends, mostly because Lauren, as a teenager, was understandably enthralled with adolescent clothing. And Ann was simply uninterested in traipsing through teenybopper stores in pursuit of the perfect tank top, hip-hugging jeans, and chunky, clunky shoes. Teenagers, Ann told her friends, always thought they looked special when in fact they looked just like everyone else their age. In time, Ann hoped to cultivate in her daughter an interest in designer fashion.

What Ann didn't admit to herself was the fact that Lauren, like her mother, preferred shopping with her friends. While Lauren did like her mother's American Express Gold card and definitely got a kick out of the oversolicitous behavior of the store clerks as soon as they saw ANN BARONS embossed along its bottom edge, she didn't like being manipulated. Her mother arched her eyebrows at almost everything Lauren thought was cute, and tried to steer her into the old lady section, toward houndstooth pants, coordinating blazers, and hot pink tops for that "pop of color." Lauren looked at her mother; was it worth it? "Sure," she said. "I could use a couple of sweaters."

"Me too," said Ann, reaching out to move a strand of Lauren's hair away from her eye. "Let's try that new store downtown."

Lauren backed away. "Isn't that a ladies' boutique?"

"Yes," said Ann, finishing her latte. "I hear she has some really cute things."

Houndstooth heaven, thought Lauren as she got up from the table.

Three hours later, Lauren was reminded of other reasons why she couldn't stand shopping with her mother. One, she moved randomly from rack to rack with the speed, intensity, and unpredictability of a tornado. And two, she was demanding and bossy with the saleswomen—actually snapping her fingers once for attention from a trainee—which was embarrassing to witness. Carrying her bags containing clothing more appropriate for her mother than herself, Lauren walked from the garage into the kitchen. Nate was sitting at the table eating a bowl of cereal. "How many bags? One, two, three—score!" he said as Lauren set them down and took off her coat.

"Shut up, Nate."

Ann walked in from the garage also carrying four shopping bags, two in each hand. Nate stood and slowly clapped his hands several times. "Here's a woman, folks, who knows how to use her AmEx," said Nate, extending a fisted hand toward his mother as if he were holding a microphone. "What do you say, Ann? A few words of advice for the beginner shoppers in our audience?"

"Are you just getting up?" asked Ann, hanging her black leather car coat on a peg.

"I might be," said Nate, returning to his cereal at the table. "Then again, maybe I've been up for hours doing my homework for Monday."

"Does that mean," said Lauren, looking in the refrigerator, "you'll do a bit better than a C-minus on your next math test?"

"Maybe," said Nate, shoving another spoonful of Wheaties into his mouth. "Then again, I could just kiss my teachers' asses like you do for good grades. God knows it's not intelligence."

"That's enough, Nate," said Ann, washing her hands.

"Enough? I'm barely getting started."

"Mom," said Lauren, "why is there always nothing to eat in this house?"

"There are lots of things," said Ann, drying her hands on a fresh tea towel from the drawer next to the sink.

"Sure," said Lauren, "if you like low fat, low sodium, and no taste."

"Order something," said Ann, making herself a latte.

"I'm hungry now," said Lauren. "I don't want to wait forty-five minutes for some random pizza guy to find our house."

"Everyone knows where we live," said Ann, tucking her hair behind her ears.

"Because we're really important," said Nate, pouring more cereal into his bowl.

Ann scooted past Lauren and grabbed the half gallon of skim milk for a latte. "Now that I've got you here together," she said, turning around to face her son and her daughter. "I want to talk to you about something."

"Too late," said Nate. "We already know about the birds and the bees."

"It's about our party Monday night," said Ann. "I was wondering if you might want to help serve." In reality, Ann was hesitant to have Nate and Lauren at her party. Teenagers were such wild cards. But when they dressed properly, they were very attractive kids. Plus, a suggestion of family unity at Christmastime was corporate smart. Everyone would see that the CEO and his wife spent time with their children, just like everyone else.

"Do you mean, would you like another salmon puff, Mrs. Fatso?" asked Nate. "Tell me you're kidding."

"I thought it might be fun," said Ann, trying to sound convincing.

"What might be fun?" asked Eileen, coming through the back door.

"Come on in," said Ann pointedly. "It's open."

"Passing hors d'oeuvres at Mom's party," said Lauren, examining the expiration date on a package of cheddar cheese, the fridge door still open. "She thinks that would be fun."

"So do I," said Eileen, pulling her arm out of her coat. "You get to see a bunch of fancy, dressed-up people and eat great food in the kitchen."

"Nobody said a word about eating the food," said Lauren, looking at her mother.

"The food," said Ann, "is for my guests. Close that door, Lauren."

"Oh, we already know that," said Nate. "If it were a party for us, there would be no food."

Eileen smiled at her grandson. "Come down to our house Monday night, and I'll make anything you'd like."

"Like what?" asked Nate, interested.

"Well, how does roast beef, mashed potatoes, buttered lima beans, and homemade cherry pie with vanilla ice cream sound?"

"Wow," said Lauren, who had abandoned the cheese, closed the door, and was now looking in the "snack cupboard" for something other than her mother's 100-calorie packs. "That sounds great."

"Nate?"

"I must admit, that does sound pretty good," he said.

"It's done, then," said Eileen. "Selma's going to take a couple of days off, so it will be just the four of us. Dinner is at seven. But come early and we'll have a few hors d'oeuvres of our own."

"Are you sure you don't want to come to the party?" Ann, sipping her drink, asked her mother.

"Your father doesn't do well at parties," said Eileen. "We'll meet your friends another time." Ann nodded her head. It was the perfect arrangement. She could now tell her guests that the kids were having dinner with their grandparents.

"I may have plans, Gran," said Nate tentatively.

"You do have plans," said Eileen, "to be at my house at six thirty." Temporarily resigned, Nate poured himself another bowl of cereal and turned his attention to the sports section of the local newspaper. He had two days to think of an excuse.

Nate turned down his music when his phone vibrated. It was Josh, reporting back about the lack of social activities that evening. "You can't tell me there's nothing going on," said Nate.

"There's a lot going on," said Josh. "For one, your parents are having a huge party and Tim, Brad, and Kevin are stuck home babysitting their younger brothers and sisters because of it. Tom's still grounded. Kyle has some family thing happening, and Ed's already gone for Christmas vacation. There's no action anywhere tonight."

"Shit," said Nate. "What are you doing?"

"A pile of relatives are coming for dinner," said Josh. "The highlight of the evening will be when my uncle George slaps me on the back after a couple of scotches and asks me for the thousandth time what college I'll be attending."

"I hate that," said Nate.

"Tell me about it," said Josh. "What's Jenny up to?"

"Big Christmas dinner at her aunt's house," said Nate.

"Why don't you tag along?"

"I wasn't exactly invited," said Nate. "According to Jenny, only husbands and fiancés get to join the party."

"I hope that wasn't some kind of hint, man," said Josh.

"If it was, I missed it," said Nate, even though he had already wondered what it would be like to one day ask Jenny to spend the rest of her life with him.

"So what are you going to do?" asked Josh.

"Unless I come down with some funky disease in the next thirty minutes, I guess I'm going to eat dinner with my grandparents."

"That's a drag," said Josh. "Is Lauren wrapped up in that, too?"

"Oh yeah," said Nate. "I wouldn't even think about going if she didn't have to go. My old man actually feels kind of bad about it. He gave me fifty bucks."

"That's cool," said Josh.

Nate hung up the phone and turned up the volume of his music. He lay back on his bed, closed his eyes, and hoped for a miracle.

In her bedroom, Lauren was in the middle of a dream about Judd Acker. They were alone together in the school gym, only it didn't look like the gym at Dilloway High. He had lost his car keys and asked Lauren to help him look for them. He thought they might be under the bleachers. Taking Lauren's hand, Judd led her under the gigantic metal structure and into the darkness. Just when

Lauren was wondering how they would be able to look for keys in the pitch-black darkness, Judd flipped a light switch, illuminating an underground city. "We should stay together," he said. "Let's look over here first." Lauren followed him, all the while looking at the ground for his keys. He said her name and she looked up at him; only he was no longer Judd. He had somehow turned into Josh.

Lauren awoke with a start and looked at the clock next to her bed. She had fifteen minutes to get to the guesthouse. She sat up and pushed her hair out of her face. A few strands had made their way into her mouth and were sticking to her lips. She picked them out as she slowly made her way across her floor—through dirty clothing, schoolbooks, and the cut-up magazines and markers for her poster about war in Third World countries that was due the day after Christmas break (she thought that was so unfair), and several empty plates, except the one with the bagel half-covered with strawberry cream cheese that she had forgotten to eat the other night—and into the bathroom. She washed her face and brushed her hair. She pulled the sweater she had been sleeping in over her head and dropped it on the floor. After she reapplied deodorant, she walked back into her room, fished another sweater out of her bottom bureau drawer, and put it on. She walked out of her room, closing the door behind her. Down the hall, she knocked on Nate's door, but got no response. She knocked harder, then walked in. "Doesn't anybody knock anymore?" asked Nate, removing the headphones from his ears.

"I did."

"Do you want something?"

"It's time to go," said Lauren.

Nate looked at his clock. "I'll be there in a few minutes," he said, putting the headphones back on his head. Lauren turned her back and left his room. As she walked down the stairs, she could hear and smell activity. When she walked into the bustling kitchen, her mother, in a winter white silk pantsuit, looking like the Queen of Entertainment, was instructing the caterers. Three of them, dressed in black pants and white pleated shirts, hovered around her, looking attentive. Another, dressed in chef's attire, was pulling curlicues of beef out of the oven, while another, dressed in all black, washed dishes at the sink—all players in the Party Factory game; Ann Barons poised to spin them in different directions at the next roll of the dice. No one acknowledged Lauren as she grabbed her black down coat from the peg rack and slipped out the back door. As soon as she was outside, the quiet cold enveloped her, simultaneously stunning and awakening her senses. A sharp intake of air stabbed her lungs. Something at the edge of her field of vision made her look up. She missed whatever it was, but was rewarded with panorama of a million stars, each perfectly positioned like a Hollywood night sky. When she exhaled, she could see her breath. She pretended to smoke, the invisible cigarette perched between the second and third finger of her right hand as she walked down the path to the guesthouse. The salt her father had sprinkled on the walk that afternoon crackled under her clogs. As she got closer to the house, she could see her grandfather, framed by the square pane of insulated glass in the front door, staring out into the night and then focusing on her. He flicked the switch next to the door; light from the lamp above the door rained down upon her. Her grandfather squinted and then opened the door wide. He called over his shoulder, "We've got a visitor."

"Lauren," said Eileen, walking from the kitchen, wiping her wet hands on her apron before giving her granddaughter a hug, "I'm so glad you're here. Sam, take Lauren's coat." Lauren took off her jacket and handed it to Sam, who looked at it, then looked at Eileen. "In the closet, Sam," she said. "Put Lauren's coat in the closet." With deliberate, robotic movements, Sam turned around and reached into the closet. He missed on his first two attempts, but made contact with the gold metal hanger on his third try. He slid the end of the hanger into one sleeve but was unable to push the other end into the second opening. He looked for his wife, but she was gone, as was the girl. So, he wrapped the coat around the hanger and laid it on the closet floor. Knowing he might have done something naughty, Sam slid the door along its tracks until the coat was hidden from view. He scuffed down the hallway to the kitchen. "Sam," said Eileen, handing him a small bowl of cashew nuts, "take this to the living room."

"Aye-aye, skipper," said Sam, saluting his wife.

"Lauren, here's a bowl of potato chips and some onion dip for you to carry. I'll grab the cheese and crackers." Eileen followed her husband, who managed to sit down in a chair without spilling a single nut, the bowl now partially buried in his lap. Eileen set the baked brie down on a quilted pot holder, and Lauren put the chips and dip down next to it. "Wow, Gran," she said. "That looks amazing."

"Doesn't it, though? And it's so easy. I'll teach you how to make it," said Eileen as she settled her skirted bottom onto the couch. "Where's Nate?"

"He's coming," said Lauren, eyeing the cheese. "He's always late."

Sam brought the bowl of nuts from his lap to his chest. Eileen gently removed it from his fingers and set it down on the table. She smiled at Lauren. And then she quickly stood. "I'm going to get the drinks," she announced. "I've made something special."

"I'll come with you," said Lauren, getting up from the couch.

"You stay here and chat with your grandfather, dear," said Eileen. "I won't be a minute."

Lauren watched her grandmother disappear behind the kitchen cabinets. Then, she very slowly turned her gaze to her grandfather. He was looking at her intently, like an interviewer sizing up a job applicant. "Where do you go to school?" he asked, liquid gurgling in his throat.

"Dilloway High School," said Lauren, sitting on the couch next to his chair.

"Do you like it?"

"Yes," said Lauren, "I do."

"I went to Pembroke High School," said Sam, looking at the food on the coffee table. "It was a good school. They had all the usual classes there, of course. And there were other things, too."

Saliva ran out the corner of Sam's mouth and down his chin. From there, it fell like a miniature waterfall, a long, shimmering stream dropping from his face to his shirt. Lauren momentarily averted her eyes. She took a deep breath and then leaned forward to cut into the brie. She put a small slice onto a cracker, then centered it on a cocktail napkin busy with holly leaves. She extended the holiday treat to her grandfather. "Is this what you want?"

"I'd love one," he said, balling up the napkin and moving it toward his wide-open mouth. Lauren put her hand up, traffic police–style.

"Just the cheese, Gramps," she said. Sam looked at her, but his gaze was unfocused, unclear. Lauren took the napkin out of his hand and unwrapped the cheese. She placed the warm bundle in the palm of his outstretched hand, and he popped it into his mouth as if there had been no issue at all. She then brushed the pastry crumbs from his face with the napkin. Up close, it was not as disgusting as it looked from the couch, and Lauren wondered if young mothers felt similarly when they removed puréed carrots from the faces of their babies or digested ones from their bottoms.

"You don't have to do that," said an apron-less Eileen, appearing from the kitchen with two tall glasses of light green liquid leading the way in her hands.

"It's okay, Gran," said Lauren.

"Thank you," she said, handing Lauren a drink. "This is a frozen lime concoction I read about in a cooking magazine. Go ahead, take a sip."

"It's delicious," said Lauren, meaning it.

Eileen gave the other drink to Sam, who looked it at, and then set it down on the table next to him. Eileen was headed back to the kitchen, when she heard a knock on the door. She turned to Lauren, as if to ask, "Are you expecting anyone?" Then she gently slapped her forehead with her hand. "Nate," she said, smiling at her granddaughter. "Will you get the door while I get the other drinks?" Lauren jumped up from the couch and jogged to the door. Seconds later, Nate walked into the living room, preceded by an icy breeze. "Man, it's cold out there," he said.

"Well, look who's here," said Eileen, appearing from the kitchen with two more lime drinks. "All your friends have plans tonight?"

"Who *is* here?" asked Sam, moving his gaze from the cheese to Nate's face. When their eyes locked, Sam's rubbery face shifted.

His left eye narrowed slightly. His eyebrows rose, and his lips moved. He looked like he was making a mental list or adding a column of numbers in his head.

Nate looked back at his grandmother. "That's right, Gran," he said, flashing a smile. "And I called everybody."

Eileen laughed. "I'm glad you're here," she said. "Come join us."

Nate removed his coat, revealing clean, unwrinkled jeans and a black V-neck sweater worn over a red plaid collared shirt, and set it down on an unoccupied side chair. He ran his fingers through his hair, the color of Northern Michigan beach sand and cut so it stopped a couple of inches above his shoulders. It was the exact color, Ann had once told Lauren, of Ann's hair in her teenage years; a color her hair stylist sought to duplicate every eight weeks at Antonio's Salon. Lauren was dark, like her father. Her hair, with his wave, fell well below her shoulders. However, most of the time, tonight included, it was held captive by a coated elastic and jutted out the back of her head like a horse's tail.

"Hello, young man," said Sam. "I'm Sam Sanford."

Nate approached his grandfather and shook his extended hand. "I'm Nate Barons, your grandson."

"Of course you are," said Sam.

Eileen set the drinks down, cut several slices of brie, placed them on crackers, and offered them to Lauren, Nate, and Sam before taking one for herself. "So, how's everything at the big house?" Eileen asked after she had swallowed her cheese. "Are people starting to arrive?"

"It's like Black Friday at Walmart," said Nate. "The flood of people coming through the front door pushed me right out the back."

Eileen clapped her hands together. "I love a good party."

Nate took a chip and scooped up some onion dip. "I can't say anything about the quality of the guests," he said, taking a bite. "But the quantity is right on track."

"Why the hell weren't we invited?" said Sam, looking at his wife. "We've known these people for years."

"We have company," said Eileen. "We're busy." Sam nodded

his head longer than necessary to signal comprehension. "Nate," Eileen said, "tell me about football. How did your last game go?"

"We won," said Nate, "in overtime."

"Now that must have been exciting," said Eileen. "Did you have any wonderful tackles like the one in the Thanksgiving game?"

"Just one," said Nate, smiling. "It's really no big deal."

"Oh yes, it is," said Eileen. "A good tackle can turn the game around."

He shrugged. "Sometimes," he said. "I got to start a couple of games this year."

"That's great," said Eileen. "I thought only the seniors started."

"Yeah, well, mostly they do. They don't like it much when juniors take their place."

"Next year, you'll be a star," said Eileen. "Just like your sister. She's going to be the queen of that volleyball court."

"You think so?" asked Nate, looking at Lauren.

"Oh yes," said Eileen. "By next Christmas, you two will be signing autographs."

Eileen's genuine interest fascinated Nate. Her attention was flattering and sweet, not invasive like his mother's. The tension he had felt earlier, that he felt often—stiffness in his neck and a tight jaw—eased as they chatted about sports, school, and what they wanted for Christmas. Their one-sentence responses to Eileen's questions turned into paragraphs; their descriptions filled out with adjectives and flexible punctuation. And while Sam looked like he was mostly lost and only occasionally regained the thread of the conversation, he was calm, peaceful. When they finished their drinks and had their fill of hors d'oeuvres, Lauren helped Eileen clear the coffee table. In the kitchen, Lauren wrapped the leftovers with aluminum foil and quietly asked about her grandfather. "He's gone downhill so quickly," said Eileen, tying her apron around her waist. "Six months ago, he was still fairly alert. Now, he seems to be in a world of his own."

"Are you scared, Gran?"

"Of your grandfather? No," said Eileen, switching off the oven and then stirring the gravy with a whisk from the stove top. "Of the future, yes. But for now, I just try to go day to day. It's not easy,

Lauren. I do get irritated, sometimes, by his inability to do just about anything for himself."

"You never seem irritated," said Lauren, rinsing the dishes and putting them into the dishwasher.

"That's because he's sick, Lauren. He's got a disease that's wreaking havoc on his mind as well as his body," said Eileen. "What I feel most is sadness—at his condition and at the way he's spending the last part of his life."

"I feel sad for both of you," said Lauren. "It's your life, too."

Eileen set the whisk back down on the gravy-stained stove top and hugged her granddaughter. "It's easier when I'm with all of you," she said softly over Lauren's shoulder. "I'm so happy to be here." Lauren, who had been standing with her arms awkwardly at her sides, briefly encircled her grandmother's waist. When Eileen pushed back, her hands lingered on Lauren's arms. "Thank you," she said, "for asking." And then she returned to her task of putting on dinner: taking the roast beef from the oven, lifting the lid to the pot of mashed potatoes and stirring them, asking Lauren to set the kitchen table with the water glasses, napkins, and flatware already waiting to be arranged, and moving the dinner plates and cherry pie from the counter into the oven to warm. She added a clump of butter to the lima beans, as well as some salt and pepper, before replacing the lid to the pot. She ducked her head under the cupboards and called to Nate through the cutout in the wall. "Nate, will you please come in here?"

Nate stood, and as he did, Sam's eyes followed him. Sam had been telling Nate something about the navy destroyer that was his home during the Korean War, but he couldn't remember where he left off or where he started. He'd have to ask the boy. "I'll be right back," said Nate.

"Where are you going?"

"To the kitchen. Gran needs me."

Sam watched Nate leave the room before he looked at his watch. He couldn't tell for sure, but he guessed the interview had lasted more than an hour, a good sign in the navy. Sam next studied the palms of his hands. He had no idea why the admiral wanted him to be the skipper of this new ship. Maybe he was handpicked;

maybe he was just lucky. Either way, Sam knew he was the man for the job.

"What's up, Gran?" asked Nate, walking into the kitchen.

"I need you to carve this roast," she said.

Nate looked at the roast beef on the counter. "I have no idea how to cut meat," he said, an uneasy feeling germinating in his gut.

"Well, come here," said Gran, "and I'll show you." She plugged the Sears electric knife she had brought from home into the outlet, then pushed the ON button. "You slice on the diagonal," she said over the hum of the twin blades, moving fast enough, Nate thought, to spark flame. "Start from the top and work your way down." She handed the knife to Nate, who took it gingerly, wondering if it would be hot, if it would burn his hand, even though his grandmother had just used it without crying out in pain. Eileen then put her hand over his as a guide. They sliced two pieces together before she let go of the knife. Eileen patted his back and moved back to the stove. She rewhisked the mashed potatoes, tasted them, and added three more shakes of black pepper. "How are you doing?" she asked him, looking over her shoulder to watch.

"Fine," he said, mesmerized by the powerful tool sliding through the beef. "This is actually kind of fun."

"That's fine carving, Nate," she said. "You've got a Thanksgiving turkey in your future."

During dinner, Lauren asked Eileen about her childhood. And at first, she waved off the question, saying, "You wouldn't be interested in that." But when Lauren and Nate both insisted they would, she told them about growing up on a farm in eastern Pennsylvania, much like their mother had. It was a working farm, as they had become known in modern times even though real farmers thought the term was redundant, with cows, pigs, chickens, tractors, and three hundred acres. Eileen's two older brothers, along with several hired men, helped her father with the animal care and crop oversight—they grew corn, mostly, occasionally rotating in other grains when the soil demanded it. Eileen and her mother tended the family garden—tomatoes, pole beans, squashes, lettuces, peppers, potatoes, beets, and onions, as well as a flower garden—and took care of the house, which meant cooking, baking, cleaning, sewing, canning, and anything else her mother could think of, and she thought of things more often than not. Consequently, Eileen was busy during the week with chores and school from five in the morning until ten at night. Saturdays were different. She was allowed to stay in bed until eight before starting her chores. On Sundays, they went to church from nine until eleven, had dinner, which Eileen helped prepare and serve, and then she had the afternoon off. Lauren finished chewing the meat that had been sitting in her mouth while her grandmother talked. She swallowed, and then asked, "When did you have fun?"

Eileen reached for her water glass. "I didn't have much time for fun," she said. "Sometimes, on a summer evening after all my chores were done, my mother and I would sit on the front porch swing and drink a tall glass of cool lemonade. We'd talk quietly and listen to the crickets."

"That was your fun?" asked Nate, eyebrows raised.

"Well, sure," said Eileen. "I can't tell you how good that lemonade tasted after a day filled with hard work. You have to understand how nice it was just to be sitting."

"Did you ever go out?" asked Nate.

"Occasionally," said Eileen. "Sometimes, we'd go to the Grange Hall for a dance on a Saturday night, but that was just two or three times a year. Most of the time we were home."

Nate swallowed a forkful of mashed potatoes. "Were you bored out of your mind?" he asked, smiling.

"No," said Eileen. "We didn't have time for that."

"I get bored with some frequency," said Sam through a mouthful of lima beans.

"It was a different time," continued Eileen. "We worked hard for what we had. We spent time together as a family. We didn't get into a whole lot of trouble. It's different today."

"Yeah," said Nate, "and about a million times better. I don't think I would have survived back then. I think I'm allergic to work."

Eileen smiled at her grandson. "That's only because you don't work. If you did, you'd actually feel better about a lot of things, including yourself."

After dinner and dessert—the best cherry pie, Nate announced, that he had ever tasted—they all did the dishes at Eileen's suggestion. Lauren cleared the table and scraped the meager leftovers into the garbage. Nate loaded the dishwasher, and then relinquished the sink to Eileen, who washed the pots and pans. Sam ran a dish towel over the wet pots, and then laid them on the cleared kitchen table. When everything was done, Eileen walked her grandchildren to the door, kissed their foreheads, and sent them off into the cold darkness.

"I like the life Gran lived," said Lauren, walking up the path with her hands in her coat pockets.

"You're kidding," said Nate, kicking at the salt on the bricks.

"I'm not," said Lauren. "It sounds like a good life to me."

"It sounds like a whole lot of work to me," said Nate, two steps ahead of his sister.

"But they felt good about what they did," said Lauren, stopping. "They were proud of themselves. I mean, I can't really think of anything I'm proud of and I'm fifteen years old."

Although Nate kept walking, he tried to think of something that made him proud. Nothing came to mind, other than the fact that for his sixteen years he hadn't put more than 50 percent effort into anything and seemed to get away with everything. It had never occurred to him until that very moment that pride and effort are related.

Inside the big house, Nate dodged the roaming caterers in the kitchen like a hero avoiding aliens in a video game. Just as he was about to walk though the doorway into the hall, someone bumped him on the arm. Game over. "Sorry, man," said a kid about his age, carrying two large buckets of ice. "I didn't see you."

"No problem," said Nate.

The boy hurried past him and down the hallway, before disappearing into the living room, where the bar was set up. No wonder he was rushing; this crowd could put away the alcohol. The poor bartender was probably six-deep in customers waiting for rocks for their single-malt scotches. Nate walked down the hallway cleared by the kid with the ice, with the exception of two men dressed like twins in gray flannel pants, crisp white shirts, red Christmas ties, and navy blue blazers citing stock market numbers. Just as he placed his hand on the banister, Mrs. Nelson, drink in hand, found him. "Nate!" she said enthusiastically as she entered the hallway from the dining room. "Where have you been hiding all evening?"

Nate pasted a smile on his face and turned to greet his mother's friend. She moved toward him like a big cat slinks toward its dinner. Men her age probably thought she was hot—frosted blond hair cut in a youthful style, expensive clothing and jewelry, ultra-thin like his mother, and willing—but Nate found her grotesque, an overdone circus sideshow ("Rich Lady"). Plus *she* thought she was hot, which made it worse. What kind of forty-five-year-old woman approached a teenage boy looking for the wrong kind of attention? Her husband worked for Dilloway and probably spent as many hours making money as Nate's dad did. Men like that were married to women like Mrs. Nelson. "I was having dinner with my grandparents," said Nate, backing into the banister.

Mrs. Nelson stopped just shy of bumping into him, her face inches from his. Her eyelids were heavy with taupe eye shadow and from drinking. He could smell wine on her breath. She grinned at him, as she shifted her body, blocking the stairs. "You look delicious tonight," she said, putting a gem-bedecked hand against his chest. "Let's run away together." Nate felt the sweat push out of his forehead pores, a hundred tiny epidermal dams burst. He swallowed hard and blinked at her. She smiled and then laughed, throwing her head back.

"Nate!" called Lauren from the end of the hallway. "Mom needs you in the kitchen."

Nate deftly ducked away from Mrs. Nelson. As he slid past Lauren on his way to the kitchen, he murmured, "Thanks." Lauren carried on down the hall when Nate was gone.

"Hello, Mrs. Nelson," she said as she turned the corner and started up the stairs. "Nice to see you again." But Mrs. Nelson was already moving on, toward the living room, toward the bar.

In the kitchen, Nate leaned against the wall, counting in his head. His heart rate, which first matched the pace of his counting, eventually slowed. He looked at his watch, and then poked his head around the doorway. The hallway was deserted. He inched around the corner, jogged the length of the hall, and flew up the stairs. He ran to his room and shut and locked the door behind him. He stood against it, listening for her; his breathing was deep, as if he had just sprinted an entire football field. Convinced she had not followed him, Nate exhaled and crossed the room to his bed. He grabbed the remote control from his nightstand, lay down, and turned on his television. He flipped through eighty-seven channels, stopping briefly for motor-cross racing and a *Baywatch* rerun, and then clicked it off. He sat up and rooted through his backpack for his iPod. He covered his ears with headphones and selected his "Kick Ass" playlist as he made his way to his desk and laptop. He pushed his laundered bath towels from the chair to the floor, sat down, and played three games of Deadly Invader, losing interest when he lost the last game. He reached for his cell phone and called Josh, who didn't pick up. Nate didn't leave a message.

Nate looked back at his spring break screen saver and thought about what his grandmother had said that evening about boredom. She said she had never been bored because she was too busy. Nate was perpetually bored. Was there a correlation between working and satisfaction? Maybe, thought Nate, maybe not. His father busted his balls working and he was never satisfied. Nate thought he heard something and looked at his door. If that tramp Mrs. Nelson had the guts to come up here, he'd tell her where to go. He walked quietly to his door and put his head against it—nothing. He opened it, ever so slowly, just an inch and looked out—no one. He closed the door and went back to his bed. Something was different. Nate looked around his room, but found nothing amiss. He lay down and listened. It was quiet. That was it, Nate realized; it was the quiet.

Instead of creating noise with his iPod or another computer game, Nate stayed put, closed his eyes, and thought about Christmas morning. It would be uneventful, like it always was. He got whatever he requested—this year it was money to buy a new music system for his car. The same applied to Lauren, although lately Ann had presented Lauren with a corny Christmas keepsake, an idea she no doubt stole from one of her lifestyle magazines. Two years ago, it was a homemade quilt from the Amish in Pennsylvania, and last year, it was an antique chest of drawers. A piece of furniture for a teenager. Of course, it was no mystery what she herself would receive. She always got a huge piece of jewelry, hand-selected at Cartier or Tiffany in New York, which sent her squealing from the couch to the chair, where his dad sat with a smug look on his face as if he actually had something to do with it. His mother was the one who flew to New York and secured the purchase, so it was really more of a surprise for his dad, especially when he got the bill. He put up with it, though, just to see his wife happy.

Nate rarely saw her that happy or animated, except when she had too much alcohol. She drank every night, as far as Nate could tell, starting at 6 p.m. Many of his friends' parents did the same, to melt away the stresses of the day, he guessed. It was when his dad found out about his mom's daytime drinking that the blind eye suddenly got vision.

Nate remembered the argument between them. He had been sitting in their den, with the TV on mute and the latest issue of *Sports Illustrated* in his hands. He paid attention when he heard their raised voices simply because they rarely raised them. And he was interested in hearing what his dad had to say. He might not have said anything, if Lauren hadn't told him that their mom "smelled like wine" and "drove erratically" on the way home from volleyball practice. Nate hadn't been aware of her afternoon wine breath, or if, in fact, it was routine. He was busy after school, at practice or hanging out with friends at the mall or someone's house. By the time he got home, it was almost dinnertime, and she was already into her first evening glass.

"You will not endanger my children with this behavior," Mike had said. "You're an adult, and you need to start acting like one. Being Ann Barons does not put you above the law."

"Lauren was exaggerating," countered Ann. "I had one glass of wine with Sally after a shopping trip."

"That's a lousy excuse, if it is one. You don't need anything in the afternoon. You drink every night."

"As do you!"

"When my daily responsibilities are over, and I don't have to get in a car and pick up a child, yes."

"God, Mike, it was one time. You're overreacting."

"It's one time that you've been caught. Because I am not your babysitter, I don't know about other times. Although I have my suspicions."

"What the hell does that mean?"

"Stop it, Ann. It's indefensible behavior. And if you can't stop it, get help."

And that had been the end of it. Neither Lauren nor his dad had said anything since, and Nate had seen no evidence. But he wondered if she continued to imbibe every now and again, because an occasion arose or just because she had nothing better to do. Nate couldn't blame her for drinking. If he had to live her life, he'd be bored out of his mind, grabbing a drink whenever one was offered.

Nate sat up, got off his bed, and walked over to his computer. He had forgotten to order the sneakers Lauren wanted for Christmas. He had found the website a few days before and saved the link, so it was quick and easy. He clicked "yes" to the exorbitant overnight shipping charge and to the "Bill Me Later" payment option, so the gifts, like the others he had purchased, wouldn't show up on his mother's credit card statement.

Maybe being home for Christmas would make it different this year. While he liked the prime rib and gravy, fruit pies, and hearty egg dishes his grandmother always prepared when they went to their farm for the holidays, Nate was looking forward to waking up Christmas morning in his own house. Christmas had always been at home when he was little. It was the one day Nate could count on his father to play all day with him and his new toys and his mother to make whatever he and Lauren wanted for breakfast.

Eileen didn't share her plans for Christmas morning with Ann, mostly because her daughter pooh-poohed everything she suggested. A Christmas Eve dinner together, for example, was out, Ann said, because they already had plans to go to the Kendalls' house for holiday drinks and an out-of-this-world dinner buffet. Lydia was a world-class cook who dazzled her guests with her colorful and inventive presentations. Ann offered to call Lydia to double-check, but she was certain Eileen and Sam could join in on the festivities. Nate often backed out, Ann explained, but Lauren usually tagged along. Eileen told Ann not to bother; she and Sam would spend Christmas Eve as they always had, at home. And Nate and Lauren were welcome to join them.

As it turned out, all of the Baronses went to the Kendalls' party. Jenny's family had been invited this year, so Nate was keen to go. And Lauren, hoping other families had been added to the list of attendees, was eager, too. No one wanted to go to church. So Eileen bundled up Sam in his red wool scarf and worn gray overcoat and drove him to St. Paul's, where she had gone with Ann. Father David remembered her, or at least pretended to, and seemed pleased to meet Sam. The service was packed with people Eileen suspected were "Chreasters," those attending church only on Christmas and Easter, but she enjoyed the service nonetheless. Sam sang all the hymns boldly, not needing the book to remind him of the words. Afterward, she and Sam ate pork roast, wild rice, and fresh green beans, followed by decaf tea and apple turnovers. They did the dishes together—Sam drying the pots, then laying them on the cleared kitchen table as usual. Afterward they changed into their pajamas; Sam settled into the chair and Eileen covered him with a blanket. She sat on the couch and turned on the George C. Scott version of *A Christmas Carol*. Sam recited Jacob Marley's opening lines, but quickly lost steam. He was asleep before the visit from Christmas Past.

Just after nine o'clock, Eileen heard a knock on the door. It was Lauren. "Come in," said Eileen, opening the door wide.

"I just wanted to wish you a Merry Christmas," said Lauren, her eyes bright from the cold.

"Well, Merry Christmas to you," said Eileen, ushering Lauren into the living room.

"Oh!" said Lauren, switching to a whisper when she saw her grandfather slumbering in the chair. "You're watching *A Christmas Carol*."

"Yes," said Eileen. "Would you care to join me?" Lauren smiled at her grandmother as she took off her coat. "You sit on the couch, and I'll make some popcorn," said Eileen, heading into the kitchen. Lauren settled onto the warm cushion, pulled her legs up underneath her, and covered herself with the fleece throw next to her. She glanced over at her grandfather. His head was tilted back at an improbable angle, and his mouth was open enough for Lauren to hear the air get sucked in and then blown out. His scratched glasses lay on the table between them. For a moment, Lauren watched him before turning her attention back to the movie. Several minutes later, Eileen joined her on the couch, setting the bowl of buttered popcorn between them. She handed Lauren a napkin. And together, they watched the uplifting transformation of Ebenezer Scrooge.

In the morning, Eileen and Sam joined the festivities in Ann's living room. Mike plugged in the lights wrapped around the sixteen-foot tree the party planners had erected and decorated the week before. Dressed in jeans, a red cashmere V-neck sweater, and Gucci loafers, he then sat down amid the pile of presents to play Santa. At his insistence, the presents were opened in rounds, one at a time, starting with Lauren and ending with Sam; witnesses were encouraged to coo their approval, at which Eileen excelled, until it was her turn to open her gifts. "Another for me? Ann, this is too much, dear," she said more than once. "I thought we agreed you weren't going to go overboard." Sitting next to her mother on the couch, Ann smiled, winked, and sipped a large mug of coffee. She and a bottle of Bailey's Irish Cream had been up until two o'clock wrapping gifts and arranging them under the tree, a task she enjoyed doing alone.

When all the presents were opened, and Sam and Mike were picking up the layer of crumpled-up wrapping paper and yards of ribbon that covered the living room floor, Eileen invited everyone back to the little house for breakfast. Ann protested, saying she had already bought a Christmas coffee cake, but Mike held up his hand. "Eileen," he said, "we'd love to come." Carrying Sam's and Eileen's new flannel shirts and nightgowns, books, winter boots, and two shopping bags filled with gourmet food items and other miscellaneous holiday treats purchased by Ann, they all trudged down the path Mike had shoveled a few hours earlier. As soon as they had shed their coats and set the gifts down on the living room carpet, Eileen disappeared into their bedroom. She reappeared with a soft stack of gifts, wrapped in green tissue paper, red ribbon, and a sprig of holly. She instructed them to open the gifts simultaneously, as they were all the same. But they weren't. The hand-knitted scarves were different colors, patterns, and wools. Lauren's looked like spring meadow grass. She wrapped it around her neck and kept it there as she ate her grandmother's Christmas sausage and egg casserole and cinnamon swirls, and as she much later chatted on the phone with her friend, Pammy. "You won't believe how soft it is," said Lauren, sitting on her bed in her new flannel pajama pants and a white T-shirt, stroking the scarf.

"Tell me more about the diamond tennis bracelet," said Pammy. "Are you allowed to wear it to school?

"I guess so," said Lauren.

"I can't wait to see it," Pammy said. "I'll bet it's gorgeous."

Several days later, when the holidays were over and the business of Christmas had been cast out to the curb with the naked tree, Lauren's bracelet was still in the box.

CHAPTER 8

$\overline{}$

Ann cleared the weekend with Mike's secretary, then booked two nights at her favorite hotel/spa in San Francisco. She called Sally and told her they needed to take an emergency shopping trip. Then she called her mother. "You can just walk down the path, Ann," said Eileen into the mouthpiece. "I feel foolish talking to you on the phone."

"The phone is much more efficient," said Ann, spooning nonfat Greek yogurt into the blender. "If I walked down there, we'd get sidetracked and talk for an hour."

"God forbid," said Eileen, pulling a chair out from under the guesthouse kitchen table.

Ann hit the PULSE button, transforming the additives into a smooth purple liquid. "I'm calling because Mike and I are going away."

"When?"

"This weekend," said Ann. "We haven't gone anywhere since you arrived and, frankly, I've got a serious case of cabin fever. I've got to get out of here."

"Where are you going?"

"San Francisco," said Ann. "It's not the best time of year to go, but it really doesn't matter. My plan is to get lost in the spa for a couple of days."

"The spa?" asked Eileen. "Do you mean a hot spring?"

"Tell me you don't know what a spa is, Mother," said Ann, pouring her shake into a chilled mug from the freezer.

"I just told you what I thought it was."

"It's a luxury facility," said Ann. "For massages, facials, pedicures, general body toning."

"You won't lose weight while you're there, will you?" asked Eileen.

"It's not a fat farm, Mother," said Ann, grabbing one of her pads with ANN'S LIST printed on the top and jotting down some of the clothing she planned on packing. "It's a spa."

"Because you certainly can't afford to lose more weight."

"Thank you," said Ann. "I'll take that as a compliment."

"Why are you so thin, anyway?" asked Eileen. "You used to have some meat on you."

"I lost that *meat* years ago," said Ann.

"Why?"

"Because it's good to be thin. It's healthy."

"You don't look particularly healthy to me," said Eileen, looking out the kitchen window at Ann's kitchen window.

"I'm very healthy," said Ann.

"You look, actually, honey, a little like a bag of bones."

Ann sipped her shake. "Why are we discussing this?"

"Because I don't like to see you wasting away into nothing."

"I'm a good distance from nothing," said Ann.

"Not from where I'm standing," said Eileen, standing.

"Well, you're standing in the nineteen-fifties," said Ann. "You have no idea what attractive, fashionable women are today."

"Bags of bones, I guess," said Eileen.

"That's your opinion."

"Hold on," said Eileen. "I'm coming over." She put down the receiver, grabbed her cable-knit sweater from the hall closet, and wrapped it around her shoulders. She told Selma she was going to the big house, then walked as quickly as she could up the path. Before Ann registered what was happening, her mother was at her back door. Ann sighed loudly and looked at her watch as Eileen walked in and shut the door behind her.

"I've got a lot of things to do today, Mother," said Ann, finishing her drink. "We're not turning this discussion into a marathon coffee-drinking session."

"Who said we were?" asked Eileen. "Maybe I've got a lot of things to do, too." Ann looked at her mother. "I just think it's ridiculous to talk on the phone when you could be talking face to face," said Eileen, shrugging off her sweater and draping it over the back of a kitchen chair. "Now, what is the situation with Nate and Lauren?"

"The situation?"

"Do you have someone staying with them, or do they stay on their own?"

"They're sixteen and fifteen, Mother," said Ann. "They can stay on their own. Plus, Emma said she is willing to work this Saturday. She can cook for them—although they'll probably eat takeout all weekend as usual—and clean up after them Monday morning."

"Why not send them down to our house?" asked Eileen, arms akimbo.

Ann looked at her mother with raised eyebrows. The notion that teenagers would prefer to stay with their grandparents rather than on their own was pure fantasy. "They're fine here," said Ann, fighting the urge to smile at her mother's suggestion.

"I know they'll be fine," said Eileen, sitting in the same chair that held her sweater. "There's a difference between fine and well cared for."

Ann walked her empty mug to the sink. "They'll be fine here," she repeated over her shoulder. "They're comfortable in their own surroundings."

"Fine," said Eileen. "I'm happy to stay here."

"Mother," said Ann, turning and facing her, "why are you doing this? I've already talked about it with the kids and they're content with the plan. You don't need to get involved."

"I am involved," said Eileen, folding her arms across her chest. "I'm their grandmother."

"It's a little early in the day for drama," said Ann, getting a bottle of water from the fridge.

"I'm not being dramatic," said Eileen, chin out and stomach in.

"You're *always* dramatic," said Ann.

Eileen stood—dramatically, thought Ann. "We can discuss this," said Eileen, putting on her sweater, "when you're in a better mood."

"I'm in a fabulous mood," said Ann, raising her voice. Without another word, Eileen opened the back door and walked out. "Have a nice day!" Ann yelled at her mother retreating down the path.

"Can you imagine that?" Ann asked Sally as they got out of Ann's car and walked toward Nordstrom. Ann hit the LOCK button on her key fob, and then pushed it again, reassured only by the second toot of the horn that her car was secure.

"You are a saint," Sally said to Ann. "I mean, do you know anyone who could put up with living with her parents for—how long is it now?"

"Seven weeks," said Ann, dropping her keys into her purse and grabbing a bottle of water. "A very long seven weeks. And I swear to God, Sally, it's so much harder than I thought."

"You poor thing," said Sally, putting her hand on Ann's shoulder.

"She won't leave me alone, for God's sake," said Ann, cracking the seal on the water bottle while Sally pulled open the large glass door to the mall. "I don't have a minute to myself. She just walks in my back door whenever she's got a free moment, several times a day." Sally shook her head sympathetically. "I have never needed a vacation more," said Ann. "At this point, if Mike cancels on me, I'm going alone."

"Good girl," said Sally.

They scurried into the women's department, Ann in the lead by the usual step.

Sally pinballed from rack to rack, trying to match Ann's frenetic shopping pace, searching for the perfect outfit for herself or an adorable shirt or sleek pair of pants Ann would find worthy of adding to her own stack of possibles. *Oh Ann,* Sally might casually say, *this would look just darling on you.* Ann would then look up from her avid hunt and do one of two things: shake her head and quickly return to business or smile and approach Sally. Sally flipped through the size two skirts and found nothing Ann did not already have or would find attractive enough for a second glance.

"Sally, come here," called Ann from several circular chrome racks away. "Look at this skirt. It's so cute." Sally walked through the maze of clothing to where Ann was standing. "I tried to find it in my size," said Ann, "but had no luck. Try this on. It's perfect for you."

Sally took the skirt from Ann and looked at the inside label. "It's a four," she said.

"That's right," said Ann.

"I'm a six," said Sally, looking at the skirt instead of at Ann.

"Oh my," said Ann, "I'm sorry. I keep forgetting."

"I'm working at it," said Sally, who couldn't imagine eating any more fruits and vegetables than she already did.

"That's the important thing," said Ann, taking the skirt back from Sally. "We never want to lose sight of our goals."

"Right," said Sally with false enthusiasm. "I'm actually starting to like balsamic vinaigrette."

"Excellent," said Ann, patting her on the back. "You'll be shopping side by side with me in no time." Sally returned to the area she had been browsing in before Ann beckoned her. When she wore the same size as Ann, they would always shop together. Sure, sometimes Jesse and Paula would come along, but they, by their size, would shop away from Ann and Sally, the size twos. When she wore the same size as Ann, people in town would take notice. Some people had already told her she looked like Ann, as she had almost the same color hair cut in almost the same style, and she made a point of tucking in her shirts and wearing a belt. A belt, Ann once told her, was a constant reminder of waist size.

They walked out of Nordstrom and into the mall just after one o'clock. Ann had bought two pairs of light wool slacks, two blazers, and three pairs of shoes. Sally, unable to seriously consider a size six purchase after her pep talk from Ann, was empty-handed and, regrettably, hungry. She followed Ann past several restaurants, including Bohemian Bliss, her favorite. "Are you hungry?" asked Ann, turning her head to look back at Sally.

"Not really," Sally lied.

"Great," said Ann, reaching into her enormous black patent leather purse like a magician into a hat and producing two protein bars. "Eat one of these to tide you over and we'll continue to shop while all the amateurs stop for lunch." Sally forced a laugh as she took the peanut butter bar from Ann. She ate it in four bites, finishing the last one as they reached Neiman Marcus. "Another?" asked Ann.

"I'm full," said Sally, patting her stomach for conviction. "That hit the spot."

"Didn't it, though? I find them so satisfying," said Ann, again reaching into her bag, this time for her half-empty bottle of water. "I am so dehydrated, though. These malls are incredibly dry."

"I know," said Sally, who was suddenly thirsty for a Diet Coke. If she had been at home, she would have simply descended her basement stairs, as she did most afternoons, and reached into the spare refrigerator, where she kept an extra gallon of milk and a variety of pop and bottled juices. Here, Sally pressed on. Ann, she knew, thought anything but water, coffee, and alcohol was for teenagers.

An hour later they had gone through most of the department stores and $2,000 of the Baronses' fortune. They strolled out of Macy's and back into the mall, Ann announcing her dire need for a large latte. They walked to Java Hut in the food court, next to Mrs. Fields Cookies. As they waited in line, Sally's eyes wandered over to the brightly lit glass cases of treats. Behind them, a hair-netted woman was removing a large tray of what looked like white chocolate macadamias from the oven. Sally was so hungry she would have paid twenty dollars for just one of those warm cookies. "Go ahead," said Ann, following Sally's gaze. "You've been good today."

"Oh no," said Sally, flustered, "I'm fine. The cookies, they just remind me of my childhood. I hardly ever eat them now; they're just loaded with fat."

"Too true," said Ann, stepping forward in line. Large lattes in hand, Ann followed by Sally sat down on a vacant bench. After

Ann rubbed hand sanitizer onto her hands and squirted some into Sally's, she took her first sip. "Where to next?"

"I don't care," said Sally, who honestly didn't. What she wanted most at this point was to go home and make a tuna melt.

"Well, I've got everything I need," said Ann, "but I'm worried about you. You haven't bought a thing."

"That's okay," said Sally, brightening at the prospect of leaving. "Some days you find things and some days you don't."

Ann sipped her coffee drink. "I always seem to be able to find something," she said. "I've got that fashion show coming up at the end of the month, so I'm motivated. I wouldn't want to be caught in something everyone's seen."

"Don't they give you the clothes for the show?" asked Sally, still sensitive about not being asked to participate.

"Well, yes," said Ann, "but Marge Simon told me they're doing furs this year. Well, you know that; you were with me that day. But I'm thinking about wearing my own clothes underneath. I've got several combinations that haven't been out in public yet."

"That's a good idea," said Sally. "You never know who's been wearing those fashion show clothes."

"Last year," said Ann, "they put me in a blouse that smelled like it had been through gym class." Sally chuckled. She would be happy to wear a smelly fashion-show blouse, if only Marge would ask her. Being a local celebrity, Ann was asked every year. But so were ordinary people, like school principals and real estate agents. Sally made a mental note to call Marge after the show to congratulate her on a job well done. Maybe Marge would sign her up for the following year. Wouldn't Paula and Jesse just die to know she and Ann would be doing the fashion show together?

"Are you ready to go?" asked Ann, standing.

"Absolutely," said Sally, popping up from the bench and grabbing four of Ann's six bags. If they didn't have too much traffic, she could be eating that tuna melt in just over an hour.

Eileen knocked on the back door just after Ann had returned downstairs from organizing her purchases in her closet. "Oh, for God's sake," said Ann, walking to the door and opening it.

"I've got it all figured out," said Eileen, brushing past Ann and taking off her sweater. "I checked with Selma and she's fine with my staying here."

"What are you talking about?" asked Ann, standing by the open door, one hand still on the handle.

"Close the door, honey," said Eileen, hanging her sweater on the back of a kitchen chair. "I'm talking about this weekend, of course. I can stay here this weekend with Nate and Lauren."

"We've been through this," said Ann, closing the door. "They don't need you to stay here."

"I understand that," said Eileen, "but it would make me feel better."

Ann walked to the fridge to get a bottle of water. "This isn't about making you feel better."

"I know," said Eileen. "It's about making you feel better. And I hope a weekend in San Francisco will do that for you. But I don't want my grandchildren coming home to an empty house."

"We've got a very sophisticated alarm system," said Ann.

"I don't care about your alarm system," said Eileen, waving her hand in the air as if she were coaxing a housefly to move on. "I'm talking about making them dinner and keeping them company."

"They don't care about that," said Ann. "They'll be grateful, in fact, for not having company."

"I don't think so," said Eileen.

Ann took a sip of her water and counted to five, as Mike had instructed her. "They like to be alone."

"Let's ask them," said Eileen. "Let's ask them what they want to do. If they don't want me here, I'll back away."

"That sounds good to me," said Ann, knowing her children would loudly protest having their grandmother hovering over them for the weekend.

Eileen put on her sweater. "I'll come over after dinner and talk to them," she said. "Don't say anything about it until I arrive."

"Oh, I won't," said Ann, "trust me."

Nate and Lauren sat at opposite ends of the kitchen table eating a large pizza. Nate's half had cheese and pepperoni, and Lauren's half had peppers, onions, mushrooms, sausage, and black olives. The bagged iceberg lettuce, red cabbage, and shaved carrot salad Ann had insisted Lauren order along with the pizza had been emptied into a wood salad bowl and was untouched. Ann looked at her watch; Mike wouldn't be home for another hour. She picked up the phone and called her mother.

"They're almost done," she said into the receiver. "You can come over anytime."

"Who's that?" asked Lauren.

"Your grandmother."

"Why is she coming over?" asked Lauren, taking another slice from the pie sitting between her and Nate.

"She wants to talk to you," said Ann, hanging up the phone.

"Ooooh," said Nate with a mouth full of pizza. "Lauren's in trouble."

"I'm not in trouble," Lauren snapped back.

"She wants to talk to you, too, Nate," said Ann, wiping the island top with a sponge. Lauren stuck her tongue out at her brother.

"What'd I do?" asked Nate, taking his last slice from the pie. Pizza was the one food he ate consistently and without complaint. And while Ann knew it wasn't the most nutritious option, it was better than a fast-food burger and fries.

"I don't know, Nate," said Ann. "What have you done?"

"Nothing," said Nate, jerking his bangs out of his eyes. "I haven't done anything."

"Then you've got nothing to worry about," said Ann. Less than a minute later, Eileen came in the back door. "My God, Mother," said Ann. "You must have been waiting by the door with your sweater on."

"Something like that," said Eileen, taking off her sweater and draping it over her arm.

"Hi, Gran," said Lauren. "Are we in trouble?"

"Absolutely not," said Eileen, "unless there's something I don't know about." Nate figured he could devote an entire website to all the things his grandmother and mother didn't know about. "Hello, Nate," said Eileen. "How's your pizza?"

"Good," said Nate. "Lauren, are you going to eat that piece?"

"Yes," she said, even though she was beginning to feel full.

"Did you have pizza, too?" Eileen asked Ann.

"I'm going away in two days," said Ann. "Why would I be stuffing my face with grease-laden, calorie-packed pizza?"

Lauren looked at the half-eaten piece in her hand and then at Nate. "Go ahead," she said. "You can have it." Nate scraped off the black olives and shoved half of the piece into his mouth.

"Okay," said Eileen, joining her grandchildren at the table, "this is why I'm here."

Nate and Lauren both looked at her. "I want to stay with you this weekend."

Shit, thought Nate. He had already made preliminary plans for a party at his house Saturday night. Jenny was spreading the word to her friends, while Josh was rounding up the boys.

"I will not get in your way," continued Eileen. "If you want to have friends here, that's fine. I expect you to introduce them to me, and then I'll disappear into the den. Lauren, if you want to go somewhere, I'll drive you."

Lauren smiled. Maybe her grandmother would let her drive. Even though she had had her permit for six months, her mother was always in too much of a hurry to relinquish the steering wheel.

"I'll cook your meals, whatever you want, within reason." Nate thought about his grandmother's roast beef and mashed potatoes.

"What's in it for you?" asked Nate, leaning back in his chair.

"I get to spend time with you," said Eileen.

"Why would you want to do that?" asked Nate skeptically.

"Because I like you," said Eileen.

"Yes," said Lauren. "I want you to stay with us."

Nate shot his sister a look. "What?" said Lauren.

"Nate?" asked Eileen. Nate looked at his mother, who was sitting at the center island and looking at him with raised eyebrows. He knew she thought he would say no. He always said no because it bugged her so much. In this case, *yes* was the right answer.

"Okay," he said. "You can stay with us."

"Why would he say yes?" Ann asked Mike the following evening as they were packing their bags for the weekend. Mike walked out of his closet with a navy blue blazer in one hand and four neckties in the other. He held the ties out to Ann. "The blue one and the yellow one," she said.

"I don't know," said Mike. "Maybe it's the food. Your mother is an awfully good cook."

"So you've said," said Ann, turning her back to Mike to place the first of eight pairs of shoes in her large bag.

"Or, more likely," said Mike, approaching Ann and playfully slapping her bottom, "he's just getting inside your head." Ann wheeled around to face her grinning husband.

Mike kissed her forehead. "He's sixteen," he said. "And boys will be boys."

When Lauren arrived home from school the next day, her parents were gone and her grandmother was in the kitchen, making chocolate chip cookies. "Well," said Eileen, putting two warm cookies on a plate and handing it to Lauren, "how was your day?"

"Pretty good," said Lauren, taking a bite of a cookie on her way to the table. "I got an A-minus on my history test."

"Good girl," said Eileen. "Would you like some milk?"

"Yes," said Lauren, turning back to get a glass.

"Stay where you are," said Eileen, holding up her hand. "I'll bring some for both of us. I could use a cookie, too."

Twenty minutes later, Nate walked through the garage door, a stuffed backpack hanging from his right shoulder. He tossed his car keys into the wicker basket. Before he had his coat off, Eileen had set another place at the table. "Did you treat Mom like this when she was growing up?" asked Nate.

"Yes," said Eileen. "I was always in the kitchen when she got home from school."

"She's *never* here," said Lauren.

"And she definitely never makes cookies," said Nate, sitting down and taking one from his plate. "She thinks she'd jump a couple of pants sizes if she ate one."

Eileen chuckled. "I think she could stand to jump a few sizes."

"Tell me about it," said Lauren. "Everyone in town calls her The Scarecrow."

"Was she always skinny?" asked Nate, finishing his second cookie.

"No," said Eileen, remembering the hurtful verbal battles she and Ann had had about weight. "I thought she was just right. She disagreed. But enough of that, now. Who would like more?"

Just after seven o'clock, Lauren took a deep breath and knocked on Nate's door. "What?" Nate bellowed. Lauren opened the door and stood in the doorway. Nate was lying on his bed, looking through *Sports Illustrated*.

"We're going to the video store," she said. "Do you want to watch a movie with me and Gran?"

"Do I look like a loser to you?" asked Nate. "No wait, don't answer that question."

"It's was Gran's idea," said Lauren, looking at her hands. "She thought we could all watch something together."

"What, like *Old Yeller* or *Mary Poppins*? No thanks," said Nate, returning to his magazine. "I'd rather jump off a cliff."

"Why *don't* you jump off a cliff?" said Lauren angrily. "I can drive you there."

"Getting in a car with you driving would be like the same thing," Nate retorted.

"Let's go then."

"Get lost," said Nate, turning the pages of the magazine.

"With pleasure," said Lauren, grabbing the door handle and backing out of Nate's room. "It smells in here anyway!" Lauren slammed the door and ran down the stairs to the kitchen. Eileen was waiting next to the door leading to the garage with her coat on, keys in hand. "He's so mean," said Lauren, grabbing her coat off its hook. "I hate him!"

"He's your older brother," said Gran softly. "Older brothers are always mean."

"You had older brothers, too," said Lauren, lifting her ponytail out of the coat's collar.

"Three of them," said Eileen. "And I'm alive to talk about it." Lauren wiped a tiny tear from her cheek. She looked into her grandmother's warm brown eyes. "Let's go," Eileen said, handing

Lauren the car keys. "Now we can rent a chick flick and eat all the popcorn."

"Who needs him anyway?" Lauren said, opening the door to the garage.

"Not us," said Eileen. "It's Girls' Night."

When they got back from the video store, they found Selma in her long down coat waiting in the driveway, waving her arms. She ran to the car as soon as Lauren stopped it and opened the driver's side door. "He's gone!" she said, her eyes wide open, her voice warbling with fear.

Lauren looked at her grandmother, who was unbuckling her seat belt. She pushed herself out the door and ran around the front of the car to reach Selma. "What happened?" she asked, holding Selma's hands.

"I don't know," said Selma, her facial features contorted with concern. "I don't know how he could have gotten out that door. I had it locked at the top and the bottom."

"Take a breath and tell me what happened," said Eileen.

"He was on the couch, watching a John Wayne Western, and he seemed settled in for the night. He asked about you, and I told him you went out, but that you would be back soon—just as we decided. He seemed fine with that answer—fine in general—so I went into my bathroom to take a bath. And I checked the locks beforehand, so I knew he was secure. I was in there for twenty minutes or so and when I got out, Sam wasn't in the house." Selma was shaking.

"Okay," said Eileen, putting her arm around Selma's shoulder. "It's going to be okay. Let's go into my daughter's house. He's probably wandering around inside."

The three of them searched the main floor, as well as the basement level, but found no clues to his whereabouts. When they walked back into the kitchen, Lauren noticed the partially open microwave door and its illuminated empty interior. The bag of popcorn Lauren had left there for the movie was gone. The realization that he had been in the house and was now absent was somehow worse than if he had never been there at all. Lauren bolted out of the kitchen and up the stairs to Nate's room. She opened his door and found her brother lying on his bed listening to music. "Gramps is missing!" she shouted. Nate sat up and stuffed his feet into his sneakers. Together, they ran back down the stairs and into the kitchen. Eileen told Nate to put his coat on. It was below freezing.

CHAPTER 9

W̲earing flannel pajama bottoms, a sweatshirt thin from many washings, slippers, and a long black Windbreaker one of Ann's female guests had left in the front closet of the guesthouse, Sam walked on the frozen, snow-covered ground in the woods behind the Baronses' property. In one hand, he carried the bag of popcorn, provisions for his journey, and in the other, he carried a section of the local newspaper, specifically the want ads. He desperately wanted to know what time it was—he was worried he'd be late for the interview—but he didn't have his watch. He hoped it was back at the hotel or Eileen would hit the roof. He shuffled through the tall, bare trees along a narrow pathway, which he guessed had been there for a hundred years. The company's founder probably ordered it made so he could walk home from work without soiling his shoes and pant legs on wet grass or mildew-laced leaves. This path was like all paths, welcoming those who trod up them, giving direction and hope to their followers. Sam knew that if he stayed on it, he would reach his destination. Aside from not knowing the time, Sam's only other concern was his feet, which were moist and chilled, like two bottles of wine sunk in twin ice buckets at a fancy restaurant. He tried to lift them out, but no matter where he stepped, they sank back in. And he was wearing his new shoes, too.

At the end of the path was a wide clearing framing a large house-like structure some 100 yards away. All of the windows were dark, however, which seemed odd. Was he that late that everyone would have gone home? He quickened his pace as much as his numb feet would allow. As soon as he was excused from the interview, he was going to sit down and write a letter to the manufacturer of his shoes. They were plenty comfortable, but they were absolutely worthless for wearing outside, which, as everyone knew, was the reason shoes existed in the first place. Sam shook his head. The world was changing, and not for the better.

He walked through the snow around the building to the front. It really did look like a house, with gabled windows, clapboard siding, and a porch that ran the width of the building. And even though it was very attractive—any family would think it hit the jackpot to live in such splendor—the company's headquarters, he thought, ought to have more of a corporate presence. This down-home, informal image showed weakness, something a business should always go to great lengths to hide. What would the stockholders think? It might appeal to the women in the group, but most men would feel exactly as he felt, disappointed. Did he want to work for a company that housed its most important officers in a huge Dutch Colonial? Never mind, thought Sam, grabbing the handrail to climb the front steps. He could argue the merits of manliness over friendliness after he was hired. He'd add that to his growing mental list of concerns, which was just one of the reasons he wanted to work for the company. Frankly, they'd lost their edge. Sam was willing to help them regain it, for a competitive salary and a healthy pension. Surely their future was worth that much.

Now take the fellow at the hotel they were staying in—what was his name? Mark? Mike, that was it. He was part of the new generation, the men that wanted to get in and get out as fast as they could, taking a wheelbarrow of cash on their way out the door. The pension was all but dead in today's business world, replaced by the almighty bonus. They had all the answers, these newcomers, and thought themselves smarter, more connected to society's pulse than their forebearers. What they didn't realize was that sound business acumen never went out of style. In fact, if there was one good thing about this Mike, it was his judgment. He knew what he was doing. And, after their heated discussion the other day, he ought to tell him as much.

Up on the ice-covered porch, Sam slowly made his way to the front door, flanked and brightly lit by large brass lanterns attached to the house. He rang the illuminated doorbell, and then waited for what he thought was a reasonable amount of time before he rang it again. No one answered. Sam reached into the pocket of his coat, where he had stuffed his interview invitation, and found it empty. Oh God, he needed that letter. Sam swung around to scan the ground and lost his footing on the slippery surface. He fell hard on the cold, unyielding floor, his head hitting the icy surface with a loud *thump*.

Nate drove at ten miles per hour, as instructed by his grand-mother, around the neighborhood. They all agreed Sam couldn't have gone far in just twenty minutes, well, forty minutes now. Eileen had successfully calmed Selma, mostly by telling her about the time she had lost Sam at the mall (she found him trying to buy a cell phone from a Verizon salesperson so he could call her) and by assuring her they would secure or change the locking system on the doors so this would never happen again. Selma was an excellent caregiver and cook, and Eileen didn't want to lose her because of this one incident. Prior to tonight, her record had been perfect. Yet Eileen knew she uttered false promises. Sam, albeit sick, was a clever, persistent man. If he wanted to escape, he'd find a way. The only way Eileen could deter him from future escapes was to lengthen the time it would take him to get out.

Caught in their headlights was a couple walking a dog. Eileen told Nate to pull the car up next to them. Eileen lowered her window and asked them if they'd seen her husband. They shook their heads; they had not seen anyone at all. Eileen wrote her name and Nate's cell phone number down on a pad she had grabbed from Ann's kitchen and asked the couple to contact her if they saw him. Nate continued driving. He stopped after turning the car around in a cul-de-sac. "I've driven down all the streets in the neighborhood, Gran," he said. "What do you want to do now?"

"We've got to keep going," said Lauren. "We've got to find him."

"Let's go home," said Eileen.

"Gran," said Lauren, "it's cold outside. We can't stop now."

"I know it's cold," said Eileen. "I think it's time to call the police."

Twenty minutes later, Officer Terry Handley arrived at the house in freshly falling snow. While the department usually waited twenty-four hours before acting on missing person claims, older people with health problems fell into a different category, especially in winter. What Officer Handley didn't tell them, as he took down Sam's physical description and mental status, was the window for finding people like Sam was smaller than those for finding any other group, including very small children. There was no rational pattern to what a confused elderly person would do. Every case was different, and many of them ended badly. "There is some good news," Officer Handley said. "With this snow on the ground, we just might find some footprints. And we've got a full moon to help us see."

"I'm going with you," said Lauren, popping up from her chair at the kitchen table.

"Me too," said Nate. "Gran, you and Selma stay here, just in case he comes home. Lauren, turn the volume up on your cell phone; I'll leave mine with Gran."

Eileen nodded, accepted Nate's phone and quick instructions on how to use it, and then watched Officer Handley and her two grandchildren put on their coats, hats, gloves, and boots before walking out the back door. Eileen turned to Selma, who looked like she might cry, and asked her to make tea. "They'll find him," Eileen said aloud to the lime-green walls of her daughter's kitchen. "I know they'll find him."

They did, indeed, find footprints in the snow that started on the path between the big house and the guesthouse and then veered off into the yard. "We may be in luck," said Officer Handley.

Lauren ran ahead, holding the flashlight she had taken from the toolbox in the garage. "Gramps!" she shouted into the blackness.

"Not too far," called Officer Handley, more concerned about what Lauren might find than about her safety.

She ignored him and ran faster. The cold night air flattened her lungs. "Gramps!" she shouted again.

Nate ran after his sister. "Wait for me!"

Lauren stopped and waited for her brother, who was quickly next to her. They walked together into the woods, following the uneven, muted trail of footprints while Officer Handley lagged behind, shining his flashlight this way and that. "We've got to find him," said Lauren, her voice breaking. "We can't leave him outside all night."

"We'll find him," said Nate, trying to sound strong.

"Why did he run away?" asked Lauren.

"He's confused," said Nate. "He doesn't think like you and me."

"That's so unfair," said Lauren. "To have that happen to you is so unfair."

"A lot of things are unfair," said Nate, looking into the dark spaces between the trees to his left. Would his grandfather have gone in there? They continued along the narrow path until they reached the Nelsons' spacious backyard. Officer Handley was twenty yards behind them, directing his light into the woods.

"Some footprints go this way," said Lauren, shifting her light from the path to a set of new tracks in the yard. She started running; Nate caught up with her. Soon, they were at the front of the house, at the top of the front steps, and upon their motionless grandfather. A pool of frozen blood surrounded his head. "Oh God," said Lauren in a voice that was barely above a whisper.

"Run and get the cop," Nate ordered his sister. "Tell him he's hurt." Nate watched as Lauren flew down the stairs, around the corner, and out of sight. As soon as she was gone, Nate got on his hands and knees and lowered his ear to within an inch of his grandfather's mouth. He listened carefully. At first, he heard nothing but the wind swirling around the porch. He moved closer, putting his ear against his grandfather's cold lips. Only then did he feel a shallow breath. He was alive! Nate took off his coat and folded it in half. He gently lifted his grandfather's head and slid the coat underneath. Then, he removed his wool cap, which he had worn every day to school lately because it was considered both retro cool and Rastafarian, and put it on his grandfather's head. He took off his gloves and put them as best as he could onto his grandfather's frozen hands. "They'll be here soon," said Nate to Sam's icy, immobile face. Moments later, Lauren and Officer Handley appeared at the side of the house. "He needs an ambulance," called Nate. "He's cold and he's hurt."

"I've got one on the way," said Officer Handley, navigating the icy steps. The officer took off his thick black gloves and knelt down next to Sam. He took clear plastic gloves from a leather pouch on his belt and quickly pulled them over his fingers. He checked Sam's pulse, at his wrist and then his neck. He listened to Sam's slow but consistent breathing. He looked up at Lauren and Nate, who were watching him. "Call your grandmother," he said. "Tell her we'll be taking him to Grace Memorial Hospital."

As soon as the ambulance arrived, Lauren asked if she could ride to the hospital with her grandfather. Then she and Nate silently watched the technicians go about their ministrations, bundling their grandfather into blankets and then onto a cot with wheels, inserting an IV into his wrist, strapping an oxygen mask to his hard face. Officer Handley stood a short distance away, reporting the incident into a radio device he had unclipped from his thick belt. Soon enough, Lauren was whisked into the vehicle alongside Sam and various equipment boxes, and the doors were shut. The driver waved and then eased the ambulance out of the driveway. On the street, he hit the lights, the red flashes broadcasting distress and urgency into the night. Nate and Officer Handley waited until the ambulance had turned the corner before starting back through the Nelsons' backyard. As they forged a new path to the woods, the icy layer on top of the snow gave way under their feet, crunching like the punch noises in one of Nate's video games—a thunderous noise Nate had not noticed with his sister. After a few moments, Officer Handley spoke. "Does your grandfather have Alzheimer's disease?"

"He's got dementia," said Nate. "I don't know about Alzheimer's."

"So he's forgetful?"

"Yeah," said Nate. "He has a hard time tracking normal conversation. Sometimes, it seems like he loses his place in time."

"Yes." Nate glanced at the officer. "I think your grandfather's going to be okay," he said. "The cut at the back of his head may require stitches and will probably give him a bit of a headache, but I've seen worse."

They walked several more steps. "Why would he go outside in his pajamas?" asked Nate. "It's freezing out here."

"Your grandfather's brain is not working the way it's supposed to," said Handley. "It tricks him now into thinking he's dressed appropriately or he's a different person or it's summer instead of winter."

"That sucks," said Nate.

"Yes, it does," said Officer Handley, looking ahead to the lights of the Baronses' house.

Nate pulled his car out onto the road for the second time that night. Eileen sat in the front with her grandson and Selma sat in the back. During the ten-minute ride to the hospital, Nate told them about finding Sam. He told them about the cut on the back of his head without going into detail about the frozen blood. He told them Sam looked okay without mentioning the fact that he'd urinated himself. And he repeated Officer Handley's optimistic prognosis. All the while, Nate's stomach churned. He could not erase from his mind the picture it had made of his grandfather on the front porch. It was the picture of a dead man, a street person in a rumpled, rotting heap at the end of a Detroit alley. And because Nate barely knew his grandfather and was afraid of his affliction—now more than ever—he had been tempted to run away from the Nelsons' front porch. Like city dwellers passing homeless people on their way to the subway, Nate didn't want to know how bad it was.

They met Lauren in the waiting room, busy and noisy with patients, family members, and medical personnel. They all made their way around children drawing in hospital-issued coloring books on the floor, parents trying to console crying infants, and older women in wheelchairs stenciled with GRACE MEMORIAL to the far end to several empty chairs. Eileen's coat had barely touched the molded plastic when she started asking questions about Sam. Lauren told them what the emergency medical technicians, or EMTs, as Lauren called them, told her—that the wound was superficial, that the biggest issue was getting him warm. He'd lost a lot of body heat on that front porch. Nate made eye contact with his sister; Lauren stopped talking.

A half hour later, they were called to the desk, where a balding, trim doctor told them he wanted to keep Sam for the night. They'd stitched his head and stabilized his vital signs and everything looked okay. Dr. Moyer said Sam needed rest more than anything else, and a ride home would prove more detrimental than beneficial to that goal. Dr. Moyer was very encouraging in general about Sam's recovery. "You and I know he's not well," he said to Eileen. "But he's surprisingly strong for a man in his condition. A lesser man would be in a very different position right now, Mrs. Sanford."

"It's all the years on our farm," said Eileen, explaining.

On the way home, they all talked about making the guesthouse more secure. Two locks already bolted the top and the bottom of the front door. And just last weekend, a handyman had installed a stopper-lock on the slider in the master bedroom after Eileen had seen Sam fiddling with the handle's locking mechanism. "The answer is not more locks," said Eileen. "He does have clear moments when he's perfectly capable of unlocking a door."

"Maybe we need an alarm," offered Nate. "You know, one that goes off every time the door opens."

"That can be an awful lot of times in one day," said Selma.

"It doesn't have to be an eardrum breaker," said Nate. "Just a long beep, or something, so you know the door has been opened."

"That's a good idea," said Eileen. "I'll talk to your father about it when your parents get home. I think we'll be safe for a couple of nights. Sam will most likely be too sore and exhausted to attempt another escape right away."

Nate pulled the car into the garage and they all sat for a moment before slowly getting out and walking into the kitchen. The lights were on, as if they had never left, but the charged atmosphere Nate felt several hours earlier, created by the prospect of a Friday night in a parentless house, was gone. Instead, Nate felt depleted. He walked around the island to the microwave and shut the door, putting out the interior light that had been shining on nothing since Sam had taken the bag of popcorn. Still, no one said anything until a few moments later, when Selma spoke what they all were thinking. "I'm tired," she said.

"Yes," said Eileen. "Nate, would you walk Selma back to the guesthouse?"

The guesthouse lights were still blazing from Selma's search earlier, and yet it felt cold inside instead of warm and inviting. "Let's have a look around," said Nate. Together, they checked the sliding glass door in Sam and Eileen's bedroom that led to a small deck behind the guesthouse. It was locked and the stopper was in place. Sam had, apparently, focused his efforts that evening on the front door only. Selma drew the thick drapes across the door and turned out the bedside lamp. One by one, they checked all the windows and found them locked. After each was inspected, Selma pulled the blind, lowered the shade, or closed the curtains, as if the vinyl, cotton, or polyester could fend off the demons of the night. Nate, who was increasingly spooked by the evening's activities, did not question her motives. If he could not quell the uneasiness in his own body, certainly he could not convincingly allay Selma's. "Well," he said, after checking the final window, "it looks like everything is okay."

Selma put her fingers to her forehead and gently massaged her light brown skin. "It's been a long night," she said, eyes closed.

"Are you okay here?" asked Nate. "You are welcome to stay at the other house."

"Thank you, Nate," said Selma, looking at him. "I'm as good as I'm going to be until the morning."

"Okay," said Nate, zipping his coat and walking to the door. His hand on the knob, he turned to again face Selma. "My grandfather is a pretty smart guy. He could have fooled any of us." Selma nodded her head. "Lock behind me," said Nate, opening the door.

"I will," she said.

Nate heard the bolts lock into place just after he shut the door.

He gave Selma a quick wave, then shoved his hands in his pockets. Halfway up the path, Nate turned. At the side of the guesthouse, lit by the moon, were the footprints of his demented grandfather, joined by those of Lauren, Officer Handley, and himself. Nate shook his head and turned to face the big house, his house, and the realization that he, too, was now responsible for his grandfather. His walk through the woods and trip to the hospital earned him admission to Sam's circle of caregivers. His parents, Nate guessed, walking the rest of the way to the back door, would never truly enter the circle. They understood a lot about money and business, but they didn't understand outsiders, especially those in a weakened condition. Nate turned the knob and pushed himself into the warm kitchen, where his grandmother and his sister were sitting and talking at the kitchen table. A pot of tea was sitting between them; a third, unused cup had been paired with a vacant chair. "How's Selma?" asked Eileen as Nate took off his coat and hung it on a hook.

"She's okay," said Nate. "A little scared, I think."

"I would imagine so," said Eileen. "This evening has been unsettling for all of us." Nate stood next to the table, hands in his jeans pockets. "Sit with us," she said. "It's decaffeinated tea; it won't keep you up."

Nate smiled. "I'm not really worried about staying up, Gran. I'm usually up until midnight anyway."

Eileen looked at her watch. "Well then, you've got a couple of hours yet."

His mind made up, Nate took a step back from the table. "I'm going to head upstairs." Gran stood and approached him, and before he knew what was happening, she had reached up and put both her soft palms on his cold, weather-reddened cheeks. She pulled him to her and kissed his forehead. Nate blushed.

"Thank you," she said, releasing him. "Thank you for everything you did tonight. I don't know if I could have done this myself."

"Of course you could have, Gran," said Lauren.

"I'm not so sure," said Eileen, the last word catching in her throat.

Nate took a step back. "It's okay," he said, turning to leave. "Good night now."

"Good night, Nate," said Lauren, able in her grandmother's presence to speak her brother's name.

"Okay," said Nate, leaving the kitchen. He walked through the dark hallway and up the stairs to his room. He closed the door behind him and then emptied the pockets of his pants: wallet, keys, and cell phone his grandmother had given back to him at the hospital. It had vibrated several times when they were there, but Nate had forgotten about the calls. One message was from Jenny, who had texted him from a movie she described as totally disgusting, and the other messages were from Josh, who was wondering just where the hell he was, since they were supposed to meet Bill and Andy at the community center in thirty minutes (message one) and five minutes (message two). Nate sat down on his bed and called Josh's phone number. "Dude," said Nate.

"Where the fuck are you?" asked Josh.

"Home," said Nate.

"Well, that's nice," said Josh sarcastically. "And you decided not to respond to your text messages and blow off your friends for what good reason?"

"Because I was out looking for my grandfather, who walked out of the guesthouse in his pajamas."

"What?"

"My grandfather," said Nate, flopping down on his bed, "walked out of his house, wearing his pajamas and slippers and a woman's raincoat. He walked in the snow through the woods to the Nelsons' house behind us. We found him on their front porch, unconscious from a fall he had taken that put a nasty gash in the back of his head. And an ambulance came and took him to the hospital. So, actually, I've been pretty busy."

"Shit," said Josh. "I'm sorry. Is he okay?"

"The doctor says he's going to be fine," said Nate, removing his shoes and peeling off his socks. He smelled them and then threw them in the direction of his laundry basket.

"Why would he do something like that?"

"Because his brain's all fucked up," said Nate.

"That sucks," said Josh.

"It does suck," said Nate, "and what sucks even more is my parents don't have a fucking clue about my grandfather, or my grandmother, for that matter. They're off at some resort in California—because my mother can't stand to be around us for more than a few weeks at a time—and her father is half-dead in a hospital." Nate lay back on his bed, grabbing his remote control on his way. He clicked on the radio, then lowered the volume so he could hear Josh.

". . . this will change things," said Josh.

"I don't think so," said Nate.

"How's Lauren?" Josh asked. "Was she with you?"

"Why do you care?" asked Nate.

"I don't know," said Josh. "Girls can get funny about this kind of stuff."

"We're all a little weirded out," said Nate.

"Yeah," he said. "So, are we still on for tomorrow night?"

Nate ran his fingers through his hair. "I don't know. Who's in?"

"Billy, Andy, Todd, Steve, Tom, and Nick," said Josh. "Jenny's working on the girls, but I know she was hoping to get eight or ten."

"That sounds good," said Nate. "I'll call you tomorrow, when I know a little more about what's going on here."

"Okay," said Josh, already thinking they could move the party to Steve's house. His parents were in town, but they were the coolest adults he knew. Whenever the boys sneaked beer from the old man's fridge, he just looked the other way. The old man sometimes wanted to join in on the fun—relive his high school days, he called it—which was awkward but tolerable, as long as he didn't hang around too long.

Nate hung up the phone, took off his belted pants, and got under his covers. He turned out his bedside light and closed his eyes. There, as clearly as if he were still outside, bending over his grandfather on the Nelsons' front porch, was the clay-like face. There was the congealed blood. Nate opened his eyes, turned on his light, and hit the remote for his television. He clicked to his favorite music video channel and propped himself up on his pillows to watch.

Downstairs, Lauren and Eileen had finished the pot of Orange Sleep Well tea. Eileen rinsed the pot out in the sink, while Lauren put the two remaining homemade oatmeal raisin cookies of the original six back in the red tin her grandmother had brought over from the guesthouse. "Maybe I should just give up on him," said Lauren, continuing their discussion about Judd Acker, the out-of-reach captain of the high school football team.

"Oh, I don't know about that," said Eileen, wiping her hands on the dish towel hanging next to the sink. "It's always good to have dreams. But it's also good to play the field. Don't let Judd think he's the only one."

"Gran," said Lauren, putting her hands on her hips, "we've gone over this. He doesn't know I exist."

"Maybe he doesn't," said Eileen, approaching Lauren and putting her arm momentarily around her granddaughter's shoulder, "and maybe he does." Together they walked up the main stairs and down the hall to Nate's closed door. Eileen gently knocked on it and called "good night." At Lauren's door, Eileen kissed her granddaughter's cheek and then carried on down the hallway to the spare room she was occupying that weekend. At the doorway, she looked back.

"Good night," said Lauren, removing the coated elastic from the back of her head, setting her hair free.

"Sleep tight," said Gran, before she disappeared into the room.

Lauren walked into her room and flicked on the light. She drew her curtains, undressed, put on her favorite flannel pajama pants and a clean T-shirt, and got into bed. She was worried about her grandfather, but tired of thinking about him. She took the latest *People* magazine from the bedside table and opened to the cover story, again about Brad and Angelina.

CHAPTER 10

Nate drove his grandmother, Selma, and Lauren to the hospital the next morning to get Sam. The doctor gave Eileen care instructions for his stitches and said Sam might be even more disoriented as a result of his head injury. Eileen thanked him, and then folded the photocopied instructions and tucked them into her handbag. Sam held Nate's arm like a prom date as they made their way through the hospital lobby and across the windy, snow-drifted parking lot to the car. The plow had been through the lot once, but the snow, relentless in its descent, continuously recovered the pavement. The roads were slippery and the visibility was terrible; Nate had to concentrate just to see the road in front of him. He took his time, knowing an accident right now might further injure his grandfather. Everyone was quiet, concentrating with Nate as he drove along one wintry street to the next, winding his way across town. Halfway home, Lauren, up front with her brother, fiddled with the radio tuner until she found an easy listening station with music she thought appropriate for grown-ups. Nate reached for the scan button when he heard the opening bars of a Neil Diamond song he'd endured several times while eating at the mall, but reconsidered. Music was better than the silence, interrupted only by the depressing sound of his grandfather clearing the phlegm from his throat. "Who lives here?" asked Sam, when Nate pulled the car into the driveway.

"I do," said Nate, driving around to the back.

"You've done quite well, young man," said Sam.

"Thank you," said Nate, pulling his car in next to Selma's.

As soon as they were parked, Selma got out and hurriedly made her way along the path. She took her keys from her purse and unlocked the front door to the guesthouse. Inside, she turned up the heat and turned on the burner underneath the teakettle. She hung her coat in the front hall closet and then swept the snow off the front mat with a broom. Eileen was the first to reach her and then Nate, guiding Sam, and then Lauren, carrying the mystery woman's raincoat Sam had declared stylish but snug. Eileen thanked everyone and then announced that she and Selma would get Sam into bed. She asked Nate and Lauren to head back to the big house to tidy their rooms, taking any clothes needing washing to the second floor laundry room and any cups, plates, and silverware to the kitchen sink. The crisis was over; it was back to business. Nate looked at Lauren, who gently shrugged. "Are you okay here?" Nate asked his grandmother.

"We're fine," said Eileen, hanging her coat in the closet. "Selma and I will take care of Sam and have a cup of tea. You two have been so good to both your grandfather and me this morning—it's time for you to run along. Get your chores done, so you can enjoy your day. I think your grandfather just needs to rest now."

Lauren and Nate walked back outside, Nate closing the door behind them. "That was weird," he said.

"What?"

"We get our grandfather, who could have died, out of the hospital, and the next thing out of Gran's mouth is about cleaning our rooms?"

"I don't think it's so weird," said Lauren, zipping her coat. "She wants to put it behind her. She's embarrassed by what happened, I think."

"Yeah, well, I think it's weird," said Nate, putting his hands in his pockets. They walked the rest of the way without talking. When they reached the back door, Nate turned to his sister. "Are you going to do it?"

"Do what?" asked Lauren, coating her lips with the stick of balm she took out of her jacket pocket.

"Clean your room." Lauren looked at her brother blankly. "Hey," he said, punching in the alarm code and then opening the door, "don't look at me like I'm some kind of gigantic moron. It's not like you clean your room all the time."

"Gran asked us to do it," she said, walking into the kitchen and taking off her coat. "Are you going to say no to her?"

"I don't know," he said, checking his cell phone for messages.

"Well, I'm not," said Lauren, walking across the kitchen floor to the hallway. "I think she's been through enough."

Nate took off his coat and hung it on a peg next to his sister's. He took her coat off its peg and dropped it to the floor. "Kiss ass," he said. He grabbed a Coke from the fridge and headed upstairs. He opened his bedroom door, which he always kept closed, and noticed an odor that had not been there yesterday. He pulled open his blackout drapes, allowing sunlight to shine on the rumpled clothes that covered his carpet. He grabbed his empty laundry basket from the corner of his room and began stuffing shirts, pants, boxers, and socks into it. When it was overflowing, he hauled it to the hallway and set it down. When he returned to his room, he again noticed the odor. After opening a window an inch, Nate searched for the source. In doing so, he threw all the paper from his desk into the trash can. He put three Coke cans, four used glasses, and a plastic bowl coated with what looked like dried, melted chocolate ice cream, out in the hall next to his pile of clothes. Still, the smell remained. Determined to find it, Nate looked under his bed. He pulled out a dust-covered sock and three *Sports Illustrated* magazines that instantly reminded him of the other magazines he had hidden under his mattress. Nate stood, crossed the room, and locked his door. He went back to the bed, lifted the sheet-covered mattress, and smiled at the two vintage issues of *Playboy* he had found years ago during one of his forages in the woods behind their old house. He grabbed both worn copies before repositioning the mattress, and then he sat on the floor with the rest of his Coke and flipped to the centerfold to have a look at Miss April. She looked like Jenny, kind of, even though Nate hadn't yet seen Jenny completely naked. And like Jenny, Miss April was turned on by funny, sincere men, and turned off by rich phonies. Just as Nate reached into his pants, someone knocked on his door. "What!" said Nate, shoving the magazines under his bed.

"It's Gran," called Eileen. "How's everything going?"

"Okay," said Nate, scrambling to his feet.

"Can I come in?"

"Just a minute," said Nate. He bent down, grabbed the *Playboys,* and slid them back under his mattress with one hand, while he adjusted his pants with the other. His large flannel shirt covered his crotch. He had a quick look around his room, took a deep breath, and then unlocked his door.

"Well," she said, walking in and glancing from his desk to his bureau to his closet, "it's coming along."

"Yes," said Nate, putting his hands in the front pockets of his jeans.

"Do you notice an interesting odor?"

"I was just trying to find out what that was," said Nate.

"It smells like old cheese to me," said Eileen. "Check under your bed."

"I'll do that," said Nate.

"You're doing a great job."

Nate closed the door behind her and made a face. "This is bullshit," he said, reaching for his iPod. "Complete bullshit." He flopped down on his bed, resolved to stand up to his grandmother. He was done cleaning his room. It was their housekeeper's job, not his. He plugged his headphones in and closed his eyes.

When Eileen walked into Lauren's room, she found her granddaughter sitting on the floor painting her toenails. Crumpled clothes lay in a heap in the corner, but nothing else looked like it had been touched. Lauren's small desk, partially covered by a laptop computer, was cluttered with textbooks, notebooks, lined paper, balled-up tissues, and brightly colored pens and pencils. Dusty knickknacks stood atop an antique doily on her bureau, the drawers of which were in various stages of closure, depending on the number of shirt sleeves and pant legs sticking out of them. Glancing into the bathroom, Eileen saw a tipped-over can of hair spray, a tube of hair gel without a top, myriad plastic containers of blush and eye shadow, at least four vials of mascara, and too many lipsticks and eyeliners to count without actually doing so. She looked back at Lauren, who smiled at her. "Isn't this the greatest color?" she asked. "I found it under some clothes in the corner, and I couldn't believe it. I've been looking for this forever."

"Yes," said Eileen, wondering why even a fifteen-year-old would want to paint her nails lavender. "How's your room coming along?"

"Pretty good," said Lauren, sticking cotton balls between her toes. "I'm just going to let these toes dry, then I'll do some more."

"Okay," said Eileen, turning to leave. "As soon as you're done, I thought we'd make a couple of cherry pies."

"That sounds great," said Lauren, painting the thumbnail of her left hand.

Eileen left Lauren's room, leaving the door open behind her, and then walked back down the hallway, down the stairs, and into the kitchen, where she had laid out all the ingredients for the pies. She ran the garbage bags back up the stairs and left them outside Nate's door. When she returned to Ann's kitchen, she wrote Nate and Lauren a note, telling them she'd gone back to the guesthouse and to come and get her when they were done. She put on her coat and walked out the back door thinking about her childhood bedroom that she never had to tidy because it didn't occur to her to make a mess.

She opened the front door to the guesthouse and walked down the short front hallway to the kitchen, where Selma was chopping vegetables.

"How's he doing?" Eileen asked, sliding her coat off one shoulder.

"He's still asleep," said Selma, looking up from her task.

"Good," said Eileen. "He needs the rest."

"The medication the doctor gave us is helping him do that," Selma said. "I haven't heard a peep out of him all morning."

Eileen walked across the living room to the bedroom door, which was ajar. She gently pushed it open enough to fit her head through. There, lying in a fetal position on the bed, was her husband of almost forty-nine years. His face, bruised by his fall, was limp, but nonetheless peaceful, a state Sam increasingly seemed to achieve only in sleep. Eileen walked into the room and sat down on the bed. She put her hand on his shoulder; Sam blinked several times, then opened his eyes. "How are you feeling?" she asked.

"I've been better," said Sam, still focusing. "That was some party last night."

"Yes."

"Is there some work to be done?" Sam asked sleepily.

"No," said Eileen, patting him. "You can get some more rest."

"What a treat," said Sam, closing his eyes. "I can't remember the last time I slept in on a Saturday."

Eileen got up off the bed and walked back through the living room and into the kitchen. The vegetables had moved from the cutting board on the counter into a large pot on the stove. "What can I do here?" Eileen asked.

"I'm okay," said Selma, measuring chicken stock in a large glass cup.

"Are you really?" Selma looked at Eileen. "I have a feeling this is more than what you bargained for."

Selma took a deep breath. "What happened last night was very scary, I must admit," she said, wiping her hands on her apron.

"I don't blame you for what happened, and I hope you don't blame yourself," said Eileen. "It could have happened with both of us here."

"I don't know," said Selma, turning back to the sizzling vegetables.

"I do know," said Eileen. "He can be so docile sometimes that he fools you into thinking he's just getting old. And then you turn your back and he's up to something that reminds you just how sick he is."

"He is a sick man," said Selma softly.

"And I won't leave you for a weekend like this again," said Eileen. "I wanted to spend some time with my grandchildren alone, to see what they're really like. But I can see it's too much of a strain on you. I'm sorry for that."

Selma turned her head. "I understand your need to be with your grandchildren," she said. "And for the most part, I really am okay. Underneath his illness, your husband's a good man."

Eileen looked briefly at the floor. "Thank you," she said, raising her eyes to meet Selma's. "Sometimes I feel like I'm the only person on earth who knows that."

When Eileen walked into Lauren's room thirty minutes later, she found her granddaughter in the bathroom in front of the mirror. "Hi, Gran," she said. "I found this lavender shadow to go with my nails. Do you think it's too much?" She turned and faced her grandmother.

"No," said Eileen, being honest. Lauren, she could tell, was good at applying cosmetics. Most teenagers overdid it. "I think I'm going to start those pies."

"Oh good," said Lauren. "I'll help you."

Eileen looked around Lauren's room, which was still in need of attention. "I'll tell you what," she said. "You dust and vacuum in here and then you can help me. Deal?"

"Deal," said Lauren, putting on pink lipstick. "I just have one problem."

"What's that?"

"I have no idea where the vacuum is."

"It's a central vacuum," said Eileen, pointing to the outtake valve on the wall. "Look in the linen closet down the hall for the attachment. If you don't find it, come get me in the kitchen and we'll look together." Eileen left Lauren's room and walked back down the hall to Nate's closed door and the sound of muffled music behind it. She hesitated a moment, her fist poised to knock on the door, and then retreated and walked on.

Nate turned down his music to answer the vibrating cell phone in his pocket.

"Okay," said Josh, "everyone's on board. Now we just need to know where we're going to party."

"Can we still go to Steve's?" asked Nate, lying on his bed.

"Yeah," said Josh. "You need to back out?"

"I think so, man," said Nate. "My grandmother's got me cleaning my room."

"Ouch."

"Who's getting beer?"

"I'm still working on that," said Josh. "Tom's older brother said he'd buy it, but he wants a commission."

"Since when?"

"Since now," said Josh. "A buck a six-pack."

"What an asshole."

"He is definitely an asshole, but he's our best shot."

"We'll pay the jerk," said Nate. "I'm not drinking Coke at the party."

"You got that right."

"So, you're making this happen?"

"Yeah," said Josh. "I'll make a few more phone calls and we'll be in business."

"Perfect," said Nate, sitting up.

"I've got more," said Josh.

"Yeah?"

"Billy's trying to score some weed."

"Awesome," said Nate, smiling.

"It's party time," said Josh.

Nate made a face as he ended the call. That putrid smell seemed even stronger now. "Okay," he said, getting onto his hands and knees, "one of us is leaving this room."

He looked back under the bed again. This time he found a pair of navy blue sweatpants, two more socks, a brand new Frisbee still in its packaging, a pair of plaid boxers, a whole lot of dust, and a plate holding a half-eaten piece of New York cheesecake. Green and blue mold sat like a hairpiece over the top. Nate gagged, then put it into a garbage bag, plate and all. He stuffed the Frisbee, the socks, and the boxers into the bag, too. The sweatpants he walked to the mound of laundry already in the hall.

Lauren, who was walking past his open door, stopped. "I'm done! I'm free!" she said, smiling.

"Good for you!" sang Nate sarcastically.

"And I'm going to get pie!" sang Lauren back.

It was late enough in the day that Nate was starting to get hungry. And he couldn't think of anything better to eat than his grandmother's cherry pie. "Are they done?" he asked.

"Of course not," said Lauren. "Gran and I are making them together."

"One of them is mine."

Lauren looked past him into his room. "Not by the looks of that room, mister."

"Tell me you're done with your room."

"Neat as a pin," said Lauren.

"Suck up," said Nate.

"I think I'll have my pie with ice cream," said Lauren, walking away.

Nate forcefully shut his door. He went back to his bed and put on his headphones. He listened to four songs from his favorite CD, then sat up. Slowly, he got off the bed. He reached for the half-drunk bottle of Mountain Dew on his desk and dropped it into a garbage bag.

After dinner, Nate had two pieces of pie. He cleared the table and then headed upstairs for a shower. Lauren, who was going to the movies with two friends from the volleyball team, helped Eileen with the dishes. She found that fitting everything into the dishwasher was like doing a puzzle: the dessert plates fit best in the rack at the back, and the bowls slid in perfectly along the sides. When they were done, Gran patted Lauren's back and thanked her for helping. Then, saying she'd be back before Lauren left, Gran went to the guesthouse to check on Selma and Sam. Lauren walked into the den and turned on the TV. Halfway through the stations she found an *Entertainment Tonight* story about Charlie Sheen. Just as she was settling in under a blanket, the doorbell rang. She lazily got up from her seat and walked to the front door. When she looked through the side windows, Josh waved at her. "Hi," he said, when she opened the door. "What's up?"

"Not much," she said, smiling at him as she closed the door behind him. "Nate's in the shower."

Josh looked at his watch. "That's not surprising," he said as they walked down the hallway to the kitchen.

"What are you guys up to?" Lauren asked, getting a bottle of water from the fridge.

"Party," said Josh, biting into an apple he took from the bowl on the counter that Eileen filled the day before. "Want to come?"

"Very funny," said Lauren

"I'm serious," said Josh, chewing.

"My brother would rather die than be seen at a party with me."

"That's probably true for him," said Josh "but not for me."

Lauren blushed. "I'm going to the movies," she volunteered.

"That's cool," he said. "You going on a date?"

Lauren laughed. "I wish. No, I'm going with Pammy and Katie."

"Blow them off," said Josh, taking a step closer to Lauren and taking another bite. "I'll blow the party off and you and I can go sit in a dark theater."

Lauren looked at Josh. He was several inches taller than she, and he had long, lean arms. If she took one step toward him, she would walk right into his chest, and he could wrap those arms all the way around her. He looked into her eyes, smiled, and then reached over and tucked a strand of loose hair behind her ear. Her face tingled where he touched it before putting his hand back into his pocket. A moment later, watching him take another bite of the apple, Lauren thought she could have imagined the whole thing, even though her face was still hot.

"What's up?" asked Nate, walking into the kitchen.

"An evening of fun, my friend," said Josh, turning to face Nate. Lauren slowly backed away from Josh and, for something to do, she opened the cupboard above her head and grabbed a box of low-fat crackers. "Who's driving?" asked Josh.

"You are," said Nate. "I am so out of gas."

"Cool," said Josh. "Are we picking up Jenny?"

"No, she's going with the girls," said Nate, looking at his watch. "They should be there by now."

"Let's roll," said Josh. Their conversation took place around Lauren, as if she weren't there. And then, just as Josh was walking out of the kitchen, with Nate a few steps ahead of him, he turned to Lauren and winked.

Steve Jansen-Smith lived on the other side of town, a ten-minute drive. On the way, Josh and Nate each drank a Red Bull. When they arrived at Woodview Court, it was already crowded with badly parked cars, forcing Josh to circle the block and park on Timber Lane. The boys threw their aluminum cans into Josh's backseat before easing themselves out of the car and into the snowy night. "I am so pumped for this party," said Nate, briefly removing his hands from the pockets of his worn jeans to thrust them into the air. "It has been way too long."

"Months," said Josh. "It's been months, maybe years, since anyone in this town's thrown a decent bash."

Nate laughed. "Allison's coming," he said, teasing his friend.

"Allison who?" asked Josh.

"I don't know why you don't like her," said Nate. "She's cute."

"Yeah," said Josh, "in the dark maybe."

"Man, you're getting really picky."

"Says the man who's got Jenny."

"Point taken," said Nate. "But hey, maybe Allison will look better to you after some beer."

"Ask me after I've had three or four," said Josh.

As instructed, the boys walked around the side of the enormous brick house and down a snow-covered slope into the backyard. Through the floor-to-ceiling basement windows, Nate and Josh saw a crowd of people, drinking beer, smoking cigarettes, dancing, laughing, talking, and shouting to each other over the thumping beat of the music. "We've arrived," said Nate, smiling as he opened the sliding glass door to an instant blast of party sounds. Josh followed Nate inside, where Steve, the host, approached them immediately. "Welcome, gentlemen," he shouted. "Your beer is in the fridge—bottom shelf, Budweiser."

"Cool!" Nate shouted back. "Have you seen Jenny?"

"Yeah," yelled Steve, pointing to the other side of the room. "She's over there, making out with Tom."

Nate twisted his smile. "Fuck you, man," he said, moving in the direction of the white refrigerator at the end of the hallway. As promised, he and Josh found two six-packs of Bud among several six-packs of imported beer. Nate grabbed two from Josh's, marked with a black Sharpie, and handed one to his friend.

"I saw that," said Josh, smiling.

"Yeah, yeah," said Nate. "You can get them from mine next time."

Beers in hand, Nate and Josh walked into the party room and stood, with their backs against the wall, surveying the scene. To their right was a sitting area, two couches and two chairs arranged in a crooked oval. On the couch, Tom really was making out with someone, but it wasn't Jenny. It was Tiffany from their chemistry class, the girl who asked dumb questions and laughed at whatever the teacher said. Josh shook his head; Tom was such a smooth operator. He could talk almost anyone into a make-out session. Next to them, Andy had on his lap a girl Josh recognized but couldn't name. He rubbed her back with one hand while he sipped a beer with the other. She held a Coors Lite in her hand but didn't appear all that interested in it. In fact, after Andy had taken the last sip of his beer, she leaned into him and gave him a long drink from her can. Andy moved his hand down and began to caress her lower back. Sitting in the chairs and on the other couch was a group of girls from the field hockey team. They were gorgeous, all five of them, and dressed exactly alike: extra skinny jeans, little pastel tops with words written across the chest—Patti's said BABY—and generous slices of flat, toned tummies visible between the top of their low-rise pants and the bottom of their short shirts. They all had long hair—three blondes and two brunettes—that they had twisted up at the back of their heads. They talked and laughed; Ashley smoked a cigarette. Soon, they were joined by their soccer-team boyfriends, who circled them like stagecoach settlers. Josh turned his attention to the dance floor and saw Jenny on the other side. "There's Jenny," he said to Nate. Nate wove through the dancers like a determined laboratory rat working a maze. When he reached Jenny, she smiled and kissed his lips, surely a better reward than a piece of stale cheddar. Nate immediately put his arm around her shoulder, a high school code of possession more than an act of passion, and said something into her ear. She laughed. Josh gulped the last of his beer before working his way back to the fridge for another. Trying to fit her wine coolers onto the overcrowded top shelf was Jenny's friend, Allison Haynes. "Oh, hi, Josh," she said, giving him a big smile. "Great party."

"Yeah," said Josh, already thinking of ways he could extract himself from her company. If he didn't come up with something quickly, he'd be listening to her babble all night.

"How long have you been here?" she asked.

"A while," said Josh, looking beyond her into the fridge for his Budweiser.

"Same here," she said. "Jenny was wondering when you'd get here. She was thinking that maybe you'd changed your minds and were doing something else. But I told her, 'Oh no, Jenny. They'll be here.' " Josh glanced back at Allison. "She's crazy about him, you know," she said. "Then again, I guess I don't have to tell you that— you have eyes, don't you? Anyone who looks at the two of them can see how crazy they are about each other. How nice it would be to feel that way about someone, you know? And to have him feel that way about you, too."

Josh nodded his head. "I'm going to grab a beer," he said. "Do you want one?"

"Sure," said Allison, setting her wine cooler down on the floor. "I don't really like these anyway."

"They're on the bottom shelf," he said. "Let me just get by you."

Allison moved to Josh's right, propping the door wide open with her body. When Josh bent down to get to his beer, she put her hand on his head. He looked up at her. "Sorry," she said. "Lost my balance for a moment." Josh looked back at the bottom shelf: no Budweiser. He checked the other shelves: Coors Lite, Heineken, Sierra Nevada, and St. Pauli Girl. Josh stood. "Did you drink it all?" asked Allison. Josh quickly surveyed the hallway and spotted several Budweiser-sporting girls. One of them had her hand wrapped around a can with NATE written on the side. He left Allison at the fridge and strode up to the gaggle. "Where did you get that beer?" he asked.

"From the fridge," one of them said. "Steve told us to help ourselves."

"Well, I think that's my beer you're drinking."

"Oh," she said, looking at the can. "Actually, it's Nate's beer. But hey, sorry. There's lots more in there, though."

"Yes," said Josh. "And it belongs to other people."

She took another sip. "Well, hey, I don't think anyone would, like, care."

"I do," said Josh, turning to leave.

"What happened?" asked Allison, scurrying after him.

"My beer's gone," said Josh. "I'm going to find Steve."

"What?" asked Allison, having trouble keeping up with Josh, who moved through the crowd like a bouncer at a bar.

"I'm going to find Steve," Josh shouted back at her.

"I'll wait here," she yelled.

Working his way through the mass of warm bodies crowding the dark hallway adjacent to the party room, Josh lost his enthusiasm for being there. Parties were great when everything went his way, he thought, as he passed another girl drinking Budweiser: when no one touched his six-pack, when a cute girl flirted with him, when his mother didn't wait up and sniff his breath like a bloodhound when he got home. But they could turn from sweet to sour in an instant. An ember of hope presented itself when Josh found Steve, Todd, and Nick, illuminated by a red lightbulb hanging over the hot water heater at the end of the hallway, smoking pot. "Dude!" said Steve when he saw Josh. "What's up, man?"

"Someone drank my beer," said Josh.

"Shit," said Todd. "That is such a drag."

"Take someone else's," said Nick. "With all these chicks here, there's got to be a huge supply of, like, Amstel Light, dude."

Steve and Todd cracked up. Josh looked at the three of them and waited for someone to ask him if he wanted a hit off the roach. Even though they all knew one other, it was considered poor form to ask for it. They all stared back at him. "You are so fucking tall," said Todd, breaking into laughter. Steve and Nick joined him and Josh knew it was a lost cause. They were all too stoned to realize what pricks they were. Josh turned and walked through a doorway, finding himself on the far side of the dance floor, where Nate had been standing earlier. He was no longer there; he was slow dancing with Jenny. Josh found a piece of wall and, folding his arms across his chest, leaned against it to wait. As soon as the music stopped, Josh approached Nate, whose heavy eyes and rubbery lips broadcast his alcohol-induced relaxation. "I'm out of here," he said.

"Oh man, don't go," said Nate, hooking Jenny's trim waist with one arm.

"Jenny, can you get him home?" Josh asked.

"Yeah," said Jenny. "I need to drive Allison, too, but I can drop her off first."

The music started again and Nate groped for Jenny. "Are you drinking?" shouted Josh.

"Nursing one," Jenny shouted back, showing Josh her beer can.

"Cool," said Josh. "Thanks."

Josh cut a path through the middle of the room. He grabbed his coat from the pile on top of the washer and dryer and walked out the sliding door, pulling it closed behind him. The relative quiet soothed him, as did the cold, clean air. He walked back along the crunchy trail of footprints to his car and started the engine. It was just ten o'clock; he had no interest in going home. He pulled out onto the road and drove; ten minutes later, he was in front of Nate's house, Lauren's house, and the lights were on. Josh drove up the driveway and parked in front of the garage. He got out of the car and walked along the shoveled path to the back of the house. Almost to the back door, he could see into the kitchen. Lauren, wearing pink gingham pajama pants and a Nike T-shirt, was sitting at the kitchen table eating a bowl of ice cream. Her hair was down, framing her face before spilling over her shoulders. At school, she wore it up in a tight ponytail Josh was always tempted to tug whenever he passed her in the hallways. He hesitated for only a moment before knocking on the thick glass panel separating them. Visibly startled, Lauren shifted her attention to the door. When she saw Josh, she got up, deactivated the alarm, and opened the door. "You scared me," she said, one hand covering her heart.

"I'm sorry," said Josh. "I didn't really think you'd be here. Didn't you go to the movies?"

"I was supposed to go to the movies," said Lauren, shutting the door behind Josh. "My idiot friends got last-minute dates and blew me off."

"That sucks," said Josh. "I would have gone with you."

"Oh yeah," said Lauren, sitting back down at the table, "and not gone to the party."

"Yeah, well, the party sucked, too," said Josh, pulling off his coat.

"Where's Nate?"

"Still there," said Josh. "Jenny's going to give him a ride home."

"So, why didn't you stay?" asked Lauren, putting a spoonful of ice cream into her mouth.

"Because someone drank my beer and there was no way I could talk to Allison Haynes all night without some kind of buzz."

Lauren laughed and held up her bowl. "Do you want some?"

"Sure," said Josh. "Thanks."

Lauren got up and got the Brownie Batter ice cream her grandmother had bought out of the freezer. She scooped some into a bowl, put the carton away, and set the bowl in front of Josh. Josh looked at the ice cream, then looked back at Lauren. "Can I have a spoon?" he said, smiling. "I know where they are, but you're already up." As Lauren walked back across the room for a spoon, she considered her outfit. Being seen in pajamas wasn't the best option, but it was far better than being seen in sweats or mismatched home-all-day-on-the-weekend clothes. She thought about pulling her hair back and wrapping it with the coated elastic around her wrist, but decided to leave it alone. Josh never saw her this way.

"So," said Josh, taking the spoon from Lauren when she returned and scooping up some ice cream, "why don't you go on dates?"

"Because nobody asks me?" said Lauren.

"And why's that?"

Lauren shrugged, putting a small spoonful of ice cream into her mouth.

"Because everyone knows you're wild about Judd Acker?"

Lauren's face got hot and pink. "What's that got to do with anything?"

"It's got everything to do with everything," said Josh. "If boys know you're interested in someone else, why in the world would they ask you out?"

Lauren took another bite of ice cream. "Because I'm cute?"

"You are very cute."

Lauren cocked her head at Josh, wondering if he was teasing her, but he looked very serious. Never breaking eye contact, Josh switched chairs and sat next to Lauren. He smiled at her, then lightly kissed her forehead. Lauren shut her eyes. He kissed the tip of her nose. Lauren breathed in deeply. He kissed her mouth, and then kissed it again. "Oh God," said Lauren, barely above a whisper.

"Oh God, what?" whispered back Josh, inches from her face.

"That felt so good," said Lauren, opening her eyes.

"Well, good," said Josh, "because there's more where that came from."

Lauren laughed, which make Josh laugh. "Why did you kiss me?"

"Because I wanted to," said Josh. "Did you want me to?"

"Oh yeah," said Lauren. "I wanted you to. This is just so weird. I mean, you're my brother's best friend."

"I don't talk about you with him."

"You want to keep it a secret?"

"Keep what a secret?" asked Josh.

"This," said Lauren.

"What?" asked Josh.

"Don't tease me."

Josh put his hand under Lauren's chin. "When I ask you to go somewhere and you say yes—if you say yes—it will no longer be a secret."

"Are you going to ask me to go somewhere?"

"Yes," said Josh, pulling back. "Let's go into the den and watch TV."

"I'm in my pajamas," said Lauren.

"Consider yourself lucky," said Josh, standing. "I wish I were in mine."

They walked down the short hallway at the back of the house and into the Baronses' den, a room Josh had been in many times, watching TV with Nate. Even though Nate had a television in his room and an extravagant entertainment center in his basement, Josh preferred the den's comfortable leather furniture and close atmosphere. "Are you cold?" he asked.

"A little," said Lauren, arms crossed over her chest.

Josh took a blanket out of the antique wood chest at the end of the couch and then sat down. "Sit with me," he said to her. She sat down next to him and he covered both of them with the blanket. He reached for the remote on the glass coffee table, turned on the TV, and then wrapped his right arm around Lauren's shoulders and drew her to him. He brushed her hair from her face with his fingers.

"What do you want to watch?" asked Lauren.

"Anything," said Josh. "I'll watch anything you want to watch."

An hour later, Josh heard a knocking sound. "What's that?"

"Someone's at the door," said Lauren, getting up.

They walked through the hallway to the front door. Jenny's face was framed in the beveled glass, her breath fogging the lower half. Lauren opened the door. "I need help," said Jenny. "Nate's had too much to drink."

Lauren looked past Jenny to the front driveway, where Nate, with his head at an uncomfortable-looking angle against the headrest, was slumped in the passenger seat of her car.

"Can he walk?" asked Josh, moving through the doorway.

"Not very well," said Jenny, following him. "It took two guys to get him into the car."

Josh walked the short distance to the car and leaned down to talk to his friend. "Nate," he said. "You're home, buddy. Let's go."

Nate opened his eyes and looked up. Unable to focus on Josh's face, his eyes gave up and rolled back in their sockets. "I'm fucked up, man," he said.

"I know," said Josh, bending down and putting his arm around Nate's shoulder to ease him out of the seat.

"Everything is fucking spinning," said Nate.

"Let's get some air," said Josh. "What you need is some fresh air."

"No," said Nate. "What I need is a large pizza. Will you call for me?"

"Yes," said Josh. "We'll get you inside, and then I'll call." Josh pulled him out of the car easily enough but, not expecting to completely support 160 pounds, lost control. Nate sank to the ground. "Maybe you're the one who drank my beer," said Josh, teasing his friend as he leaned over to help him up.

"That's possible," said Nate. "I'm quite sure, at this point, that I had more than my share."

"Up we go, pal," said Josh, lifting Nate from behind. "Let's get you moving." With Josh half-carrying him, Nate made it to the front steps.

"Maybe we can make him some coffee or something," said Jenny.

Josh pulled Nate through the front door and into the hallway, where Eileen, in a white terry-cloth bathrobe, was now standing. Nate looked at her and said, "Oh shit," and then threw up.

CHAPTER 11

With a glass of pinot grigio in her hand, Ann lay back on the fluffed pillows of the king-sized bed, admiring her fresh manicure. A ninety-minute massage had taken care of the company jet ride ache in her lower back, and her legs still tingled and glistened from their waxing and conditioning treatment. Tomorrow, she would immerse herself in a rejuvenating body bath, guaranteed to restore youthful oils and nutrients, followed by a butt polish. Finally, some attention to her needs. Ann took another sip of wine and closed her eyes.

Minutes later, Mike walked in the room from their bathroom, wearing a towel around his waist. That afternoon, he'd spent an hour with the tennis pro, an hour with a massage therapist, and $6,000 in the men's shop. He smiled at his wife as he stood over the bed. "Don't you look like a new man," she said.

"I feel better than I've felt in months."

"See?" said Ann. "It's like pulling teeth to get you away from the office, but whenever I do, you're grateful, aren't you?"

"I am indeed," he said, removing his towel to dry his hair. "There's just one more thing that could make me the most grateful man on the planet."

"Really?" asked Ann.

Mike dropped his towel to the carpet, sat down, and stroked one of her exposed legs. "Your thighs are perfect."

"They ought to be," said Ann, finishing the wine. "God knows I work them."

"I can work them, too, you know," said Mike, climbing onto the bed.

"Mmmm," said Ann, setting her glass down on the bedside table. "I know you can." He straddled his naked body over hers, and she wrapped her arms around his neck. "You're the only man who turns me on," she whispered.

"Oh God," said Mike, entering her.

It's so easy, thought Ann as Mike rocked back and forth. A few words, a touch here and there, a well-timed moan; it took ten minutes. Early in their marriage, Ann had tried to inject her own sense of romance into their relationship. She held his hand whenever they walked together. She wrapped his arm around her when they sat on the couch watching TV. She told him how much she loved fresh flowers—all in the hopes that he would realize it was his attention she sought. She wanted him to think about her, for thirty seconds even, think about what she wanted or what would please her. His attention, when he looked at and listened to her with intensity, was much more of a turn-on for Ann than his naked body. They approached their physical relationship from opposite ends: she wanted to feel loved before they had sex, and Mike thought sex was the proof.

For a while, Ann had tried a few "No Fail" options described in a Valentine's Day article in a women's magazine: watching sports on TV with him, giving him back rubs, calling him at work to tell him she was thinking about him. *Shower him with your affection, and he will shower you with his* (Suggestion #6). He seemed to appreciate these efforts, especially the back rubs, but they didn't change his behavior. In his defense, he had always been that way. He had never been the suitor with a bouquet of red roses, offering instead a post-hockey game freshly showered body and a six-pack of beer. And Ann had fallen just the same.

While Mike groaned, Ann decided what she was going to wear to dinner. After, Mike lay on his side, looking at his wife's naked body. "What are you thinking?" she asked.

"About last year's fourth quarter," said Mike.

"Well," said Ann. "There's an honest answer."

"And?"

"It's okay to be satisfied, Mike. To linger in the moment rather than launch yourself into the last or the next business quarter."

"Because you're basking in postcoital bliss right now? Tell me you weren't just deciding which shoes you're going to wear to dinner." Ann wrapped her robe around her and sat on the edge of the bed. Mike reached out, his long arm just an inch or two short of touching her. "Hey," he said, gently. "We're on vacation. Just relax."

Ann rubbed her temples. The light buzz from the wine circulating earlier had settled there, threatening, a storm cloud on the horizon. "I'm going to take a bath," she said, reaching for her wineglass, looking for the on switch. "Then we should probably get ready for dinner."

"I'll get you some," said Mike, sitting up and taking the glass from his wife. "Go get in the tub."

Mike got out of bed and walked naked to the wet bar, where he poured himself a scotch. He took a sip, concentrating on the warmth of the liquid as it traveled from his mouth, down his throat, and into his gut. One of the best things about vacation was the freedom to drink whatever and whenever he chose. He'd had a martini at lunch and a beer after tennis and it didn't matter to anyone. He had no meetings scheduled. He had no phone calls to make until tomorrow. He had nothing and no one except his uptight but very sexy wife to attend to. Pleasing her was no less challenging than satisfying his stockholders.

Her demands were different now that they were approaching middle age. She examined her face every night in the bathroom mirror, lamenting the inevitable "aging process" and rubbing expensive cream into the tiny lines around her eyes and mouth before yanking the occasional gray hair from her scalp. Her obsession with being thin had burgeoned over the last few years, with exercise and diet knocking everything else off her priority list. And the children, as teenagers, didn't need or want her in their lives.

When Nate and Lauren were young, they defined her mission, perhaps even more than other mothers because getting pregnant had been difficult with Ann's endometriosis. And as a mother of young children, Ann had been playful, silly even, like she was in college when they first met. She was competitive and determined as well, capable of outdoing and outshining those who challenged her. And it was this trait that Mike most admired, that drew him to her, and made him choose her over the girls who wilted in this presence.

She was drifting now, his stalwart wife, searching for what mattered. And he could not help her, either define it or acquire it. She would find her ground, but she would do it as she did most things, on her terms and by herself.

Mike took another sip of scotch; his thoughts switched to work and the juxtaposition of where he was that moment and what he was usually doing. The pressures on him were continual, like the chemicals running through a pipeline in one of his manufacturing plants, twenty-four hours a day, seven days a week. He poured Ann a half glass of wine. And there was certainly no room for drinks in that design. At business lunches, he sipped mineral water. Those who chose less wisely quickly lost the thread of the conversation, nodding their heads in false comprehension while he steered the discussion. Mike walked Ann's wine into the bathroom, where he found her sitting in a bubble bath, surrounded by candles. He handed her the glass, wrapped a fresh towel around his waist, and then sat down on the pink marble steps leading up to the tub.

"Did you drink the other half?" she asked.

"There is plenty more where that came from, Ann. Pace yourself."

"We're on vacation, remember?"

"Which means you can drink yourself into a stupor?"

"No," said Ann. "I didn't mean that."

"What did you mean?"

"Never mind," she said. "If you're going to play Alcohol Cop, I can't stop you."

"Somebody's got to," he said, drinking his scotch. "At some point you need to realize that she who drinks the most wine and champagne does not necessarily win."

"Win what?"

"Exactly," said Mike.

"Can we stop now?"

"Yes," he said, knowing her overindulgence with alcohol was part of her search. Yet whether or not this dependency would fade was far more troublesome to him than her excessive exercise and shopping. Her drinking was escalating in spite of, or perhaps due to, his periodic lectures.

They sat in silence.

"Thank you for taking me away," Mike said, changing a tired subject. "I'm enjoying this immensely."

Ann took a sip of her wine, then set the glass down on the edge of the tub. "We really have to do this more often."

"Let's do that."

"You say that," said Ann, "but you don't mean it."

"I do mean it," said Mike. "This life looks pretty good compared to working my ass off."

"Retire," said Ann impulsively.

"At forty-six?"

"It's not like we need the money," said Ann, reaching for her glass.

"The way you spend it," said Mike, smiling, "we could always use more money. And as much as work is constant, it is rewarding. I work with a great bunch of guys and I'd miss that. What would we do with ourselves?"

"Travel the world," said Ann.

"You've seen quite a bit of the world already."

"The world's a big place."

"And we've got lots of time. The kids will both be out of the house in a few years and then we'll have no ties whatsoever."

"God, I dream about that," said Ann. "A quiet, clean house—

no fighting, no talking back, no lying. Of course, we'd have that already if you'd just said yes to boarding school."

Mike stood and stretched his arms over his head. "And we've had this conversation a thousand times," he said. "No go."

"We could send them to the best schools in the country," said Ann.

"I know that," said Mike, looking into the mirror behind the tub and wondering if he should shave again.

"And?" asked Ann.

"As you already know, I spent my entire childhood at boarding school," said Mike, rubbing his chin to assess the stubble. "I won't do that to my kids. End of discussion."

Ann took another sip of her wine. "Fine then," she said. Mike glanced down at her. "You definitely need to shave," she said, sinking lower into the tub.

"Okay," said Mike, dropping his towel to the heated floor. "I'm going to take a quick shower, then dress for dinner. What's the drill for tonight?"

"Formal," said Ann. "Wear your tux. I got you a new tie and cummerbund."

"Not floral," he said, turning on the shower.

"MacAndrews plaid," said Ann. "You'll look fabulous."

At dinner, they sat with the same three couples as the previous night. Ann had requested major league players at their table and she was not disappointed. Then again, most of the people who stayed in five-star resorts didn't have their money in 529 college funds—like most Dilloway people at home. Those Midwestern wives had absolutely no fashion sense, thinking Talbots was an upscale place to buy clothes and jewelry. Sometimes three or four showed up to the same company dinner in their new faux pearl earring and necklace sets. Awkward in social situations above them, they blushed frequently and seldom talked. When one did speak, it was often a failed attempt to sound up-to-date on current politics or an ignorant compliment on Ann's outfit. And their husbands were, in some ways, harder to take. They spent the evening trying to outdo one another in the presence of the big boss. "You know Mike," one would say, before launching into a supposedly impromptu economic theory that everyone within earshot knew he'd rehearsed at home. Ann had to resist the urge to shoo such people away like fruit flies from ripe bananas. This crowd wasn't like that. They all had money and power, although by Ann's quick calculations, not quite as much as she and Mike, the Big Cheeses.

After dinner, they all danced to Tunes by Taylor, a fabulous deejay who played music from the 1970s through the 1990s. Ann had always been an avid fan of eighties pop. Duran Duran, Boy George, Fine Young Cannibals, the Bangles—she could shake her bones to anything with a beat. Again and again, she pulled Mike away from business conversation with the boys to romp and stomp on the dance floor. She sang the words, clapped her hands over her head, and let the champagne she'd drunk at dinner work its magic. The disco ball hung from the ceiling sent circles of colored light spinning around the room, while Mike, a capable dancer, spun Ann around the floor.

Back at the table, they had brandy. Everyone was in a good mood, such a good mood that Ann decided to share some bawdy stories from college. She had them all in stitches with her favorite—Pencil Dick—when the first wave of nausea hit. She stopped abruptly and looked at Mike. He said something to her that she couldn't understand. When the second wave came, she stood up. Excusing herself, she walked as fast as she could around tables and people to the nearest exit. Gagging, she threw herself through the French doors out onto the terrace where they'd had cocktails several hours earlier. Across the flagstones and out onto the grass, Ann ran with her hand over her mouth. She ducked behind a hedge just as the evening's festivities roared out of her like water released from an uncapped fire hydrant. Falling to her knees, she retched again and again, into the bushes. A few minutes later, Mike found her, picked her up, and carried her through a back hallway and up two flights of stairs to their room. Closing the door behind them with his foot, he walked her to the bed and set her down gently. "Where is everyone?" asked Ann sleepily.

"Still at the table, I would presume," said Mike, undoing his tie. "Are you all right?"

"I'm drunk," said Ann.

"Well, yes," said Mike. "I think everyone knows that."

"How do they know?" asked Ann, shielding her eyes from the light when Mike turned on the bedside table lamp.

"Pencil Dick's a pretty good barometer for that sort of thing," he said.

"Oh shit," said Ann, rolling over and hiding her face in the pillows. "How will I face them again?"

"I told them you were on medication," said Mike. "They all seemed to understand completely."

"Why did you let me drink so much?"

"I think you did it all by yourself," said Mike, helping Ann out of her dress.

"I was having such a good time," said Ann. "Until I threw up."

"Well, yes," said Mike.

"What time is it?" asked Ann as Mike pulled back the duvet for her.

Mike looked at his watch. "It's time for bed."

Ann awoke early the next morning with a hazy, hot, throbbing head that felt like it weighed a hundred pounds. With her eyes still shut, she lifted it off the pillow, making it pulsate. She slowly put it back down. "Oh God."

Mike rolled over to face her.

"I think I'm going to die," she whispered.

"I would imagine you do," said Mike, getting out of bed and walking into the bathroom. "How many do you need?"

"Four."

Mike returned with a glass of water and four Advil. He handed them to Ann, who put them in her mouth and swallowed them. She then drank the water.

"Thank God for hangovers," said Mike.

"That's mean."

"No, Ann, that's justice. You've got to learn when to stop," he said. "And it's not my job, it's yours."

"But I've been so good."

"You have been okay. Since your parents arrived, you've been a bit better about watching your intake."

"I just let loose last night, Mike," said Ann. "You have to give me a longer leash when I'm away from home."

"Your leash is as long as you make it," he said. "I cannot be your babysitter."

"You're mad at me."

"I'm not mad at you, Ann. I am simply frustrated by your lack of control. Because you decided to let loose last night, I will have breakfast without you, and our final vacation day will be spent with your hangover concerns."

Ann rolled over, away from Mike. "Are we done?"

"For now," said Mike. "But we aren't really done until you're done."

"Fine," she said. "I'll never drink again."

Mike smiled. "You'll have a glass of wine in your hand by five o'clock today."

Ann rolled over and looked at him out of one eye. "You don't think I can go one day?"

"No, I don't."

Ann's gut tightened. "What's riding on it?" she asked.

"A blow job," said Mike. "The blow job you promised to give me this morning."

Ann searched her disconnected brain for the section that controlled memory. Had she said that? She licked her dry lips. "And what do I get if I win?"

"New shoes," said Mike, "from Paris. And you can fly there to find the perfect pair."

"You're on," said Ann, picturing the strappy gold sandals she had seen on a Hollywood actress at a gala. She then told Mike she desperately needed a bubble bath and room service. There was no bad hangover a white cheddar cheese, egg white omelette and a toasted English muffin with sugar-free strawberry jam couldn't cure, even though the idea of eating that much fat came close to making Ann sick again. Since she'd lost her dinner the night before, however, Ann figured she could eat whatever she wanted this morning and not gain more than eight ounces. And that she could easily shed tomorrow at the gym if she did a double session.

Mike called room service, then started Ann's bath, squirting in the organic bubble bath she'd bought at the spa the day before. He looked at his watch and debated going to breakfast with the group. There was some talk the night before about meeting at 9:30, which would give Mike thirty minutes to shower. Maybe it was best to just leave it alone. The only one he was really interested in seeing was Paul Rosenberg's wife, Sharon, and Mike knew better than to pursue that idea. He grabbed his bathrobe and walked back into the bedroom, where Ann was sitting up.

"Your tub's ready," he said, "and your eggs are on the way. I'm going to get a Coke."

"Don't we have some in the fridge?"

"I drank them."

"You could call room service."

"Yes, but I want it now," said Mike, "not forty-five minutes from now. There's a Coke machine down the hall."

"You're going like that?"

"There are only four rooms on this floor," said Mike, opening the door. "What are the chances I'll see anyone?" Mike walked around the corner and down the hall. He took six quarters out of his pocket and put them into the Coke machine. He bent down to get the can, and then turned around to find Sharon Rosenberg standing in front of him. "Hello," he said, smiling.

"Aren't we two peas in a pod," said Sharon, wearing the same hotel-supplied bathrobe.

"Yes, we seem to be," said Mike.

"I had fun last night," she said, running her fingers through her long red hair. "You're a fabulous dancer."

"You're kind," said Mike.

"Are you going to breakfast?"

"I don't think so," said Mike. "Ann isn't feeling well this morning." Sharon laughed. "I imagine not."

"Can I buy you a Coke?" asked Mike.

"Sure," said Sharon.

Mike took more quarters from his own pocket and put them into the machine. "Regular or diet?" he asked.

"Do I look like I need diet?" asked Sharon playfully.

"Absolutely not," said Mike, pushing the button and sending a can of regular crashing into the receptacle. He turned to give the can to Sharon and immediately noticed the tie to her bathrobe was undone. The sides of her robe, moments ago cinched tightly around her small waist, were now slightly parted, allowing Mike an inch glimpse of her tanned tummy. She smiled at him and reached for the can, parting her robe even farther. Mike knew he should turn from her and walk away, but he didn't.

"Paul's at a tennis lesson," offered Sharon.

"That's an early lesson," said Mike, using every bit of strength he had to look at her face and not her visible breasts.

"No one's in the room," said Sharon, fingers on her chest. "It's just down the hall. Would you like to see it?"

"Very much," said Mike, before he could stop himself. "But I've got to get back to Ann."

Sharon took a step closer to him, fingers now on his chest, and said, "Are you sure?"

Mike looked down at her and swallowed hard. He had been in this position before, but not for some time. It was a business trip, about a year ago. Ann was shopping in New York and had not been able to accompany him, but many of the other wives had tagged along with their husbands. They were all staying at a gorgeous, secluded resort in the Florida Keys, where they spent their warm days on the golf course and cool evenings eating and drinking in a private outdoor dining area. It was the youngest and most attractive wife who approached him after dinner one night. He had gone back to his room and was undoing the tie to his tuxedo when he heard a soft knock on his door. He opened it to find her standing before him in her clingy gold dress, looking like a piece of chocolate waiting to be unwrapped. She'd claimed she'd lost her way, but when Mike pointed her in the right direction, she didn't move. Instead, she suggested they have a nightcap in his room. Mike had opened his mouth to speak, having no idea what he was going to say—he still didn't know what he would have said to her, to Rachel—when she caught sight of her husband at the far end of the corridor and scurried away. And while Mike knew then as he knew now that women approached him because of his position in the company, he occasionally got caught up in the notion that he was, indeed, magnetically attractive and they couldn't stop themselves from falling for his charms. "No," said Mike, smiling. "I'm not sure, but I've got to get back."

Sharon pressed her body into his and then slowly pulled away. "Perhaps another time," she whispered.

Mike awkwardly thanked her, then turned before she could see the result of her suggestions. He walked quickly back to the room, where Ann was still in the tub. "You must have gone to the front desk for that Coke," Ann called from the bathroom.

"Something like that," said Mike, taking a sip from the can and adjusting his hard-on in his boxers.

"Are my eggs here yet?"

Mike looked around the room. "No," he said. "I'll call and check on them."

"Good," said Ann. "Then come in here and tell me all about last night. I can't seem to remember a thing."

Mike sat down on the bed and dialed the phone. While he waited for an answer, he thought about living in a hut in Greenland. By the time he was put on hold and then was assured the eggs would arrive within fifteen minutes, he was physiologically able to face his wife. He got off the bed and walked into the bathroom and found her—pink cream covering her face—lying up to her shoulders in bubbles.

It was always hard for Ann to leave. She loved the luxurious, pampered life expensive spas and hotels provided, preferring it to the routine of everyday life at home. She pouted as she packed her bags. "Honey," said Mike from across the bed, where he was packing his suitcase, "we can do this again."

"You say that," said Ann, "but it will be months before I can get you out of the office again."

"That's not true," said Mike gently. "We've been home so much because your parents are living with us."

Ann stopped what she was doing and looked at her husband. "What do you mean by that?"

"Exactly what I said," said Mike.

"Well, I think that's a rotten thing to say," said Ann.

"There's nothing rotten about it," said Mike, returning to his task. "It's factual."

Ann refolded a sweater she hadn't worn and put it into her large bag. "You don't want them there, do you?" she asked, her eyes on the pink sweater.

"I said nothing of the kind," said Mike. "Their presence doesn't affect my life one way or the other."

"Of course they affect our lives," said Ann. "You've got your head in the sand if you don't think so." Mike walked into the closet and grabbed his bagged tuxedo. He brought it back to the bed and set it down beside his suitcase. "Did you hear me?" said Ann, throwing her shoes into another suitcase. "I said you have your head in the sand!"

Mike walked around the bed to his wife, who was glaring at him, and put his hand on her shoulder. He knew better than to hug her, at this point. "We don't have to do this," he said softly. "We've had a lovely weekend."

Ann's eyes began to water. "Let's stay another day," she said, suddenly smiling. "We could be recklessly spontaneous and stay another day."

Mike now leaned forward and gathered her into his arms. "We'll come again," he said. "On the way out, we'll book another weekend."

"When?" asked Ann, pushing against his chest and looking at him.

"Soon," said Mike.

One of Ann's tears spilled over the rim of her eye and down her cheek.

"I hate that word," she said. "It means nothing. 'Let's get together soon!' people say when they rarely mean it. 'I'll call you soon!' promise people who've got no intention of calling at all. 'Soon, it will be just the two of us,' say married men to their mistresses, knowing they will never leave their wives. It's a hateful, deceitful, overused word that makes me crazy."

Mike took his BlackBerry off the bedside table. He looked at his calendar, then looked at Ann. "How does the weekend of March twentieth sound?"

Ann immediately brightened. "Really? Are you serious?"

"Completely."

"I think the Gallagher Gala is that weekend," said Ann, "but I don't care. What shall we do?"

"Whatever you want to do," said Mike. "I have only three or four days, so don't book us too far away."

"Do you want to come here again?"

"I'll do anything you want to do," said Mike, kissing his wife on the forehead.

"I'll ask around," said Ann. "You can leave that with me, and I'll take care of everything."

Mike kissed her on the lips. "You always do," he said.

At the airport, Ann bought a stack of teen magazines for Lauren and a Stephen King book for Nate. She always brought them a souvenir from wherever she and Mike stayed, but she had forgotten about it over the weekend. In fact, she and Mike hadn't talked about the children at all. Ann decided that was healthy, a sign that she and Mike had really needed the time away to focus on each other. She also bought a large, skim milk latte, with a half shot of sugar-free chocolate syrup and a half shot of sugar-free caramel syrup and a black coffee for Mike. "I don't know how you can drink that," said Ann, holding out the foam cup to her husband, "when you could be drinking this."

"Because I'm a boy," said Mike, folding the *Wall Street Journal* in half and setting it down on the vacant seat next to him to accept the coffee, "and you're a girl."

"That I am," said Ann, sitting down beside him.

Mike looked at his watch. "Well, in five hours we'll be home."

"Don't remind me."

"I like going home," said Mike. "I like unpacking my bags and sitting in my study. I'm at ease there."

"Of course you like sitting in your study," said Ann, cupping her hands around the latte. "That's where your computer is."

"I'll grant you that," said Mike. "It's nice to work at home."

"Not after you've put in twelve hours at the office," said Ann. "That's not nice, that's obsessed."

"And who would you rather have running the company?"

Ann put her hand on Mike's knee. "No one," she said. "You're the best big boss there is. It's just hard on me sometimes."

Mike laughed. "You poor millionairess."

Ann smiled at him. "It's not always about money."

"Really?" asked Mike, arching his eyebrows. "What then?"

Ann thought a moment and took a long drink from her cup. "Never mind," she said. "It is about money."

Mike kissed her forehead and then returned to the newspaper.

The reality of going home hit Ann again as they sat in their lounge chairs on the jet. She didn't feel in control of the decision to go home, even though she'd booked the flight with Mike's secretary for that very day. Nothing but a stack of unread newspapers and unpaid bills awaited them at home, so what was the big rush? After that came the phone calls mandated by the messages left in her absence, and the gargantuan grocery list for Emma. Lauren had probably polished off her bottled water and 100-calorie pack stash. Ann knew that before long, she would be so successfully reimmersed into her home life that she would barely remember the soft hands of the massage therapist or the state-of-the-art fitness room with a view of the San Francisco Bay. "Where's Jenna?" Ann asked Mike.

"Doing whatever flight attendants do, I guess."

"Ring for her, will you?" said Ann. "I want a drink."

"I thought you weren't drinking today."

"Oh Mike, that was hours ago," said Ann, looking out her window. "You're not going to hold me to that, are you?"

"No," said Mike, putting his BlackBerry back into his pocket. "I won't hold you to that. I will, however, hold you to your bet."

"What bet?"

"You know very well what bet."

The blow job. Oh God, she had forgotten all about the blow job.

"Well?" asked Mike.

It would take five minutes, Ann told herself. "I'll have some pinot," she said.

Mike smiled at her. "Coming right up."

CHAPTER 12

Nate opened his swollen eyes and rolled over to look at the clock. It was five in the afternoon and the pain in his head from that morning showed little sign of diminishing. He sat on the edge of his bed and rubbed his face. When he felt ready to stand, he lifted himself off the mattress, slowly walked into his bathroom, and took three Advil from the bottle on the counter. This was his third trip to the bottle that day, but the ibuprofen had still not delivered on its promise. In fact, Nate knew from experience that nothing would help except heavy, greasy food and the passing of time. Tomorrow morning—he told himself as he swallowed the medication—it would be as if the party never happened.

He walked down the stairs and into the kitchen, where he found his grandmother stirring something on the stove. He winked at her, even though she had woken him at nine o'clock that morning to clean out the garage. After that, she sent him to the grocery store with a long list of items, and after that, she told him he needed to spend a couple of hours with his grandfather. Cleaning out the garage, she told him, was penance for throwing up all over the front hall. That had been the most disagreeable thing she'd had to clean up in years. Going to the grocery store was a favor. As she had cleaned up after him, he would do something nice for her. And visiting with his grandfather was an act of kindness. It was important, she told Nate, to think beyond oneself. The people who dictated the morals and ethics of today's society didn't do enough of that.

Nate complied with his grandmother's wishes, mostly because he really did feel bad about barfing all over everything and then passing out. He still couldn't figure out why he puked. He drank five, maybe six beers. And while that was a good amount, it certainly wasn't enough to blindside him. He couldn't even remember how he got home. Jenny must have driven him because she was with him when he got sick, but he had no idea how he got from Steve's basement to his front hall.

Cleaning the garage was a piece of cake because his dad was compulsive about keeping things in order. The bright red Lamborghini sat under a protective cover in the third bay, and the Aston Martin followed suit in bay four. Why his father owned two incredibly cool and expensive cars mystified Nate. Mike took them out only three or four times a year. The rest of the time, they just sat there. Occasionally, his father took a male party guest into the garage for a cigar and a peek at them, but that was that. Still, nothing could be close to them—no bikes, no skateboards, no power scooters, no flower baskets, nothing. To that end, Mike had painted lines on the floor, between which four unused bikes leaned on their kickstands. He had also installed shelves, which he numbered, that held everything else, from the gardener's tools to the outdoor Christmas lights. Nate simply checked the master list on the garage wall to see that everything was in its place—which it was, as usual—then picked up the broom and pushed a thin layer of dust and dirt out the second bay door.

His trip to the grocery store turned out to be more enjoyable than he thought. He walked a cart up and down the aisles at a leisurely pace, checking out the products that lined the shelves like brightly colored paper box soldiers. Everything looked so good. The background music was a little lame, but the atmosphere was relaxed, soothing even. No one seemed rushed, except a couple of mothers with young, crying children. They scurried through the aisles like they were in a reality show race, throwing cans and boxes into their carts and shoving fish-shaped crackers into their toddlers' pudgy hands. When he heard them coming, Nate simply wheeled his cart to one side, letting them roar past him. And then it was peaceful again. After he bought everything on his grandmother's list, he bought a few things with his own money—chocolate-covered pretzels, Smartfood popcorn, and a six-pack of orange pop—which he decided to store in his bedroom for his occasional nocturnal hunger attacks.

When he had unpacked and put away the groceries and his treats, his grandmother thanked him, and reminded him of his final obligation: a visit with his grandfather. Selma, Eileen said, had been with him all weekend and could most likely use a little fresh air. Eileen didn't care what Nate and Sam did—they could watch TV, have a snack, read the newspaper—but she expected Nate to spend two hours with him. After that, Eileen said Nate could take a nap. Selma, who had been filled in on the plan, grabbed her coat from the closet when Nate knocked on the guesthouse door. She put her finger to her lips. "He's sleeping," she whispered as she opened the door.

"Perfect," said Nate, who thought he might get his nap early.

"There are some chocolate chip cookies on the counter," she said, easing her coat over her shoulders. "They're your grandfather's favorite."

"Mine, too," said Nate, taking off his jacket and hanging it on the hanger that had just held Selma's.

"You'll be here for a couple of hours?" she asked, looking at her watch.

"That's the plan," said Nate.

"Have fun," she said on her way out.

When Nate heard the click of the latch, he turned from the door and walked into the living room. "That," he said, flopping down on the couch and putting a pillow under his head, "should not be a problem." He took the remote control from the coffee table and clicked through several stations: movie, shopping channel, cooking, weather, movie, movie, Spanish channel. He settled on golf, even though he thought the game was a huge waste of time and nothing close to a real sport like football. What he loved about it was listening to the whispering commentators; they made him sleepier than Mrs. Annon's English class lectures. He woke with a start to find his grandfather standing over him.

"What are you doing here?" asked Sam.

"I'm here for a visit," said Nate, sitting up. "I guess I fell asleep."

"I do a lot of that," said Sam.

"I'm still tired," said Nate, yawning and looking up at Sam. "Do you want to sleep some more?"

"I'd love to," said Sam, shuffling back toward the bedroom, "but there's no time for that. We have to be at the airport in an hour."

Oh shit, thought Nate. "What airport?" he called, getting off the couch and following Sam into the bedroom, where a small canvas suitcase with leather trim was sitting on the bed. The only things in it were a toothbrush, three pairs of black socks, and a book about space travel.

"The airport we always go to," said Sam. "I'm almost packed. How about you?"

Nate looked at Sam and knew he was serious. "It won't take me long to pack. I just have to confirm the flight first."

"Good thinking, young man," said Sam. "Do you have the number?"

"Oh yes," said Nate. "It's in my head." Nate walked into the kitchen and sat down in the chair next to the phone. He dialed the 800 number of Columbia House and listened to the recording. When prompted, he punched in his membership number and ordered three DVDs. When Sam called, "Is it on time?" from the other room, Nate grabbed a pad and pencil from the counter and wrote down a bogus flight number. He also wrote the words FLIGHT CANCELLED—TECHNICAL DIFFICULTIES, which he showed to Sam, who had made his way across the living room carpet onto the tile floor in the kitchen and was now standing at his side. Nate hung up the phone.

"Technical difficulties?" asked Sam. "What kind of excuse is that?"

"I guess it's a pretty good one when it comes to planes," said Nate. "You wouldn't want to get on a faulty airliner."

"I don't think there's any such thing," said Sam, batting the air with one hand. "It's a conspiracy, son. The government is so concerned now with the comings and goings of normal citizens that, I think, it randomly cancels commercial airline flights."

"I had no idea," said Nate.

"Most people don't," said Sam. "It's a well-kept secret. Did they say when the next flight was scheduled to go?"

"No," said Nate, jerking his head to the side to move his bangs off his face. "They said nothing about that."

"It figures," said Sam dejectedly. "The inconvenience to John Q. Public means nothing whatsoever to the United States of America."

"How about a cookie?" asked Nate.

"I'd love one," said Sam, "but first I'm going to call that airline and give them a piece of my mind."

"You can do that," said Nate. "But if the U.S. government is the culprit, aren't you simply shooting the messenger?"

"Good point," said Sam. "I'll call the White House."

"I think it's closed on Sunday," said Nate.

"Isn't that just perfect," said Sam sarcastically. "What if there was a national emergency on a Sunday, another Pearl Harbor?"

Nate shrugged, then crossed the kitchen and grabbed the plate of cookies Selma had left for them on the counter. He brought them back to the table, where Sam was leafing through the yellow pages of the Michigan phone book. "Let's have some cookies," he said, holding out the plate to his grandfather. "Do you want milk?"

"Absolutely," said Sam, showing the first smile Nate had seen that afternoon. "A nice, tall, cold glass of milk would hit the spot right about now."

"Coming right up," said Nate, walking to the fridge for the half-gallon jug.

"Wow," said Sam, biting into a cookie. "That's the best cookie I've ever had."

"That's good news," said Nate, bringing the glasses of milk to the table. "I could use a good cookie right now."

Sam chuckled. "That's very funny," he said.

"Well, thank you," said Nate, chewing.

Sam took another cookie and put the whole thing in his mouth. After he finished chewing, he sat back in his chair. "So," he said, "what are we going to do about this trip?"

"Not go?" asked Nate.

"That's a defeatist attitude that I didn't expect from you."

"What do you want to do?"

"I think we should go," said Sam. "I'm all packed. Let's just get in the car and go."

"Where, exactly, is it you want to go?"

Sam looked surprised. "To the meeting, of course."

"Which meeting?"

"Oh, for Christ's sake, son, the farm insurance meeting in Hartford."

"Oh, that meeting."

"Do you want to drive, or shall I?" asked Sam, pushing back from the table.

"I'll drive," said Nate. "Let's get your bag."

"Now you're talking," said Sam, rubbing his hands together. "It will be an adventure. I haven't taken a road trip in years."

Nate followed Sam back into the bedroom, where the suitcase lay untouched. Sam closed the top and pushed the brass flipper latches down until they clicked. "Do you have everything you need?" asked Nate.

"I like to travel light," said Sam.

"We're off then."

"What about your bag?" asked Sam.

"It's up at the big house," said Nate. "I'll run and get it and then come back here to get you." Nate jogged up the path to his parents' house and into the kitchen, where his grandmother and sister were sitting at the kitchen table playing cards.

"How's it going?" asked Eileen.

"Fine," said Nate. "Do you mind if I take him for a drive?"

"No," said Eileen. "Do you want company?"

"Nope," said Nate, grabbing his keys from the wicker basket and his backpack from the floor. "We're going on an adventure."

"Well, have fun," said Eileen, smiling.

Nate ran back down the path to the guesthouse, where his grandfather was standing in the front entrance with the suitcase in his hand. Nate held up his backpack. "I'm all set," he said.

"Let's go!" Sam said. "Let's get out of here before we change our minds."

"Good plan," said Nate, taking Sam's suitcase and leading the way to the garage. Halfway there, Nate realized Sam was not beside him. He turned around and discovered his grandfather had made very little progress from the front door. Sam moved slowly even though he looked like he was moving as fast as he could. Stooped with his eyes to the ground, he shambled along the sidewalk, an old man on an urgent trip to nowhere. It would have been hilarious, Nate thought, if it hadn't been so terribly sad. Nate walked back to meet him. "The first thing we should do," said Nate, taking his arm, "is fill the tank with gas."

"Excellent idea," said Sam, winded. "I always fill up at the beginning of a trip. That way, you can accurately calculate the gas mileage."

"That's right," said Nate, walking at Sam's pace. "I'll leave that to you, if you don't mind."

"I'd be honored," said Sam.

They walked the rest of the way to the garage in silence. Finally there, Nate punched the code into the keypad and the large steel door began to rise. Sam ducked, even though they were nowhere near the moving metal, and didn't straighten up until the gear box lifting the door stopped grinding. They walked inside and split company—Nate moving toward his car and Sam moving toward the Lamborghini. He lifted the protective covering and peeked underneath. "Let's take this one," he said.

Nate laughed. "You have good taste, Gramps," he said. "My father, however, would kill us both." Nate led Sam instead to his silver BMW and opened the passenger door. Sam ducked his head, but not quite far enough, and bumped it on the car's cloth hood.

After the impact, he reeled backward. Nate dropped the suitcase and caught him, almost falling to the floor himself. "Are you okay?"

"I'm fine," said Sam, holding his forehead with one hand. "I have no idea why that happened."

"It happens to lots of people," said Nate. "Let's try again."

Nate put his hand on top of Sam's head and guided it under the roof of the car like a police officer would a crime suspect. Next, he helped him swing his body around so he could ease himself down to the seat. Once seated, Sam told Nate he was fine. Nate buckled his seat belt, then grabbed Sam's suitcase and put it and his backpack in the trunk. He hopped into the driver's side of the car and turned on the engine before he realized his grandfather's legs were still hanging out the passenger side. *This,* thought Nate, *is where caregivers lose it.* He'd seen the stories on various news shows, depicting the abuse of the elderly. Grown-ups hit, pushed, and slapped their husbands, their wives, their mothers and fathers, or their paid responsibilities, treating them like misbehaving toddlers who couldn't understand instruction. And, if Nate had had an even larger headache than he did, he might have walked around to the other side of the car and roughly adjusted his grandfather's legs. But something stopped him. Perhaps it was because they had all the time in the world. They weren't on their way—late now—to a doctor's appointment or another scheduled event; they were embarking on a fictitious adventure. What did it matter? When Nate did walk around to the passenger side, he gently lifted Sam's legs and tucked them into the car. "All set?" he asked, when he was again sitting in the driver's seat.

"Ready to roll," said Sam. "Where are we going?"

"That," said Nate, backing the car out of the garage, "is a very good question."

Nate chose Route 10, which quickly took them out of town and into the country. Nate drove out there occasionally with Jenny, who loved animals. The more cows and chickens she saw, the more likely she would consent to a make-out session on an old dirt access road. They drove past farm after farm in silence until Sam urgently beckoned Nate to pull over and stop the car. "Back up," he said.

Nate put the car in REVERSE and backed slowly along the deep irrigation ditch at the side of the road. A hundred yards back, Sam again asked Nate to stop the car as he pointed at a white clapboard farmhouse set back from the road. "That's my house," Sam said. 'I'm sure of it."

"Gramps," said Nate, "you grew up in Pennsylvania. This is Michigan."

"Then somebody moved my house," said Sam, still pointing. "That's where I grew up."

"Okay," said Nate neutrally.

Sam turned to look at Nate. "Can we go in?" he asked quietly.

Nate looked into his grandfather's eyes and saw, more than anything else, fear. Was he afraid Nate would say no, or was he afraid of something else, less tangible or inexplicable? "Sure," said Nate, turning the car around.

"Do you think my mother's home?"

"No," Nate said. "But someone else might be there."

Nate pulled the car into the rutted driveway and stopped next to the worn, warped brick walk that led to the front door. He helped Sam up and out of the seat to a standing position. "Do I look all right?" asked Sam, reaching up but not quite touching his hair.

"You look great, Gramps," said Nate. "Let's go."

Together they walked slowly along the salted path and up three cracked cement steps to the front door. Nate pushed the doorbell button. A middle-aged woman, wearing jeans and a red turtleneck, partially obscured by a brown and white bib apron with little skipping bears along its waistline, opened the door and smiled at them. "Hello," she said.

"Hello," said Nate. "I'm Nate Barons and this is my grandfather, Sam Sanford. He grew up in Pennsylvania, but he thinks he may have grown up in this house."

"I did grow up in this house," said Sam.

The woman looked at Nate and then Sam. Her eyes lingered there, as if she were trying to read Sam's mind. Soon enough, she stepped aside and pushed the door open wider. "Would you like to come in?" she asked. "I've got some brownies in the oven that are just about ready."

"I love brownies," said Sam, lifting his foot to step up into the house.

"We won't stay long," said Nate apologetically.

"It's no trouble," said the woman, leading them into the living room, where she took their coats and laid them over the back of a large, overstuffed armchair. "The house was built in the nineteen-twenties by two brothers. One of the brothers lived here for fifty years; the other brother lived in the house next door, which is the one they built just after this one. You can see it through the window over the couch." Sam took the few steps to the couch, then peered out the window. Across a lawn, maybe seventy yards away, was another house that looked very similar to this one, only it was different. "They're opposites," said the woman. "The square footage is the same. The layout is opposite."

"That's clever," said Sam. "They're the same, but they're different."

"Exactly," said the woman, walking toward a doorway. "You wait here. I've got to check those brownies."

"Who lives there?" called Sam after her.

"The Taylors," she called back. "They're actually the ones I'm making the brownies for. It's my turn for dessert." A long minute later, she walked back into the living room. "I've set them on the counter to cool. Let's sit a few minutes and then I can give you hungry travelers one for the road." Nate sat down next to his grandfather on the couch. "What looks familiar to you?" the woman asked Sam. Sam stared at her blankly.

And then they all looked around the room. The walls were covered with paper that featured what might have been tiny pink roses, but it was hard to tell, as whatever was there had faded into tan dots. Sheer curtains, lifeless without a summer breeze, hung at the windows, just like those from Sam's childhood. The navy blue couch they sat on had worn arms and cushions and a number of visible stains, in spite of its dark color. Sam wondered if over the years people had gathered for Saturday night dinner parties and eaten as they sat upon it. He could picture them, awkwardly holding china plates on their laps, gasping when they dropped a chunk of lasagna, a dribble of coffee, or a bite of cheesecake. After school, the children, with small bowls of buttered popcorn on blue-jeaned laps, had watched cartoons, absentmindedly eating their snack. Sometimes the popped kernel had gone into their mouths, and sometimes it had gone into the couch. Sam shook his head. While he had grown up sitting on a similar couch, it had been, most definitely, light brown.

Nate saw the stains on the couch, too. They matched the stains on the chair across the room that held their coats. And that was all that matched. It was as if the furniture had been purchased separately, one garage sale at a time. It was inviting furniture, not like the arranged pieces in a showroom window, and certainly nothing like what filled the living room in his parents' house. That furniture, while attractive to the eye, was not welcoming to the body. And no one with a piece of chocolate cake or a mug of tomato soup would dream of sitting on his mother's white living room furniture. Nate had trouble just breathing in that room. He went in there only when summoned by his parents in an attempt to impress a visiting dignitary with the domestic tranquility of the Barons family. Nate sank deeper into the couch, resisting the temptation to close his eyes. He was suddenly very tired in this stranger's house. He wondered what she'd think if he announced his intention to nap, and quickly decided she wouldn't think anything. She'd probably get him a pillow and blanket from the scarred wood hutch in the corner and tell him to rest as long as he needed. She'd encourage him to put his feet up on the couch because the wet salt on the bottom of his shoes wouldn't matter to her. And this was not because she was a slob and didn't care about her house; of course she cared. She would never apologize for its appearance because it wouldn't occur to her to do so. "Let me get those brownies," she said, standing. "Would you like a glass of milk?"

"Yes, please," said Sam like a child practicing his manners. Nate watched the woman walk into the kitchen. He looked over at Sam, who gave him a wink. "I can't believe we stumbled across my childhood house," he said. "I haven't been here in sixty years."

"It's a nice house," said Nate.

"And my daughter," said Sam, smiling. "Didn't I tell you you'd like her?" The woman walked back into the room carrying a tray, with two glasses of milk and two plates with brownies. She set the tray on the table in front of Sam and Nate, then handed each of them a plate. Sam took a huge bite, then immediately began to talk. "Who are the Taylors?" he asked, his mouth full.

"Our neighbors," said the woman. "Karen, the mother, slipped on some ice and broke her leg. She's having trouble getting around, so all of us neighbors are helping with meals for a while."

"All of you?" asked Nate.

The woman laughed. "I know what you're thinking," she said. "We live on a straight road out in the country—where's the neighborhood, right? But we do have a neighborhood, of sorts. We all look out for each other."

"Like people used to," said Sam, chewing. "Nobody looks out for neighbors anymore. They all keep to themselves."

"Not around here," said the woman. "We get together once a month for dinner, and twice every summer for picnics and games. And, of course, we see each other when we're out working in the yard or shoveling show."

Nate never saw his neighbors; he didn't even know who some of them were. It was not that the houses were all far apart. It was simply because nobody worked in their yards. The landscaping companies raked the leaves in the fall, weeded the gardens and mowed the lawns in the spring and summer, and plowed the long driveways in the winter. Two guys, in their red pickup truck, washed the windows, outside and inside, twice a year. Cleaning crews arrived on Friday mornings, just in time for weekend entertaining. (Since Emma cleaned the Baronses' house daily, the cleaning agency came just twice a month to do what his mother called "deep cleaning.") And AquaMan, in his blue van, maintained all the neighborhood pools, including the Baronses' kidney bean. Nate and Lauren had been excited about the pool at first. Their parents had even thrown a couple of pool parties the summer after they moved in. But then everyone got too busy or lost interest or something. Occasionally now, his mother would have a party around the pool, floating candles on the surface of the clear, still water, but never in July or August. Because even though Pete's Pest Control had thoroughly sprayed the yard that afternoon, the mosquitoes would inevitably drive everyone inside at dusk.

Nate did know one neighbor, Katie from next door. She was in his math class, and that was the only time he saw her. He knew she was inside the black Suburban that pulled out of their driveway every morning as he was driving out of his, but they never talked about it. He had once thought about offering her a ride to school, mostly because she was gorgeous, but had never done anything about it. Jenny probably wouldn't have liked the idea anyway. Nate finished his second brownie and swigged the last of his milk before returning the glass to the tray. "We should get going," he said, standing.

"I guess you're right," said Sam.

"Thank you for stopping by," said the woman. "It's nice to have company."

"Where is your family?" asked Sam.

"At church. There's a father/child Bible study twice a month. I just send all four kids with Bob," she said, smiling.

Sam leaned forward, grabbed the edge of the heavy oak coffee table, and then pulled himself up. His agility was like a light switch, thought Nate, on or off. "Good for you," Sam said to the woman. She took their coats from the back of the chair and handed them to Sam and Nate. Nate helped Sam with his coat. "I'm glad we came," he said, allowing Nate to zip him in. "I've missed you."

"And I you," said the woman, giving Sam a quick hug.

Nate led Sam to the front door. He thanked the woman, and then took his grandfather outside and helped him into the car. Nate backed the car out onto the road and headed for home. They rode for several minutes in silence. "I don't know why we don't go there more often," said Sam. "It's so close and we're family." Nate said nothing. "I don't even know if my mother knows about this," said Sam. "It's uncanny."

"What is?" asked Nate.

"The fact that we've had these people living in our backyard and hadn't the slightest idea."

Nate yawned. The events of the day coupled with his alcohol abuse the night before were catching up with him. All he could think about was his bed and a nap. Nate saw that Sam, too, was tired. Before Nate turned onto the main road, Sam, with his head against the window, was asleep. Ten minutes later, Nate pulled into the driveway and directly into the garage. He gently nudged Sam before helping him out of the car and along the path to the guest-house. It was an extra slow journey; Sam was still sleepy. When they reached the door, Nate led Sam inside to the couch, where he was eager to lie down. Nate covered him with a blanket. Selma, who was in the kitchen cooking, waved at him. "Thank you," said Sam softly.

"My pleasure," said Nate. "Get some rest, Gramps."

"That won't be a problem," he said, closing his eyes.

Nate nodded at Selma on his way out the front door. He walked quickly up the path to the main house. In his mother's kitchen, Eileen was making oatmeal raisin cookies. "Well, how did every-thing go?" she asked.

"Fine, Gran," said Nate. "Gramps is sleeping on the couch at your house."

"Good," said Eileen, looking at her watch. "How are you feeling?"

"Okay," said Nate. "Tired."

"Head upstairs then. You've earned your nap today."

"Thanks," he said. "I'm going up."

"Thank *you*," said Eileen, taking a tray of cookies out of the oven. "I'll wake you when your parents get home, and then we can all eat together."

Nate walked out of the kitchen, up the stairs, and down the hall-way. His hand on the doorknob, Nate turned his head when his sis-ter called him. She was standing just outside her room. "Josh called," she said.

"How would you know?"

"Because I talked to him."

"You answered my phone?" asked Nate, patting his empty pockets.

"No," said Lauren. "He called on my phone."

"Why would he do that?"

Lauren wondered how much, if anything, Nate remembered from the night before. She shrugged. "I guess he couldn't get in touch with you."

"What did he want?"

"To talk to you, I guess," said Lauren.

Nate walked into his room and closed his door behind him. He looked for and found his cell phone, sitting on his desk. It was off. Too exhausted to check his messages, Nate took off his jeans and slid into his bed, where he pulled his down comforter up to his chin. Within seconds, he was warm. If someone offered him a million dollars, in cash, he wouldn't have moved from that bed.

CHAPTER 13

Mike pulled his Jaguar out of the executive parking garage and circled around to pick up Ann and their bags at the curb. The lightly falling snow pleased him, even though he knew it would depress Ann. He liked winter in Michigan, where the ground was covered from early November to late March, and his car seat heaters and vents were the only source of outside warmth. It was scientifically proven that humans were more effective, more alert in cooler temperatures—perhaps an ancient survival technique. Mike's office thermostat was set at sixty-seven degrees all year; frequent visitors knew to keep their suit jackets on. On the other end of the spectrum was Ann, who craved sunshine and warm weather, a bad match for half of the year. They had a condominium in the Florida Keys, but managed to get there only a few times a year. Occasionally, Ann flew down with a few of her friends. But her parents moving in had put an end to that. Then again, her parents moving in had put an end to a number of things. The changes were real, but hard to name, like a lost thought.

Ann had told him it would be easy, that having her parents live with them would change very little. And in some ways, she was right. Sam and Eileen did, in fact, spend most of their time in the guesthouse. And Selma, for the most part, took care of them by attending to the grocery shopping, cooking (with Eileen, Mike guessed, usually by her side), cleaning, and watching over Sam (again, with Eileen's conscientious guidance and assistance). Ann's parents didn't go out much, which didn't affect Mike one way or the other. At work most of the time, Mike saw very little of them. And Lauren and Nate had stopped complaining about them.

It was Ann who was different and, even though Mike couldn't describe how, he knew she wasn't the same. For example, she didn't want to go out to dinner several times a week anymore, and yet she hated eating at home night after night. She didn't take off with her friends for days at a time, and yet she resented not going. She loved it when people complimented her on inviting her parents to stay, and yet she found their presence burdensome. Sam and Eileen brought hardship with them, which no one in the Barons family had felt for years, his wife in particular.

Mike pulled up to the curb and got out. As he loaded their bags into the trunk, Ann sat down in the car and turned up the heat. She shivered, though she was wrapped in fur from her neck to her ankles. Mike got back in the car and drove out of the airport and onto the expressway. "Let's go to Café Annette," said Ann, reapplying lipstick in the visor mirror.

Mike looked at the car clock. "Really?" he asked, surprised.

"Really," said Ann, taking her phone out of her purse. "I'll call and see if they've got a table."

"I thought your mother was expecting us for dinner."

"She is," said Ann, holding the phone to her ear. "That will be my next call."

Ann booked the reservation for six o'clock, which was early, but available and perfect, really, since they were only five minutes from the restaurant. She pushed the buttons for her home number and Lauren answered the phone. "Hi, Mom," she said. "How was your trip?"

"Great, honey," said Ann.

"Are you on your way home?" she asked.

"Yes," said Ann, "but we're going to take a little detour. Will you put Gran on the phone?"

"Hello, dear," said Eileen, her voice full of cheer and warmth. "Did you have a good time?"

"Fabulous," said Ann. "I couldn't be more refreshed. How was everything here?"

"Just fine," said Eileen. "We can talk about it at dinner."

"That's why I'm calling," said Ann. "Mike and I won't be home for dinner. We've made other plans."

"I thought you were going to be home," said Eileen. "I've got a ham in the oven."

"You're sweet to make dinner, Mom," said Ann. "I'll be happy to have ham tomorrow night."

"What kind of plans have you made?" asked Eileen, her vocal thermometer dropping.

"We're just looking for another couple of hours alone," said Ann.

"Haven't you been alone all *weekend?*"

"Yes and no," said Ann. "You always spend a good amount of time away with new friends."

"Well, that's your choice, isn't it?" said Eileen, opening the oven door and sticking a fork into the ham.

"Yes, it is, Mom," said Ann. "And it's also my choice to do what I want when I want. I'm a grown-up now."

"Yes," said Eileen. "I've come to learn how very grown up you are."

"We'll be home by eight thirty or so," said Ann. "I'm sure you can manage until then. It's not like the children are toddlers."

"I can manage just about anything," said Eileen, turning off the oven, "just about anything."

"Well, good," said Ann. "We'll see you when we get home."

Ann pushed the END CALL button before her mother had a chance to respond. "She makes me feel like a teenager again," said Ann, putting the phone back in her purse.

Mike said nothing. "I'm serious," said Ann. "I didn't have to call her at all."

"You were good to call," said Mike, putting his hand on his wife's thigh.

"Not in her eyes," said Ann. "I get absolutely nothing but grief for checking in. Next time, I won't bother."

Mike pulled his car into the lot behind Café Annette, a restored farmhouse fifteen miles outside of town. He opened Ann's door, then held out his arm to escort her into the restaurant. "We've got a few minutes," she said, looking at her watch. "Let's get a drink in the bar."

As soon as Selma and Sam came through the kitchen door, Eileen pulled the scalloped potatoes and buttered rolls from the oven and set them down on the dining room sideboard. Nate got up from the kitchen table, where he had been looking at *Sports Illustrated* and enjoying the savory smell of an imminent dinner, strode to the island, and picked up the electric knife. Lauren stood at the stove and spooned buttered green beans and slivered almonds out of a saucepan and into a china serving dish. When it was full, she covered it and then took it into the dining room and set it down on the hot pad next to the potatoes. Eileen stood next to Nate, watching him carve. "You are good at this, Nate," she said.

"Thanks," said Nate, glancing at his grandmother.

"What can I do to help?"

"Nothing," said Nate. "Go sit with Selma and Gramps. I'll bring the platter in."

Eileen hesitated. "Go," Nate said gently. Reluctantly, Eileen left the kitchen. Lauren returned from the dining room and stood next to Nate. She had never watched anyone carve before, except the chef at the club, and she was mesmerized by the pink folds of meat falling away from the whole and onto the warmed oval platter. Nate stopped carving and told his sister to join the others. "I'll bring it in," he said.

Eileen sat at the head of the table, where Ann usually sat. Only then did Lauren remember her parents were supposed to be home. "Where are Mom and Dad?" she asked as Nate walked in from the kitchen.

"They've been delayed," said Eileen evenly.

"Now there's a surprise," said Nate, setting the platter down in

front of his father's chair and then sitting. "Late plane or early dinner reservations at Tony's?"

"They did go out to dinner," said Eileen, not making eye contact with anyone as she unfolded her napkin in her lap.

"Because what we have here certainly isn't good enough," said
Nate. "My mother needs salmon poached in a parchment bag and
a carafe of wine to get her through a Sunday night."

"Nate," said Eileen. "Will you say the blessing?"

Nate made a face. "I don't want to do that, Gran."

"It's not hard," she replied. "Just tell us what you're thankful
for and then we can eat."

Nate looked at his sister. "I'm thankful," he began, "for this
weekend. I'm thankful for Gran taking care of us. And I'm thankful Gramps is feeling better."

"Amen," said Eileen. "Thank you, Nate."

"Did you say anything to my mom about, uh, the events of the
weekend?" asked Lauren, looking at her grandmother.

"No," said Eileen. "And the more I think about it, the more I
think we should just keep it to ourselves."

"Keep what to ourselves?" asked Sam. "If you're going to have
secrets, you might as well let me in on them."

"It's nothing, really," said Eileen. "We can all talk about it later.
Let's eat." They all ate hungrily, especially Sam. Eileen cut his ham
into bite-sized pieces, which he shoved into his mouth. And while
watching him eat could be disgusting at times, Nate also found it
fascinating. His grandfather was like a caveman with no concept of
table manners. He ate because he was hungry. And the faster he
could get the food into his body, the faster his hunger would be
sated. It was a very honest way to eat. People could make such a big
deal out of a meal. They employed tricks like putting the fork down
on the plate after each bite, or taking a sip of water after each swallow, all in an effort to slow themselves down. It was a game, really,
like the rest of life. Nate was beginning to understand the time involved in making a meal, since his grandmother seemed to be in the
kitchen all day long doing whatever was required to produce one
awesome dinner after another, so he could also understand why the
cook didn't want the meal rushed. But why not eat quickly, like

Sam, then sit back at the table, digest, and talk about how good the food tasted? Wouldn't a cook appreciate that as much as watching people pick at their food so slowly that half of it would be cold before it passed through their lips? Nate looked back at his grandfather, who had finished his meal and was holding his plate out for more. He had a lot of problems, but showing his true feelings wasn't among them. And for that, Nate thought, he was better off than most.

After dinner, they had vanilla ice cream topped with Eileen's homemade fudge sauce. Then they all helped in the kitchen, with Sam drying the unbreakable things with a dish towel, then setting them on the island. When the work was done, Selma and Sam put on their coats and walked out the back door. Eileen, who was wrapping up leftovers, promised she'd join them after Ann and Mike got home. Lauren gathered her homework from the kitchen table, stacking her books against her chest. "So, do you not want us to talk about what happened with Gramps?" she asked. Nate, who had just picked his backpack up off the floor and hoisted it onto his shoulder, stood still and listened.

Eileen brushed a curl from her forehead. "It's not that I don't want you to say anything," she said. "It's just that I don't want to worry your mother and father. It's over and I'd just as soon forget about it. We'll all be more careful. And, of course, if anything like this happens again, I'll tell your parents everything. Does that sound okay to you two?"

Nate shrugged. "What about the locking system?" asked Lauren.

"I will have to talk to your father about that," said Eileen. "But I will do it in a vague way, something about Sam fiddling with it or being able to unlock it. What do you think?"

"Sure," said Nate.

"Lauren?"

"I'm okay with that, Gran," she said. "You're probably right." Lauren walked over to Eileen and kissed her on the cheek. "Aside from what happened to Gramps, this has been an incredible weekend," she said. "You're a great babysitter."

"And you," Eileen said to Lauren, "are a great kid."

Lauren looked at Nate. "See?"

"Clearly, she doesn't know you too well," said Nate. His headache was finally gone, his stomach was full of delicious home-made food, and his parents were elsewhere. He hadn't felt this good since Josh picked him up for the party the night before. He, too, kissed his grandmother's cheek, and then followed Lauren into the hallway. "Tell me again why Josh was here last night," he said when they reached the bottom of the stairs.

Lauren's heart thumped. Josh had told her to keep his visit a secret. "He just stopped by," she said, trying to sound casual.

"Why?"

"I guess someone drank all his beer at the party," said Lauren, walking up the stairs, "so he left."

"I know that," said Nate. "I'm wondering why he came here."

"Maybe he wanted to make sure you got home all right." Leaving her brother standing at the top of the stairs, Lauren walked down the hallway to her room. She shut the door behind her. Nate lingered a moment, then walked into his room, flopped down on his bed, and called Jenny. She picked up, as she always did, on the third ring. "How are you feeling?" she asked.

"Better," said Nate. "I'm sorry I put you through that. I don't know what happened to me."

"I do," said Jenny. "You drank too much."

"You are a genius," said Nate, smiling. "Are you mad at me?"

"No," said Jenny, "but cleaning up your vomit was absolutely disgusting."

"You cleaned it up?"

"Did you think I was going to leave it all to your grandmother?"

"Thank you," said Nate.

"Did you have fun at the party?"

"From what I remember, I guess I did. Did you?"

"I guess so," said Jenny. "It was kind of weird, though. A lot of people were messed up. I don't like that."

"I know you don't," said Nate. "Let's do something different next weekend—just you and me."

"Like what?" asked Jenny.

"I'll think about it and you think about it and we'll come up with something," said Nate. "Do you still love me?"

"Of course, I love you," said Jenny, meaning it.

"I love you, too," said Nate. "I'll see you tomorrow."

"Okay," said Jenny. "Good night."

Nate called Josh next. "Hey," said Josh. "How's the Spew King?"

"Very funny," said Nate. "What were you up to last night?"

"Other than cleaning up your barf, not much," said Josh.

"Why did you leave the party?"

"Someone drank my beer," said Josh. "I guess it put me in a bad mood, so I just wanted out."

"What did you do?"

"Just drove around, really," said Josh. "I ended up at your house later on."

"Were you spending time with my sister?"

Josh hesitated. "Nate, you're my best friend," he said. "I spend a lot of time with your sister."

"Does she like you?"

"She's over the top about Judd Acker," said Josh. "You know that."

Nate laughed. "I can't believe he actually talks to her sometimes."

"He's a nice guy," said Josh. "And your sister's not ugly, Nate."

"She's no Angel."

"There's only one Angel," said Josh.

"Okay, man," said Nate. "I've got to open my history book or I'm toast on that test tomorrow."

"You and me both," said Josh.

The kitchen was immaculate and deserted, just the way Ann liked it, when she and Mike walked in from the garage. She washed her hands at the sink and then walked quickly across the floor, through the hall, and into the den, where her mother was reading. "We're home," she said.

Eileen looked up from her book and smiled. "Well, so you are. How was dinner?"

"Wonderful," said Ann. "How's everything here?"

"Just fine," said Eileen, closing her book and getting up from the chair. "Nate and Lauren are upstairs in their rooms and Selma and Sam are down at the house."

"It's so quiet," said Ann, taking off her coat and folding it over her arm.

"Well, yes," said Eileen. "We've had a busy weekend. We're all tired."

"Did you have any trouble?" asked Ann.

"Not really," said Eileen. "Your father was, well, your father, but he's okay."

"And the kids?"

"Great," said Eileen. "You've got terrific kids."

"Really?" said Ann, smiling. "You'll have to tell me more about that."

"In the morning," said Eileen, moving toward the hallway. "I'm ready to hit the hay."

"Thank you," said Ann, following her mother back into the kitchen. "Mike and I really needed to get away."

"Here she is," said Mike, approaching his mother-in-law when she walked into the kitchen, "Saint Eileen." Eileen smiled and accepted a scotch-scented kiss on her cheek. "It looks like you survived," he said, putting his arm around her shoulder. "I'm impressed."

"I'm impressed with your kids," said Eileen. "We had fun."

"It's nice to know they're good for someone," said Mike, patting her on the back.

"Okay," said Eileen, "Well, I'm going to head down to the house."

"I'll walk you down," said Mike, taking her Irish-knit sweater from the wall peg and wrapping it around her.

"And I'm going to take a bath," announced Ann. "I'm exhausted."

Mike and Eileen walked out the back door and Ann climbed the stairs. Nate heard her walk past his door on her way to see Lauren.

He turned off his light. Ann knocked on Lauren's door and entered when granted permission. "Hi, Mom," said Lauren, looking up from the pile of books and papers at her desk. "Did you have fun in California?"

"Lots of fun, honey," said Ann, setting the stack of magazines down on Lauren's desk, then giving her daughter a gentle hug. "I'm completely refreshed."

"That's good," said Lauren.

"And how were things here?" asked Ann. "Did you survive the weekend with your grandmother?"

"Oh yes," said Lauren, smiling. "She's great. We really had a good time."

"You didn't tire her out?"

"She's got more energy than anyone I know," said Lauren. "And she's an unbelievable cook."

"Did you miss me?" asked Ann, putting on the same exaggerated pout she always wore when looking for attention.

"Of course," Lauren lied, wondering how a mother who was no longer involved in her child's everyday life could ask that question in earnest. Lauren used to miss her mother when she was away because her absence was as obvious as a blue sky without the sun. But for the past couple of years, Lauren had been somewhat relieved when her mother left town, taking her puppy dog look with her. Not that they spent much time together, but when they did, her mother either tried too hard or treated her like a child. She had trouble gauging the distance Lauren wanted between them. Lauren knew this was partly her fault because she wanted to be close with her mother one day and have nothing to do with her the next. But her friend Pammy's mother seemed to understand this, knowing that a "You're awesome!" note in her backpack the day of a volleyball game was cool—Pammy had, in fact, shared these notes with the entire team—and that hugging her in the car when she dropped her off at school in the morning was not. Lauren's mother didn't seem to understand this delicate balance. If Lauren pushed her away, her mother took it personally.

"That's my girl," said Ann, turning to leave. "I'm going to take a tub, then crawl into bed. I'll see you in the morning." Lauren made a face at the door after her mother left. She hadn't even noticed Lauren cleaned her room. Ann walked back down the hall to Nate's room. She lifted her hand to knock on his door when she noticed his light was out. Her mother had probably kept him hopping all weekend, doing chores and running errands. He must be exhausted to be asleep at nine o'clock. Instead of knocking, Ann simply said good night to the door. On the other side, Nate, lying in bed and waiting for her departure, raised the third finger of his left hand in the air. As soon as she left, Nate switched on his light and picked up his favorite vintage Gameboy. Not tired enough to sleep, but not awake enough to do homework, Nate played Super Mario Brothers for half an hour. His father never came to see him.

Lauren was just about to turn off her light when her cell phone rang. She picked it up on the second ring. "Hi," said Josh.

"Hi," said Lauren, cannon blasts in her chest.

"Did you have a good day?"

"I had an awesome day," said Lauren, "until my parents came home." Josh laughed. "I wish my grandmother could be here all the time. She's easy to be around."

"Nate says she makes you guys work."

"A little bit," said Lauren. "I don't think that's so bad for you."

"You're kidding," said Josh.

"I'm not kidding."

"Then you can come live at my house," he said. "My parents work us to death."

Lauren laughed. "You have very nice parents," she said.

"That's in public," said Josh. "In private, they're slave drivers." Lauren laughed again. "I thought about you today," Josh said quietly. Lauren blushed. "Did you think about me?"

"Yes."

"Are you okay with last night?"

"Yes."

"I want to take you out next weekend," said Josh. "Do you want to go to the movies Saturday night?"

"Sure," said Lauren excitedly.

"Good," said Josh. "I'll call you this week and we'll figure out what we want to see, okay?"

"Yes," said Lauren, feeling like warm water was running through her veins.

"And I'll talk to your brother," said Josh. "I don't want you to worry about it."

Mike walked into their bathroom, where Ann was soaking in a bubble bath. "Your mother's a piece of work, isn't she?"

"You're just finding this out now?"

"No, but maybe I'm just finding out what an unbelievable woman she is."

"In what way?"

"In every way," said Mike. "She's just very principled."

"And I'm not," said Ann, sitting up.

"I didn't say that," said Mike. "I said she was."

"But you were implying I wasn't."

"I was doing nothing of the kind," said Mike, unbuttoning his shirt. "This is not about you."

"I beg to differ."

"I'm not going to get into an argument," said Mike, looking in the mirror. "You owe me something."

"And what in the world would that be," said Ann, sitting back in the tub.

"Think about it a moment," said Mike. "I'll undress and wait for you in the other room."

Oh God, thought Ann, *the blow job.* Slowly, she stood and slid her hands down her body to remove the bubbles. If she had only passed on that pinot on the plane, she wouldn't be in this position. Of course, she had two glasses of wine at the restaurant, but, again, she wouldn't have had those if she hadn't had the damn pinot. But it had tasted so good. There was nothing like alcohol to dissolve the stress of a travel day, any day, for that matter. The first sip from a graceful glass was her absolute favorite—the tangy taste of the wine pooled in her eager mouth, the aroma filling her nose and the welcome fire sliding down her throat. The world always looked better through an empty bottle. She stepped out of the tub and dried herself. She wrapped her robe around her naked body and walked into the bedroom. Mike was lying in their bed, propped up against two pillows. The sheet and blanket covered his legs and waist, but his hairy chest and large shoulders were exposed, a mating posture. He was lean, as many powerful men are, with a stomach that was almost as flat as when Ann had met him in college. He didn't always watch his diet the way Ann wanted him to, but he was fairly good about getting exercise. He ran on the weekends from home and three days during the week from his office. Three or four of his top men ran with him, like the Secret Service accompanying the U.S. president. They talked sports, no business, on the four-mile loop around headquarters, Mike and his boys. He smiled at Ann as she sat on the bed. He told her to remove her robe, which she did, slowly. She enjoyed showing him her body because she worked so hard to maintain it. She weighed less now than when she graduated from college, a fact that circulated around town whenever Ann and Mike made a public appearance together for the company. The local newspaper reporters seemed to enjoy describing her toned arms as much as her designer outfits. And while she outwardly whined about such frivolous description, she inwardly basked in the spotlight every other woman in town could or dared not enter.

As she drew closer, Mike slid the covers down from his lap, revealing his hard cock. Ann smiled at it, making Mike's chest swell with anticipation. She climbed onto him, straddling her legs over his. Ever so slowly, she lowered her head to his penis. She kissed the tip, causing Mike to shudder. She then ran her tongue around the head and down the shaft, while Mike whispered, "Yes, baby." She took it in her mouth and began to gently suck. She knew it would be only a matter of seconds at this point and her mind drifted to the tasks that faced her tomorrow. She would get up and make herself a double-strength latte before calling Sally to arrange a workout and possibly lunch at Susie's Kitchen. She couldn't get enough of Susie's no-fat sesame noodle salad. After that, she needed to talk to Dede about redecorating her living room. The whites and beiges were no longer interesting. Everyone had them. She sucked. She was ready for some color in that room—maybe warm cranberry tones, something dramatic but inviting. Suddenly, there was an explosion in her mouth. Brought back to her task, she swallowed dutifully, avoiding making a face. "Thanks, baby," said Mike.

Ann met his eyes, then got off the bed and walked into the bathroom, closing the door behind her. She bent over the toilet bowl and stuck her finger down her throat. Moments later, the fluid she'd just ingested, flew into the water. Ann gagged, then stood, wiped her mouth, and brushed her teeth. She walked back into the bedroom, where Mike was reading *Businessweek*. He looked up at her and smiled. She crawled into her side of the bed and turned on the lamp on the table beside her. She picked up *Architectural Digest* and flipped through the glossy pages of an article about sunrooms. She closed her eyes and pictured such an oasis off their family room. Yes, that would be the perfect solution to the long Michigan winters.

Chapter 14

Mail in hand, Ann walked into her kitchen after a morning workout and lunch with Sally to find her mother, bent over, taking cookies out of the oven. *Good God,* thought Ann, *what in the world will get the message through to her that this is not her house?* "Hello," said Eileen cheerfully. "How did your exercise routine go?"

"My *workout,*" Ann said, "was just fine."

"I don't suppose you want a cookie."

"No," said Ann, setting the mail down on the counter to take off her coat.

Eileen coaxed the sugar cookies onto a wire rack with a spatula. "Nate and Lauren love them," she said.

"Mmm," said Ann, flipping through the stack of magazines and bills. She stopped when she saw the American Express envelope. She opened it with the bone-handled letter opener she kept in the basket on her desk and inhaled deeply as she quickly scanned its contents. She folded the bill in half and put it into the pocket of her yoga pants.

"Your friend Jesse called," said Eileen, spooning more dough onto the cookie sheet she had just emptied.

Ann looked up from the mail. "You answered my phone?"

"Well, I was standing right here," said Eileen.

"Isn't that an invasion of privacy?"

Eileen smiled. "I'd call it secretarial," she said, peeling the page with Jesse's name and phone number off Ann's message pad and handing it to her daughter. "She said she tried your cell phone."

"Tell me again why you're in my kitchen making cookies," said Ann.

"I'm making them," said Eileen, "for Lauren and Nate, who will be home soon from school."

"They don't need cookies," said Ann.

"We all need cookies," said Eileen.

"Well, I certainly don't," asked Ann, giving her mother a sarcastic look.

Eileen bent down and opened the oven door. "I think you do," she said.

Go to hell, thought Ann as she walked out of the kitchen and up the stairs to her bedroom, where she shut the door behind her. She sat down on the bed and called Jesse.

"You know," said Jesse, "if you want people to be able to get in touch with you, you have to turn your cell phone on."

"Then my children might call me," said Ann.

"You gave them your number?"

Ann removed her shoes and then lay back on the duvet. "My mother is driving me crazy."

"So what else is new?"

"I'm not kidding, Jesse."

"Your mother," Jesse said, "is delightful. I don't know why you say the things you do."

"You don't live with her," said Ann. "She's in the middle of everything."

"She sounds like she's a tremendous help. I can't believe how often she makes dinner for you."

"She makes dinner all the time," said Ann, rubbing her temples.

"How can you not love that?"

"First of all, I'm not a meat and potatoes girl and haven't been since the ninth grade," said Ann. "And second, if I eat one more tuna casserole, I'll explode."

"That I'd like to witness."

"She just likes to show me up," said Ann, sitting back up.

"I doubt that's her primary motivation, Ann."

"And I'm quite sure it is."

"At any rate, she was just delightful on the phone," said Jesse. "And it seems quite silly and rude of me, actually, that I've made no effort to spend any time with her."

"Trust me," said Ann, taking the bill out of her pocket and putting it in her bedside drawer. "You're better off."

"And so," said Jesse, "I have a proposition."

"This is why you called?"

"No, I called because you have to be at the fashion show tomorrow at one instead of one thirty," said Jesse. "But my proposition is to invite your mother to the show and we all have lunch together beforehand."

"I'm not sure I can get a ticket," said Ann.

"I've got an extra," said Jesse. "Janice Parker can't come."

Ann hesitated and then breathed into the phone. "Do we have to do this?"

"I'll take care of everything," said Jesse. "You extend the invitation. We can meet at the Marriott. I'll make reservations in the Peach Tree Café for eleven thirty."

Ann opened her mouth to protest, but Jesse hung up.

At eleven ten the next morning, Ann walked through the garage door into the kitchen and found her mother, dressed in a wool skirt, freshly ironed white shirt, green cardigan sweater, and pearls, sitting in her kitchen and reading the newspaper. "Didn't I just find you here yesterday?" said Ann, setting her keys down on the counter.

"That you did," said Eileen, looking up from the newspaper and smiling at her daughter. "But today, I was invited."

Ann looked at her watch. "We're not due there until eleven thirty," she said.

"Are you going like that?" asked Eileen.

"Don't be ridiculous," said Ann. "You know these are the clothes I wear to the gym."

"Well, you'd better change then, hadn't you?"

Ann left the kitchen and ran up the stairs to her bedroom.

"Well, you'd better change then, hadn't you," said Ann, imitating her mother with a whiny, nasal twist to her voice. She walked into her closet, took off her clothes, and stuffed them into the hamper. She pulled on her jeans with the map of Italy print and then a camel-colored, scoop-neck cashmere sweater over her head. She wrapped a black leather belt around her waist, slid her feet into three-inch black heels, and grabbed some amber jewelry from her safe. She snipped the price tag from her charcoal black leather blazer and put her arms through the sleeves as she walked out of her room.

Downstairs, Eileen was standing by the garage door. She looked at her watch as soon as Ann walked into the kitchen. "It's eleven twenty," she said through tight lips.

"And the restaurant," said Ann, grabbing her black leather purse from the countertop, "is ten minutes away."

"Then we'll be late," said Eileen, turning to open the door.

"Fashionably so," said Ann, walking into the garage behind her mother. "Didn't anyone ever teach you to be fashionably late?"

"Not when friends are waiting for me," said Eileen, opening the passenger side door to Ann's car. "That's not fashionable; that's rude."

"Trust me," said Ann, sitting down in the driver's seat, "we'll be the first ones there."

When they arrived at the restaurant, Jesse, Sally, and Paula were sitting at the table with Betsy Weyerman, who was given complimentary tickets every year mostly because her great-grandfather was partly responsible—100 years ago—for the startup of the company that Mike and others before him had coaxed and nurtured into world-class excellence. "Hello, girls," said Ann brightly. "This is my mother, Eileen."

"Yes," said Jesse, standing and giving Eileen a quick hug. "It's so good to see you again. It's been too long. Please, sit and join us."

Eileen reintroduced herself to Sally and Paula, both of whom she had met years before. Betsy extended her hand and said, simply: "I'm charmed." Two minutes later, Janet Bellows and Jean Stefanski, two pigeon-breasted women in their midfifties, arrived together as they did everywhere. Pat Waters arrived next and sat down beside Ann. Introductions were made again around the table and the small talk began. Ann narrowed her eyes at Jesse, annoyed at being tricked. She had no idea this lunch would include anyone other than Sally, Jesse, and Paula.

"Ann," said Pat, "it's so good to see you. Where have you been hiding?"

Ann glanced down the table at her mother, who was busy chatting with Jesse and Paula. "At home, I'm sorry to report," she said, keeping her voice down. "My parents arrived in the fall. My dad's got Parkinson's and dementia, and we've all been doing our best to make him comfortable."

"Oh, you poor dear," said Pat through thick frosted lips. "I had no idea. Do you need anything?"

"We're doing pretty well right now, Pat," said Ann, lifting her water glass and wondering when the server would arrive and take drink orders.

"You must be exhausted," said Pat, tucking her dyed black bob behind her ears as she always did when she had new earrings to show off; the diamond studs were maybe two carats each. "Call me if you need a hand or a sympathetic ear. And you know I mean that."

"I certainly do," said Ann.

Pat patted Ann's hand. "Call me anyway," she said, already looking past Ann to Janet and Jean cackling at the other end of the table. "Maybe I can sneak you away for a facial."

Finally, the server arrived and announced the specials. Ann ordered two carafes of pinot grigio for the table and a spinach salad—no bacon, cheese, olives, or dressing—for herself. She sat back and listened to the others order everything from quiche Lorraine to chef salad with blue cheese dressing on the side. She wondered, not for the first time, how these women with thick middles could stand in front of a mirror. What were they—size tens? twelves? Janet and Jean looked like they could be on the verge of size fourteen.

Ann's first glass of wine went down like water. A touch sour, it awakened her dormant taste buds and emboldened her tongue. She poured herself another glass as the bread baskets arrived and another with the presentation of the entrées. She raved about her various treatments at the San Francisco resort spa, calling the massage therapist a genius, even though he was gayer than a male nurse. At that, the clicking of stainless steel forks and knives against china plates stopped—led by Pat, whose son was in nursing school—as if frozen by a metallic power failure. And the cloud of silence hovering over the table near the window, where a couple married for twenty-five years ate their matching burgers without speaking, shifted, surrounding Ann and the others. Ann lifted her glass and took the final sip. By the time she set it back down on the table, the cloud had moved on. Jesse switched topics to the charity the fashion show was supporting, and everyone eagerly joined in on the conversation. Ann quietly picked at her salad, feeling suddenly deflated and having no idea why. *It must be my mother,* she thought as she speared a dry mushroom and raised it to her mouth.

The server returned with the dessert menus as Ann was pouring herself more wine.

"Look at these choices," cooed Jean. "They're absolutely sinful!"

"You can take their cheesecake," added Janet, "and just apply it directly to your hips!"

Or your big fat abdomen, thought Ann.

"How's the apple cobbler?" asked Paula.

"Fabulous," said Jean, closing her eyes and slowly shaking her head as if she were scanning her brain for a picture. "They make it here."

Paula bit her lower lip. Right now, Ann thought, Paula was doing her best to muster up the willpower to decline on dessert. At the same time, she was wondering how bad it would look if she ordered it without the mountain of whipped cream that came with it. Then, Ann guessed, she would announce that she could order it with the whipped cream and simply skip dinner. Paula was always talking about skipping dinner.

"Well," announced Jean, "I'm going to get the cheesecake."

"Oh, you naughty girl!" said Janet, chuckling. "I'll join you."

The server, pencil on pad, looked at Paula. Paula hesitated. "I'll have the cobbler," she said finally, as if there were really any choice in the matter.

"Whipped cream?" asked the server.

Paula looked at Jean, who gave her the thumbs-up sign. "Yes," said Paula, smiling.

"Bravo!" said Janet. "I knew you had it in you."

"Looks like I'm going to have to skip dinner," said Paula.

Jesse ordered a cup of lime sorbet, and Sally, looking at Ann, declined. Eileen ordered a "small wedge" of cherry pie. The server looked at Ann, who was sipping more wine. Ann waved her away.

When the desserts arrived, the true celebration began. "Doesn't this look marvelous?" asked Jean, holding up her cheesecake.

"Gorgeous," said Janet. "I'm going to eat mine one decadent bite at a time!"

"And look at that cobbler!" exclaimed Jean. "That's the freshest-looking crumble I've ever seen."

Paula, who had already shoveled a piece into her mouth, said, "It's delicious."

Ann looked down the table at her mother, who was talking to Jesse. "Does this look like a small wedge to you?"

Jesse smiled at her. "Just eat what you want, Eileen. The portions here are always ample."

"Yes," said Eileen, taking a bite.

Jesse touched Eileen's hand with hers. "Enjoy it," she said. "It looks terrific."

"It is," said Eileen, smiling. "Would you like a bite?"

"No," said Jesse, "but thank you."

A moment later, Jesse was on her feet. "I'd like to thank you all for coming," she said. "Ann and I have to scoot over to the arts center to get gussied up for the show. You still have some time to enjoy yourselves. We'll see you over there."

Eileen called down to Ann, "Do you want me to come now? I've just started my pie."

"No," said Ann. "Sally will take you."

Able until now to hide her disappointment about not being chosen for the show, Sally's face flushed. She raised her glass to her lips to cool the fire kindling in her cheeks, but her shaking hand missed its mark, sending water down her chin and onto her suede vest. Immediately aware of her miscalculation, Sally grabbed her napkin from her lap and dabbed at the repelled wetness. "Are you okay?" asked Jesse, putting her hand on Sally's shoulder.

"Fine," said Sally, focusing on her vest instead of Jesse. "It's just water."

After Ann slipped her mother three twenty-dollar bills to cover their lunches, she and Jesse walked away from the table as Sally continued to dab at her chest, much longer than was warranted by a missed mouthful of water. Why hadn't Jesse told her she was in the show? And why had they chosen Jesse over Sally? Sally continued to blot her vest, willing herself not to tear up. How could they pick Jesse? Was it because of where she lived in town? Jesse certainly had a lovely house, but it was not—like Sally's—in the historic district. Was it Jesse's car? She drove a Lexus, but who didn't? Year after year, the committee had snubbed her for no good reason. And year after year Sally had taken some solace in the knowledge that Paula and Jesse, too, didn't cut the mustard. And now it was just she and Paula.

In the car, Ann began to laugh.

"What's so funny?"

"Could you believe that dessert scene? As if any of them were actually thinking about *not* having dessert."

Jesse smiled. "Dessert isn't evil, Ann."

"Not when you have sorbet," said Ann. "You made the only sensible choice at the table."

"I must admit, I was thinking about having the cobbler."

"Oh, you were not," said Ann, allowing the car to roll through a stop sign. "That cobbler must have six hundred fifty calories, without the whipped cream."

"Are you okay to drive?"

"Of course I am," said Ann. "What kind of question is that?"

"You hit the wine pretty hard at lunch."

"Oh my God," said Ann. "Am I driving with my friend or my mother?"

"Your friend," said Jesse. "A concerned friend."

"Don't start, Reverend. I'm not in the mood."

Jesse stared out the windshield, thankful the center was only a few blocks away. After they arrived, Ann parked the car and they hurried inside. They walked, as instructed, directly backstage. Lit up like a car dealership with Frank Sinatra crooning from the sound system, the cavernous dressing room area looked like a movie set. A half dozen harried-looking women scurried about with clipboards in one hand and cardboard cups of coffee in the other, emitting signals of controlled panic. Marge Simon, the fashion show organizer, approached Ann with a worried look on her face. "I'm so glad you're here," she said, dismissing one of her assistants. "Everyone's running late."

"What can we do to help?" asked Jesse.

"Go talk to Pam. She'll tell you what you're going to wear and when you're on," said Marge. "She's in the middle of reworking the schedule, but she should have a good idea by now."

Pam Rogers, a take-charge type who had been Marge's Girl Friday for years, was on the other side of the room encircled by four women talking at once. "Ladies," she finally said, holding up her free hand. "Let's all calm down."

"How can we calm down?" asked Penny Martin. "The show starts in thirty minutes and you have no idea what you're doing."

"Actually I do know what I'm doing," said Pam, consulting her clipboard. "You are all matched up by size. Penny, you're a size ten, which puts you in the sable and sheared beaver."

"Wonderful," said Penny, hugging herself.

"Where's Ann Barons?" asked Pam.

"Right here," said Ann, stepping forward.

"You're in white fox all day long," said Pam.

"They're all size two?" asked Ann over the buzz of conversation.

"Yes," said Pam. "We ordered them in especially for you."

"Excellent," said Ann, grinning. "When can I try one on?"

"Talk to Jennifer," said Pam, pointing to the other side of the room. "She's our release captain. And I've left further instructions in your room."

Ann winked at Jesse and strutted over to Jennifer, a slim, perpetually tanned, bleached blonde who dressed in Lily. She smiled falsely when she saw Ann, then kissed the air beside her left cheek. "Where have you been hiding?" she asked. "I haven't seen you in a dog's life."

"At home," said Ann. "My parents are visiting."

"Yuck!" said Jennifer. "I break into hives whenever my parents stay longer than dinner."

Ann laughed. "My mother actually *makes* dinner."

"Worse!" howled Jennifer. "Don't tell me—it's Casserole City! Either that, or meat loaf smothered with creamed mushrooms, baked potatoes with butter and gobs of sour cream, and green beans with slivered almonds. God, my mother can't serve a bowl of beans without those slivered almonds. You need a wheelbarrow to leave the table." Ann laughed again; someone finally understood her situation. She should have known Jennifer would come to her defense. After all, she was the only other size two in town. Ann had always admired her thinness, even though it was maintained by cigarettes instead of exercise. At least Jennifer understood the importance of appearance. Ann made a mental note to ask her to do something other than lunch or the gym. Maybe they could go shopping in the city, just the two of them. "However, I must admit, you look marvelous," said Jennifer, putting her hand on Ann's arm. "Have you been sneaking the meat loaf to the dog?"

"I just leave it on my plate," said Ann. "I'm hoping my mother will catch on that her dinners should be sent back to the nineteen-fifties."

"Any luck?" asked Jennifer, feigning interest.

"Not yet," said Ann. "I think we're having breaded pork chops tonight."

Jennifer rolled her eyes. "Well, you continue to fight the fight," she said, turning to face the rack of furs. "In the meantime, let's get you suited up."

In a tiny side dressing room, Ann put down the note from Pam requesting she wear the clothing provided and sniffed the armpits of the black suede pantsuit Pam wrote was new. Ann had not wanted to change her clothes, but Pam's note indicated that the show's theme extended beyond the furs. Ann ran her hands along the material, which felt expensive, then shed her clothing. The suit fit like it was tailor-made for her, feeling like bathwater against her chilled skin. She slid her feet back into her calfskin heels and strode out of the room, looking for Jesse and an assistant who could find her a low-fat latte. As she rounded the corner, the heel of her left shoe caught the edge of an area rug, and she went down, landing on her bottom and then back and head, biting her tongue. "Shit!" she said.

"Oh my God, are you all right?" asked a woman who had opened the curtain to her dressing room when she heard the thud. She knelt down and then gently lifted Ann's head and back so that Ann was sitting. "Stay right here. Breathe," she said, still on her knees next to Ann. "What happened?"

"I'm not sure," said Ann, whose head felt like it was full of sand.

"Let me get you some water."

"And some coffee," said Ann. "Would you please get me some coffee?"

"Don't get up," said the woman. "I'll be right back." She returned in five minutes, with a glass of ice water in one hand and a cardboard cup in the other. "Let's get you into my dressing room. There's a folding chair in there, if you feel ready to move."

"Yes," said Ann. "I'm okay."

The woman set the water and coffee down on the floor, took off Ann's heels, and then helped Ann to her feet. She led her into the dressing room and onto the chair. She then grabbed the water and coffee from the floor and handed the water to Ann. "Take a sip," she said. "Nice and easy." Ann took a small sip and then another. Her head was beginning to clear. "You stay here, don't move," said the woman. "I'm going to find Pam so she can change the schedule."

Ann held up her hand. "I'm okay. You don't need to do that."

"It's an easy switch," said the woman. "You're near the beginning of the show, and I'm near the end." And before Ann could further protest, she disappeared behind the curtain. When she was gone, Ann set the water glass down and reached for the coffee. She took two long pulls from the tepid latte and then two deep breaths. Why in the world would someone put a rug in a dressing room area on a stage?

"Done," said the woman, reentering their tiny space. "This will give you another thirty minutes or so to recuperate. How are you feeling?"

"Good," said Ann, even though the sand in her head had been replaced by intense heat. "If you could just point me back to my dressing room, I'll be fine."

"I'll walk you back," she said, helping Ann to her feet. They walked over the offending rug and around the corner to the back row of rooms. Ann could again hear the busyness of women around her: talking as they wrestled their clothes off and on in shared dressing rooms, laughing, shouting, squealing, and scurrying around her in the narrow hallway.

"This is it," she said, pointing to a room with its red curtain pulled across. The woman held the drapery in the air so Ann could pass through. Inside, Ann sat on her own folding chair and looked at her watch. "Would you get me some Advil? It's in my purse." The woman spun around, grabbed Ann's bag from the floor, and handed it to her.

"I'm going to head back to my room to get ready," said the woman. Ann noticed then that she was still in her changing robe. "Can I find someone to be with you?"

"I'm okay, really," said Ann. "Once these Advil kick in, I'll be good to go."

"All right, then," said the woman. "I'm off. Wish me luck."

"Good luck," said Ann. "And thank you." As soon as she was gone, Ann closed her eyes and focused on her throbbing head. It was like a hangover, she told herself. She knew how to function with a hangover.

Five minutes before her turn, Ann slipped the white fox car coat over her shoulders. On Marge's cue, she walked out from behind the cityscape set design and onto the carpeted runway that took her to the center of the stage. The audience *oohed* its approval. "You all know our lovely Ann Barons," said Susan Barry, chair of the Ladies Charitable Society and the event's announcer. "She's dressed in casual, but elegant evening wear from Fashion Sense." At this, Ann parted her coat to reveal her outfit. As instructed, she spun slowly, then removed the coat and slung it over her right arm. "This outfit, ladies, will take you anywhere," oozed Susan. "Dinner with your husband at a cozy restaurant in town. Or get those diamonds out of the safe for a dazzling look, appropriate for a night in the city." Some of the ladies in the audience nodded at one another knowingly. Ann slid the coat back on, hugging it closed, which sent ripples of laughter through the auditorium. "Oh yes," said Susan, smiling broadly. "You'll absolutely love yourself in this white fox car coat. Of course, it's perfect for a night out, but it's also a great coat to grab and wear over jeans. Dress it up or dress it down. It's incredibly versatile."

Eileen, who was sitting between Sally and Paula, made a face. She hated fur coats on anyone except Eskimos and Arctic explorers. And the very notion of wearing such a thing on errands was nothing short of grotesque. She leaned over and whispered in Paula's ear, "Would you really wear that to the grocery store?"

"Oh, lots of women here do," whispered Paula back. "I think it's kind of a status thing. It seems as though anyone can wear a fur to dinner or to church, but if you wear one to the grocery store that means you definitely have more than one in your closet. Doesn't Ann look fabulous?"

Eileen returned her attention to the stage, where her daughter was prancing like a circus horse down the runway away from the audience. "She certainly thinks she does," she said, more to herself than to Paula. It was one big farce was what it was, the fashion show. It was housed in the halls of charity, but it was really a chance for the town's finest to show themselves off and it sickened Eileen. Then again, thought Eileen putting her hands to her stomach, it could be the cherry pie. She had eaten the whole thing, in spite of its enormity. Quick calculation told her she had consumed one-sixth of the pie, when, at home, she normally ate no more than a tenth, or at the very most, an eighth. What in the world made her do it? Maybe, she thought shamefully, she'd just wanted to show Ann's friends that she could.

Sally offered to drive Eileen home after the show, but Eileen declined. Even though she was tired and anxious to see Sam, she decided the right thing to do was to wait for her daughter in the lobby. She sat in an industrial-looking chair with a thin red padded seat and watched the women clear out of the arts center. Most of them chatted happily as they moved from the auditorium to the glass doors that led to the parking lot. Snippets of conversation filled Eileen's ears.

". . . the most beautiful thing I've ever seen. I'm going to put *that* on my Christmas list!"

". . . marvelous charity."

"Did you see the . . . ?"

". . . always does such a nice job."

Eileen shut her eyes and the voices became discordantly musical, a symphony of words. Her stomachache was beginning to ease.

". . . the original bitch."

"Who does she think she is? Strutting around the stage like a peacock."

Eileen opened her eyes and saw two women standing several feet away from her. Others were still milling about, digging car keys and cell phones out of purses, saying their good-byes, but most of the women were already on their way home. These two lingered, appearing to prefer the warmth of the carpeted, red brick lobby to the ice-covered parking lot. They talked freely, seemingly unaware of Eileen's presence. "I used to think she was pretty, but I think she's gone overboard," said the redhead in black pants and an emerald green top.

"Completely overboard," said the other, a blonde in a royal blue outfit. "She really *does* look like the scarecrow everyone calls her." They laughed. "Maybe she'll keep dieting until she just disappears altogether!"

"No one would miss her. How refreshing this town would be without the presence of the Baronses." Tempted to approach the women, to scold them for their unkindness, Eileen instead held her ground and her tongue. But she could not stop herself from listening.

"Except for Mike. God, he's gorgeous."

"How does she hold on to that handsome husband of hers?"

"How do you think?"

"Sex, sex, and more sex?"

"Exactly. That's all any man really wants."

"Well, if that's the case, I'd be happy to take him on."

"He'd be grateful for something to hold on to!" They laughed again.

Just then, Ann appeared in the lobby. Eileen waved and Ann approached her, walking past the two gossipers, who were now chatting about March break vacation plans. "Have you been waiting long?" she asked.

"Not really," said Eileen, standing and making eye contact with her daughter before briefly shifting her gaze to the two women. One of them looked back at her. Eileen gave her daughter a quick hug.

"What was that for?" asked Ann, steering Eileen toward the exit.

"You did a good job today," said Eileen.

"Why, thank you," said Ann.

"Do we need to drive Jesse home?"

"No," said Ann. "She's all set." Ann pushed open the heavy glass door to the outside. Her headache was finally gone. "Well, that was fun," she said. "Did you have a good time, Mother?"

"I did," said Eileen. "And lunch was wonderful. Thank you."

Ann stopped and looked at her mother. She smiled warmly. "You are most welcome."

CHAPTER 15

⁓

Lauren first heard the news in chemistry class. She heard it again in American History and a third time in gym. By noon, it was everywhere. When she sat down for lunch, the first thing out of Katie Allan's mouth, in whispered urgency, was, "Did you hear?"

Judd Acker and Angel Spiller had broken up.

The details were sketchy. Katie said she heard Angel was cheating on him—had been, in fact, for months—with Danny Haynes, another football player, who had moved into town just last summer from St. Louis. Jenny Robson said Jamie Palumbo told her it was the other way around: Judd dumped Angel because he wanted to play the field. Katie looked at Lauren. "Looks like today's your lucky day."

"Yeah, right," said Lauren. "Like the guy even knows I exist."

After lunch, Lauren had study hall in the library. She sat down at the table farthest away from the ancient but eagle-eyed librarian and opened her history book. Before she had finished the third paragraph of chapter 12, Stephanie Pappas, a volleyball teammate, sat down and asked her if she'd heard the news. Lauren gave her a weary stare. "About forty-seven times," she said.

"Well, how does it make you feel?"

"What do you mean?"

"I don't know," said Stephanie, flipping her dark brown pony-tail over one shoulder. "It makes me kind of sad."

"You're kidding me."

"I'm not," said Stephanie. "Judd and Angel are like the king and queen of the school. They're our leaders; we all look up to them. If they've broken up, what does that mean for the rest of us?"

"I hadn't thought about it that way," said Lauren.

"Because you've got the hots for Judd," said Stephanie, smiling with heavily glossed lips.

"Who says?"

"Everybody knows that," said Stephanie, taking her math book from her backpack. "I read it on a stall in the girls' room the other day."

"Get out!" said Lauren, closing her book. "Which one?"

"It doesn't matter," said Stephanie, choosing a pencil from the wallpapered coffee can on the table. "Everybody knows."

"Well, shit," said Lauren, thinking about Josh and wondering how this looked through his eyes.

"Anyway, it's the end of an era," said Stephanie, routing through her backpack again. "It's kind of like Brad and Jen."

"That's going a bit far," said Lauren.

"Not really," said Stephanie, now taking everything out of her backpack. "I'm borderline mourning."

"You're borderline psycho," said Lauren, returning her gaze to her history book.

"Crap," said Stephanie, using the word she uttered whenever she missed a shot in volleyball. "I left my science notebook in my locker. Think that nasty Mrs. Filhaven will give me a hall pass?"

"Smile sweetly," said Lauren, not looking up from the page. "And tell her you're disoriented because of the breakup."

Stephanie stood and put everything back into her backpack. "You'll see I'm not wrong," she said, slinging one strap over her shoulder. "You have to be in touch with the pulse of the school."

Lauren watched Stephanie walk through the turnstile, before turning back to her book. But her thoughts wouldn't focus on the War of 1812. Judd Acker was a free man. It was an absurd notion, really—a concept so far out of normal space and time that Lauren wondered if the rumors and stories had all been a part of a dream. She looked around the library and found that everything was as it should be. People were talking quietly at the study tables or roaming through the beige metal stacks in search of a book. The computers were all occupied, as usual. The librarian and her student assistants were busy behind the large circulation desk in the center of the room. And the afternoon sun was shining through the large windows above the lounge area, where two boys were dozing in matching plaid armchairs. It was all happening, including the breakup of the prettiest girl in school and the boy Lauren had fantasized about since last spring, when he said hello to her for the first time in the hallway near the gym. He was so beautiful, so perfect, godlike in every way imaginable. His thick, wavy blond hair swept across his face and hit the top of his shoulders, which were broad and, in football gear, looked like they could support her mother's jewelry safe. His stomach, Lauren had seen last summer that blessed day at the lake, was flat with a thin trail of light brown hair that ran from his belly button into the top of Hawaiian-style jammer shorts. His butt looked firm in the faded jeans he wore on his hips, like the male models in Hollister ads. He had muscular arms and perpetually tanned, soft-looking hands that could on weekends throw a football seventy yards into the eager hands of a wide receiver and during the week delicately steer Angel through the crowded school corridors. Judd's best feature, however, were his eyes, which were a green and blue combination like the water in the Virgin Islands and intense, like Lauren's father's eyes. That day he looked at her—when he said hello in the hallway—she felt pulled into them, as if sucked off the edge of a cliff into a deep lagoon.

What she wouldn't give to be in an isolated lagoon in the Caribbean with Judd, their sailboat bobbing in the distance as they lay on the beach, far away from Angel and the sad memories; far away from her parents; far away from Josh; far away from anyone. Judd would be an excellent skipper, of course, and would confidently sail them from bay to bay, day after day, in radiant unerring sunshine. Lauren, who in her daydream transformed her body into that of a Victoria's Secret model, would sit by his side, occasionally popping up to retrieve more lemonade or fresh fruit from the cabin. In the late afternoons, after they had anchored their boat for the night, they would swim together; Lauren in a fabulous floral bikini and Judd in brightly colored trunks that accentuated his tanned, toned abdomen. Afterward, he would cook local fish on a barbecue attached to the boat's stern, and they would feed each other, sipping island drinks between bites.

"Where are you?"

"What?" said Lauren, rocketing from the Caribbean back to the library.

"You're lost in thought," said Stephanie, sitting down.

"What time is it?"

"About five minutes before the bell. I went all the way to my locker and emptied it looking for that stupid science notebook. I must have left it at home, which means another stupid detention from Willouer."

"Can't you just use another notebook to take notes?"

"No way," said Stephanie, frowning. "Willouer's as compulsive as they come. He checks our notebooks every day."

"Sweet-talk him," said Lauren, checking her cell phone for text messages.

"I've tried," said Stephanie. "I think he's allergic to it."

"Bummer," said Lauren.

"Tell me about it," said Stephanie as the bell rang.

Lauren put her history book back in her backpack and realized she, too, had forgotten something: her worn school-issued copy of *Othello* for English class. She searched again, then closed her eyes, focusing on where she'd put the book.

"Are you coming?" asked Stephanie.

"Yes and no," said Lauren, standing and slinging the backpack over her right shoulder. "I've got to run to my locker before English."

Lauren walked as quickly as she could out of the library and into the overpopulated hallway, down two flights of stairs and another hallway to her locker, the second one in from the End of the World. Even though she continually vowed to carry everything she needed for the day in her backpack, she inevitably forgot something. And each time she made a hurried trip to her locker, inconveniently located near nothing that had anything to do with her life, she swore to herself that it would never happen again. The bell rang just as she flung open the metal door. She grabbed the book from the shelf, slammed the door, and sprinted back down the hallway and up one flight of stairs. She ran down the now empty halls, around the corner to her classroom, and saw the shut door.

"Shit," she said, breathing hard.

Mrs. Bennigan shut her door precisely sixty seconds after the bell. She said that was adequate time for the prepared student to be in his or her seat, silent, and ready for instruction. Those unable to do so were expected to get a late pass from the office. They would be admitted to class at the halfway point, when Mrs. Bennigan allowed another full minute for what she called a Fidgety Stretch. She timed all kinds of things on the stopwatch she wore around her neck.

Lauren took her time walking to the office, where she found several people already in line for passes. When she reached the head of the line, she gave the office assistant her name, the teacher's name, and the classroom number, all of which were written on a green slip, torn off the pad, and given to her. Slip in hand, she meandered back to Mrs. Bennigan's room. She arrived with another fourteen minutes before the door would open and sat down on the floor, resting her back against a locker. She thought about taking her book out of her backpack and having it open to the murder scene, the topic of discussion for that afternoon. But she had plenty of time for that. Shakespeare made her kind of crazy anyway. Nobody talked directly about anything. Instead, they relied on messages that always got lost or the advice of a friend who turned out to be an enemy. If the characters only communicated better, there would be no need for the senseless violence. Lauren closed her eyes.

"Hi," said a boy's voice. Lauren opened her eyes to see Judd Acker standing in front of her. She blinked, thinking she was imagining his image, and then blushed.

"Hi," Lauren said meekly.

"What are you doing here?" asked Judd.

"I'm late for Mrs. Bennigan's class," said Lauren, explosions in her chest, cheeks hot.

Judd smiled. "And so you can't go in until she opens the door, right?"

"Yes," said Lauren.

"I had her last year," said Judd. "She's a great teacher, but she's kind of a nutcase."

Lauren smiled. "What are you doing here?" she asked tentatively.

"That's my locker you're leaning against."

Lauren thought his locker was in the U hall. Now she knew it must be Angel's—and Judd no longer kept his things there.

"Oh God," said Lauren, jumping up. "I'm so sorry."

Judd put his hand on her right shoulder, his touch sending a current of energy through her entire body. "Hey, it's okay," he said. "I've got plenty of time. I'm in study hall."

"Oh."

Judd turned the combination wheel on his locker. "You're Nate Barons's little sister, aren't you?"

Lauren swallowed, trying to moisten her dry throat. "Yes," she said.

"What's your name?"

"Lauren."

"I'm Judd Acker," said Judd, extending his hand.

"I know," said Lauren, putting out her hand and blushing again.

"How do you know?" asked Judd, taking her hand in his.

Lauren looked down at their joined hands and couldn't speak. The warmth of their hands spread up her arms and into her lungs, now ablaze. His hand fit perfectly around hers, like the worn oven mitt she used at home to remove tuna and melted cheese sandwiches from the toaster oven. "I'm sorry," Lauren said.

"What are you sorry about?" asked Judd, releasing her hand but still looking intently into her eyes. Lauren, convinced she would combust at any moment, took a deep breath, then looked at the floor.

"I'm sorry about you and Angel," she said softly.

"Thank you," said Judd, as softly as she had spoken.

"You must be sad," said Lauren, feeling strong enough to attempt looking into his eyes. When she got there, he looked away. He opened the door to his locker and grabbed a book from the shelf.

"It's okay," he said quietly. "It was time."

He bent down and extracted another book from a neatly stacked pile on shelves at the bottom of his locker. It was one of the neatest lockers she had ever seen. No mass of crumpled notebook paper at the bottom. No tests with bad grades that never made it home, no old lunch bags, or fast food cups, or broken pencils, or plastic pen shards, no pieces of erasers—just stacks of books and notebooks, and a pencil case hung on a hook next to the navy blue pea coat she loved. Judd shut his locker door just as Mrs. Bennigan opened her classroom door. "Ready to join us, Miss Barons?" Mrs. Bennigan asked with an amused expression.

Lauren looked at Judd, willing him to ask her to run away with him.

"Hey, Mrs. Bennigan," said Judd. "How's it going?"

"It would be going perfectly," she replied, "if my students would arrive at my class on time."

"Don't be too hard on her," said Judd. "She's a friend of mine."

"Ah," said Mrs. Bennigan, nodding her head.

"See you, Lauren," said Judd, turning to walk down the hall.

"Bye," Lauren said to his back.

"Come join us, Miss Barons," said Mrs. Bennigan. "Desdemona is in terrible trouble!" Lauren walked past her teacher and took the empty seat in the front row that was reserved for late people. She opened her book, looked down, and daydreamed about Judd until the bell rang. As she put her book, notebook, and pen into her backpack, Mrs. Bennigan approached her desk. "I'll see you at two thirty-five," she said.

"Okay," said Lauren dejectedly. She had hoped Mrs. Bennigan would skip the detention, as a favor to Judd. Lauren walked down the hallway and was just about to walk into her writing workshop when she heard Josh's voice. She turned around.

"Hey," he said.

"Hi."

Josh led her out of the doorway. "I called you last night."

"I'm sorry I didn't pick up," said Lauren. "Pammy was in crisis mode. I was on the phone with her until eleven, and then I didn't want to wake you."

"And I'm sorry this whole dating thing isn't turning out too well," he said. "I want to take you out. My parents have been driving me absolutely crazy with weekend plans."

"That's okay," said Lauren, meaning it. Judd was *free*.

"I think we're around this weekend, though," said Josh as the bell rang. "I'll call you later."

After her writing class, Lauren walked back to Mrs. Bennigan's room. There she sat, flipping through *Othello* but for the most part looking at the clock, until three fifteen. Mrs. Bennigan thanked her for her time, a practice Lauren found annoying, and excused her, along with several others, thanking them all. Lauren dragged herself down the hall and down the stairs; she had no money for a cab and it was a long walk home. Her mother wouldn't pick her up; she was always too busy. And Nate, even if he did answer his phone, would only laugh at her. She scuffed her feet all the way down the empty hallway to her locker and exchanged the books she didn't need for those she did. She slammed her locker door as hard as she could, gratified by the amount of noise generated by metal hitting metal. If school had been in session, she would have received another detention for that little trick. She walked back down the hallway and up the stairs to the back of the school. Outside, she sat down on the cold cement wall to fortify herself for the walk and wish for a miracle, like her mother, on a whim, swinging by school on her way home from Nellie's Nail Salon. Two minutes later, Lauren slid off the wall and heaved her loaded backpack onto her shoulders. She walked on the sidewalk down the hill to the access road, and then out to the main road, where she readjusted her backpack as she waited for the light.

"Hey, Lauren!" Lauren turned her head and saw Judd Acker's black Jeep next to her. The passenger side window was down and he was looking at her from the driver's seat. She took the few steps needed to reach the car and was met, for the second time that day, by his beautiful face. She smiled at him and said hello, using his name. "What are you doing?"

"I had a detention, from Mrs. Bennigan," Lauren explained.

"Ah, yes," he said. "No ride?"

"Nope," said Lauren. "My brother refuses to be seen in public with me."

Judd laughed. "Hop in," he said. "I'll take you home." Lauren took a quick look around to see if anyone could serve as a witness, then opened the car door. She put her backpack down on the floor, sat down, and started memorizing details about the car's interior so she could tell her friends. "Where do you live?"

"Foxwoods Lane," said Lauren. "It's off Wayward."

Judd pulled the car onto the main road. Lauren leaned back against the seat and concentrated on inhaling and exhaling. Sitting in Judd's car reminded her, somehow, of her grandmother. She couldn't think of a single reason why that would be true until she saw the flat, yellow cardboard pine tree hanging from the rearview mirror. It was scented, Lauren realized at that moment, like her grandmother. Whenever Gran walked into their kitchen, she smelled sweet and pure and fresh, as if surrounded by a fine vanilla mist. Lauren reached out and touched the tree. "I like it," she said. "Your tree."

Judd turned down the music and looked over at her. "You like vanilla?"

"Yes," said Lauren. And before she could stop herself, "It reminds me of my grandmother."

"Do you like vanilla ice cream?"

"It's my favorite," said Lauren.

"Me too," said Judd. "The people at B&R think I'm crazy whenever I go in there. They've got a million flavors, but I get plain vanilla."

Lauren laughed. "I do the same thing."

Judd slowed the car at a stop sign and looked at his watch. "Do you want to go get some?" he asked. "Do you have time?"

"I'd love to," said Lauren.

Judd drove down Plymouth Street, then took a left onto Elm

and parked the car a few blocks from the ice cream shop. He got out, walked over to Lauren's side as she was unclipping her seat belt, and opened the car door. Warm and flushed, Lauren stepped out of the car and onto the sidewalk next to Judd, who was taller than she'd remembered from their chat at his locker. They walked into Baskin-Robbins, ordered vanilla waffle cones, and took them back to the car. Judd again opened the door for Lauren, then walked around the car and opened his door. He sat back down in the driver's seat, started the car, and turned on the heat. Instead of shifting into DRIVE, he turned in his seat, leaning his back against the door window. "Is this good, or what?" he asked.

"Unbelievable," Lauren managed to say.

Judd licked his cone and Lauren licked hers, all the while watching him. He ran his gorgeous tongue all the way around the outside of the cone three times. After that, he used it to push the center mound of ice cream farther down into the cone. When the ice cream was even with the top of the cone, Judd took his first bite. "How am I doing?" he asked.

Lauren blushed and then laughed. "Fine," she said.

"I'm teasing you," said Judd. "I like to watch people eat, too. You can learn a lot about people by their eating habits."

"Like what?" asked Lauren.

"Let's look at you," said Judd. "I can tell you really do love ice cream, but you're trying not to be a pig about it because you don't know me very well and you're not that comfortable in this situation. So, you're eating slower than you'd normally eat, and you're being especially careful because you'd be absolutely mortified if you dropped something on your jacket."

"Pretty close," said Lauren, blushing again, as if her head were a lighthouse, with a hot red light that shone through her face every sixty seconds. Judd took another bite of his cone, then shifted the car into DRIVE.

"I'll take you home now," he said, pulling out of their parking space. Too soon, he pulled the Jeep into her driveway. Lauren thanked him again for the ice cream and for the ride. He thanked her for her company, but made no attempt to open his door. Did he not want Nate to see him? Lauren grabbed her backpack with her left hand and the door handle with her right and pushed herself out of the car. She shut the door, waved through the window, and watched him drive away. When she walked into the kitchen, her aproned grandmother was chopping celery.

"Well, hello," said Eileen. "How was school?"

"Wonderful," said Lauren, twirling once before setting her pack down next to the table.

Eileen stopped chopping. "You're positively glowing," she said. "Something marvelous must have happened."

"Better than that," said Lauren, smiling.

"Did you get an A on a test?" asked Eileen, still holding the knife midair over the half-chopped celery.

"Gran," said Lauren, moving closer to the kitchen island and her grandmother, "getting an A on a test and dancing around the kitchen are mutually exclusive."

"Not for me," said Eileen, chopping again. "An A was hard to come by."

"Guess again," said Lauren.

"You're in love," said Eileen. Lauren flashed her grandmother a broad grin. "Is it Josh, Nate's friend?"

Lauren's smile faded. "No."

"Oh," said Eileen. "Well, that just shows you how much I know. I thought you two had feelings for each other."

"We do," said Lauren, her mood sinking like a helium balloon the day after the birthday party.

"But you have stronger feelings for someone else?" said Eileen, putting the knife down on the countertop. Lauren told her grandmother, again, about Judd Acker, this time in greater detail. She told her she'd essentially been in love with him forever. She told her about his eyes and his voice and his hands and his manners. She told her about that very afternoon, about how he opened the car door for her, about how he bought her ice cream. When Eileen wondered why a modern-day knight like Judd was unattached, Lauren told her about Angel and about the breakup that shocked everyone at school. "If Judd and Angel have just broken up after a three-year relationship, do you think he's ready to start dating again?" asked Eileen.

Lauren thought for a moment. "What you're saying is if Judd is interested in me, it would be nothing but a rebound relationship," she said.

"Not necessarily," said Eileen, scooping the celery with cupped hands into a mixing bowl. "I just think it's a matter of poor timing." Lauren's eyes welled up with tears. Eileen wiped her hands on her apron and then wrapped her arms around her granddaughter, steering her toward the kitchen table. They both sat down on the window seat cushions. "I've said the wrong thing," said Eileen, thumbing away a tear from Lauren's cheek.

"No," said Lauren, looking down at the tabletop. "I think you're right, but I just don't want to think about it like that. I want to believe he wants to be with me as much as I want to be with him. Spending time with him today was like a dream come true."

"I am glad you had a nice time with him," said Eileen.

Lauren looked up at her grandmother. "Maybe he's different, Gran," said Lauren. "Maybe he's been wanting to break up with Angel for a long time but couldn't because of circumstances in her life."

"I thought she broke up with him."

"No one really knows," said Lauren. "The rumor mill is unreliable that way."

"Ah," said Eileen, putting her arm around Lauren's shoulders. They sat a bit longer before Eileen stood. "Want to help me cook?"

"Okay," said Lauren. "What are we making?"

"I'm making a casserole," said Eileen, "but you could make the chocolate pudding."

"Perfect," said Lauren. She got her mother's apron out of the broom closet. It was made of a sheer pink fabric and had black martini glasses printed all over the skirt. The olives in the glasses were green. It was part of a naughty housewife costume Ann had worn to a Halloween party several years ago. It had never been worn as just an apron until Eileen and Sam moved in. Whenever Eileen and Lauren cooked together, which was now a couple of times a week, Eileen wore the white cotton apron with apples on it that she had brought from Pennsylvania and Lauren wore the pink martinis, the only apron her mother owned. They were both standing over the stove when Ann walked in the door from the garage.

"What a day," announced Ann wearily as she tossed her keys into the wicker basket. "If I don't have a caramel cappuccino immediately, I'm going to die." She opened the fridge and grabbed a gallon of skim milk. "The Garden Tour Committee is made up of complete idiots," she said to no one in particular. "That meeting was a huge waste of time. And the line at the Coffee Connection drive-through was backed onto the street. What are you two cooking up for dinner?"

"Chicken casserole," replied Eileen, "green beans, and corn muffins."

"Oh goodie," Ann shouted over the noise of her cappuccino maker. "At this rate, we'll all need cholesterol medication by summer."

"I've been eating chicken casserole for years," said Eileen, "and look at me."

"The picture of health," said Ann. God, she had a headache.

"I like Gran's casserole," said Lauren, in defense of her grandmother.

"Of course you do," said Ann. "You also like ice cream, Brie cheese, and every chip known to man."

Lauren frowned. "What's that supposed to mean?" she asked.

"It's supposed to mean you're a young woman now and you should be monitoring your intake," said Ann.

"Nonsense," said Eileen, spooning the contents of the mixing bowl into a large casserole dish. "She's an active girl and will probably never need to diet."

"She will if she doesn't want to be a size twelve," said Ann.

"There are worse things in life than being a size twelve."

"I can't think of one," said Ann, pouring her drink into a large ceramic mug.

"I can," said Eileen, turning her back on her daughter. Lauren watched her grandmother wash her liver-spotted hands in the sink. She had working woman hands, with large knuckles and thick fingertips. Yet the thin skin that stretched across the bones on top was smooth and soft to the touch. Lauren looked over at her mother's hands, one of which was reaching for the large plastic bottle of ibuprofen in the cupboard above the coffeemaker. Her hands were smooth, too. Aside from the absence of age markings and the active-length, sweet plum–colored, manicured fingernails, they looked like Gran's. Lauren looked at her own hands, padded with teenage fat and adorned with silver friendship rings. Her orange nail polish was chipped. Lauren looked back at her mother's hands, now holding her favorite mug and turning the pages of the new *House Beautiful*.

"Do you feel okay, Mom?" asked Lauren.

"I have a raging headache," said Ann, not looking up. "I just need a few minutes of quiet."

"What you need is some nutrition," said Eileen. "A good meal."

Ann held up her hand. "Don't start, Mother. It's been a long day."

Eileen joined Lauren at the stove. "How's that pudding coming along?"

"It's starting to thicken," said Lauren.

Eileen stuck her right index finger into the pot and tasted Lauren's creamy brown mixture. "That's perfect," she said. "I couldn't have done better myself."

CHAPTER 16

⤳

When Nate hit his teenage years, Mike started paying attention to his birthday. Before that, he had often missed his son's parties, and not necessarily because he couldn't extract himself from work. No, on many occasions he had chosen to be working rather than participating in whatever Ann had cooked up for the occasion: a sleigh ride, tobogganing, or ice skating outside and professional clowns, jugglers, and caterers inside. The level of noise and excitement rivaled that at a state fair midway, and Mike wanted no part of it. Nate's birthday was a day over which Mike had no control—until Nate turned thirteen, and Mike talked Ann into letting him take his son to New York instead of her trying to top the previous year's and everyone else's festivities. They flew to Manhattan, just the two of them, on the Dilloway corporate jet, dined at an exclusive men's club in Midtown, and then strolled the streets of the most powerful city in the world before sitting in the front row at a New York Knicks game. When Nate was fourteen, they went to Houston, where Mike just happened to have a business meeting. The best part for Nate was not the lavish Mexican food and real cowboy boots, but the fact he got to miss school and watch TV in the hotel suite while his father worked. For Nate's fifteenth, Mike took him to San Francisco for an entire weekend—no business meetings, just periodic cell phone calls and laptop time. They drove up and down the hilly streets, and they visited Alcatraz to hear firsthand the daunting tales of failed escape. They viewed the Golden Gate Bridge from a dozen locations, its color captivating Nate. A red bridge should be in the desert, he told his dad, where it would span a gazillion grains of sand, its hard surface providing temporary relief to travelers weary of the soft, sinking, shifting sand underfoot.

A European business trip took Mike away for Nate's sixteenth birthday. He had a five o'clock flight out that Monday morning for a four-day meeting in Zurich, and Nate couldn't go. Ann didn't want Nate to miss that much school, although she was also protesting the fact that Mike wouldn't take her. She understood it was an important event for the company and that Mike would be incredibly busy, but she resented being thought of as a distraction. And if she wasn't going, certainly Nate wasn't going. Mike had explained his conflict to Nate the week before and offered him several alternatives, all of which Nate turned down. Mike had seen then that his son would not be bought off cheaply. Nate now expected his father to come through on his birthday, and Mike was not someone who broke his word. A new car would do it, Nate told his dad the day before Mike left for Switzerland. So, that afternoon, Mike picked up Nate from school, drove him to the BMW dealership, and wrote a check for a $55,000 car.

This year, Nate was turning seventeen, and Mike had rearranged his schedule to take him to Colorado for a long weekend. They would leave Wednesday after school and return Sunday in time for dinner. Eileen told Nate she would make him his birthday dinner, anything he wanted. And while she preferred to serve a birthday dinner on the actual day, Friday this year, she agreed to serve it on Sunday night when he returned with his dad. And so the preparations began. Mike and Nate went snowboarding, and Eileen and Lauren planned, shopped, cooked, and baked. For an appetizer, Nate requested escargot served with toasted French bread. The salad, he said, should not be too girly; no curly misshapen exotic lettuce, no avocados, no pineapple or mandarin oranges, and definitely no roasted pine nuts, the ingredient most restaurant chefs could not stop themselves from sprinkling on the top of their house salads. For the main course, Nate wanted ribs and lots of them. And he wanted potato salad and he wanted real baked beans, nothing out of a can. For dessert, he was clear and resolute. He wanted no part of a cake with candles. Nothing would do except his grandmother's cherry pie.

Ann was busy and unavailable Thursday and Friday and then visible and grumpy, what Eileen called out of sorts, most of the weekend. She didn't want to help in the kitchen, but she didn't seem to do much else, either. She went to the gym Saturday morning, then hung around the house all afternoon, for the most part flipping through magazines. It was almost five o'clock when Ann, from the living room, and Sam, through the back door, walked into the kitchen simultaneously. Eileen and Lauren were sitting at the kitchen table halfway through a 500-piece jigsaw puzzle called Niagara Falls in the Spring. "Who wants a drink?" asked Ann.

"I do," said Sam, taking off his coat.

Ann walked to the refrigerator and took a large bottle of white wine from the bottom rack. There was no need for French champagne tonight. "What would you like, Dad?" she asked, taking the corkscrew from its magnetized home on the wall.

"I'll have what you're having."

"White wine?" asked Ann. "I thought you were a scotch drinker."

"It's all the same to me," said Sam, trying to hang his heavy wool coat on a wall peg. He had already dropped it, but received no help from his wife, who firmly believed he had to do something for himself once in a while.

"Oh, for God's sake," said Ann, swiftly crossing the room and hanging her father's coat. "They're not all the same."

"It's alcohol," said Sam, moving toward the kitchen counter like a windup toy in need of a key turn.

"Good point," said Eileen, placing another water piece into the puzzle.

"That's ridiculous," said Ann, pouring herself a glass of wine. "That's like saying food is all the same. That it doesn't matter if you have broccoli or ice cream for dessert."

"Well, it doesn't matter to you," said Eileen, standing. "You don't eat dessert anyway." Lauren giggled.

"You're very funny, Mother," said Ann, taking a large sip from her glass.

"Am I going to get my wine or not?" asked Sam, reaching for the bottle.

"Yes," said Ann curtly. "Mother?"

"Oh, why not," said Eileen. "Let's throw discretion to the wind." Ann poured two more glasses of wine and refilled hers. "Anything for you?" Eileen asked Lauren.

"I'd love some wine," said Lauren, smiling.

"Nice try, little girl," said Ann, taking her glass and walking across the kitchen floor and into the hallway.

"You're welcome to a soft drink, Lauren," said Eileen, when Ann was gone. "Join us in the living room if you'd like."

"No thanks, Gran," said Lauren. "I'm going to stay here."

"Don't do that whole puzzle on me, now," said Eileen. "We can do more together later."

"Sounds good," said Lauren, fitting in another piece. As soon as her grandparents left the kitchen, Lauren took one of the real Cokes her father occasionally brought home from the refrigerator. She popped the top, then sat back down at the table. She had inserted three more pieces into the puzzle and was on the verge of completing the lower left-hand corner when she felt her phone vibrate. She reached into her pocket and checked the caller ID. It was Josh.

By the time Eileen and Sam reached the living room, Ann was sitting on the couch, reading the newspaper. "Mind if we join you?" asked Eileen, holding a small bowl of peanuts.

Ann put the paper down and looked at her mother. "Wasn't that the point?"

Eileen held Sam's glass while he lowered himself into Mike's favorite armchair. Ann thought about protesting—knowing he would either spill his wine or dribble chewed peanuts down his shirt front and into the cracks around the seat cushion, creating indelible oil stains on the imported silk fabric—but she had no idea where she would prefer he sit. She briefly considered the family room, but decided against it since it would take so long to relocate. She finished her wine as Eileen gave Sam a handful of nuts and then sat down on the other end of the couch. "Peanut?" asked Eileen, holding the bowl out to Ann.

"Not for me," said Ann, holding up her hand.

"They're delicious," said Eileen, popping a few into her mouth.

"What I need," said Ann, standing, "is some more wine."

"That's the last thing you need," said Sam after Ann had left the room.

"Sam, honey, are you with me?" asked Eileen.

"I'm always with you."

"I'm worried about her, Sam," she said, leaning forward on the couch cushion, looking at her husband's kind face. "I'm worried about our daughter."

"With good cause."

"She drinks an awful lot. And I'm afraid," said Eileen, looking at the carpet beneath her feet, "that she isn't very well-liked."

"What on earth do you mean?" asked Sam, taking a sip of his drink and appearing interested.

"Remember I went to that fashion show with Ann—last week, I guess it was. Well, afterward, I was waiting in the lobby for her and happened to overhear two women, who were complete strangers— I had never seen either of them before—talking about our Ann. And they were saying derogatory, uncharitable things."

"Women are gossipers," said Sam. "It's nothing to concern yourself about."

"But it happened in church, too, Sam, people talking about our daughter, like they do about a movie star or someone in national politics. I don't understand it," said Eileen. "And I don't like it."

"I don't like it any better than you do."

"She's vulnerable, Sam. She seems strong, but she is soft inside. She appears to be on top of things, but I think she's lost. And I don't know how to help her."

"And I can appreciate that," said Sam, "because until I got to know these people we are staying with a little bit better, I might have said the same things." Eileen briefly searched her husband's face with her eyes, and then scooted back on her cushion and took a sip of her wine.

In the kitchen, Ann poured herself another glass, drank half of it, and then replenished what she'd consumed. She opened the refrigerator door to put the bottle back, then, changing her mind, carried it to the living room, where her parents were sitting in silence. "More wine?" she asked, showing them the bottle.

"Goodness no, dear," said Eileen. "I've still got half a glass."

"Dad?"

"What?"

"Would you like some more wine?"

Sam looked at Eileen. "Do you know what she's talking about?"

"She wants to know if you want more wine, Sam," said Eileen.

"I don't even drink wine," said Sam. "How could I possibly want more?"

"Because your current glass of wine is almost empty," said Ann.

Sam looked at the wineglass sitting on the table next to him. "That's not mine," he said.

"Suit yourself," said Ann, carrying the bottle to the couch and setting it down on a magazine on the coffee table. "Any news from Meadowbrook?"

"Nothing available yet," said Eileen. "But it shouldn't be much longer. We're moving up the list." *Not fast enough,* thought Ann. "So," said Eileen, "what do you think the boys are up to tonight?"

Here we go, thought Ann: Hypothetical Who Cares, one of her mother's favorite games. She loved to wonder aloud what someone, anyone, in the world was doing and encourage everyone in the room to discuss it. It could be someone the game participants knew, in this case Mike and Nate. It could also be someone no one knew personally, like the president of the United States. Who, what, and where didn't really matter, as far as Ann could tell. Hypothetical Who Cares was simply her mother's method of getting people to talk. It was what people referred to as an ice breaker, but Ann thought it was old-fashioned and boring. "I have no idea," she said, pouring herself more wine.

"What do you think, Sam?" asked Eileen.

"What do I think of what?"

"What do you think Mike and Nate are doing tonight?"

Sam stared blankly at his wife. "How would I possibly know something like that?" he finally said.

Ann smiled. "Good point, Dad."

"Well, *I* think they've just finished their last run of the day," said Eileen, looking at her watch. "I think they're heading to the lodge for some hot chocolate."

"Maybe," sang Ann, who guessed Mike hadn't had a hot chocolate in ten years.

"Is there a lodge meeting?" asked Sam, putting his hands on the arms of the chair in an effort to lift himself.

"No, no, Sam," said Eileen, waving the air in front of her. "We're talking about a ski lodge. Mike and Nate are in Colorado celebrating Nate's birthday."

"No kidding," said Sam. "That sounds like a fine idea. I wish I could have gone with them."

"I'm sure they would love to have you along," said Eileen to Sam. Ann drank the rest of her wine, then reached for the bottle. "Haven't you had several glasses already?" asked Eileen, touching Ann's hand.

"I'm a grown-up," said Ann, "so I can decide for myself what I think is an appropriate amount of wine."

"My mother always told me . . ." started Eileen.

". . . that two drinks was all anyone needed in an evening," finished Ann.

"Evidently, I've told you that before."

"About a billion times," said Ann, refilling her glass. "Obviously your mother didn't have much fun."

Eileen pursed her lips and stood. "Who's ready for dinner?"

"I am," said Sam. "What's on the menu?"

"Meat loaf, baked potatoes, and lima beans," announced Eileen.

"Give me a trucker's portion," said Sam, lifting himself out of the chair. "I could eat a horse."

"I'm going to pass," said Ann, picking up the newspaper.

"Ann, you've got to eat something," said Eileen.

"I'll find something a little later," said Ann, from behind the Region section. "I'm not hungry right now."

"You're going to waste away into nothing," said Eileen.

Ann poked her head out, looked at her mother, and smiled. "That's my plan," she said.

In her room, where she walked when her phone rang, Lauren was still talking to Josh. Images of Judd ran in and out of her mind. She was lying on her back on her bed, holding the phone in her right hand and looking for split hair ends with her left. Pammy had told her that by the time most girls were fifteen, half of their hair ends were unhealthily divided. "Do you need to check with your mom?" asked Josh.

"What do you think?"

"No," said Josh.

"I'll tell her I'm going out with friends. You don't even have to come inside."

Josh hesitated. "Do you want me to come inside?"

"No," said Lauren. "She'd want to know the whole story and then she'd probably tease us."

"What is the whole story, Lauren?"

"What do you mean?"

"I mean with us," said Josh softly. "Are we really going to do this, or was it a spur-of-the-moment thing the night of that party?" Lauren inhaled and held it. She slowly let out her breath. She wasn't thinking about Judd anymore. "I want to be with you," Josh said, "but only if you want to be with me. I don't want to potentially lose my best friend over a girl who's not that interested."

"That's not very nice," said Lauren.

"Maybe not," said Josh. "But I'm about to come out of the closet here with Nate, and I don't want to look like a fool, Lauren."

Lauren sat up. "You're not a fool," she said, more interested in Josh than she had been in the last fifteen minutes.

Josh said nothing, and then asked her about Judd. "He's free," Josh said. "He's free for the first time in three years."

"I know," said Lauren, picturing sitting in his car.

Lauren heard a knock on her door. It was her grandmother, telling her dinner was ready. Lauren hollered she would be right down. "I guess you have to go," said Josh, laughing.

"Yes," said Lauren. "It's time for dinner."

"Okay, then. Do you want to go to the movies tonight?"

Lauren bit her bottom lip and thought about what her grandmother had told her about rebound relationships. Judd probably already had a date for that very night. He would certainly want to play the field and Lauren knew she wasn't first-string material. "Yes," she said.

"Good," said Josh. "I'll pick you up at eight thirty, at the front door."

Lauren, Eileen, and Sam sat at the table in the guesthouse kitchen. Selma was having dinner with her sister, but would be home in time to help Eileen settle Sam in for the evening. Lately, he had been getting out of bed and walking around in the middle of the night. On the one hand, his behavior told Eileen he was comfortable in the guesthouse, comfortable enough to think he belonged there and had things to do at two o'clock in the morning. On the other hand, his nocturnal wanderings were a source of concern. How long would it be before he figured out the new locking system on the doors and wandered off again into the darkness? He was an intelligent man—had been, anyway—and his moments of lucidity brought with them opportunities for everything from coherently participating in a conversation to working a mechanical device. Eileen knew Sam would eventually discover the new locks and consider their conquest an honorable pursuit; she just didn't know when, because he was different now. Sometimes he was her husband, but most of the time he was a stranger, more animal than human. She watched him shove a large chunk of meat loaf into his mouth. He ate ravenously. It pleased Eileen to know that after all these years he still loved her cooking. But he'd lost his sense of decorum, which disturbed her. Proper speech, dress, and manners had always mattered to him. As a healthy man, he was always aware of how he was perceived by others, much more so than most in their farming community. He changed his shirt and washed his hands rigorously before sitting at the dinner table, his fingernails rid of the field. Now, he sometimes reminded her of a feral dog grazing in a diner Dumpster on castoff daily luncheon specials, unaware of anything but what was right in front of him. Food was so important to him now; maybe because it was the only thing he had to look forward to. Sam looked up and caught Eileen looking at him. He smiled at her, and she patted his hand. Good boy.

After dinner, Sam watched a movie in the living room while Eileen and Lauren did the dishes. "Gran," said Lauren, drying a pot, "can I talk to you?"

"Of course you can," said Eileen.

"It's about Josh."

As promised, Josh rang the big house doorbell at eight thirty. Lauren, who had already told her mother she was going to the movies with some friends, called good-bye and bolted out the front door. Josh, who was suddenly standing six inches from her, laughed. "I guess you really don't want me to come in," he said.

Lauren smiled at him. "It's just my mother in there," she said. "We don't need to talk to her."

"Your mother's okay," said Josh, putting his arm around Lauren and steering her toward the car.

"And you're just being polite," said Lauren.

"Ah," said Josh, opening the car door for Lauren. "You've caught me." Lauren sat down and Josh shut her door. She watched him as if for the first time as he walked around the front of the car through the headlights. He had beautiful skin, clear and the color of an early June tan. His cheeks were rosy, as if he had run to their house instead of driven. He was an inch or so taller than Nate, who was five foot, ten inches. Judd was six feet, two inches. She'd seen that somewhere—maybe a football program. Josh had nice teeth, the result of spending his junior high years in braces and nighttime headgear, and lips that were red enough to warrant a second glance. His lazy brown eyes and long dark lashes made him look like he was from another country. A lot of girls at school thought he was cute and asked Lauren what it was like having him around her house all the time. But she had always shrugged off their questions. She had not been seriously interested, until now, and wasn't sure why. He was such fun. Lauren had a mental picture of him from a couple of summers ago on their pool deck, his broad, hairless chest and strong, wiry arms flexed into an Incredible Hulk imitation, done without the slightest hint of self-consciousness. He was a good friend to Nate because he was loyal, but also because he didn't let Nate run all over him. Josh opened his door, allowing a blast of cold air into the warm exterior. Lauren shivered and Josh turned up the heat. "You look pretty," he said, looking at her. "I'm glad you're going out with me tonight."

"Me too," said Lauren, who had spent more time than usual on her appearance. While she was certainly aware of what other girls wore to school and to parties, and, consequently, had much of the same clothing, she didn't linger in front of the mirror. Tonight, she did, brushing the tangles out of her hair, brushing her teeth, applying light makeup. Just before she left her room, she sprayed perfume into the air and then walked through it. She'd read about that in a magazine.

Josh leaned over and kissed her cheek. He slowly pulled away from her before shifting the car into DRIVE. "Okay, let's go."

Ann opened her eyes and realized she was lying on the couch in the living room with the newspaper, refolded, sitting on her lap. She looked at her watch; it was just after nine o'clock. She must have fallen asleep. Slowly, she sat up, put the newspaper on the coffee table in front of her, and gently rubbed her eyes. She had a headache. She got up off the couch and walked into the kitchen. There, she took the bottle of ibuprofen out of the cabinet above the sink and spilled three terra-cotta-colored tablets into her hand. She filled a glass with water, then, leaning against the counter and closing her eyes, swallowed the tablets one at a time. She ran her hands over her abdomen and realized she was hungry. When she opened the refrigerator, the first thing she saw was a Tupperware container filled with the leftovers of one of her mother's casseroles. Fat from the hamburger or bacon or sausage or whatever meat her mother had mixed into it had congealed, forming a half-inch layer of pale yellow lard on top. Ann gagged. With her thumb and index finger, she lifted the container from the shelf and threw it into the garbage. Next in line was another container, this one half-filled with green beans. Again, Ann threw the whole thing away. Three pieces of well-done steak wrapped in aluminum foil; two spoonfuls of crusty scalloped potatoes in a small glass jar; dressed salad so soggy it could have been served with a spoon (Ha, thought Ann—send *that* to the starving children in China); chocolate pudding with its crust peeling away from the sides of a plastic bowl; and three one-inch cubes of cantaloupe wrapped in plastic wrap all sat on the second shelf of her refrigerator, as if it stood in the one-bedroom apartment of a single mother in the city's projects. While disgusted, Ann was not surprised to find leftovers in her fridge. Her mother simply could not throw food away. It didn't matter if it was sixteen kernels of corn. She would find them a temporary home in a plastic container she had once purchased at the grocery store, eaten the contents of, and then washed out carefully for future use. As a child, Ann had been the one assigned to find the perfect container for whatever leftover her mother wanted contained. The bottom was never hard to find; Eileen had a hundred of them in varied sizes. It was finding the matching top that proved vexing to Ann. Often in utter frustration, Ann had called her mother away from the sink to help. And it was then, time and again, that Eileen had explained the Ring on Deli tops always went with the A&P Forever bottoms. Together, Eileen and Ann would package up whatever they didn't eat and refrigerate it. On Friday nights, Eileen served what she called the Week's Review, declaring, "Waste not, want not!" as she set her creation down on the middle of the kitchen table. Ann's father always smiled appreciatively as Ann held her stomach in anticipation of the ache it would inevitably suffer later. Even then, as Ann silently prayed for survival when her father was saying grace, she vowed to never eat another leftover as soon as she was on her own.

No longer hungry, Ann made herself a decaf, sugar-free, skim-milk vanilla latte. She sat at the kitchen table and slowly sipped it. Her head was pounding. She took her coffee up the stairs to her bathroom, where she set it down on the side of the tub. Taking off her clothes, Ann stepped on the scale and was pleased to see she'd lost ten ounces. She then poured her favorite, special order, French bubble bath into the running water and watched it foam. She stepped into the tub, lay back against the cool ceramic, and closed her eyes. In twenty minutes she would towel off and get into bed, where—without Mike, an active sleeper—she could get a decent night's rest. Tomorrow, she would talk to her mother about the left-over situation. Tomorrow, she would sterilize the refrigerator. Tonight, she would do nothing for anyone but herself for a change.

CHAPTER 17

$\sim$

February always chilled Ann to the bone. She had enough trouble with January and its obligatory New Year's resolutions. What was she supposed to do, lose ten pounds like everyone else? Get into shape? At forty-five, she was in the best shape of her life. And January was too damn long. It was as if every day someone secretly tacked on another, of skin-freezing cold and endless snow. Yet it was February and its deceiving twenty-eight-day length that tried Ann's patience. She pulled her car into a parking space half-cleared by the overworked snowplows and prepared herself for the wall of winter she would slam into the moment she opened her door to step outside. The wind blew harder than ever and the sleet stung her face as she ran from her car to the offices of Noble and Robertson, the best and most expensive architects in the area.

Peter Noble and Tim Robertson knew the Barons family well because they designed and built their $3.4 million house and guesthouse. In Ann's mind, they were worth every penny. It was all in the details, she told Mike, who had asked about it every time he wrote them a check. Four-inch molding around the windows and along the floor and ceiling didn't come cheap. Neither did imported Italian marble or hardwood floors or six-panel solid wood doors or custom windows. Her house was a testament to the finest building materials available. During construction, Ann was ecstatic. Peter or Tim visited the site every day throughout the nine-month project, both joking this was the Baronses' third and final baby. They worked closely with Ann, catering to her whims. Ann hadn't received such attention since she and Mike were dating.

She was hoping to recapture that feeling of power and feminine authority with her sunroom proposal. What she had in mind was a sunny, tropical room off the family room end of the main hallway. The southern exposure was perfect for it. Floor-to-ceiling windows would ensure light and warmth throughout the day; the month of February would pass in a blink. Casual and inviting, the room would serve as a perfect location for anything from an afternoon of reading and napping to an informal luncheon spot for close friends.

"Hello, Ann," said Peter Noble, with a warm smile. He ushered her out of the waiting room and into his spacious office, impeccably decorated with contemporary furniture, carpeting, and window treatments in soothing earth-tone colors. "It's good to see you again. Sit down and tell me what you have in mind." Just before he closed the door, he called back to his receptionist: "Darlene? Please get Mrs. Barons a sugar-free, caramel latte with skim milk."

Ninety minutes later, the preliminary plans for Ann's sunroom were mapped out. Peter suggested a semicircular room, mirroring the shape and intensity of the sun, and Ann readily agreed, even though she had pictured something square or rectangular. Peter acknowledged his suggestion would give her less useable space, but it would certainly be more dramatic and more architecturally pleasing from both the outside and the inside. It would make a statement, said Peter, knowing how much Ann Barons loved and lived to do just that. Ann left his office after promising to talk to Mike that very evening. She ran to her car and called Sally, hoping she would be free for lunch. Sally was on her way to a library committee meeting. "You don't need to go to that meeting," said Ann. "You need to have lunch with me."

"I can't," said Sally, who, truth known, had not fully recovered from the fashion show snub. Ann had called her just twice since— once to go shopping and another time to have coffee after exercise—and both times Jesse had been asked, too.

"Of course you can," said Ann. "Those library committee meetings are excruciating."

"How would you know?" sniffed Sally. "You haven't been on the library committee."

"Mike's been on that board," said Ann. "And he said it should have been called a B-O-R-E-D instead of a B-O-A-R-D." Sally allowed herself to smile. "Come on," said Ann. "I need my best friend. I'll treat."

Best friend? Sally's heart swelled. "Okay," she said. "Where do you want to go?"

"I'll meet you at Tony's in thirty minutes," said Ann. "Believe it or not, I'm absolutely craving carbs."

As they ate linguini drizzled with olive oil and garlic and drank house wine, Ann told Sally all about the sunroom. Feeling envy but feigning enthusiasm, Sally nodded her head, smiled, and said, "Ooh, sounds lovely," in the appropriate places. As the story dragged on, Sally realized Ann didn't need *her*, in particular. She merely needed an audience, anyone to listen to her talk about her money. Maybe she'd tried Jesse or Paula before she called her. Maybe she hadn't thought of the best friend trick until the other two had declined her invitation. Sally glanced at her watch—a well-established signal of boredom in Ann's little coterie—but Ann, oblivious, carried on. It wasn't until their plates were empty that the topic turned for the better. "So, here's what I think," said Ann, filling her wineglass for the third time. "We need a little trip to Florida for some sunroom inspiration. Just the girls."

"Now that sounds marvelous," said Sally, meaning it. "When do you want to go?"

"Before the end of the month," said Ann. "You know how much I hate February, and this year is no exception. It's been nothing short of horrendous."

Sally took a sip from her water glass. The two glasses of wine she'd consumed had gone to her head and she was feeling slightly dizzy. "Have you spoken to the others?" asked Sally, referring to Jesse and Paula.

"No," said Ann. "I thought I'd run it by you first."

Sally smiled. "Let's go!"

* * *

Ten days later, Ann and her friends were at the airport, headed for the Baronses' four-bedroom duplex in the Keys. Mike had given Ann permission to go ahead with the sunroom and construction was penciled in for the fall. Eileen had volunteered to "look in on" Lauren and Nate while Ann was away, and Emma—knowing Eileen would again give her time off in secret while Mike was at work—had declared herself available for extra help. The Baronses' Fun Only bank account was full, thanks to Mike exercising some stock options; Ann was as giddy as a high school senior on prom night. When everything was as it should be, she loved her life. And she was generous with those close to her.

When they stepped off the second plane in Florida, the weather was perfect—a cloudless sky and brilliant warm sunshine. Ann removed her cherry red leather blazer and slung it over her arm as they walked into the tiny terminal. A hired car and driver were waiting, courtesy of Mike, enabling the women to get away quickly, without going through some of the procedural hassles that arriving in the Keys could include. Twenty minutes later, they arrived at the beachside condo. It was clean and bright and fresh—Ann having made all the arrangements ahead of time. The windows were wide open, allowing the ocean breeze to flow from one room to another, leaving its salty scent behind. As soon as the driver deposited their luggage into the foyer and accepted his generous tip and drove away, Ann opened the refrigerator door and pulled out a pitcher of margaritas. "Welcome to the Islands," she said, filling the first of four glasses.

"Oh, honestly, Ann, you think of everything," said Paula.

"That I do, my friend," said Ann, handing a glass to each woman. "When you've got a limited amount of time, it's best to use it wisely."

"Cheers," said Jesse, clinking glasses with everyone.

"Now," said Sally, after her first sip. "Where is everyone going to sleep?" In fact, Sally had mapped out who was sleeping where and cleared it with Ann beforehand. She and Ann would share the master bedroom. It was so big, and Ann didn't like staying in it by herself. And Paula and Jesse would bunk in at the other end of the hall in the next biggest room, simply called the East Room. The two bedrooms on the lower level—where Nate and Lauren stayed—would remain vacant. Sally told Ann it was much more fun to share a room than be alone.

"I'm easy," said Jesse. "And I don't snore."

Ann laughed, her carefree mood enhanced by half a margarita.

"Great," Sally said. "I was thinking it would be fun to share rooms."

"Well, the last time we were here, I was in that room at the back," said Paula. "You know, the one that gets the morning sun."

"Yes," said Jesse. "The East Room; that's lovely."

"Then it's settled," said Sally, a little too quickly. "You two will share that room."

Jesse smiled at Sally. "And where will you sleep, Sally?"

"Well," said Sally, avoiding Jesse's amused gaze, "I guess I could keep Ann company."

"Whatever," said Ann, refilling their drink glasses. "Let's unpack and go to the beach."

"Sounds good," said Jesse, putting her untouched refill down on the counter. She had made a pact with herself and her husband that she would not spend three days living in a wineglass. Jesse could not match Ann's drinking capacity and had long ago stopped trying. For the first few years of their friendship, Jesse got drunk whenever Ann did. It didn't matter if they were meeting for lunch or a late afternoon catch-up, Jesse drank whatever Ann was drinking, glass for glass. For Jesse, it was an effort to be social more than it was a desire the consume alcohol. She didn't want Ann to drink alone. It finally came to her one night when she was kneeling on the bathroom floor in front of the toilet, waiting for the next round of nausea, that Ann didn't care if she drank alone.

The women walked up the stairs with their suitcases and parted company at the top. "Let's meet on the deck in fifteen minutes," announced Ann, walking toward her bedroom with Sally in tow.

"Perfect," said Paula, downing the rest of her margarita and setting the glass down on a table in the hallway.

As soon as she and Jesse reached their bedroom, Paula sat down on one of the two queen-sized beds separated by a wicker nightstand. A moment later, she lay back, appearing as exhausted as her coral-colored capri pants straining to imprison her generous thighs. "Phew!" she said. "I'm feeling a little dizzy."

"Close your eyes for a moment," said Jesse, looking at her watch. "You've just had two drinks in twenty minutes."

"Oh God," said Paula, following Jesse's advice. "I can't do this."

"You don't have to."

Down the hall, Sally closed the door to the bedroom as soon as she and Ann were inside. "Did that go okay down there?" she asked.

"Did what go okay?" asked Ann, rolling her bag across the floor to a whitewashed pine bureau.

"The bedroom discussion," said Sally, setting her drink on the pine table next to the king-sized bed. "I hope no one has hurt feelings."

Ann unzipped her suitcase and pulled out a stack of T-shirts in bright colors, freshly ironed by Emma. She carefully laid them in a bureau drawer. "And why," asked Ann, returning to her suitcase, "would anyone have hurt feelings?"

"About the sleeping arrangements, silly," said Sally, hands on her hips, standing over her unopened suitcase. "Honestly, Ann."

"And honestly, Sally," said Ann, removing the first of eight pairs of sandals from her shoe bag. "You think about this stuff too much."

Sally opened her suitcase. "I'm not sure that's true," she said, taking out three pairs of capri pants and setting them on the bed. "Because I know Paula can have issues with this kind of thing. You know how easily her feelings get hurt."

"Paula has a lot of issues," said Ann, placing six of her favorite cotton sweaters in the bureau's bottom drawer. "But I don't think sleeping with me is one of them."

Sally smirked. "That's cute, Ann," she said sarcastically.

Ann, several bathing suits in hand, turned and looked at Sally. "Let's move on," she said. "I'd like to get to the beach before dark."

"That's fine," sniffed Sally. "I just like to bring these things up so they don't blow up on us later."

Ann turned her back on her friend, walked into the master bathroom, and closed the door behind her. She took off her clothes and checked out her body in the mirror that sat above the double sinks embedded in pink marble and ran from one side wall to the other. The dieting she had done in the last week had paid off. Her stomach was completely flat, almost concave. She slipped on the first of three bikinis she recently bought, then twisted and turned in front of her image. When she wheeled all the way around, she frowned; her bottom looked big. The second suit was better, from every angle. Ann walked toward the mirror, then away from it, looking over her shoulder. Yes, this was the suit for the day. Ann smiled at her reflection before opening the door to the bedroom. Sally was sitting on the bed, examining her new pedicure, and wearing the same suit. "Oh my gosh!" said Sally, smiling. "We're twins!"

Not smiling, Ann said, "Where did you get that suit?"

"Going Along Swimmingly," said Sally. "At the Sunset Mall."

"That liar Candace," said Ann. "She told me she'd just unpacked the suits and that no one had bought one."

"It's no big deal," said Sally. "Jesse and Paula will get a kick out of it."

"I don't think so," said Ann, hands on bony hips. "One of us will have to change." Recognizing an order, Sally slowly stood and walked to the bureau that held her clothes. She grabbed her other suit, last year's aqua one-piece with a low-cut back, and walked silently into the bathroom. Two minutes later, she emerged. "You look fabulous," said Ann, grinning. "Let's find the others."

Sally watched as Ann quickly pulled a pink diaphanous cover-up over her head, the same cover-up Sally had purchased from Candace because it matched the suit. Luckily, Sally had packed her white, terry-cloth cover-up. When she put it on, Ann told her how versatile it was, a word Sally well knew meant uninteresting.

Paula, wearing a black tank suit under a large black and white vertical striped tunic, and Jesse, wearing a pale yellow one-piece with a matching sarong tied around her hips, were already sitting on the porch when Sally and Ann walked downstairs. As soon as compliments were paid all around, Ann suggested they head down the cement pathway to the beach, where they would find chairs, towels, umbrellas, and—most importantly—the bar. Wearing her new straw hat and Juicy sunglasses, Ann led her friends under the palm trees to the sand. She told the beach boy to set up four chairs and a table under two umbrellas. She then ordered four frozen margaritas for delivery. "Now this," said Ann, as soon as she sat down in a chair, "is what it's all about."

"I'll second that," said Sally, taking the chair next to Ann.

"All I need now is that drink," said Ann, craning her neck around to see if the margaritas were on their way.

Jesse sat in the fourth chair, giving Paula the seat next to Sally. Paula hadn't been sitting thirty seconds when she pulled a romance novel from her beach bag and started reading. "Oh, here we go," said Sally. "Has the prince invited the scullery maid to the ball yet?"

"No, no, no," said Paula. "This one takes place in the here and now, in Manhattan,"

"Let me guess," said Ann, grinning at the muscular, tanned, Speedo-clad beach boy offering her a margarita on a Lucite tray. "She's an ad executive, and he's a well-mannered office boy who doesn't yet know he's heir to the throne of a faraway kingdom."

"They're in retail," said Paula dismissively.

"I don't know how you read those books," said Sally, taking a sip from the drink just handed to her. "They're really kind of silly, aren't they?"

"Haven't we had this discussion?" asked Paula, taking her drink from the tray but keeping her eyes on her book.

"Well," said Sally, removing the latest thick issue of *Vogue* from her canvas beach bag, "perhaps we just haven't found your answer satisfactory."

"And since when has my goal in life been to satisfy you?" said Paula, looking up from her book and through the gray lenses of her aviator sunglasses at Sally.

"Touché!" said Ann, giggling.

Jesse took her drink from the beach boy and set it down in the sand next to her. "There's a good reason women read romance novels," she said, gathering her shoulder-length brown hair into a ponytail. "They're hugely popular."

"And why is that?" asked Sally, still smarting from Ann's remark.

"Women love romance," said Jesse. "Ninety-nine times out of a hundred they don't get it from their husbands of twenty years, so they read about it in books. Experience it vicariously, so to speak."

"My husband can be romantic," said Sally defensively.

"Think about when and why he's romantic," said Ann, drink in hand. "Isn't it because he wants sex? Then again, Jack's ahead of the rest of his gender if he's romantic at all, Sally. Most men hop into bed and expect their wives—wild with lust after a day of caring for the children, running errands, and doing housework—to jump on top of them and beg for it." Paula laughed out loud.

"Are you saying making love isn't romantic?" asked Sally, removing her sunglasses, looking confused.

"It can be very romantic," said Jesse, "especially if both people want it at the same time. However, if the husband wants it and the wife simply acquiesces to get him to focus on something else, that's not all that romantic."

"Amen to that," said Ann. "Sex comes first and everything else comes afterward."

"You see, Peter, in the book, isn't like that," said Paula, swatting at but missing a horsefly that landed on her fleshy knee.

"That's why it's called fiction," sang Ann.

"It used to be true, though, didn't it?" asked Jesse. "Remember when we were dating our husbands? Remember how attentive they used to be?"

"Absolutely," said Paula. "My husband was the original Prince Charming."

"Flowers, dinner reservations, sunset strolls on the beach," said Jesse, smiling. "They know exactly what it takes to win us over."

"Then we get married, thinking we've met the man of our dreams," said Ann, "and everything changes. After all, he now gets sex for free!"

"Not in my book," said Paula. "Peter waits on Linda. He gives her foot massages."

"Now that's nice," said Jesse, turning her attention to the *Time* magazine she'd bought for weekend reading.

Sally took the last sip of her drink and then spoke slowly, as if recalling a dream from the previous night. "So, are you saying all men really want is to make love?"

"Yup," said Ann. "You've got it. Well, that and have power and money. Speaking of sex, where is that darling cabana boy?"

Sally sat back in her chair and covered her tiny tummy bulge with her hands. "That's depressing."

Paula leaned over and patted her shoulder. "That's why I read these books," she said. "You can have it when I'm done."

Sally didn't respond, deciding against talking to her friends about her love life. It certainly wasn't what Ann and Jesse described, and it wasn't found in the pages of Paula's romance novels. Her husband, Jack, was tired when he came home from work, often not until eight thirty or nine in the evening. Most of the time he had eaten dinner at his desk and wanted nothing more than a quick look at the evening newspaper, a twenty-minute bath, and a good night's sleep. Occasionally, when Sally would offer herself to him in the middle of the night, without saying a word to each other, they would make love. Until now, Sally actually thought this was quite normal. Neither of them seemed to require much physical passion. Of course, when she and Jack were first married, they made love regularly. They were in their early twenties and full of energy and, well, lust. *That's just what being twenty-two is all about,* was what Jack, grinning, would say to her afterward. Now, they were close to fifty. And Sally assumed her lack of interest in making love mirrored her husband's; that they'd just moved into another stage in their relationship and, frankly, didn't need to prove their commitment to each other by groaning and grunting in the bedroom. She and Jack had never discussed it, and, until today, Sally hadn't given it a lot of thought. Women made jokes about it, but Sally had taken them as simply that, jokes.

Paula put down her book and took a sip of her melted drink. She looked up at the horizon, composed of nothing but ocean and sky, one green and the other blue, stacked like colored sand in a gift shop jar. "Who wants to go for a swim?" she asked.

"Good Lord, no," said Ann, reaching for her glass. "I was about to order another drink. Who wants one? Sally?"

Sally looked at her empty glass and, not wanting to disappoint Ann, nodded her head.

"I'm all set," said Jesse.

"Me too," said Paula.

"I'll take you up on that swim, though," said Jesse, getting out of her chair.

When Jesse and Paula had left, Sally watched Ann make her way to the bar. The sand impeded her progress, sometimes causing her to check her balance like a sailor on a ship in stormy seas. Halfway there, she was met by the beach boy, who had run to meet her. He bowed and ran back in the direction of the bar. Ann wheeled around and, appearing lost, scanned the sparse crowd, hand shielding her eyes. Instead of signaling Ann, Sally turned to watch Jesse and Paula work their way into the water. They stood, hands on their hips, in knee-deep ocean. She wished she had gone with them. She was light-headed and drowsy and had no use for the drink Ann had ordered for her. Perhaps she could just get up and join Paula and Jesse before Ann made it back. Sally looked back at Ann, then quickly stood and removed her cover-up. She had just finished reapplying sunblock to her nose when Ann ducked under the umbrella shading her chair. "God, that sand is hot," she said. "My feet are on fire."

"Come swimming," said Sally.

"We've got cool drinks coming, my dear. That's all the liquid refreshment I need at the moment."

"Mmm," said Sally. "I'm just going to test the water. I'll be right back."

"Suit yourself," said Ann, settling into her chair.

Released, Sally walked quickly to the water's edge. She called out a greeting to Paula and Jesse, who had made little headway. "Have you come to brave the salty waters with us?" asked Paula, turning around at the sound of Sally's greeting.

"I don't know," said Sally. "Is it cold?"

"It's lovely," said Jesse. "I'm just not ready for full immersion."

Sally walked into the water to meet them, lifting her feet up high with each step, as if she were wearing clothing she didn't want to get wet instead of a bathing suit.

"We were just talking about Ann," said Paula.

"Oh?" said Sally. "What's up?"

"Well, Jesse's worried about her drinking."

Sally tucked her freshly highlighted bob behind her ears. "We're on vacation, Jesse. She's just cutting loose."

"She has had a drink in her hand since we walked into the condominium," said Jesse.

"The Ann I know does like her alcohol," said Paula.

"We all like our alcohol," said Sally.

"This is different," said Jesse. "She's been drinking more lately— she had too much when she was away with Mike, and she drank like a thirsty frat boy at lunch before the fashion show."

"How do you know she had too much with Mike?" asked Sally. "Did she tell you?"

"I don't know about the fashion show," said Paula. "We all had a couple of glasses that day. Pinot grigio goes down like water."

"So you think I'm worried about nothing," said Jesse, hands on her hips.

"No," said Paula, reaching out to touch Jesse's shoulder. "I know Ann drinks a lot. I just don't know if that amount has increased enough to warrant worry or action."

"Action?" said Sally. "What are we talking about here—an intervention? I don't think that's necessary, girls. We're on vacation."

"Just watch her with me," said Jesse. "I know we're on vacation, and I know she's going to drink more than she usually does. I'm telling you, I'm worried. She's been different since her parents arrived."

"Do you think that's what it is?" asked Sally, her brain racing, searching for details. What had Ann said about her mother?

"Partly," said Jesse. "Having long-term company is stressful, no matter who it is. But when you are face-to-face with your parents, your own history, every day of the week? Well, I can't really imagine how strange and unsettling that must be."

"You've got a point there," said Paula, wading a foot deeper into the water.

"It can't be that cold!" The three women turned their heads toward shore. Ann, holding her empty margarita glass, was standing on the sand dampened by the surf. "Go for it!"

Paula, Jesse, and Sally all looked at one another and then dove under the surface.

After late afternoon showers and a drink on the porch, they walked down the path to The Beachcomber, the resort's casual beachside restaurant. The tables and chairs, made from bamboo, sat on a cement floor that had been swept free of sand. The grass roof, sheltering them from unlikely rain, was supported by four corner posts, and the clear plastic sheets that served as walls in bad weather were rolled up and fastened at the roofline. They were shown to a table at the far end of the outdoor room, away from the resort kitchen and close to the beach. As they sat and chatted about the sound of the waves and the brilliant moonlight, Ann ordered an expensive bottle of white wine and insisted they all try the local fish, which was delicious as well as low-fat. Jesse closed her eyes. The warm breeze moved the stray hairs at her temples and cooled her hot skin. When she opened them, Ann was facing the bar in search of their wine; Paula was looking at the menu; and Sally was gazing into a compact, touching up her lipstick. As soon as the waiter arrived and filled Ann's glass, she took a mouthful.

"Ann," said Jesse softly, as soon as their waiter had left the table. "Where's the fire?"

"No fire," said Ann. "I'm just ready to get there."

"Get where?" asked Sally, shutting her compact.

"To an altered state," said Ann, taking another sip. "That's where I'm going."

"Take a look around you, Ann," said Jesse. "From where I'm sitting, it looks like we're already there. We're not in Kansas anymore, honey."

"We sure as hell aren't," said Ann, raising her glass to toast no one and nothing and then draining its contents. Normally, Ann could tolerate three small drinks in an hour, when she was home on her living room couch with nothing but the newspaper for company. But the effect of being in the sun all day, combined with the margaritas she'd sipped most of the afternoon, caught up with her, its power sudden and irreversible. Her head lost its weight, feeling like a helium balloon attached to her neck. When she spoke, her words echoed in her ears. And when her friends spoke, she couldn't understand their muttering. It was all incredibly funny to Ann, until she tried to order another bottle of wine and Jesse laid her hand on Ann's wrist and suggested they order bottled water instead. Ann pulled her arm away with such force that she rocked back in her chair. She was on her way down, her head seconds away from connecting with the shiny cement floor, when the waiter—who had just set their salad plates down on the table—reached out with his giant forearm and stopped the chair midair. He gently righted it, and then walked away as if nothing had happened. Ann burst out laughing.

"Are you okay?" asked Sally, hand at her throat.

"Absolutely," said Ann. "That was fantastic!"

"What are you talking about?" asked Jesse.

"Where are your eyes, girl?" asked Ann. "I just fell off a cliff and survived! That calls for another round. Where's our waiter?"

"He's done with his shift," said Jesse. "They're closing up." Ann looked at her friend with squinted eyes, as if she couldn't quite make out who she was talking to. Sally and Paula also looked at Jesse, waiting for what would happen next. Jesse pushed her chair out from under the table. "I'm going to take Ann back," she said, standing. "You two go ahead, and I will join you when I can."

"I'm not going anywhere," said Ann.

Jesse looked down at Ann, a rubber doll somehow able to talk. "It's time," said Jesse.

"Fuck you, it's time," said Ann, reaching for her empty wineglass.

The waiter returned to the table with a stout, middle-aged woman dressed in the crisp royal blue and white uniform of the resort. Her black hair was pulled back into a bun, the side hairs held in place by a glistening gel. She smiled at Ann, exposing coffee-stained teeth through pulpy burgundy lips. "I've turned down your bed, Mrs. Barons," she said. "And I've put a jigger of brandy on your bed stand, just the way you like it."

"Who the hell are you?"

"Let me help you to your place," she said, bending down.

Ann slapped her on the arm. "I don't need your help," she said, swaying as she got to her feet. "I'm forty-five years old. I know how to fucking walk." She zigzagged around the other dining tables, making her way past the bar to the restaurant entrance. The maître d' looked up as she approached. Ann raised the middle finger of her right hand and thrust it toward his face. "Thank you," she spat, "for a wonderful evening."

"Stay here," Jesse said to Paula and Sally, who were half-standing. "I'll go after her and come get you if I need you."

"We want to help," said Sally.

"I know you do," said Jesse. "But if the three of us confront her, it may be overwhelming. Let me just see if I can get her into bed. I'll be back."

Jesse walked quickly out of the seating area before jogging along the path to find Ann. She found her friend fumbling with keys at the door and stepped forward to help her. "Where the hell did you come from?"

"Let's go inside," said Jesse, sliding open the glass door that had not been locked.

Ann opened her mouth to speak, but no words emerged. She charged past Jesse and plopped down on the living room couch. "Get me a glass of wine, will you?"

Jesse sat down opposite Ann. "I think we went through the bottle before dinner," she said. "Why don't you lie down and I'll see if I can get one at the restaurant."

"Excellent idea," said Ann, already leaning into the couch cushions.

"I'll be right back," said Jesse.

She jogged back along the path to the restaurant, where she updated Sally and Paula. "I think she's going to pass out," she said. "I'll get her settled and then come back and join you."

"Can't we do something?" asked Sally, straightening her cutlery. "I feel useless sitting here."

"Don't feel useless, Sally. I know you're here. It may be that tomorrow is the day you can help instead of tonight. Nothing is going to get through to her right now."

"Do you want us to just come with you?" asked Paula. "We don't have to say anything."

"Ask them to hold my dinner," said Jesse. "I'll be right back."

When Jesse got back to the condo, Ann was not asleep. Instead, she was standing behind the bar, fiddling with a corkscrew and the bottle of wine she had pulled from the fridge. Jesse heard the pop of the cork. "I found a bottle in the fridge," said Ann, eyes half-closed. "I've got two glasses out for us."

Jesse stood where she was, just inside the sliding glass door. "I don't want any wine, Ann. And I think you've had enough for tonight."

"What is this?" asked Ann, looking around the room. "A conspiracy?"

"Look, Ann," said Jesse, approaching her. "Let's get you to bed. Tomorrow is another day, and you don't want to miss it with a huge hangover."

"I thought I left my mother in Michigan," said Ann, pouring herself a glass.

"I'm not your mother, Ann. I'm your friend."

"A friend?" asked Ann incredulously, her voice rising in volume and pitch. "You call yourself a friend? I'm the one who invited you to stay for a weekend and you have the fucking nerve to tell me when I can and can't have a drink?"

"I think it's best for you to stop."

"You think it's best? Who gives a rat's ass what you think?"

"You do," said Jesse, standing on the other side of the bar from Ann. "Sometimes."

"Well, tonight's not one of them," said Ann, hitting her hip on the bar as she walked around it toward the couch. "Ouch! Look, I'm here on vacation. I'm forty-five years old and I can do whatever I damn well please."

Jesse watched as Ann, now stopped in front of the couch, swaying slightly, drank half her glass of wine in two swallows. Jesse thought about what to do next; the pitfalls of arguing with a drunk were well-documented. "You're absolutely right," she said, turning her back on Ann and walking toward the sliding glass door. "You can do whatever you please."

"What are you doing?" asked Ann, setting her wineglass on the glass side table. "Where are you going?"

"To get Sally and Paula," said Jesse. "I'll be right back."

Jesse closed the door behind her, walked a few steps until she was out of Ann's view, then hurried down the path. When she reached their table in the restaurant, Sally and Paula were just starting their entrées. "What's going on?" asked Sally when she saw Jesse. "Where's Ann?"

"She's back at the condo," said Jesse, breathless from running. "I don't want to leave her long because she's having another drink. Here's my suggestion. Let's all go back together and go to bed."

"Go to bed?" asked Sally, looking at her watch.

"We have to pretend we're going to bed," said Jesse. "If we all go back there and stay up, she'll have three more glasses of wine tonight."

"Won't she drink them anyway?" asked Paula, forking some garlic mashed potatoes into her mouth as she stood.

"I think she's close to crashing," said Jesse. "Let's go."

"You two go," said Sally. "I'll be right behind you."

Jesse and Paula walked out, while Sally reached for her purse. She gave her credit card to their waiter and apologized for the commotion. She then scurried along the path to find her friends, catching up to them outside the sliding glass door.

"She's always liked to drink," said Jesse, hand on the handle. "But tonight she's way out of control."

"Do you think I should talk to her?" asked Sally, breathing hard.

"I don't think talking to her tonight is going to result in anything but a fight," said Jesse. "I'm hoping if we all go to our rooms, she'll choose to do the same thing, rather than sit in the dark alone with a glass of wine."

"Okay," said Paula. "I'm in."

"Sally?" asked Jesse.

Sally bit her lower lip. She was quite certain she could talk some sense into Ann if she could just get her alone. Perhaps she could sneak back downstairs after Paula and Jesse had retreated to their bedroom. Or, perhaps she could talk to Ann when she came upstairs. That was it. She'd have her all to herself in the master suite and they could talk, just the two of them. "Let's go," said Sally.

When they walked into the living room, Ann was on the couch. An almost-empty wineglass was sitting on the table beside her. "Well, here they are," she said, "the party poopers."

"I *am* pooped," said Paula, in a loud voice. "That sun was brutal today. Anyone mind if I go up?"

"I'm with you," said Jesse, feigning a yawn. "I'm exhausted."

"Me too," said Sally.

They all looked at Ann. "Good night," said Jesse. "It's been a great day. Thank you."

"You've got to be kidding me," said Ann, her words slow and weighted with wine. "The three of you are going to bed?"

"I'm whipped," said Paula. "A little aloe for my sunburn and I'll be in dreamland in fifteen minutes."

"Sally?" asked Ann. "You won't stay up and talk with me?"

Sally hesitated. She looked at Jesse. "Come upstairs," Sally said. "We can talk for a few minutes before bed."

"I'll come upstairs when I'm ready to come upstairs," said Ann. "So, don't wait up."

Jesse headed for the stairs, followed by Paula, and, reluctantly, Sally. Ann called after them, "Next time, I'll invite some adult friends, not schoolchildren."

"Let it go," Jesse whispered to the others.

When they were gone, Ann got off the couch. She reached for her wineglass, but bumped it instead, sending it flying off the table and onto the straw rug, where it spun several times before rolling under the dining table. "Thank God for plastic," said Ann aloud. She got down on her hands and knees and ducked under the table to get the glass. She would have just one more before joining the losers upstairs. She grabbed it by the stem, then—forgetting she was underneath the table—raised up her back and head, smacking it against the glass top. "Shit!" she said, ducking again, and then backing out into open space. She crawled to the couch, put her head back onto a seat cushion, and closed her eyes. And she slept in that position for an hour, when Jesse came back down the stairs and helped her friend into bed.

CHAPTER 18

Eileen made a big breakfast that Saturday. She had agreed to accommodate Nate, who asked to sleep in, as well as Mike, who wanted to take a long run outside, and serve the meal at eleven o'clock. Preparations, however, began at nine, when Eileen walked up the path to the big house and made a pot of green tea, Lauren's favorite. Lauren, who had begun to appear earlier and earlier on weekend mornings, came down at nine thirty, ready to help. Eileen handed her a mug of tea, then put her to work making waffle batter while she fried the sausages. Still wearing his pajamas, miraculously dry, under his overcoat, Sam ambled into Ann's kitchen through the back door and—after saluting Eileen—reported that Selma was taking a shower and would arrive on time. He then sat down in the window seat and looked at the newspaper Eileen had retrieved from the front walk.

At quarter to eleven, with the sausage, bacon, and waffles in the oven, Eileen started the scrambled eggs and Lauren cut up the cantaloupe. Everything was going according to Eileen's schedule. She and Lauren chatted about Josh, high school gossip, and Eileen's early married life while the eggs cooked to fluffy perfection. When they were done, Eileen scooped them onto a platter and put them into the oven along with everything else. It was just shy of eleven, when Lauren set the melon slices on the island. Breakfast would be a buffet, Eileen had decided, with everyone serving themselves and eating around the kitchen table.

At eleven, a wet-headed Mike walked into the room, followed by Nate, who had a notable bed head and was dressed in jeans and a sweatshirt wrinkled from spending the night on the floor of his room. Selma, looking squeaky clean, blew in the back door. "Something smells awesome," said Nate, yawning. "I didn't even need my alarm."

"Well, I hope you're all hungry," said Eileen. "We've got enough food for an army."

It was just after Lauren and Eileen had removed the warm platters from the oven and set them on the island with the melon that Sam made his remark. It was not expected, or even, seemingly, remotely possible because there was nothing that portended its arrival. "She used to love me," he said.

Selma looked at Sam and then at Eileen. "Sam," Eileen said softly. "Get a plate."

"You have no idea what it's like," continued Sam, lowering the newspaper and looking at Eileen. "You don't know what it's like not to be loved by your own wife."

Red-faced, Eileen said, "Okay, everyone, let's eat."

"Is it because you love someone else?" Sam asked, his voice rising.

"Gramps," said Lauren. "Gran loves you."

"It's okay," said Eileen, whose watery eyes told everyone in the room otherwise.

"Are you having an affair?" asked Sam. "Go ahead and tell me. 'Fess up to it, for Christ's sake!" Eileen looked at her husband for a moment, and then ran out of the kitchen and into the hallway. Lauren followed her.

"You two go ahead and eat," said Selma to Nate and Mike. "I think I'll take Sam back to the house and fix him something there for breakfast."

"I'm not going anywhere," said Sam, slamming the table with his open hand.

Mike took Nate aside. "See if you can get him down to the

guesthouse," he said. "You have a way with your grandfather, and he may just listen to you. I'm going to find your grandmother."

As soon as his father left the room, Nate approached Sam. "Gramps?" he said. "Can we talk somewhere? I need your advice."

Sam looked at his grandson. "Of course we can," he said. "What's on your mind, son?"

"Let's go to your house," said Nate, reaching down to help his grandfather up from the window seat. "We can talk there."

Sam glanced over at the food on the counter. "What about breakfast?"

Nate looked at the platter of cooling scrambled eggs, then at Selma. "Selma will put everything back in the oven," said Nate. "We can eat in a little while."

Sam licked his lips. "This can't wait?"

"No," said Nate. "I'd like to talk now."

"Very well then," said Sam, accepting Nate's help to stand. They walked slowly toward the back door, which Selma opened. She closed it after them, then scurried over to the oven and turned it back on. She re-covered the food with the aluminum foil tents Eileen had left on the counter, then slid the platters into the oven. When she was done, she stood next to the oven with her hands on her hips, wondering what to do next. She didn't, particularly, want to find Eileen, who was already with Lauren and Mike. And she didn't want to interrupt Nate and Sam. She sighed as she removed the pot holders, and then sat at Ann's kitchen table. She picked up the newspaper Sam had discarded and started reading the front page.

In the living room, Eileen was sobbing. Embarrassed by her emotions, but seemingly unable to stop them, Eileen told Mike and Lauren she would be okay.

"It's okay to cry," said Lauren, sitting on the couch next to her grandmother and holding her hand. Mike, with his hands in his pockets, stood over his daughter and mother-in-law. For the second time that morning, he was glad Ann was somewhere else. She wouldn't handle this scene well. The first time was just after nine o'clock, when Sharon Rosenberg, the woman who'd come on to him at the resort in San Francisco, called him. He wondered how she'd found his private cell phone number before realizing he had given it to her husband, Paul.

"I just knew you'd answer," she said, after purring her name and asking if he remembered her. "Powerful, attractive men always answer."

"How are you?" asked Mike, his groin warming.

"I would be just perfect if I could see you," whispered Sharon. "I'm in Detroit, with Paul on business, so I thought I'd call."

"What do you think of Detroit?" asked Mike, unable to think of anything else to say.

"What do you think I think of Detroit?" asked Sharon, chuckling. "It's dreadful."

Mike laughed.

"I hear there is a good mall, some restaurants, and a four-star hotel about an hour from here," said Sharon. "That would be about an hour from you, too. We could meet this afternoon."

Oh God, thought Mike, his warm groin now tingling. He remembered her open robe in the hallway of the resort. He remembered her lovely large breasts. In an instant, he pictured her naked, on top of him, her nipples inches from his mouth. She had a wide, fleshy ass he could hold on to, so unlike Ann's. "I can't," said Mike, closing his eyes and leaning back in his chair.

"Please," said Sharon slowly. "I would just love to see you."

Mike sat up. "And I'd love to see you," he said, meaning it. "I just can't today."

"Your loss," said Sharon flippantly. *Yes,* thought Mike. "I'm going to give you my number," she said, "just in case you change your mind." Mike wrote it down. "I always answer my phone. Day and night."

"Okay," said Mike, looking at the number he had just written.

"Call me, Michael," said Sharon. "Any time at all."

"He doesn't mean it," said Lauren to her grandmother. "I know he doesn't mean what he says."

"I know it, too," said Eileen, blowing her nose. "I don't know why it hurts so much."

Not knowing what else to do, Mike sat down in the chair across from the couch where Lauren and Eileen were sitting. It was the chair he sat in when he and Ann had drinks in the living room, and so he was comfortable. He tried to focus on the conversation at hand, on Eileen and Lauren, but his thoughts kept drifting back to Sharon. Should he call her? Should he meet her, just for a drink?

"It hurts because you love him," said Lauren. "And he loves you."

At this, Mike decided he was in the wrong place. "I'm going to check on Nate and Sam," he said, standing. "I'll meet you in the kitchen in ten minutes or so."

"Fine," said Eileen, taking a deep breath. "I'm sorry to be so silly about this."

Mike gave his mother-in-law a hug and then left the room.

"You're not being silly," said Lauren. "He hurt your feelings."

And at that, Eileen's tears flowed again. "I can take his physical disabilities," she said, dabbing at her eyes with the crumpled tissue. "I can take changing his sheets and helping him get dressed and, sometimes, feeding him. In many ways, it's like having an infant again." Eileen blew her nose with a fresh tissue from her apron pocket. "I can take anything," she continued, "except when he insults me." Lauren wrapped her arm around her grandmother's shoulders. "When he tells me he doesn't love me," said Eileen, softly, "I die inside."

Lauren's eyes blurred with tears. "He does love you," she managed to say.

"How do you know?" asked Eileen, looking at her granddaughter. "He never tells me anymore."

"I can see it," said Lauren. "I can see it in his eyes."

On his way through the kitchen, Mike told Selma, who was still at the table reading the newspaper, that everyone would be ready to eat shortly. Selma smiled at him as he walked out the back door and returned her attention to the story she had been reading about show dogs. Mike signed her paychecks, but she would have breakfast on Eileen's schedule.

In the guesthouse, Mike found Sam and Nate, side by side on

the couch, watching the History Channel. "Anybody hungry?" asked Mike, standing next to the couch with his hands in his pockets. Neither Nate nor Sam responded. Mike spoke louder, over the volume of the television. "I said, is anyone hungry?"

"You said is any*body* hungry," said Nate, still looking at the images of tanks and army men on the screen.

"Let's go, guys," said Mike, walking in front of them to turn the television off.

"Dad!" protested Nate. "We're watching something here."

"And your grandmother," said Mike, standing in front of the set, "has worked all morning to prepare a breakfast that's drying out in the oven."

"I'd like to watch the program," said Sam quietly.

"I'm not going to listen to that," said Mike, pointing his finger at Sam. "You started this."

Nate got up from the couch. He turned the television back on, then told his father to go outside with him. On the way out, Nate stuffed his bare feet into his grandfather's slippers that were lined up next to Eileen's pair in the entranceway closet and grabbed his jacket from the hanger next to the one holding Sam's overcoat. Outside, Nate explained to his dad how agitated Sam had been and how the television was sometimes the only thing that would get him refocused. In another ten minutes, Nate suggested, Sam would be calm enough to join them for breakfast. In fact, Nate thought, he would have forgotten the entire incident. Arms folded across his chest, Mike listened to his son talk, and then said, "I understand what you're saying, and I appreciate that you have a relationship with your grandfather. In fact, I commend you on that. But I'm a little tired of these games we have to play. I'm hungry, and I'd like to eat the meal Eileen prepared. And I don't see why we need to wait any longer. As far as I'm concerned, he can eat with us or he can have a bowl of cereal in front of the TV."

"He's part of this family," said Nate.

"Yes," said Mike. "And he and your grandmother are living here temporarily by the good graces of your mother. We are doing our best to make this work. But it cannot be all one way, Nate. Nothing in life is one way."

"Meaning Gramps has to give back?" asked Nate.

"Something like that," said Mike, knowing how ridiculous that statement sounded as soon as it left his mouth.

"He has Parkinson's disease and dementia," said Nate. "What kind of giveback are you looking for?"

Mike looked, briefly, at the ground, and then back at Nate. "Look," he said. "I don't understand his disease. I don't know how it works."

"It doesn't work, Dad," said Nate. "His brain doesn't work like it should. Do you think he said those hurtful words to Gran on purpose? Sometimes he has no idea what he's saying."

"I know that, Nate," said Mike. "I just don't know how to handle it."

"You can't just handle this. It's not like a business decision."

"Well, that's what I'm good at, Nate."

Nate lifted both of his arms, pointing his hands at the big house. "Obviously," he said. "And if you're that good at business, you can certainly figure this out."

"To what end?" asked Mike. "What am I going to do with this information?"

Nate turned to go back inside. With his hand on the doorknob, he said, "You will not profit from this information, Dad. There is no financial gain. But if you make an effort to understand him, you will learn other things, things that matter more."

Mike put his hand on Nate's shoulder. "Maybe I should just leave that in your capable hands," he said. Nate turned the doorknob and opened the door. "Can we eat soon?"

"I'll push him a little," said Nate. "Gramps and I will be in the kitchen in ten minutes."

"I'll go tell the others." Mike waited until Nate went back inside and shut the door before he turned and walked back up the path to the back door. In the kitchen, Selma was still reading the newspaper and breakfast was still in the oven. Mike assumed Lauren and Eileen were still having a therapy session in the living room, so he went to his office, where he was needed, and sat down behind his desk. Sitting on his calendar was the phone number Sharon gave him that morning. He picked it up and looked at it. "Sharon," he said aloud, before crumpling up the paper and throwing it away.

It wasn't until almost twenty minutes later that Eileen, looking both composed and apologetic, appeared in the doorway of Mike's office. "Are you still hungry?" she asked softly.

"Sure," said Mike, getting up from his chair and wondering what food that had been sitting in a warming oven for almost an hour would taste like. "Are you okay?"

"Yes," said Eileen. "I don't know what made me react that way."

"Where are the others?" asked Mike, putting his arm around Eileen's shoulder as they walked down the hallway.

"Lauren's putting the finishing touches on everything," said Eileen, "and Selma's gone to get Sam and Nate."

In the kitchen, Lauren was setting tall glasses of orange juice on the table. Mike sat down and drank his immediately. "Well, everything looks pretty good," said Eileen, surveying the food Lauren had arranged on the island. "It would have been much better when it was fresh."

"At this point," said Lauren, "I'd eat the foil." Mike smiled, realizing again that his daughter could be funny.

Moments later, Selma, Nate, and Sam walked into the kitchen through the back door. "Something smells good," said Selma, taking off her coat.

"You're kind," said Eileen. "Sit down—everyone. I'm going to bring the food to you."

Mike looked at Nate, who winked at his dad. Lauren chatted with Selma, and Nate resumed his conversation with Sam while Eileen went back and forth between the table and the counter with plates of food. Mike sat silent, with his hands across his chest, until he was served. "This looks wonderful," he said to Eileen, putting his napkin in his lap and lifting his fork. He had already eaten his first bite of scrambled eggs when he realized no one else was eating. He put his fork down on his plate.

Eileen served herself, then sat down next to him. She bowed her head and said aloud, "Thank You, Father, for this food we are about to receive. In Jesus' name, amen." She then cut a piece of sausage and put it in her mouth. Only then did Nate, Lauren, Selma—even Sam—begin eating.

"This is absolutely delicious, Lauren," said Selma.

"Thanks," said Lauren. "Gran did most of it. I was just her helper."

"With helpers like you, I read the entire morning paper," said Eileen, smiling at her granddaughter.

"Eileen's always been a good cook," said Sam, "all through our married life."

Eileen looked at her husband, who appeared to have no recollection of the morning's events. Even before he got sick, he was always able to put unpleasantness behind him. Throughout their forty-eight years together, he had rarely stewed about anything. Worrying, he said, was a waste of time. If something is bothering you, he had told Eileen many times, do something about it or forget it. The rest of the meal was spent in relative silence. Everyone, hungry, ate quickly. Nate got a second helping for himself and his grandfather, and Mike allowed an insistent Eileen to refill his plate. After everyone was done, Lauren stood and began clearing the dishes from the table. Nate stood and, announcing he and Sam were anxious to get back to watching the documentary about World War II on the History Channel, helped his grandfather out of his chair. "Hadn't we better do the dishes?" Sam said to Nate. "After all, the women prepared the meal."

"You're right, Gramps," said Nate. "I'm ready if you are."

"You two go ahead and finish the war," said Eileen. "I'm happy to do the dishes. Selma—bless her heart—has already done the heavy work."

"Are you sure, Eileen?" asked Sam, using her name for the first time in weeks.

"Yes," said Eileen, kissing him on the cheek.

Mike stood. "Do you want to join us, Mike?" asked Sam.

Mike looked at his father-in-law, again wondering what was behind the mask. What was it that Nate saw? Sam had been an intelligent man, who could speak about the stock market and current events as ably as he had about the farming industry. When they had spent time at the farm over a number of Christmases, it was Ann who had been uncomfortable, restless, not Mike. But things had changed in the last year, rendering Sam unable to talk capably about anything. Mike had always surrounded himself with exceptional people, from his hockey teammates in college, to his study group in business school, to his inner circle at Dilloway. "No thanks," he said. "I'm going to head back into my office."

"Dad," said Nate. "Dilloway can survive for an hour without you."

"Young man," said Sam, "you need to treat your father with respect. It's his hard work that paid for the food that sits in your stomach."

"Thank you," Mike said to Sam.

"And a father who spends no time with his child is not really a father at all," said Sam, shifting his gaze to Mike.

"Okay, then," said Eileen to no one in particular. "I'll just get started on those dishes."

"I'm ready," said Lauren, pushing the leftover sausages from their platter into a plastic storage container.

"And I know you are, my dear," said Eileen. "But I want you to run off and do something with the rest of your day. Saturdays are precious."

Lauren hesitated. "Are you sure?"

"Positive," said Eileen. "You know how I like to putter in the kitchen." Lauren kissed her grandmother and disappeared into the hallway. Selma tucked the newspaper under her arm and said she would walk down to the guesthouse with Nate and Sam. And then it was quiet; no one else said a thing while Nate helped Sam with his coat and then guided him out the back door with Selma following. Feeling oddly foolish, Mike took his hands out of his pockets and walked out of the room.

CHAPTER 19

Her head throbbing, Ann rolled over in bed and looked at the clock. It was almost five in the morning. She closed her eyes, trying to summon the energy to get out of bed and walk to the bathroom, where she could pee and take a handful of Advil. She silently counted to ten, then sat up. Big mistake; her head exploded with pain. She lay back down on the pillow. "Sally," she whispered to her friend sleeping next to her.

A light sleeper, Sally opened her eyes and blinked a few times. "Yes?"

"Be a darling and get me some Advil," said Ann.

Sally threw back her covers and got out of bed. She yawned and stretched and then went into the bathroom. "Where are they?" she asked, looking around in the dimness and long shadows cast by the night-light plugged in next to the far sink.

"On the counter somewhere," said Ann. "And bring me a glass of cold, cold water."

Sally grabbed the bottle of pain reliever with one hand and turned on the tap with the other. She stuck her finger in the running stream and, when it was cold, filled the glass next to Ann's toothbrush. She took them to Ann, who had propped herself up on her pillows.

"Four should do the trick," she said, holding out her hand.

"Four?" asked Sally, who had shaken one tablet into her hand. "I think you're supposed to take just one, two at the most, at a time."

"And I want four," said Ann, reaching over and taking the Advil bottle from Sally. Sally watched her friend take the tablets and swallow them. Then she drank the water. Ann put the glass down on the bedside table, lay back on the pillows, and closed her eyes, hoping that if she didn't move the feeling of nausea would pass.

"Are you okay?" asked Sally, still standing next to the bed.

"Barely," whispered Ann.

"Are you getting up now? Do you want to talk?"

"Good God no," said Ann. "Get back into bed."

Sally walked around to her side of the bed and got in. She pulled the covers up to her chin and turned away from Ann. "Let me know if you need anything," said Sally, eyes closed. *A bucket,* thought Ann, at that very moment. She bolted out of bed and ran to the toilet, where she vomited up the Advil and paltry remains of lunch from the day before. Sally was two steps behind her. "Are you all right?"

Ann wiped a string of saliva from her chin with her wrist. "No," she said, her head a funeral pyre.

"What can I do?" asked Sally.

"Go back to bed," said Ann. "This will be over in a minute."

Quickly, Sally left the bathroom and got back into bed. From there, she could clearly hear Ann retch another three times. Jesse was right: Ann *had* had too much to drink. It was so hard to keep track, especially on vacation, when glasses were replenished before they were empty, when beach drinks frequently tipped over and sank instantly into the sand. Ann could drink like no one Sally knew, male or female, but she had never seen her like this. What in the world would cause someone to drink enough alcohol to expel the contents of her stomach? It was so raw and demoralizing. She reached over to Ann's side of the bed and fluffed her pillows.

Several minutes later, Ann returned to the bed. The pain had moved from the back of her head to her temples: *boom, boom,*

boom, boom. Ann lay back and closed her eyes. "I hate this," she said.

"I'm so sorry," said Sally.

"Don't be sorry," said Ann. "You didn't do anything."

"That's right," said Sally. "I did nothing to stop you or help you."

Ann turned her head to face her friend. "I did this to myself," she said. "There is nothing you could have done."

"Can I do something now?"

"No," said Ann. "This will pass. Go back to sleep."

Sally, Paula, and Jesse had been up for almost three hours before Ann got out of bed. They'd left her a note before heading out for an early morning walk on the beach and then breakfast at Fred's, a local restaurant recommended by the man sweeping the cement pathways. They'd changed into their bathing suits and were just about to head back to the beach—after Jesse assured Sally and Paula that time was Ann's best friend at the moment—when Ann walked down the stairs into the living room. "Good morning," said Jesse, giving her friend a slight smile.

"I've had better," said Ann, walking past them and into the kitchen area, where she grabbed a pitcher of orange juice from the fridge and poured herself a glass.

"How are you feeling?" asked Paula.

"Not very good," said Ann. "Are you all heading to the beach?"

"We were thinking about it," said Sally. "But we're happy to stay here instead."

"No, no," said Ann, waving her hand in front of her. "You all go ahead. I'll join you a little later."

Paula and Sally looked at Jesse. "Go on to the beach," she said, gently shooing them. "I'll stay here and get Ann going."

"I'll stay with you," said Sally. "I'm happy to lend a hand."

"I don't need a hand," said Ann. "I need a large glass of tomato juice with two raw eggs in it. Run down to The Beachcomber, Sally, and get one from Eduard, will you? Tell him I want a large." Delighted to have an assignment, to be of use, Sally followed Paula out the door, down the path, and out of sight.

"So," said Jesse from the couch. "Are we going to talk about this?"

Ann looked at her friend. "I think we're going to talk about it whether I want to or not."

"Come sit down," said Jesse, patting the seat cushion next to her.

Ann sat on the end cushion, facing out; Jesse sat at the other end, her body angled toward Ann. "What's going on?"

"What do you mean?" said Ann, looking out the sliding glass door.

"With your drinking," said Jesse. "I think we need to talk about your drinking."

"I've always liked my liquor," said Ann, folding her arms across her chest. "You know that about me."

"We all like our liquor," said Jesse. "There's a big difference between enjoying a few drinks and drinking enough to make you physically ill."

Ann looked at Jesse with hard eyes. "We're on vacation, Jesse," she said. "Ease up."

"I don't think being on vacation has anything to do with it," said Jesse. "I think something's bothering you."

"Here we go," said Ann. "The psychology major has a field day."

Jesse smiled at her friend. "You can poke fun at me all you want," she said. "I'm not going away. This issue is not going away, Ann."

Ann stood and walked over to the door. "God, how long does it take to make a tomato and egg?"

"Sit down, Ann," said Jesse. "She'll be back any minute."

Reluctantly, Ann walked back to the couch and sat. "Honestly, Jesse, I feel like crap," she said. "I really don't think I'm up for a lecture."

"And no one said I was going to give you one," said Jesse. "I just want to talk about what's going on."

"There's nothing going on."

"There is most definitely something going on if you are drinking enough alcohol to throw up," said Jesse. "You told me about getting sick in San Francisco. You got sick last night. Yesterday, you were absolutely consumed by where and when you could get your next drink. That's not normal, Ann. That's not the Ann I know."

Ann sat back and sighed. "I don't know," she said, combing her sticky hair with her fingers. "Sometimes I feel like my perfect life has gone to shit."

Sally, holding one of Ann's favorite hangover remedies and smiling like a child holding a tray of cookies she had baked herself, opened the sliding glass door. "It's absolutely beautiful out here," she said, handing the drink to Ann. "I think the fresh air and sunshine would do you good, Ann."

"We'll be there in a little while," said Jesse. "You go on ahead and warm up our beach chairs."

Sally bit her lower lip. On the one hand, she thought Ann should be talking with her. But on the other, she didn't want to undo what Jesse had started. And selfishly, the warmth of the sun and the breeze off the ocean were a million times more enticing than the salmon-colored walls of Ann's living room. "Run along," said Jesse, making up Sally's mind for her.

"Are you sure?"

"Positive," said Jesse. "We'll join you soon." Dismissed with honor, Sally picked up her straw beach bag, walked out the open door, and jogged down the path to the beach.

"You can run along, too," said Ann, taking a long sip from her large red drink. "I'll be fine here."

"How," asked Jesse, "has your perfect life gone to shit?"

Ann set the glass down on the table. "Oh God," she said. "I don't know."

"Well," said Jesse, coaxing, "when did you start to feel this way?"

Ann put her hand to her head. "Probably when my parents arrived."

Yes, thought Jesse. "It's incredibly stressful having long-term guests, especially parents," she told Ann. "You've been under a lot of pressure."

"Stressful doesn't even begin to get at it," said Ann, picking up her drink. "Every time I walk into my kitchen, *my* kitchen, my mother is there. She's baking dessert with Lauren. She's whipping up a casserole for dinner. She's doing dishes Emma should be doing. She's just there."

"She must like being in your house," said Jesse, "being near you."

"I think she likes making me feel inadequate," said Ann. "She knows I don't cook, so she goes out of her way to show me just how comfortable she is in the kitchen. I think there's evil intent there."

"Really?" asked Jesse. "She doesn't seem evil to me."

"Believe me," said Ann, "you haven't seen the look on her face when she sets the homemade cake down on the center of the table after dinner—pure smugness." Ann took another sip of her drink. "God, that's good."

"Maybe it's just pride," offered Jesse. "She likes to cook and is proud of her work." Ann shrugged. "Maybe," continued Jesse, "she likes to cook because she can control things in the kitchen. Maybe being there gets her away from her husband, over whom she has no control."

Ann narrowed her puffy eyes at her friend. "I think you're reaching."

"I'm not saying your mother is aware of doing these things," said Jesse. "It's just an idea."

"She's always loved to cook and bake," said Ann, fingers at her temples. "Way before my father got sick."

"And so now she throws herself into it with extra zeal," said Jesse, sitting forward in her seat. "It gives her pleasure."

"I'll give you that," said Ann. "I know it gives her pleasure."

Jesse stood and walked into the kitchen area. "I'm going to make some coffee," she said. "You want some?"

Ann shook her head. "This," she said, holding up her tomato concoction, "is all I can handle right now."

Jesse opened the coffeemaker and found a filter already in it. She opened the bag of ground coffee on the counter and spooned some into the filter. "We haven't talked much about your father," she said, filling the carafe with water. "He's quite sick, isn't he?"

"He's out of his mind," said Ann. "It's like every wire in his head is crossed."

"That must be hard for you," said Jesse, switching on the coffeemaker.

"It *is* hard," said Ann, taking another sip of her drink. "I can barely stand to be in the same room with him."

"Why?"

"Because it's so difficult, Jesse. He is so far removed from the father of my childhood. I hardly recognize him."

"Have you discussed how you feel with your mother?"

"She's got eyes, Jesse."

"Have you talked about him at all?"

Ann finished her drink and set her glass down on the side table. "Not too much," she said softly.

"This is part of the issue here, Ann," said Jesse. "You need to face what's in front of you."

"Which is what?"

Jesse joined Ann on the couch. "Your history," she said. "Your childhood. The parents who raised you. Your father who was so strong and is now so weak."

Ann looked out the sliding door. "Jesse, talking to my dad is like talking to a turnip. And discussing him with my mother would be uncomfortable."

"For her, or for you?"

"For both of us. This isn't easy, Jesse. None of this is easy."

"Like your life has been for the last twenty years without them."

Ann stood up. "Look," she said. "I've given them a home. I pay their bills. I put up with my mother's holier-than-thou attitude. I don't need this, Jesse."

"It's okay to admit you don't have a close relationship with your father and that you miss it."

"I haven't had a close relationship with my father, or my mother, for that matter, for—as you so smartly pointed out—twenty years."

"And why is that?" asked Jesse. "And does that make you happy?"

"How can I not be deliriously happy with my life? I've got everything."

"Except a relationship with your parents and a meaningful connection with your past."

"We're different people," said Ann, walking into the kitchen area. "I moved ahead while they stayed behind. We have nothing in common anymore."

"Except your entire childhood."

"I left the fat girl on the farm thirty years ago."

"Maybe your mother is still looking for her," said Jesse. "I think she's a lot more interested in your time than in your money."

"My life is already full," said Ann, setting the empty glass in the sink and turning to face Jesse.

"Full of what?" asked Jesse.

Ann widened her eyes and gave her friend a reproachful look. "It's full of everything anyone could ever want or need," she said, before walking past Jesse on her way out of the room. Knowing Ann would not be back and knowing better than to follow her, Jesse stood. She walked into the kitchen and rooted through the cupboards until she found a plastic travel cup with a lid. She filled the mug, snapped on the lid, and switched off the coffeemaker. Then she walked back into the living room, grabbed her beach bag from the floor, and stepped outside into the sunshine. She closed the sliding door gently behind her.

Upstairs, Ann got a glass of water from the bathroom and set it down on her bedside table. She climbed onto the king-sized bed and pulled the covers up to her chin. She was shaking, freezing. She opened and closed her legs in a scissors motion in an effort to warm the cool sheets. But still she shook. She turned onto her side and drew her knees up to her chest. And then she was crying, tears spilling out of her eyes and moans pushing out of her mouth. "Oh God," she said, flipping onto her back so her lungs could fill with air. "Oh God, help me."

She was here when she should have been there—with her mother and her father, who had been repaid for their kindness and patience in raising her with little more than silence. When she had broken free of their vine-like grip on her, resentful of their interest in her teenage likes, dislikes, and decisions, Ann had been so heady in her new independence, just like Nate and Lauren were becoming now. Her mother would always accept Ann back into her life, almost on any terms, but her father would not, could not. The hurt she had inflicted over the years had settled into his head, his heart, all his organs, like an inoperable cancer. With his run-down brain, he might not remember some of the selfish tricks she had pulled over the years, but she knew he could feel it, her betrayal. And Ann, with all her money and influence, could do nothing to change that.

At the beach, Sally and Paula were full of questions. "You don't look so good," said Paula, after Jesse had sat down. "She didn't take it well, did she?"

"Well," said Jesse, taking a bottle of sunscreen out of her bag, "no one really wants to hear she has a drinking problem."

"Do you think she has a drinking problem—really?" asked Sally, in the hushed tones of someone sharing a secret.

Jesse rubbed some lotion onto her arms. "I think she has a number of problems."

Paula closed her book. "She is always so in control," she said. "It was strange seeing her so completely out of sync last night."

"Was she that far gone, Paula?" asked Sally. "Maybe we're exaggerating here."

"I don't think so," said Jesse, rubbing lotion onto her legs.

"Maybe I just don't want to face it," said Sally.

"Face what?" asked Paula.

"That our perfect friend is not so perfect after all."

"You think Ann's perfect?" asked Jesse, glancing at Sally.

"She has everything," said Sally. "How can she not be perfectly happy?"

Jesse coated her lips with balm and then shrugged. "I think having everything breeds emptiness more often than happiness."

"You're kidding," said Paula, sipping a Diet Coke.

"I'm completely serious," said Jesse, sitting back in her chair and digging her toes into the sand.

Sally sat up in the chair, removed her sunglasses, and looked at Jesse. "You think Ann Barons's life is empty?" she asked, wide-eyed.

"I don't know," said Jesse, reaching for her hat.

Paula put her book in her beach bag and looked at Jesse. "Ann

Barons has the fullest, most exciting life of anyone I know," she said. "She has gorgeous clothes; she drives an incredible car; she travels the world, and she's beautiful. She is the absolute envy of every woman in town, and you say her life is empty? Because she drank too much last night?"

Jesse dug her toes into the cooler sand beneath the surface. "I didn't say I thought it was empty," she said. "I said I didn't know."

"Well, she sure seems happy to me," said Paula. "Every time I see her, she's got something new to show me: a piece of jewelry, some fabulous Italian leather boots—hell, she's got things before the fashion magazines come out with them. She's been on the cutting edge of everything for as long as I've known her."

"I think you're right," said Jesse. "Now you tell me what you think life on the edge is like."

Sally thought for a moment. "Scary?" she guessed.

"That's what I think, Sally," said Jesse. "I think Ann's scared out of her mind."

Ann spent most of the day in her room, sleeping, crying, and drinking as much water as she could. She had no interest in joining her friends, even though it was a perfect beach day. Every window in the room was open, allowing in the warm breeze, allowing her overworked lungs to fill with fresh air. As a child, she'd always had difficulty breathing when she was upset. Ann could remember her mother telling her to concentrate on inhaling and exhaling, inhaling and exhaling. Only then, after Ann had taken several deep breaths, would Eileen try to address the cause of her daughter's tears. It didn't matter how long it took; Eileen waited patiently while her daughter calmed herself enough to talk. And after they talked, Eileen had always sat down at the kitchen table with Ann for milk and cookies. They were homemade, as Eileen had never purchased store-made cookies, only the ingredients to make her own. Chocolate chip had been Ann's favorite, but Eileen also made peanut butter, oatmeal raisin, molasses, sugar, and a variety of specialties at Christmastime. She had the time, Ann guessed, because she did little else. Oh, she volunteered at church and baked for the Women's Auxiliary Bazaar and took the minutes at the first selectman's meeting every month (which Eileen said was the best way to keep up with town politics), but, for the most part, she was home, attending to the needs of the house, the farm, and her husband and daughter. She had the time.

It was something Ann hadn't thought about much. She'd been so busy over the years with various activities. She worked out every day. If she went to the gym, she had coffee or lunch out. She shopped several times a week. She had her weekly nail appointment and her monthly facial and pedicure. Of course, being who she was, Ann was asked to be on the board of a number of charitable organizations. And that was fine because all it really meant was a monthly meeting. Ann was thankful for that, as well as for her name on the charity literature found at benefits or in the waiting rooms of various professional buildings in town. She had no interest in what the Do-bees called "getting your hands dirty." She could think of little more depressing than actually visiting terminal patients in the hospital or serving meals to the poor. Ann got up and walked into the bathroom. She blew her nose, drank a glass of water, and returned to bed. Again, she started to cry. She tried to focus on the good things in her life: she was a very healthy forty-five-year-old woman. She had a life most people could never have. She had a firm, young-looking body. She had a pretty face.

She blew her nose again.

She was an only child who had abandoned her parents. She had pulled away from her children because they pulled away first. She thought of her husband increasingly as a paycheck. She had everything she wanted and nothing she needed.

Ann was subdued at dinner. Sally, wanting to smooth over the awkwardness, chatted about their day. "It was one of my top ten beach days," she said. "Not too hot, not too cold—just perfect. Wouldn't you agree, Paula?"

"Yes," said Paula. "It was lovely. I'm sorry you missed it, Ann."

"There will be other beach days," Ann said.

"Tomorrow," said Paula. "Tomorrow is supposed to be perfect."

"I'm just glad you're feeling better," said Sally. "It's horrible to be sick, especially when you're away from home."

Ann nodded her head and took a sip of her Perrier. She looked at Jesse, who winked.

"This food tastes so good right now," said Ann. "I'm hungry."

"Just go slowly," said Paula. "A little is better than a lot."

Ann smiled at her. "I think I've said that to you a few times."

"I'm listening," said Paula. "I've got a long way to go, but I'm listening."

"Me too," said Ann. "Me too."

They talked for several minutes about their children: braces, behavior, curfews, college applications, and homework. All the while, Ann ate her dinner, nourishing her body. When she had finished everything on her plate, she sat back, satisfied. A minute later, she pushed her chair out from under the table and stood. "I think I'm about ready to head back," she said. "I'm tired."

"Of course you are," said Sally. "We'll come with you, dear."

Ann shook her head. "It's early," she said, looking at her watch. "Stay and talk. I'm going to get back into bed and try to get some sleep."

"Are you sure?" asked Jesse.

"Positive," said Ann. "You're on vacation, girls. Enjoy yourselves. Order dessert." Paula grinned. Ann smiled and then turned her back on her friends and walked to the bar. There, she paid for the meal, as well as any other expenses her friends might incur in her absence. Afterward, she made her way to the maître d' and, after a brief exchange of words, hugged him. And then she walked along the cement path to home.

Chapter 20

No one greeted Ann when she got home, which was not unusual. She walked into the empty kitchen from the garage and hung her red leather coat on a wall peg. Strangely, there was no sign of her mother anywhere. And while she was somewhat relieved not to see Eileen stooped, poised to take something out of the oven, Ann was surprised because there was nothing *in* the oven, at least nothing she could smell. She looked at her watch. At five o'clock on a Sunday afternoon, there was always something in the oven. Ann crossed the kitchen and opened the oven door. It was cold and vacant. Puzzled, Ann spun around and surveyed the room. Nothing on the table and nothing on the island or counters. Her kitchen was completely void of any sign of activity. It hadn't looked this sterile since the day they moved in. It was as if Ann had stumbled upon a preserved archaeological site. She washed her hands in the sink, destroying the integrity of the dig.

She left the kitchen and walked down the back hallway to Mike's office. His desk light was on, as was his computer, but his desk was bare: no file folders, no legal pads, no agenda. It was inconceivable that he hadn't worked that day. Normally, he worked at least two hours on Sundays. Ann walked from Mike's office up the stairs to her bedroom. "Mike?" she called. No response. She walked to the other end of the hall, past Nate's closed door to Lauren's room. She knocked and was met with silence. Slowly, she turned the knob, opening the door just enough to put her head through the crack. The first thing Ann saw was a stack of schoolbooks sitting on Lauren's desk. The next thing she noticed was Lauren's carpet, all of it. There was absolutely nothing on the floor: no clothes, no papers, no clutter of any kind. Ann pushed the door open and walked in. Lauren's bed was made and her bureau drawers were completely closed. Ann peeked around the corner into the bathroom. The countertop—usually covered with hair products and accessories and makeup—was bare. Lauren's pink bath towel was hung up properly on its rack. Ann reached out to touch it; it was damp. Suddenly not wanting to get caught, Ann scurried out of Lauren's room and down the hall to Nate's. She put her ear to the door and heard no music. She knocked. Again, there was no response. Ann opened the door ever so slightly and found the familiar sight of Nate's belongings scattered about the room. His clothes, not on the floor, lay on the end of his bed and across his desk chair. Textbooks, notebooks, a legal pad, and a Ward Just war novel covered the area rug next to his bed. The tiny red lights on Nate's music system silently danced. Ann looked at Nate's bed, which looked like it had been occupied recently. When Ann bent down to touch it, however, there was no hint of human warmth. Feeling very alone, Ann quickly walked out of Nate's room and closed the door behind her. She hurried back down the hall and the stairs and into the kitchen, where the only sign of life, still, was the cool fluorescent light above the sink. Bewildered and oddly nervous, Ann looked out the bay window at the guesthouse. Its windows were warmly aglow with yellow light. Ann grabbed her coat from the peg, walked out of the house and jogged down the path. She knocked on the front door of the guesthouse and Eileen answered. "Hello," said Eileen, smiling and stepping aside to let Ann pass. "We were just talking about you."

"Where is everyone?" asked Ann, taking off her coat.

"In the living room," said Eileen. "We decided to play Monopoly and order pizza. It was Lauren's idea."

Ann turned the corner to the living room and found Mike, Lauren, Nate, and Sam sitting on the couch and in chairs pulled up to the large coffee table in the middle of the room. When Ann walked in, they all looked up. Nate, Ann noticed, returned his attention almost immediately to the board, while Mike stood to greet his wife. "Hello there," he said, approaching her and then kissing her on the cheek. "Good trip?"

"Yes," said Ann, wrapping her arms around his waist in an uncharacteristic display of affection in front of her children. "I'm exhausted."

"It sounds like you had a good time, then."

"Can I get you something to drink?" asked Eileen. "We're all having hot chocolate."

"That sounds great," said Ann.

"You want hot chocolate?" asked Nate. "Gran makes it with whole milk, Mom. I'd guess one mug holds your calorie intake for the day." Saying nothing, Ann followed her mother into the kitchen.

"Just have some, Mom," called Lauren after them. "It's awesome."

"Is anyone interested in playing this game we have in front of us?" asked Sam.

"I am, Gramps," said Nate, scooping the dice from the board and handing them to Sam. "It's your turn."

Sam took the dice from Nate and started to put them in his mouth. "No, Gramps," said Nate calmly. "They're not food."

Sam lowered his hand and examined the dice. "I thought we were eating these beforehand," he said. "The other day, I guess it was."

Nate took the bowl of popcorn from the side table and showed it to his grandfather. "This," said Nate, "is what we're eating, Gramps. It's popcorn. Would you like some?"

Sam put his hand in the bowl and grabbed the last fistful. Instead of putting the popcorn in his mouth, however, he threw the kernels onto the game board. Nate picked up the pieces of popcorn and ate them. "I'll roll for us, Gramps," said Nate, picking up the dice and tossing them. "Lucky number seven. That's free parking. Yes!"

In the kitchen, Ann took a sip of her hot chocolate. She winced, feeling the fat in the milk cling to her throat. "So," she said. "How did all of this come about? I was worried when I found no one home."

"I'm sorry about that," said Eileen, tying her apron at the small of her back. "I wanted to leave a note and the others told me I was being foolish. They said you would certainly find us."

"After searching the house, yes," said Ann.

"Well, as I said, this was Lauren's idea," said Gran, pouring oil into the large pot on the stove. "She said she wanted to play games. She said the basement cupboard was full of games that were almost brand new. They were birthday presents or Christmas presents that were never played because you and Mike were always too busy to play."

"I don't remember being asked to play," said Ann defensively.

"It doesn't matter," said Gran. "We all wanted to play tonight."

"Even Mike?"

Eileen poured some corn kernels into the heating oil. "I cut him a deal," she said, lowering her voice. "I told him I'd make lasagna for him tomorrow if he played with us and ate pizza tonight."

Ann sipped her drink. "He likes lasagna?"

"Loves it," said Eileen, shaking the pot. "I remember making it for him, years ago, and how he raved about it. I gave you my recipe, didn't I?"

"I'm sure you did," said Ann.

The kernels popped slowly at first, then furiously. Ann watched her mother move the pot across the burner. As soon as the popping slowed, Eileen moved the pot away from the heat. "There," she said, lifting the lid. "Doesn't that look good?"

"Delicious," said Ann, knowing she wouldn't eat any of it. The oil alone had enough fat to turn her stomach.

"All we need now is some butter and salt and away we go," said Eileen, dumping the popcorn into a bowl and then halving a stick of butter into the hot pan, where she swirled it around until it melted. She poured the liquid butter over the popcorn and then grabbed the salt shaker. Ten shakes later, she tasted it and smiled.

"I don't know how people eat popcorn without butter and salt," said Eileen, mixing the contents of the bowl with her hands. "So, you had a good trip?"

"I did," said Ann. "What were you all up to here?"

"Not too much," said Eileen, removing the apron and then walking out of the kitchen with the popcorn. She decided not to tell Ann about the drama of the previous morning, mostly because it didn't warrant the attention it received in the first place. Sam, of course, had no idea he started anything, and everyone else seemed to have forgotten it happened. "Who wants popcorn?" she asked when she arrived at the table.

"I do," said Nate, holding out his hand for the bowl. "This stuff, Gran, is better than the popcorn at the movies."

"It's the butter," said Eileen, briefly resting her hand on Nate's head.

Feeling shy, Ann lingered in the doorway until her mother looked back and said, "Ann, come join us." Ann stood next to the couch. "You can't play from there," said Eileen. "You're too far away from the board."

"That's okay," said Ann. "I'll just watch." No one seemed surprised or disappointed with Ann's answer and the play resumed. Even Mike, who was the banker, appeared absorbed in the game. Ann watched him, noticing he treated the colorful play money with reverence, as if it were real. He stacked the bills before he handed them out, placing the large bills on the bottom and the small bills on top. It was how he placed money in his wallet, the ones in the front and the fifties in the back. Ann, who shoved money into her wallet usually without looking at it, had once asked Mike about his system. He told her he liked to have the ones in the front where they were easily accessible for small purchases and tips, and he liked to have the fifties in the back so he could reach for one whenever he needed it without searching through his bills. He could pay for a two-dollar item or a forty-five-dollar item without even looking at his wallet. It was a time-saving convenience, he told his wife. Ann's idea of saving time was skipping meals, which, of course, had absolutely nothing to do with how she did or didn't organize her money. All she really cared about was having whatever amount she needed readily available. The plastic in her wallet took care of that.

Her husband was a handsome man, Ann again realized as she studied him from the short distance between them. His full head of attractively graying black hair was a source of vanity for him, especially since many of his friends were losing theirs. Paula's husband was just about bald. Mike had a well-defined angular chin that reminded Ann of the old movie stars like Rock Hudson and Cary Grant. Like them, Mike was always clean shaven, even on the weekends. He thought men with facial hair were lazy. His blue eyes were filled with color, intensity, energy, and light. When he looked at Ann, there was absolutely no doubt he was looking at her, giving her his complete attention. His gaze could be too intense, actually, and Ann had sometimes wondered what it would be like to give a report or present an argument to a man with that kind of electricity coming from his eyes. He was not looking at her now, though, apparently unaware of her scrutiny. Instead, his attention was focused on Lauren, who had just rolled an improbable three to land on Park Place, which, if she could find the cash, would give her a valuable monopoly. He grinned at her good fortune. Meeting his happy eyes, she grinned back, his grin. Her husband and her daughter were not in the habit of interacting much with each other, and it pleased Ann to witness this. Lauren had his thick hair, as well as a softer, more feminine version of his chin. And like him, she was attracted to and fueled by success.

The doorbell rang and Nate jumped out of his chair. "I'll get it!" he called on the way to the door.

"There's some money on the kitchen counter," shouted Eileen, getting up to follow him.

"Okay," said Nate, passing the kitchen.

Eileen rushed up behind him in the hallway. "Honey, you forgot the money."

"That's okay, Gran," Nate said in a whisper. He took his wallet out of his pocket, paid the deliveryman, and took the two warm boxes from his outstretched arms.

"Nate," said Eileen gently, putting her hand on her grandson's shoulder. "I wanted to pay for the pizza. That was part of the deal."

"It's my treat," said Nate, smiling. He carried the boxes into the living room, where Mike and Lauren were picking up the game. Ann sat down on the couch, next to her father.

"What do you have there, my boy?" Sam asked. "A school project?"

"A dinner project," said Nate. "And you're my guinea pig." Sam frowned. Nate set the boxes down on the coffee table, and then whispered in his grandfather's ear, "You'll love this. I got extra cheese and sausage, just for you."

"That's my boy," said Sam, rubbing his hands together.

Eileen appeared from the kitchen with a salad bowl full of colorful greens and set it down on the coffee table next to the pizza.

"You promised not to fuss, Gran," said Lauren.

"And I didn't," she said. "I knew you and your brother would be heartbroken without some kind of vegetable."

"Beyond heartbroken," said Nate.

"Now all we need are plates," said Eileen, turning to go back to the kitchen.

"Stay right there," said Lauren, reaching behind her for a brown paper bag. Inside were heavy-duty paper plates, napkins, and plastic utensils. She quickly interpreted the surprised expression on her grandmother's face. "One night," she said. "We can be wasteful for one night. And no dishes! Sit down and eat, Gran."

Resigned, Eileen sat back down in her chair, next to the couch, next to Ann, whose silence was becoming noticeable. "Are you okay?" Eileen asked her daughter softly, putting her hand on Ann's knee.

"I'm fine, Mom," said Ann. "Just a bit tired."

"Eat something, honey," said Eileen. "I always feel better with a little something in my stomach."

"I will," said Ann, even though she wouldn't touch the pizza. No one else seemed to notice Ann, however. They all drew large slices of sausage-and-mozzarella-laden pizza from the boxes and commented, again and again, at how fabulous it tasted. Even Eileen, who politely cut her slice into bite-size pieces with her plastic fork and knife, remarked on its surprising goodness. She hadn't had pizza in years. In fact, she couldn't recall the last time they'd eaten it. Sam was the one who reminded her they'd eaten it at an Italian roadhouse on their way from Pennsylvania to Florida, when Eileen was pregnant with Ann.

"That was the one trip we took as a married couple," said Eileen. "Your grandfather rarely took time off from the farm."

"I'm a working man," exclaimed Sam, arching his eyebrows. "We don't need much time off."

"Well, that was a wonderful vacation in Florida," said Eileen, setting her utensils down on her plate. "I'm so glad you made time to do it."

"I don't know why you say that," said Sam. "We had absolutely no money and had no business taking a vacation in the first place."

"The money didn't matter," said Eileen.

Lauren finished chewing a bite of pizza. "Why didn't you have any money?"

Eileen served Sam some salad. "Things were different back then," said Eileen to her granddaughter. "None of our friends had money. No one we knew had money. We were all just young couples starting out. We didn't really need anything, except each other."

"Ha!" said Sam, animated, his eyes alive with light. "You say that now! You weren't so accommodating in Daytona Beach when we didn't have two nickels to rub together that morning for breakfast."

"What'd you do, Gramps?" asked Nate, reaching for another slice of pizza.

Sam sat farther back into the couch. "It's rather embarrassing," he said, scratching his head.

"Oh Sam," said Eileen. "No one cares. It was years ago." Sam smiled at his wife and then told the story. He had awoken early that day in their tiny motel room by the highway. His bride, as he called her, was still asleep. Sam quietly dressed and stole out the door, closing it behind him. Where he was headed, he didn't know. What he did know was this: It was his job to provide his wife with some breakfast and he had no money. Of course, he had the fifty dollars he had calculated it would take to get them back to Pennsylvania, but he vowed not to touch it until they left later that day. Across the street from the motel was an orange grove. Sam crossed the highway, barely avoiding getting struck by a speeding truck going too fast for his peripheral vision, and climbed over the fence into the grove. In the trees, hanging just out of his reach, were the most luscious oranges he'd ever seen. Sam climbed a tree and was about to pick his first piece of fruit when he heard a man's voice telling him to stay put, unless he wanted to meet his Maker sooner than he'd planned.

"What did you do?" asked Lauren, wide-eyed.

"I froze," said Sam. "Not only was I caught red-handed, I also had the distinct feeling the fellow below me was not in a joking frame of mind."

"Then what?" asked Nate, fascinated with both the story and his grandfather's clear recollection of events that happened close to fifty years ago.

"I told him my story," said Sam. "I apologized first, then told him I'd run out of money and needed some breakfast for my wife, who was pregnant. Well, darned if that didn't soften his heart."

"He gave you an orange?" asked Lauren.

"He gave me a crate of oranges," said Sam. "And, to this day, they are absolutely the best oranges I've ever eaten."

"Sweet and juicy," said Eileen. "We ate those oranges all the way home."

"Of course, when things are hard to come by, they always taste good," said Sam. "Ask your parents. They know what it's like. Every marriage takes a while to get on the right track. Everyone struggles."

Nate smiled. "Tell us, Mom and Dad, about the deprivation days."

Ann blushed. "We have been blessed," she said quietly.

"By who?" asked Nate. "The money god?"

"That's enough," said Mike, putting another piece of pizza on his plate.

"Everyone's had hardships," said Ann. "Just because your father and I have always had enough money doesn't mean we didn't struggle in other ways."

"With what?" asked Nate, with a laugh. "What to wear to the charity ball?"

"I said that's enough," said Mike, looking sternly at his son. "Looking back on being poor can be romantic, but living a life of true poverty is far from that."

"I didn't mean to stir up the pot," said Eileen, clearing paper plates from the table. "We were just reminiscing."

"I know you were, Eileen," said Mike. "Everything's fine."

"Of course it is," said Sam, hands on his chest. "Take the people we're staying with now. They've got enough money to buy a small country. That doesn't mean, however, they know their ass from their elbow. Most rich people don't have a clue about real life." Nate laughed out loud. "What's so funny?" demanded Sam.

Nate smiled and looked at his grandfather. "Your accuracy," said Nate. "You're a very wise man."

"Thank you," said Sam.

Nate glanced at his father, who raised his eyebrows in return.

"Well," said Ann, slowly getting up. "I'm ready to head back."

"Me too," said Mike, taking another bite of pizza and leaving the other half of the slice on his plate.

"But you haven't eaten anything," said Eileen, looking at her daughter.

"I'm more tired than hungry," said Ann.

"But I've made a special dessert."

"Gran," said Lauren, "you weren't supposed to make anything. That was part of the deal."

Eileen smiled at Lauren. "Old habits die hard," she said. "Plus, it's just a pie."

"Pie?" said Nate. "Did someone say pie?"

"She did," said Sam, pointing at his wife. "I'll have a big slice, ma'am."

"Make that two," said Nate.

"Mike?" Eileen asked.

Mike looked at Ann, who was putting on her coat. "I'll take a rain check, Eileen," he said, standing. "Thanks for having me tonight. The pizza and Monopoly were fun."

"It was Lauren's idea," said Eileen. "I think she liked spending some time with you."

Mike kissed his mother-in-law on the cheek, and then bent down and kissed Lauren's forehead. He and Ann then walked out of the room and out the door, Mike calling his good-bye on the way.

"Where's my pie?" shouted Sam from the living room.

"It's coming," said Eileen, heading into the kitchen. "But I will serve patient people first."

"I can be patient," said Sam, folding his hands in his lap like a child in Sunday school.

Lauren got up to help her grandmother. Eileen cut small wedges from her Mile-High Lemon Meringue Pie and Lauren took them into the living room. Sam brought his plate directly to his mouth and was about to take a bite, when Nate stopped him and told him they needed to wait for his bride. When Sam gave him a quizzical look, Nate simply repeated his command. Slowly, Sam set his plate on the table, still appearing mystified. Nate patted his grandfather's hand and assured him they would eat soon. Moments later, Lauren and Eileen, holding plates with smaller pieces of pie, joined them. Eileen took the first bite, closing her eyes to concentrate on the texture. It was perfect. Opening her eyes, she saw Nate helping Sam with his fork and Lauren looking at her. "You are an amazing woman," said Lauren, smiling.

"Why do you say that?" asked Eileen, taken aback.

"You're an unbelievable cook," said Lauren. "You're an unbelievable wife. And you're an unbelievable person."

Eileen, fiddling with the paper napkin on her lap, said, "Thank you."

"You're most welcome," said Lauren, lifting her fork.

Eileen swallowed hard, trying to remove the lump that had just formed in her throat. She didn't know how to say what she knew she must. She had been unable to say it all evening. "I have some news," she said, looking at Sam.

"What's that?" asked Nate, forking another bite of pie into his mouth.

"Meadowbrook has an apartment for us," said Eileen, looking down at her plate.

Nate stopped chewing.

"What?" asked Lauren.

"Meadowbrook, the assisted-living facility in Pennsylvania," said Eileen, who then coughed in an attempt to clear her throat. "They called this morning. They have space for us now."

Lauren put her untouched pie on the side table next to her seat. "I don't know what that means," she said.

"It means," said Eileen, looking at Sam again because she was unable to meet Lauren's gaze, "that your grandfather and I can go home."

CHAPTER 21

The next week was a busy one. Eileen made several phone calls to Meadowbrook: for occupancy confirmation, apartment size, meal plan options, and medical service information. She sent checks to secure everything she talked about on the phone. She called Charlene Dennis, the real estate agent, telling her she and Sam would return shortly for the few pieces of furniture they had tagged before they left, and then Charlene could sell the house, as is, to the people currently renting it. With Selma's help, she washed and ironed all their clothing and neatly packed it into the suitcases and duffel bags that had lain dormant, holding nothing but dust in the back of the master bedroom closet for more than four months. Ann squeezed two early morning appointments out of her dentist's receptionist so Eileen and Sam could have their teeth checked and cleaned before they hit the road, and a coveted afternoon slot out of her stylist. Eileen refused to have her hair colored, which Ann gently suggested would take ten years off her appearance, but she did indulge herself with a blow-dry. She sat in the padded chair with her eyes closed, allowing the warm air swirling around her head to ease the tension in her neck and shoulders. Her list of things to do stretched from the top line of her legal pad to the bottom, and Sam, of course, could not help in any significant way.

During this time of planning and packing, Eileen had no time for puttering in the kitchen. She didn't bake a single cookie; she didn't prepare a single meal. It was Lauren who, wrapped in her grandmother's apron, rolled out the dough and baked a blueberry pie. It was Lauren who made three dozen chocolate chip cookies and froze them so they would be fresh for the trip east. And it was Lauren who made a lasagna—her father's *and* her grandfather's favorite—for dinner the night before Eileen and Sam were scheduled to get into their car and drive out the Baronses' long white peastone driveway for the last time.

The afternoon before their departure, Lauren, wearing the scarf her grandmother had given her for Christmas, knocked on the guesthouse door. Eileen, smiling but looking like a person who had too much to do in too little time, let her in. "You don't need to knock, my dear," she said, gathering her granddaughter in her arms. "After all, this is your house."

"It's *your* house," said Lauren, correcting Eileen. "It always will be."

"Come in," said Eileen, taking Lauren's hand and leading her into the kitchen. "We haven't had a moment together all week. I've been so darned busy."

"Do you have time?" asked Lauren, misty-eyed.

"Of course I do," said Eileen, opening the cupboard next to the stove and taking down the teapot. "Sit. Let's have some tea."

"I've got some cookies up at the house," said Lauren. "I'll run and get them."

"Never mind," said Eileen. "Selma brought some homemade pastries from her sister. You'll just die when you try them." Eileen took several pieces out of the large red tin that was usually filled with her cookies and arranged them on a plate. She set the plate down in front of Lauren. "How does that look for an after-school snack?" she asked.

Lauren, whose efforts at willing her eyes to stop generating water were failing miserably, said nothing. She grabbed a tissue from the box on the counter behind her and dabbed her right eye. When her bottom lip became to quiver, however, Lauren knew she'd lost the battle for stoicism. She looked up at her grandmother, who had just put the kettle on to boil, and let her tears flow freely. "Don't go," she said quietly.

Determined to stay dry-eyed for Lauren, Eileen sat down at the table and took her granddaughter's hands in her own. "We have to go, darling," she said gently. "We were meant to go from the beginning and the time has come."

"Tell them no," sobbed Lauren. "Tell them you want to stay here, with us."

Eileen laughed. "Your mother might have other ideas."

"I don't care what my mother, or my father, thinks," said Lauren. "I want you to stay here with me."

Eileen put her hands on Lauren's face and kissed her nose. "We will come back," she said, only half-believing it. "For Christmas or Easter, there will be a holiday that brings us back for a visit."

"It won't be the same," said Lauren, shaking her head. "If you leave now, we'll lose everything we've built together."

Suddenly losing her resolve to remain cheerful and upbeat at all times, Eileen frowned. Tears gathered at the corners of her eyes. "Listen to me, Lauren," she said. "We will never, ever lose what we've built. You and I have a relationship that can withstand time and distance. We will always be friends."

Lauren hugged her grandmother, pressing hard against her small but strong frame. "I love you," she said.

"And I love you," said Eileen.

Lauren pulled back. "That's the first time we've said that."

"Ah," said Eileen, smiling. "But it's not the first time I've felt it."

"Me neither," said Lauren.

The teakettle whistled and Eileen got up. She poured the hot water into the pot and set it down in the middle of the table.

"Where's Gramps?" asked Lauren, just noticing his absence.

"Nate took him for a ride."

There was little he enjoyed more, Sam said as Nate buckled him into the passenger seat of his BMW, than a car ride. While summertime was best, when he could roll down the windows and let the rush of wind fill his ears, wintertime had its benefits as well. The heater kept the car comfortable enough for occupants to go coat-less, Sam explained as they drove out the driveway. That in itself was a luxury. The only problem with winter drives was the reflection of the sun on the snow. It was damn-near blinding. Nate took his sunglasses off his face and handed them to his grandfather. "What's this?" asked Sam, putting them on.

"My sunglasses," said Nate. "They will help with the glare."

"I'll say," said Sam. "These are nifty. Are they Foster Grants?"

"Oakleys," said Nate, taking a spare pair out of the pocket on the side of his seat.

"Marvelous," said Sam, looking out the side window. "With these on, I could drive forever."

"Where do you want to go?" asked Nate, turning the car onto a side street narrowed by six-foot snowbanks on both sides.

"Anywhere," said Sam.

Nate drove through the farmland north of town. Sam talked for a half hour about his upcoming transfer to company headquarters. In his mind, Meadowbrook was a corporation, not an extended care facility, even though Eileen had done her best to give Sam a comprehendible, friendly description of their new home. She described Meadowbrook as a network of people their age, supported by community helpers who would ease their burdens as they sailed into old age. From that, Sam deduced he had been promoted by the company and was finally given the responsibility and respect he deserved. Eileen did not correct him. In fact, no one corrected him much anymore because it didn't matter. If he thought it was Tuesday instead of Thursday; if he thought he was twenty-seven instead of seventy-two—it didn't matter. The only things Eileen concerned herself with were his safety, which was Number One in her book, and his happiness. "Look," said Sam, pointing at the side window. "The children are playing in the field."

"Wave to them," said Nate.

Dutifully, Sam raised his hand in acknowledgment. "I hope they're not cold," he said.

"You know kids, Gramps," said Nate, turning to look at the vacant snow-covered field. "They never get cold." Nate drove around what he called the Northern Expanse for another twenty minutes, until Sam fell asleep. Nate liked watching his grandfather sleep. He looked so peaceful with his eyes closed and his tired brain resting.

Ann poured herself a glass of wine and took it to the living room, where she sat on the couch and flipped through Noble and Robertson's proposal for her sunroom. She was impressed, as usual, with their thoroughness and excited about the prospect of building such a grand and unique addition to her home. Half of the room would be glass. It would be a bear to heat in the winter and that would be the first thing Mike would point out. But Peter and Tim suggested solar panels for the roof of the main house, which would certainly help. Plus, with that much glass, the room would act like a large greenhouse, attracting and then holding the sun's warmth. She had to decide about the flooring. While she had originally wanted South American tiling, Peter and Tim suggested she go for something warmer, either a hard wood with a large area rug, or some kind of special covering that would allow the sub-floor to breathe, yet not have the look or feel of indoor-outdoor carpeting. Ann was leaning toward the wood, even though it was more expensive. Then again, in a $200,000 sunroom, what did it really matter?

"I thought I might find you in here," said Eileen, walking into the living room. "Do you want company?"

"Sure," said Ann, moving the paperwork from her lap to the coffee table.

Eileen sat down and Ann shifted her body so she could look at her mother. "So," she said, "are you just about ready?"

"I think so," said Eileen. "I can't fit any more in our bags. And I seem to have accumulated some more things in the last few days. Thank you, Ann, for the beautiful cashmere sweaters for your dad and me."

"Well, you've been a trouper to do it all yourself," said Ann. "Are you sure I can't help you with anything?"

"You'll have a lot to contend with when I'm gone," said Eileen. "And Selma, bless her heart, helped me wash and iron everything, so we'll be all set when we arrive at Meadowbrook."

"You're still planning on stopping for the night, though," said Ann, sipping her wine.

"Oh yes," said Eileen. "I've got a small bag packed for the hotel."

"You are so organized," Ann said. "You always have been."

"As are you. You keep your house immaculate—Nate's room aside."

They both laughed. And then Ann held her wineglass out in front of her. "Would you like some?"

Eileen hesitated. "Sure," she said. "Why not?"

"I'll be right back," said Ann, getting up from the sofa and setting her glass down on her Great Horned Owl coaster. While Ann was at the bar, her back to the room, Eileen glanced at the sunroom proposal and spotted the bottom line. She smiled and shook her head.

"What's funny?" asked Ann, returning with the glass of wine.

"Nothing," said Eileen. "It's been a long day."

Ann took another sip from her glass. It was almost empty, but she resisted the urge to refill it at the bar. While she was a long way from giving up alcohol altogether, she was trying in earnest to drink less. And she had been mostly successful in the five days she had been living according to her new, self-imposed regimen of just two glasses a day. She'd slipped and poured a third the other night when Mike shared some stock option news, but had been on track since. It was harder than she thought it would be, even as she gradually accepted the idea that she might have a problem with alcohol. God knows she didn't need the calories, but she still craved the buzz, the off switch.

Eileen took a sip of wine. "I can't thank you enough," she began.

Ann held up her hand. "Please, Mom," she said. "Let's not do this. It's been fine having you here. I'm glad we had the room to do it."

"But it hasn't been easy," said Eileen, setting down her glass. "Our living here has been a huge disruption to your life."

"It's okay," said Ann, leaning over to give her mother a brief hug and breathing in the faint vanilla scent of her childhood. Alongside the salt, pepper, and vinegar, the bottle of vanilla had always been in the counter in their farmhouse kitchen. Her mother baked every day: for Ann, for the Grange, for the church, for shut-ins, and for emergencies. Ann could remember one particular summer day that a car she did not know approached the house, its tires kicking up dust from their desiccated dirt driveway. It was hot that summer, with little rain, and her mother hadn't turned on the oven in several days, instead serving cool meals and lemonade to the overheated farmhands. Yet, she was able to send the occupants of that car—a family from the city out for a country drive who had missed the turn leading back to the interstate—on their way with a tin of oatmeal raisin cookies, her own recipe, with an extra splash of vanilla. Life on the farm seemed so easy, so peaceful and honest compared with the life she had created after leaving it.

"We'll head out first thing in the morning," said Eileen. "I think that's the best way. There's no sense prolonging our good-byes."

"We'll say our farewells tonight then," said Ann. "You can't just drive off without a proper farewell."

"Farewells are difficult," said Eileen, picking a piece of lint off her pants.

Ann put her hand on her mother's arm. "It's going to be okay, all of it," she said. "Dad will get the care he needs. You will meet people. You will have a new life that will include freedom and friendship. You deserve that."

Eileen looked at her daughter. "Thank you," she said softly.

Ann squeezed her mother's arm and then picked up the sunroom proposal. "Do you want to see the plans for our new sunroom?" asked Ann. "I want to ask your advice about flooring."

Eileen scooted over closer to her daughter and listened attentively as Ann explained the pros and cons of hardwood versus carpeting.

Lauren's lasagna was delicious. In fact, it was the main topic of conversation at the dinner table, taking the place of anyone talking about Eileen and Sam's imminent departure. Lauren had so much to say to her grandmother, but she didn't know how to say any of it. Nate wished he could be alone with his grandfather. The more people in a room or a discussion, the more confused Sam became and behaved. Ann, feeling oddly ill at ease in her own home, was close to tears. And Mike, sensing the tension but unwilling to acknowledge it, ate as quickly as possible, even though Ann had already lectured him once about wolfing his food. "I'd like another piece of lasagna," he said, chewing the last bite of his first piece.

"I'm sure you would," said Ann, dabbing at her left eye with her napkin.

"Pass your plate down to me," said Eileen, picking up the silver spatula. "Whole or half?"

"Whole," said Mike at the same time Ann said, "Half."

"We're celebrating tonight," said Eileen, picking up a whole piece and sliding it onto Mike's plate. "He can start his diet tomorrow."

"It's awfully good lasagna, Lauren," said Mike. "You'll make someone a good wife someday."

Lauren gave her father a weary look, but held her thoughts. When would he learn what she was interested in, what she might become? He scolded Nate every marking period, always asking the same question: How was he ever going to get into a decent college with a 2.95 GPA? With grades like that, Mike's only choice would be to bring Nate into the company through the maintenance department. It didn't seem to matter to her father that Lauren's GPA was 3.67, which was more than adequate, even for a competitive town like the one they lived in. Of course, it was competitive everywhere, Mike often told his children, always making eye contact with Nate. More and more people were climbing the ladder of success, and every one of them would be happy to step on the fingers, shoulders, and heads of those less eager as they ascended. While Nate wasn't compelled by such images, he did use his father's "hopes and dreams" speeches as cafeteria lunch table entertainment.

After Eileen's Black Forest cake dessert, also made by Lauren, Mike raised his wineglass. Lauren looked at Nate, smiling with her eyes. "Here's to Eileen and Sam," he began. "We've enjoyed having you here. From your mouths, we've heard wisdom. From your minds, we've gathered knowledge. And from your hearts, we've experienced kindness and love. May your journey be swift and easy and may your new home bring you happiness."

Eileen raised her glass and said, "Hear, hear. Thank you, Mike." She set her glass back down on the table, twirled its stem, and then took a deep breath. "I really don't know where to begin," she said. "Sam and I are so grateful for everything you've done. I know it's not easy having near strangers come live with you. You've been so accommodating and so loving." Eileen looked at Lauren and smiled. "I know Sam and I will be okay in our new home. I know it's the right place for us. But I shall miss you all very much. You will be in my thoughts and prayers every day. I thank God for your kindness."

While Eileen and Lauren struggled to remain composed, it was Ann who wept openly, then left the table. "Why is that woman crying?" asked Sam, who had been quiet until then.

"I'll check in a minute, after she's had a moment to herself," said Mike. "In the meantime, Eileen, can I have another slice of that great cake?"

Ann was standing at her cappuccino machine in the kitchen, making herself a decaf, vanilla latte, when Mike walked in from the dining room. He stood behind her and encircled her upper body with his arms. "It's going to be okay," he said.

She turned and faced him, and then rested her head against his chest. "How do you know? Because it hasn't been okay, not for some time. And the only people who seem to be able to make it okay are driving out of our lives forever tomorrow morning."

"It is not forever, Ann," said Mike. "We can visit them, more often than we have in the past. And you—and Lauren—can go anytime you'd like."

"It won't be the same."

"That is not all bad," Mike said. "We are a strong family. Your parents have helped us to see this. But now it's our turn. We are out of practice, Ann, on how to be a family. We—all of us, but you and I in particular—are sluggish, rusty from sitting too long on the bench."

"Is it too late?" asked Ann, tilting her head up to see as well as hear Mike's answer.

"No," said Mike, kissing her forehead. "But only if we are serious in our efforts."

After dinner, Lauren lay on her bed and looked at the ceiling instead of her history notes, the test tomorrow occupying only the back of her mind. She sighed, rolled over, and lay on her stomach, which ached. She had eaten a lot for dinner, but was sure the pain wasn't related to food. Tears again gathered in her eyes. She jumped when her cell phone vibrated her entire abdomen. Lazily, she sat up and pulled the phone out of her jeans pocket. It was Josh. "How are you doing?" he asked.

"Okay," Lauren lied.

"They leave tomorrow, right?"

"Yes," said Lauren, sliding off her bed and sitting on the floor, "in the morning."

"Can I drive you to school tomorrow?"

"Why?"

"I don't know," said Josh. "I just thought you might need to talk." Lauren smiled at the phone. Josh had always been nice to her, even and especially when Nate had not. He told Nate this was because he had three sisters; he understood females. And when his sisters were unhappy, they made him unhappy. Keeping them content was his way of secretly controlling them. Nate didn't understand this strategy, but Lauren did. She loved his kindness almost as much as she loved his handsome face. Plus, her grandmother had been right: Judd Acker wasn't ready for a relationship with anyone but Angel. Three weeks after the breakup, they had reunited. Most said it wouldn't last, that the second time was never as good as the first, but Lauren didn't care one way or the other. "That's so nice of you," she said. "What about Nate?"

Josh cleared his throat. "I've talked to him about you."

"What did you say?" asked Lauren, sitting tall, her heart suddenly alive.

"I told him I liked you, and I wanted to take you out, and I hoped he didn't have a problem with that."

"Oh my gosh!" said Lauren. "What did *he* say?"

"He just kind of shrugged," said Josh. "Then he said if I broke your heart, he'd kill me."

"Really?" asked Lauren.

"I think he was kidding," said Josh. "Sort of."

"Thank you," Lauren said, "for talking to him. That took a lot of courage."

Josh hesitated for just a moment. "You're worth it, Lauren."

"So are you," Lauren responded.

"I'll see you in the morning," said Josh. "Sleep well."

"Good night," said Lauren.

The next morning, Eileen, Sam, Lauren, and, remarkably, Nate, gathered in the driveway at first light. The car was packed, had been since the previous afternoon, and Lauren's chocolate chip cookies sat in Eileen's red tin on the front seat. Two travel mugs—another gift from Lauren—filled with steaming black coffee, stood tall in Eileen's cup holders. It appeared everything was in place for the journey. Resolved not to cry, Lauren hugged and held on to her grandmother. "I'll call you," she said. "You can solve my social problems long distance."

"Every fifteen-year-old girl would love to have your social problems," said Eileen. Lauren laughed.

Nate extended his hand to his grandfather, who took it and pulled Nate in for a hug. "You are my best friend," Sam whispered in Nate's ear. "Good luck in the Air Force."

"Thank you," said Nate, choking up. Nate hugged Eileen and Lauren hugged Sam, and then Nate helped Sam into the car and buckled his seat belt. Eileen sat down behind the steering wheel and turned the ignition key.

"Call when you get there," said Lauren.

"I will, my dear," said Eileen. "I've got your number." Eileen put the car in gear and slowly rolled forward. She put her hand out the window and waved. Nate and Lauren walked behind the car several paces as Eileen drove around the bend to the end of the driveway. She tooted the horn, then pulled the car out of sight. Lauren immediately began to cry. Before he had time to think, Nate took a step toward his sister and wrapped his arms around her.

CHAPTER 22

Ann took a towel from the stack next to the water fountain and wiped the moisture from her face as she walked through the Life-cycles to the treadmills. She checked her watch, by habit more than interest; she already knew she was right on schedule. She'd done thirty minutes on the Precor, twenty minutes of weight work, and would finish with a twenty-minute run at a nine-minute-mile pace on the treadmill. Even though the five treadmills were occupied, Ann walked directly to number four, the newest and most reliable of the bunch. She'd signed up for it and had no problem asking its occupant to get off. She bent down to retie her running shoes, then stood right next to the woman, who was apparently engrossed in a cooking show. Ann tapped her on the shoulder, and the woman turned her head, looking surprised. Ann raised her wrist and pointed at her watch. The woman looked at her own watch, smiled, and held up three fingers. "Please?" she said too loudly, overcom-pensating for her headphones. Ann looked at her watch again. She waited a moment, and then held up three fingers. "Thank you," shouted the woman.

To pass the time, Ann went to the matted area next to the tread-mills. She lay down and immediately began doing sit-ups. She counted out two hundred and then stood and returned to the treadmill. The woman, sweating heavily, was standing next to the machine spraying the handles and console with the disinfectant supplied by the center. The television had been turned off. "Thank you," she said.

"No problem," said Ann.

"I didn't mean to go over."

"It's okay," said Ann, sliding past her and stepping onto the wide belt. She entered her program while the woman stood, too closely, and wiped her wet brow. Ann settled on *The Today Show* and started walking. She inserted her earbuds, signaling the end of any social interaction, and the woman walked away. Thirty seconds later, she was into her running groove. Matt Lauer was interviewing the author of a book about child prodigies and Ann began to relax. She held on to the handrails and closed her eyes for two seconds. And that was all it took for an image of her parents, sitting in the living room of her guesthouse, to fill her mind. She opened her eyes and focused her attention on the television.

When Ann finished her workout, she showered and walked out of the center. She met Sally in the parking lot. "Hey," she said, jogging toward Ann. "I called you this morning, but I can see you're already here. Why so early?"

"I have a bunch of things to do today, Sally," said Ann, lying.

"So do I," Sally said. "But let's make time for a bagel in about ninety minutes. My treat."

"I'd love to another time," said Ann. "I've got to run. I'll call you." And with that, Ann left her friend and walked briskly to her car. She knew Sally was probably wondering what the hell was wrong with her—that was the third invitation she'd turned down since her parents left the week before. Ann started her car and turned on her seat heater. She shivered as she put the car in gear and drove out of the lot. It was only nine-thirty in the morning and Ann had no idea what to do with herself, so she drove home.

In her kitchen, filled with sunlight, she found small comforts. The sink area was scrubbed clean, smelling like cleanser. And the floor, which Emma had washed just the day before, had not yet accumulated dirt and dust. The copper-bottom pots and pans all hung in their proper place above the center island. And the gleaming cappuccino machine stood ready on the counter. That, of course, was exactly what she needed. She retrieved the skim milk from the refrigerator and the espresso beans from the freezer. Ann found solace in the *shoosh* of the machine. She poured her drink into a large ceramic mug, indulgently sprinkled chocolate powder on top, and walked to the kitchen table, where she sat amid the pillows on the window seat and put her feet up. Taking a sip and closing her eyes, she, again, saw her parents. She opened her eyes and glanced over at her sanitized stove. Her mother, of course, was not bending over the oven. She turned her head and looked out the window at the guesthouse, which was dark. She had not been in it since her parents' departure.

Coffee in hand, Ann rose from her seat and grabbed her coat from the peg and her keys from the basket. She walked down the salted path, unlocked the front door, and walked in, closing the door behind her. The cool emptiness and silence surrounded her immediately like morning fog, and for a moment, she was unable to breathe. Inhaling and exhaling slowly like her mother had taught her, Ann slowly moved the rest of the way down the front hallway and into the living room. The carpeting was freshly vacuumed. Ann spun around and entered the kitchen. The counters were bare, as were the cupboards she opened one at a time. A bowl of colorful wooden fruit sat in the middle of the kitchen table, instead of the real fruit her mother had always kept handy. It was a good tip for mothers, Eileen had told Ann shortly after her arrival last fall. If the fruit is sitting there, in full view, a child will sometimes eat it. And even though Ann had laughed at the time, she had since noticed Lauren eating apples—something she had never done before Eileen's arrival.

Ann walked through the living room and into the bedroom where her parents had slept for seventeen weeks. She sat down on her mother's side of the bed, inhaling and exhaling, and ran her fingers over the dustless bedside table. She hesitated and then opened its single drawer. Sitting in the middle of the drawer was a three-by-five recipe card: *Mama's Butternut Squash Soup*. Ann lifted it and found a note underneath.

My dear daughter,

I cannot thank you enough for the love and kindness you have shown your father and me over the past months. While we are ready for this next chapter in our lives, we will miss you, Mike, Nate, and Lauren so, so much. I finally feel like a grandmother!

I'm leaving you this recipe. Your soup on Thanksgiving was superb, better than I have ever managed to produce with the same ingredients. You are a good cook, Ann. And so is Lauren.

I'll be in touch. But until we talk, know that I love you very much.

Mother

Inhaling, she wiped away the tears on her cheeks. She was tired, so tired that all she could think about was rest. Ann put her feet on the carpet and stood, just long enough to peel back the quilt covering the bed. She sat back down, removed her Italian loafers, and then lay down, pulling the quilt over her shivering body. Emma had washed the sheets, but Ann smelled a faint vanilla scent on the pillow. She gently set the card and note down on the table, closed her eyes, and fell asleep.

**Please turn the page for a special Q&A
with Susan Kietzman!**

What is The Good Life?

That's an interesting question because it has many answers. It is defined by the person asked. To some, it means good health. To others, it means being with family, friends, or whoever brings warmth, love, and happiness to a relationship. It can mean opportunity for education, travel, leisure time, delicious food—many things, yes? And for most Americans, the good life describes an existence that includes everything already mentioned. It's a life made easy and comfortable with material possessions, entitlements, and wealth. The wealthy can afford to do whatever they choose, and many aspire to this status. However, when we have whatever we think we want, do we lose sight of what we really want? Do we even know what that is anymore? The answer, like the question, is fluid. And it changes as we age and mature, as we experience loss, when we realize what we've been missing, or when we learn something unexpectedly.

So, is *The Good Life* about this wealthy lifestyle and what we can learn from it? Why do most of us who aren't rich want to read your book about rich people?

Yes, Mike and Ann Barons are wealthy, and yes, we can learn from them. In some ways, they are very much like us. Of course, they don't have to worry about the rent or the mortgage, or the grocery bill, or the electric bill, or job security. If Mike Barons lost his job, he wouldn't need to find another one right away. But they do struggle. Ann is a wife, a mother, a daughter, and a friend, but she falls short in each of these important relationships. Mike is so occupied by his working life that he has lost track of his children and what's important to them. And Nate and Lauren experience the same ups and downs of their less wealthy high school peers. The Baronses' tremendous wealth gives them more options. But they still, like us, must overcome everyday obstacles.

What makes your book different from the others on the shelf?

The Good Life is a story about an American family. Americans, I think, are interested in their own country and in the people who live here. When we listen to or watch the news, we are often taken to other countries—to learn about power or human rights struggles or economic issues or foreign culture. There are many books that also take readers to other countries, and to other time periods. And this is good, if we are not to become an ethnocentric nation of narrow-minded thinkers. As a break from these mental travels around the world, I think it's also good to think and read about this country, about who lives here, and what makes us Americans. *StoryCorps* on NPR features short interviews by and about Americans. I am inspired by these stories aired every Friday because there is something in almost every one I've heard that I can either relate to or learn from.

Why did you write the book, and why now?

Because the question "What is the good life?" has been bumping around my brain for a long time. It's always been a relevant question, perhaps even more so in this challenging economic climate. In spite of our troubles, we all want to be taken away—to lavish summer lawn parties on perfect evenings, with fabulously dressed people drinking champagne under the stars and muted floodlights of a white marble mansion. We can be taken in by these images, thinking that those who have great wealth must in some way be more important, smarter, or simply better than the rest of us. And yet, I know this isn't necessarily true. The idea for the novel came from a variety of sources, one of which was my interest in exploring the complications or pitfalls that can come with money.

Is there a message intended for the reader about the evils of wealth?

Not at all. Wealth fascinates all of us because it is so powerful. People with money can do things; they can make a difference. They can use their money not only to enrich their lives, but also to change the dire circumstances of others. Until Ann's parents arrive, the Baronses are focused on themselves. They are not particularly charity minded, preferring to cater to their personal desires. This, much more than the amount of money they have, may be the source of their dissatisfaction or disappointment.

Is what you're saying is that it's okay to make a lot of money, as long as you share the wealth?

Well, that's up to the person with the money. We all have choices. One of the best choices I think we can make with our money and our time is to balance it. A little for me, a little for you, a little for him, a little for her. Time at the office, time at the gym, time for others, time for a good book. We all have things we have to do—whether it's working or raising children or caring for parents, or going to school—and that takes most of the time and/or the money. We also have free time and a percentage of disposable income. What we choose to do with all of this time and money can define the "goodness" in our lives.

THE GOOD LIFE

Susan Kietzman

ABOUT THIS GUIDE

The suggested questions are included
to enhance your group's
reading of Susan Kietzman's
The Good Life.

DISCUSSION QUESTIONS

1. Ann appears to have had a fairly happy childhood growing up on a farm in Pennsylvania. What do you think turns her away from it as an adult?

2. Ann is attracted to Mike in college because he is "great looking and powerful." Why is Mike attracted to Ann, especially since he might be able to choose from a large pool of young women? Ann and Mike come from very different backgrounds; what do they have in common?

3. Nate and Lauren are pretty typical teenagers: sometimes sarcastic and surly; sometimes withdrawn and insecure. With a workaholic and an avid shopper as role models, why aren't Nate and Lauren insufferable? Or are they?

4. When Sam and Eileen move in, why are Nate and Lauren drawn to them? What do Sam and Eileen provide that Mike and Ann do not?

5. Sam's Parkinson's disease and dementia unnerve Mike, Ann, Nate, and Lauren. How does each of them handle Sam's disabilities? How does Eileen treat her husband?

6. What kind of relationship did Ann anticipate having with her parents when they moved in? What happened to those expectations?

7. How does Ann's drinking fit in with her need for control? Why does Mike put up with her drinking? What happens when her drinking becomes an issue on the Florida trip with Jesse, Paula, and Sally?

8. Eileen seems to be a take-charge kind of person. Why does she often keep her thoughts to herself instead of sharing them with her daughter? What, if anything, does Sam add to Ann's adult life?

9. When Eileen and Sam leave at the end of the book, who is most upset and why?

10. In the novel, who has the good life and who is still searching?

11. What does the good life mean to you?